AN HONORABLE ESTATE

AN

HONOF

J. B. LIPPINCOTT COMPANY

PHILADELPHIA · NEW YORK

ABLE

ESTATE

ANE KAUFFMANN

FOR FAITH

People Most Often Met

The Bride's Family

Vickie Fortescue	the bride
Ruth Zimmerman Fortescue	her mother
Charles Fortescue	her father, vice president of Andean C & Z
Peter Fortescue	her brother
Jacob Zimmerman	Ruth's father
Gert Zimmerman	her sister
Dr. Morris Zimmerman	her brother
Alison Zimmerman Levy	her niece (daughter of Philip and Ann Zimmerman)
Ben Levy	Alison's husband
Susan	Morris's daughter
Tommy	Morris's son

The Groom's Family

Roger Hilliard	the groom
Owen Hilliard	his father
Amelia Booth	his mother (Owen's first wife)
Professor Stephen Booth	his stepfather
Frances Booth	his half sister
Mrs. Langstaff	Amelia's mother
Douglas Langstaff	Amelia's brother
Joan Langstaff	his wife
Eliot Clay	Stephen Booth's half brother

Friends of the Families, and Others,
in the order of their appearance:

Denise Durrell	a young actress
Barbara-the-Bitch	Owen's third wife
Carol	Owen's second wife
Dr. Jeremy Wales	medical researcher for Andean C & Z
Joyce Neilson	Stephen Booth's secretary
Louis Melmoth	a jeweler in Actonsville, Connecticut
Tony Elmendorf	Owen's friend; Assistant District Attorney
Katya Woikoveč	a successful artist
Mrs. Peabody	Charles Fortescue's secretary
Bruce Bigelow	advertising manager for Andean C & Z
Arthur Vaughan	Secretary of the League of International Disarmament
Polly Spurgeon	Owen's literary agent
Mr. Rivkin	a printer and chess player
Madge Blair	widow of Virgil Blair
Gretchen	Madge's daughter
Mrs. Godolphin	specialist in wedding gowns
Lois	Carol's three-year-old daughter
Dr. Eckhardt	Amelia Booth's psychoanalyst
Guy Abercrombie	Amelia's one-time fiancé
Rodney	Amelia's first lover
Gail Galloway	Stephen Booth's editor
Freddie Ames	jester and go-between
Bill Swan	photographer of the wedding
The Reverend Dr. Kirkpatrick	

MAN'S NUPTIAL HALF *is kindlingly concerned in the launch of a new couple; it is the business of the fair sex: and man himself (very strangely, but nature quickens him still) lends a not unfavouring eye to the preparations of the matrimonial vessel for its oily descent into the tides, where billows will soon be rising, captain and mate soon discussing the fateful question of who is commander. We consent, it appears, to hope again for mankind; here is another chance! . . . After so many ships have foundered, some keel up, like poisoned fish, at the first drink of water, it is a gallant spectacle, let us avow; and either the world perpetuating it is heroical or nature incorrigible in the species. Marriages are unceasing. Friends do it, and enemies; the unknown contractors of this engagement, or armistice, inspire an interest. It certainly is both exciting and comforting to hear that man and woman are ready to join in a mutual affirmative, say Yes together again. It sounds like the end of the war.*

GEORGE MEREDITH

DEARLY BELOVED, *we are gathered together here in the sight of God, and in the face of this congregation, to join together this Man and this Woman in Holy Matrimony, which is an honorable estate, instituted of God in the time of man's innocency.* . . .

THE BOOK OF COMMON PRAYER

PART ONE

1

In her fuzzy blue dressing gown, Ruth Fortescue stood at the hall archway looking at the living room. She was not a nervous woman, her gaze did not dart about restlessly, itemizing; rather she confronted the room with a blank, comprehensive stare, waiting for her attention to be caught by some cushion inadequately plumped up or an ashtray despoiled by a thoughtless masculine cigarette stub.

As she had thought it would be, her last-minute inspection was unnecessary. The room was expectant with preternatural tidiness. Woodwork shone and ashtrays glistened, every magazine and newspaper had been swept from sight, cut flowers in strategic vases still held their waxy, hothouse freshness. A domestic vacuum had been achieved, a void aching to be filled by a party. The hall closet stood empty, waiting for alien overcoats. From the kitchen beyond the dining area, out of Ruth's sight, came an occasional clink of china and the grave murmurings of Sam and Isabel, the couple who always catered for the Fortescues—but Ruth had been lucky to get them for this evening, on such short notice.

This end of the apartment was poised to come alive at the first touch on the doorbell; vaguely Ruth sensed that she had come here not from compulsive insecurity but because the setting suited her own mood of anticipation. She, too, was poised—for this evening and for the strenuous ten weeks or so that lay ahead. Vickie had no idea. Vickie would run around in circles, would do some few of the tasks allotted to her, would forever after be convinced that she had done all the work. "Never mind, Mummy, I'll attend to *everything*." Ruth smiled to herself. She knew this was her last moment of peace for some time to come. The thought delighted and exhilarated her.

She looked forward to day after day of not knowing where she would find the time for all that needed to be done. She looked forward to being used (like the living room) to full capacity; she even looked forward to a little mild and justified complaining of her exhaustion.

However, the delight was flawed by looking a little further ahead. Ruth was reminded of the summer, years ago, when Peter had come home from the last day of school sombre and thoughtful, without the usual manic exuberance of a freed captive. Under pretense of pushing back his cowlick they had tested his forehead, but there was no fever —merely the sobering discovery that vacation was not, as it had hitherto seemed, a boundless, limitless adventure but only a finite, ninety-day reprieve. Until the mood passed, the shadow of next autumn's school had lain over the golden promise of summer. That had been the first stirrings of adulthood in Peter's case, the first sign of that sense of perspective which, once acquired, diminished every happiness with the thought of eventualities. So now Ruth could look forward to an orgy of bustle and industry and usefulness as to a vacation, yet could not forget that in due course the fuss would die down, the job would be finished—and one of the things she would have accomplished would be to increase her own emptiness.

But having yielded to her anticipation, the sweet aspect and the bitter, Ruth characteristically shrugged mentally at both and turned back down the hallway. She had little capacity for dramatizing her emotions, a lack which she considered (when she considered it at all) as somewhere halfway between her greatest strength and her greatest weakness. At Peter's door she hesitated, and then passed on: after years of a studied contempt for clothes he had suddenly, in his senior year at Princeton, become a determined dandy and probably would prefer to be left alone with the serious matter of dressing. At Vickie's door she knocked and went in without waiting for a reply.

Vickie, who was sitting in her slip at her dressing table doing supererogatory things to her pretty eyes, promptly began to talk—or rather to externalize the monologue which had before been silent only for lack of an audience. Unquestionably she would die if Roger weren't the first to arrive; he had promised, but he was coming with his mother and his stepfather, and his professorial stepfather was every bit as absent-minded as all the jokes and would no doubt hold them up, which meant that Cousin Evelyn, with her sneaky way of getting to parties with split-second promptness, would spoil everything. . . .

Waiting for the true anxiety to emerge from this nonsense, and hoping that *her* daughter was not indulging in last-minute qualms of uncertainty, Ruth admired the girl-woman she had brought forth nineteen years ago and regretted the speed with which Vickie had laid claim to adulthood. From this point of view a son was much more satisfactory. Though Peter was three years older, his adolescence had been a long, sustained entertainment, which was still (an opinion Ruth kept well hidden) not over, whereas Vickie had flickered almost overnight from child to female, sparing her parents that ghastly, interim neuter stage but cheating them, or so it sometimes seemed, of so many rewarding anxieties. Maturing early, as her mother had done, Vickie at twelve or thirteen had already advertised the woman she would be when once the gaucheness and the puppy fat had disappeared. At an earlier stage she had talked of becoming a nurse or an actress, but after that turning point there had been no sign of interest in any career; she devoted herself first to 'boys' and then to 'men'—though to an older eye the difference was often invisible. In recent years she had been sieving her 'men' with an intolerance increasingly impatient, until Ruth had developed, well in advance, a reserve of affectionate sympathy for the defenselessness of the young man who was deemed worthy of Vickie's adoration. Peter's roommate, Roger Hilliard, seemed unaware of any need of sympathy, doubtless thought of himself as very much the masterful wooer; but after the first hint of Vickie's reaction Ruth had seen him as doomed. She quite liked Roger; if she could find little that distinguished him from a dozen other personable swains who had been contemptuously discarded, she was content to believe that this was her fault and that Vickie's discernment could be trusted.

"It would be a calamity," Vickie declared broodingly, and Ruth recalled her attention: she had learned that in her daughter's language a catastrophe was negligible, a disaster rather less so, but a calamity was to be taken seriously. This, then, should be Vickie's underlying anxiety, and so it proved: she was worried that the announcement of her engagement might fail to appear in tomorrow's Sunday *Times*, or—almost as bad—might be brushed off with a horrid little paragraph and no photograph. Monica's photograph had been

11

there and so had Sally's. There were degrees of humiliation which a girl might not survive.

Gravely Ruth argued that *The New York Times* would not be likely to snub the daughter of Charles Fortescue, gravely she recalled that the photograph had not been sent till the last moment (Vickie's fault), gravely she urged that it was the bridal portrait that really mattered, and there would be plenty of time for that. But as she went back to the bedroom to finish dressing, Ruth felt sorry that she could not share her amusement with her husband. Charles tended to feel affronted by his children's lapses in logic; he might stalk into Vickie's room to ask whether she would be any the less engaged if *The New York Times* failed to record the fact.

At the necktie stage, Charles was glowering at the tie rack. "Choose me a tie," he demanded. "When Vickie disapproves of my taste, I can put the blame on you."

"I think I'll have her give you some for your birthday," Ruth said, making sure there were no spots on the grey and red Italian silk. She was pleased to see that the bedroom was still tidy, ready to serve as a receptacle for the women's coats and furs. This was a lesson that Vickie had yet to learn: in preparing for a party she still reduced her room to a state of total squalor.

"Don't be surprised if I disappear with Morris for a few minutes," Charles said, and then, realizing this might sound alarming since Ruth's brother was also their family doctor, he added, "Nothing to do with me. It's business."

"With Morris?" she asked doubtfully. It was a family joke that whenever Morris put money into anything he lost it all.

"Yes. He may be able to help me."

"Well, don't be missing long. Vickie might be hurt."

"I doubt if she'll even notice." But his thoughts had successfully been diverted to the fact that the real business of the evening was a party. "I do hope your father behaves himself for a change," he said. She smiled at him, amused that he should worry about this instead of whether her niece Alison and Ben would bring their incessant quarreling to the celebration, and he saw the smile in the mirror and misunderstood. "I always say that, don't I?" he asked. "And your father never behaves himself and it never bothers me at the time, and if he ever acted the perfect gentleman I'd spend the evening worrying about him." Some aspect of this thought so engrossed Charles that he lost track of what his hands were doing and had to begin the knotting routine afresh. "Someday," he went on, turning to face his wife, "someday we'll be going to the engagement party of a grandchild. And Vickie and Roger will be talking like this in their room, and one of them will probably be hoping that I won't be an embarrassment. Do you suppose I'll remember this then?"

"Probably not," Ruth said, unable to see what difference it made.

"It's a depressing thought, though," Charles declared. "By the way, watch out for Roger's mother. If she takes after her father, and she does, she'll be managing the wedding before you know what's happened to you."

2

Once upon a time, presumably, these celebrations occurred more simply. A young pair would announce their mutual passion, Father would bellow out the good news, relatives and neighbors would come swarming in, somebody would uncork a jug of something or other, and without further ado a party would be in progress. But that was long ago, or somewhere else. Not in modern New York City, certainly, where people live in arbitrarily chosen crowded isolation, where it is the height of bad manners (except in unreconstructed corners of Greenwich Village) to drop in upon anybody without preparing the way by telephone, and where nothing more elaborate than a table of bridge can ever happen spontaneously.

Even the most modest festivity—"just the families and a few close friends of Vickie's and Roger's"—demanded fixing a date. This had to be on a weekend so the men would be free of business preoccupations, it had to be a Saturday so the news of Vickie's triumph could appear in the Sunday papers, it had to be Saturday the second of April because next day was the last of Roger's vacation and he would be returning to college.

Naturally it was raining: a fine, sleeting rain at a temperature just above freezing, threatening with nightfall to coat the streets with ice. Taxis would be hard to come by; buses were crowded and puddly with dripping umbrellas; subways were infrequent, overheated and even more noisome than usual. Getting to the party at all was going to be a minor metropolitan horror. Nor was the weather the only inconvenience. After all, only a few of the party-goers were themselves caught up in the oblivious rapture of young love. To the others the party might be a gala occasion, a time for encounter and gaiety and reminiscence—but also it was an interruption and a dislocation, fraught with nuisance.

In an apartment on West 55th Street Ruth's father, Jacob Zimmerman, who was rather looking forward to being the patriarch of the party, had made a belated and ill-advised effort to improve the shine on his best black shoes and overturned a bottle of liquid polish. His elder daughter, Gert, who kept house for him, emerged from her bedroom in her party best to find him making matters worse with a handful of paper towels—and burst into tears. The carpet, an extravagance which represented considerable scrimping, had been laid only the previous week.

Jacob's surviving son, Dr. Morris Zimmerman, had carefully kept the afternoon free but was now at the hospital on an emergency call, waiting for a lab report, wondering whether he would have to have the nurse call Ruth to say he would not be able to make it.

Meanwhile, other miscellaneous Zimmermans were making ready to set forth uptown, across town or downtown. The Long Island contingent, damp and irritable, was already on its way.

These people, drawn by the beacon of hospitality that shone from the Fortescue apartment, fourteen stories above the East River on Sutton Place South, had at least the consolation of knowing that when they arrived at their destination they would probably enjoy themselves. The party, however lacking in spontaneity, however laboriously arranged and uncomfortably arrived at, would nevertheless be a party. The occasion was a happy one, and this would transcend whatever strain there might be between families still mostly unknown to one another. Sooner or later, probably with the second martini, conviviality would come—it was almost obliged to come. With so many people brought together on their best behavior, determined to forget their workaday cares and to revel, to drink well and to eat well, to rejoice in old ties and be animated by new ones, it would be remarkable indeed if the evening did not prove reasonably gay and successful.

Yet to all of these promises several of the prospective guests were immune. Douglas Langstaff, for example, although delighted by his nephew's engagement, looked forward to its celebration as so many hours of apprehension and misery—an attitude which his sister had treated with scant consideration. "I'm sorry, my dear," Amelia had said, "but you and Joan simply have to be there, that's all there is to it. It's a matter of solidarity. The girl's family will be swarming—not on the Fortescue side, unfortunately; there doesn't appear to *be* any

Fortescue side left—but I gather the mother's relatives come in platoons. We have to make a showing for Roger's sake." (Amelia's maternalism was all the more devastating for coming in spurts.) "Besides, Doug, there's a question of appearances. It would seem odd if only Stephen and I were there—*and* Roger's father. We all take it for granted that Owen and I have gone right on being good friends, but some people still don't understand such behavior. It wouldn't matter so much if Mother were here, but there simply has to be one Langstaff at the party to prove we're civilized and not just bohemian. . . ."

So now, with well-concealed foreboding, Douglas Langstaff sat on the chaise longue in his bedroom, watching his wife create a cosmetic approximation of the beauty he had married twenty-four years before, wondering if this would be one of the occasions when she got drunk and made a scene, bracing himself to the task of standing guard throughout the evening.

For such conscientiousness, however, he received not the slightest credit from his sister. "I suppose I'll be busy keeping one eye on Joan," Amelia was grumbling at just about this time, one vermilion nail tapping against the clasp of her purse. For the moment they were not moving. On an eastbound street in the lower Thirties a nervous woman driver from New Jersey had become uncertain of her ability to squeeze her inflated Cadillac past a double-parked furniture van and had stalled her car. Their taxicab was trapped in the resulting tie-up. On the jump seat sat the fiancé-to-be, Roger Hilliard, fuming and fidgeting at this new delay.

Professor Stephen Booth smiled reassuringly at his stepson and received a wooden stare in reply. "That would be Douglas's problem, I should think," he said to his wife.

"Oh, Douglas!" scoffed Amelia, expecting little help from that quarter. The responsibilities of the party ahead weighed on her as heavily as if she were the hostess. She would have to keep watch over Joan, pick the right moment to buttonhole Ruth Fortescue, make sure that Stephen kept in circulation, find time to take Roger's father aside and make him face up to some of the facts of life. It was enough to bring on one of her headaches. "Douglas will be much too busy making a good impression."

"On Fortescue?" Stephen asked.

"Yes, of course."

"Oh, come now!"

"Wait and see," Amelia replied cynically.

"I admit I don't know anything about business," said Stephen, who took a certain pride in this deficiency while believing that common sense more than made up for it, "but it strikes me as farfetched. He can't believe that Charles Fortescue is in need of a stockbroker."

Amelia shook her head warningly and glanced at her son. Roger was quite oblivious, peering ahead at the jammed-up street, trying to propel the taxi forward by sheer force of will power. In any case, at this stage of his infatuation he doubtless saw his prospective father-in-law as little more than an appendage of Vickie's—a stodgy old man who was lucky to be able to manufacture a job for talented young Roger Hilliard. In time, as Douglas had made eloquently explicit, he would learn better. Despite his title of executive vice president, Fortescue to all intents and purposes *was* Andean Copper and Zinc. The Board of Directors was nothing but those members of the Barbour and Haxton families who were available to attend meetings (plus a couple of retired Generals as window dressing), while the President and Chairman, old Clarence Barbour III, was content to wield his authority mainly from Biarritz. This left the real power in Fortescue's hands, and a great deal of power it was: Andean C & Z being the second wealthiest collection of mines in the Peruvian Andes, very nearly rivaling Cerro de Pasco. "He's a very, very useful person to know," Amelia said.

"Oh, *useful!* In what way?" Stephen asked.

"Don't be tiresome."

"I'm trying to be practical," Stephen said. "Your brother is forever reminding us that he is a practical man of affairs whereas I am not."

"Once in a while Douglas is right."

"Yet since there's not the least likelihood that Fortescue will ever take your brother aside to tell him the price of copper is about to rise or fall, his usefulness will be entirely factitious."

"Thank God!" Roger exclaimed as the taxi crawled forward. After a dozen feet or so they stopped again. Roger groaned piteously.

"Douglas can let it be known that good old Charlie Fortescue is practically a member of the family," Stephen continued. "I can see that would be practical. Then his equally practical, hardheaded clients will assume that Douglas's analyses of how the stock market will behave must be all the shrewder for inside information he doesn't possess."

"Very funny," said Amelia.

"Modern practicality in action," Stephen asserted. "Influence is the people you know, wisdom is the first names you can fling into the conversation. It's progress, I suppose. A giant stride forward from the Indians who looked for a special virtue in the pronouncements of the feeble-minded."

Amelia shot a look of familiar exasperation at her husband. As always, in these moods, he wore an expression of innocent abstraction, as if he were off on some fine intellectual cloud and not likely to come down to earth again for some time. Stephen was a small man, still very elegant despite a growing paunchiness; he had unusually small feet and hands and a large bald head. From behind heavy spectacles he peered out at the world with a deceptive air of bewildered gentleness. He was a shy person who had acquired authority in the classroom, an intelligent person who tried to spare his intelligence from the humdrum of everyday reality. And he derived an endless entertainment from bringing to the society in which he lived that same clinical detachment he used on the primitive peoples who were the subject of his study. In this vein he could continue almost indefinitely, and not everybody found it as amusing as he did. "It would be nice," she said, hoping she would not just provoke him to a recital of barbarous betrothal customs, "if you tried to remember it's an engagement party we're going to."

"If we ever get there," Roger said.

"We'll get there," Amelia said. The tie-up had untangled, and now they were stopped by nothing more serious than a traffic light.

"But I promised Vickie we'd be *early*."

"It was nobody's fault if we got held up."

"If Stephen hadn't mislaid his glasses, we'd be there by now," Roger said with a petulance that called in question his readiness for marriage. "I wish I'd stayed at Dad's. At least he can get places on time."

3

As it happened, in assuming that he would have been so much better off at his second home, Roger was mistaken. At that very moment Owen Hilliard was lying sprawled on his bed, naked except for a clammy bathtowel. He had been caught by the telephone just as he was emerging from the shower. After four cigarettes he was still listening to an angry young lady explaining how she understood him so much better than any other woman he had ever known. Since he had good reasons for not wanting to hurt her feelings more than was strictly necessary, it was some time before he found a way to bring this conversation to a tactful, soothing conclusion. And then he still had to dress, an operation complicated by the fact that the first shirt he tried on revealed frayed cuffs and the second lacked two buttons; the angry young lady had not been the sort to take a domestic interest in the state of his linen. So, what with one thing and another, it was more than half an hour later before Owen finally hurried down the stairs, buttoning his overcoat as he went.

Between Fifth and Madison Avenues in the Eighties there are, behind not very impressive façades, some fine old apartment buildings left over from a time before it was considered necessary to cram fifteen stories into a height scarcely sufficient for ten or twelve. The apartments are intelligently laid out; the rooms are large, high ceilinged and often beautifully proportioned; here you will find parquet flooring and there a wood-burning fireplace that still functions. But in New York City such amenities have to be paid for, and not only in a monetary sense. Often the rooms are too large for air conditioning (and the wiring too ancient to stand for it), doormen are rare, and few of the buildings boast of a canopy out over the sidewalk.

Owen Hilliard's building was no exception. While rain streaked down inches in front of his nose, he stood in the doorway and waved at a taxi which had stopped to discharge a passenger further up the street, bracing himself for the dash across the sidewalk. He had no umbrella; Roger had borrowed it earlier in the week when he had brought Vickie around to be admired.

It was long past six-thirty. Owen was late; he was irritable, and he was feeling rather older than usual. All this was the fault of an entrancing little apprentice virago named Denise Durrell, currently playing the goodhearted call girl in *The Cascade*. Like most girls she was convinced that she enjoyed a God-given prerogative to decide when a love affair was finished and was startled when a man ungallantly proved her mistaken. She hadn't made a scene, exactly: that would have exposed a blemish in her sophistication. But, unable to imagine that a man could so quickly grow bored with being acted at, however seductively, she had felt it her duty to inform him of those weaknesses in his character which had led him to resent her bountiful, uncritical love. This was all part of the game nowadays, when every third girl came out of school with a well-grounded misunderstanding of elementary psychology, and Owen was used to it. In Denise's case he had been particularly determined to curb his impatience, wishing to keep on good terms with a girl who might very well shape into a first-class comedienne. Yet it seemed very hard that she should have insisted that he resented her *youth*—this on the very day that a man was having to adjust himself to the knowledge that his son was about to start down the skids to matrimony. She knew it, too; her lack of tact had not been accidental. "You resent not being able to keep up with me," she had explained tolerantly. "It's all very well to insist that you don't like night clubs, but I've seen you in the morning when you didn't get enough sleep. I'm not blaming you, Owen; I just hate to see you kidding yourself."

The cab drew up. With an unnaturally youthful stride he bounded across the sidewalk and hurled himself inside, and was puffing not at all when he gave the address.

The trouble with nearing the fifty mark, in Owen's opinion, was not so much that your body slowed down (except in the depths of a hangover he really felt no older than ever) but that you grew so weary of living with your own defects. It could take half a lifetime to recognize what they were, but then they lay before you as so many conspicuous obstacles which still tripped you up just as effectively as when they had been hidden—except now, when you fell, the severest bruise was to your self-respect. His greatest failing, Owen was convinced, was that he fell in love too far, too easily. He always had, no doubt, but now the law of diminishing returns was beginning to operate. More or less forced to play the role of a Don Juan (the alimony payments to Barbara-the-Bitch, his third wife, discouraged anything else), he found that he simply didn't have the temperament: he lacked the true predator's ability to keep emotions strictly at the conversational level, to be absorbed by the pursuit of novelty for its own sake, and to be content with purely ejaculatory conquests. There was a lot to be said for this point of view: it was, for instance, the only proper approach to a girl like Denise, whose surrender to a lover was more like a feigned retreat before an enemy, whose husband would need to enjoy having his soul used as a rehearsal stage, yet who was an absolute delight in bed. A lot of girls were like that, and a man should be able to take them lightly or leave them alone. Owen couldn't do it. His emotions stood as romantic sentries which had to be appeased before his desire could be acknowledged. Each new hoyden had to be invested with qualities deserving of love. Then, having invented them, Owen could enjoy the process of lovingly discovering them one by one—deluding himself, persuading the poor girl that she had aroused so much more adoration than she had any claim to. A contemptible performance. As a young man he had blamed his disillusionments on the girl, thus compounding stupidity with rudeness.

Many of his faults Owen regarded indulgently, but not this one; earnestly he hoped that he had not bequeathed it to his son. Impossible to tell, of course, and too late to remedy. At the moment Roger was caught in the full glory of a love that was sure to endure a lifetime. Owen knew the feeling well: he had been there often and in the vicinity even oftener. Perhaps Roger's confidence would prove justified; it was conventional to assume so, and normal to hope so. But any sensible person knew that the chances weren't too good. You had to be lucky, and the younger you were, the more luck you needed. What if Roger wasn't lucky? What would happen to him then? The need to love and be loved wholeheartedly was such an urgent natural impulse that only time and failure could make a fault of it, and youngsters worth their salt never listened to talk of time or failure. Quite rightly. Their confidence was a shining sword which might, just possibly, be sufficient; no concern of theirs that the sword was double-edged.

(Outside, the darkly glistening streets crawled by, punctuated by stoplights where umbrella'd huddles clumped and scuttered at the crossings. On nights like this Owen always remembered his lean years after the war, when a party had meant a trip by buses or subways which invariably left him with long wet blocks to plod. The freedom to take taxis at will still seemed the most gratifying of luxuries.)

Perhaps if he had been closer to Roger he might have prevented the boy from hurrying into so early a marriage—not by dusty cynicisms about women but by encouraging the idea that a heart was better cultivated a little before being given away, so that later on the gift might be more precious, freed of callow and egoistic impatience. Guidance of that sort, however, called for an easy relationship, and Owen had never been quite that easy with his son. The divorce was to blame, although Owen and his first wife had remained on the best of terms and the custody arrangements (the usual terms: Roger to live with his mother, his vacations at his father's disposal except for alternate Christmases) had never been strained by any competition for the boy's affections. If anything, Owen and Amelia had leaned in the other direction. Amelia, the most maternal of mothers when she remembered to be, was usually seven-eighths distracted by the conflicting claims of a cause, a husband, and a *salon*; whereas Owen, during his periodic but frenetic working bouts, was admittedly jealous of his serenity. Roger had been accommodated to parental exigencies.

On the surface, the boy had not suffered. Sturdy of mind as of body, outgoing, athletic, perhaps a trifle humorless, he had grown up with fewer problems or neuroticisms than many offspring of more conventional households. As soon as Owen could afford the expense, Roger had had a room of his own in his father's apartment, free— when he was old enough—to come and go as he pleased, free to make the most of having two homes.

Yet by its very nature the relationship had been delicate. Once Roger had grown old enough to make a choice, he could scarcely be constrained to come, yet neither could he be allowed to use this liberty as a means of escaping discipline, demanding indulgence in payment for his tentative presence. Discipline there had to be, clearly, so to compensate Owen had tried to maintain a holiday mood for Roger's visits—which inevitably meant entering into Roger's interests and ideas rather than prosing on about his own. They had had some fine times. Probably the best had been the summer up on Martha's Vineyard in the little cottage out toward Gay Head, an idyllic interlude which had never, despite the best intentions, proved repeatable. But that was eight years ago; Roger had been fourteen. You met a fourteen-year-old on the level of shared activities and sensations, not on the level of ideas. And after that, so soon, so quickly, Roger had been absorbed by the adolescent world of campus doings, sports and dating; a world from which he would emerge at intervals looking to his father for the exercise of budding sophistication, the stimulation of travel, the gaiety of shows and theatres—but *not*, according to the pattern Owen himself had set, for the tedium of playing audience to middle-aged wisdoms.

It had all happened so naturally, and it had all—allowing for a certain reasonable minimum of parental selfishness—been meant for Roger's benefit: a recompense for the divorce of which he had been the innocent victim. And the result? Roger's impetuous hurtle into marriage certainly suggested that having found neither of two homes very satisfactory, he was in a hurry to create one of his own. That might not be a fair picture (certainly it wouldn't appeal to Vickie Fortescue!), but Owen was inclined to look back on his one shot at fatherhood as a failure.

A pity, that, for he was sure he had more innate paternal instincts than most men and under more normal circumstances would have made quite a good father. In certain moods he had come to regret, belatedly, that he'd never had other children. Thank heaven he had not fathered anything on Barbara-the-Bitch—that would have been an act of criminal irresponsibility—but he could feel very differently about his second wife, Carol. In so many ways that had been an excellent marriage, and children might have made all the difference, though at the time he had been as afraid of the cliché as of the financial perils. Children would have given another focus to that ambitious restlessness which underlay Carol's surface placidity: she could have left him alone, she would not have needed to leech onto his work so passionately, trying to squeeze genius from him like toothpaste from a tube. That had been the real source of conflict, though like most marital conflicts theirs had been fought on battle-fields far removed from the point of contention.

It was ludicrous to think how drastically a man's life was shaped by the effectiveness of birth-control devices. If only Carol had had one of those 'accidents' which overtook so many of his married friends (sometimes it seemed that half the children he knew of were the result of that one scotch too many which unsettled the diaphragm), he would have been outraged at the time, but there was a strong likelihood—well, an excellent chance, anyway—that he would still be happily married today.

There wouldn't have been the years of pursuing disappointment in every skirt that flirted by. There wouldn't have been a Barbara to skim the cream from his success. There wouldn't have been evenings like this one, when, between projects, he had no earthly reason to go back to his apartment except as the logical place to sleep.

(The riverside symmetricalities of Sutton Place South loomed into view, and Owen reached for his money clasp.)

He would have come a domestic man himself to this domestic celebration of social continuity. Instead of coming, as he rather felt —the outsider, the self-made outcast, the thrice-divorced social derelict, the skeleton at the feast.

4

In one corner of the long living room was a love seat with two attendant armchairs grouped around a coffee table. It was here that Vickie Fortescue, very much princess of the evening, held court for the young people, relations and closest friends, who vied for the other seats, perched on arms or sprawled on the floor at her feet.

From time to time, like the well-bred child she was (really, Amelia grew more delighted with her at every meeting), she would detach herself to visit the room at large, bringing the surplus of her happiness to the older generations. Then, her duty satisfied for the moment, she would dart back to the joys of showing off her fiancé, lording it over her older brother for a change, and generally preening herself —but sweetly—on her true graduation into adulthood. And Roger (unless maternal prejudice had got out of hand) was looking particularly handsome, though lamentably boyish in this role of consort. He beamed, he condescended, he grimaced and he played, most unexpectedly, the comedian. At home he showed few traces of a sense of humor, but now, among his contemporaries, he was throwing forth quips, incomprehensible to Amelia, which were greeted by bursts of laughter justifiable only by the most devastating wit.

Now that the huggings and congratulations were over, however, this gay and sometimes boisterous corner, the *raison d'être* of the party, was left much to its own devices for the moment. Raising their voices slightly to be heard above the bursts of merriment from that quarter, the older people had settled into their normal cocktail-party concerns, keeping the white-jacketed Sam on the run to the makeshift bar for refills, sampling canapes from Isabel's passing tray. They talked standing in threes and fours; they talked sitting in clusters and shifted about apparently at random. This appearance was in part deceptive. Recognizing that Ruth Fortescue—a gentle soul, perhaps overshadowed just a trifle by her husband—was the sort of hostess likely to let guests fend for themselves, Amelia Booth had quietly taken charge.

If put to the question, Amelia would have insisted she found her self-appointed task distasteful. All her life she had been in rebellion against her conventional, etiquette-ridden Langstaff heritage that made of every party a formal pavan. She would have liked nothing better than to relax, just once, and let a party go its own way. But *somebody* had to make sure the different families mingled, set about bridging the unfamiliarity, finding as many affinities as could be found in one evening of this sort. And Amelia wasn't one to shirk a task merely because she disliked it.

In the event, there was one link between the families already in existence, needing none of Amelia's furtherance, and coming as a surprise to everybody. Her brother Douglas Langstaff, who had had to be nagged into coming with sisterly promises of keeping an eye on Joan's drinking, had pounced with delight on Ruth Fortescue's older and distinctly dowdy sister. "Why, Gert!" Douglas's enthusiasm had been tinged with something very like awe. "Gert *Zimmerman*, of course—but I never made the connection." And he had chatted with her animatedly for fully twenty minutes (quite forgetting his preoccupation with his wife) before turning his charm towards the more predictable target of their host. Very odd, and odder still was the reaction of the dowdy Gert—a lean and high-strung, harsh-voiced spinster. She had smiled with her mouth, she had been polite, but her eyes had remained cool and distracted; far from being impressed at being singled out by a Langstaff, she (whoever she might be) played the tolerant patrician at Douglas, and Douglas accepted it.

Musing on this minor mystery, Amelia had taken charge of Joan and deftly inserted her into a cluster of the most gallant-seeming older men, already marked down for this purpose. As long as she was flirted with, as long as she had an admiring masculine audience for those mannerisms which had been such a smashing success twenty-five years ago, Joan wouldn't need to blur over the awareness of her age.

For the moment Amelia was free. Since her husband was briefly showing an unwonted sociability (usually Stephen hovered on the fringes of a party, either inspecting the ritual with incredulity or quizzing strangers with his own particular humor), she could spread herself about, distributing nosegays of her personality to the minor relations who would not be seen again until the wedding reception. This was so practiced a maneuver for Amelia that it called for neither effort nor attention: she relied on the habit of her tongue to produce the requisite noises, reserving her private self for more consequent moments. Yes, another son, Brian . . . just fourteen . . . he's at Choate—but her focus had settled on a piece of wooden antiquity that stood beside one of the armchairs. Amelia resented knowing nothing about antiques, which meant that every few years she resolved to correct this ignorance, but as her interest was really very slight she never found the time. If a familiarity with the subject had somehow inserted itself into her mind, she would have welcomed it, for she hated ever to feel at a loss. She would dearly have liked to congratulate Ruth Fortescue on this whatever-it-was—a narrow, table-high cage of carved spindles. It had a look at once rustic and sophisticated and functional, as if it once had served some unimaginable purpose in a farmhouse where people had expected beauty to be one of the attributes of utility; now it bore with sturdy resignation its conversion to a magazine rack. Almost certainly it was a piece worthy of admiration—if one could identify it and if one could be certain it was genuine. There was grotesque humiliation in admiring an acknowledged fake. But though Amelia had no immediate use for the whatever-it-was herself, she made a firm mental note of its existence. Sometime in May her mother would return from Europe to inspect these new additions to the family and would be inclined to look down her long pseudopatrician nose at Ruth Fortescue. Common ground must be found for the two women to meet on, and Mrs. Langstaff loved antiques and knew all about them, or pretended to.

Vickie was making one of her periodic progresses through the room, and Amelia decided that the time had come. Detaching herself from the Zimmerman cousin who had been listing the rural delights of life in Flushing, she cosily captured her future daughter-in-law and drew her to one side. Amelia had news to tell. In reality it was easily told, but as Amelia planned to use her news as a means of extracting, if possible, a somewhat improper favor, she preferred to build up the story a little, make it sound as if she had gone to quite remarkable lengths to be able to bestow this benefaction.

The effect was all she had hoped for. A rapturous Vickie called over her mother to hear: "Mummy, Mummy, Amelia has arranged everything! We can have the Junior League for the reception, and you *know* there isn't a lovelier set-up in New York, but it's impossible to get in June, only Amelia has managed it!"

Most people, meeting Ruth Fortescue, liked her on sight—though the more aggressive might dismiss her, equally promptly, as ineffectual. She was short and plump; a once ordinary prettiness had mellowed into a less ordinary sweetness of countenance: she radiated warm, guileless kindliness. While pleased that Roger would be getting a mother-in-law so amiably disposed, Amelia was mildly horrified that any human should be so unselfconsciously transparent. Ruth had disciplined her children, she disciplined her household, but she had never thought to discipline her own face; emotions came and went there with indecent license.

Now she showed delight in her daughter's delight, gratification that a problem had been resolved without any effort on her part, some slight pique at the usurpation of what was properly her function, and a flicker of displeasure each time Vickie spoke the familiar name 'Amelia.' Had she chosen to, Amelia could have dispelled this last emotion. Bored by the tortuously respectful sobriquets youngsters invented for parents-in-law if left to their own devices, she had promptly invited Vickie to call her and Stephen by their first names; insisted on it, in fact. If Ruth's notions of decorum were affronted, however, this was an issue that Vickie must cope with some other time. Amelia did not feel called upon to intervene. She had wanted to catch Ruth at the disadvantage of feeling grateful, and if the gratitude was to be complicated by embarrassment, so much the better.

Eventually Vickie ran off to boast of this new triumph and Amelia moved over to the attack. For moments like this her mother had perfected an air of majestic condescension which not so much requested as implied that anyone who failed to let her have her own way must be ill-bred. On principle Amelia despised such tactics; she preferred to appeal to the best in people by suggesting that a refusal was both unreasonable and unkind. "I know you'll understand," she said with strong-minded diffidence. "Children get so wrapped up in these things. And with Vickie's brother acting as Roger's best man, my youngsters are bound to feel it's a bit one-sided, they're being left out in the cold. Especially Frances—you know how little girls are when it comes to a wedding. And since there doesn't seem to be any other child of the appropriate age in the immediate family, I wonder if you'd conspire with me to let Frances act as Vickie's flower girl?"

Several distinguishable varieties of uncertainty trooped across the stage of Ruth Fortescue's face. There was distress at being asked to make a decision without consulting the others concerned, there was dislike of seeming disobliging, there was dismay at being expected to settle, in the midst of a party where she was hostess, some minor detail of a ceremonial that was nearly three months in the future.

"It's wicked of me to plague you like this," Amelia added, before uncertainty could firm into procrastination, "but Franny was hanging around while I was *besieging* people about the Junior League, so now she's all excited to know what part she'll have to play."

"Yes, of course," said Ruth, smiling with brilliant misery at this reminder. "I don't know what Vickie's plans are . . ."

"Oh, I wouldn't expect Vickie to appreciate how much these things mean to a little girl," Amelia said. "That's why I came to you. On something like this I'm sure she'll let herself be guided—she's such a thoughtful girl."

The doorbell rang, aggravating Ruth's anxiety to escape. Amelia remained oblivious, single-minded, detaining Ruth with gentle persistence until Ruth bought her freedom with something sufficiently like a promise of support. Her surrender was not clear-cut, but neither (surely) was her memory so precise that she would later on be confident of just how far she had committed herself.

The latecomer was Roger's father, arriving as usual with the maximum of commotion—scattering raindrops, shouting apologies, generally suggesting that the party must have been a dull affair till now but henceforward everyone would have a good time. The exhibitionism of the introvert was so much more flamboyant than that of the natural extrovert. Owen Hilliard was a man of standing now, of eminence and even of glamour. If he had crept into the party as timidly as a mouse, he would have been sought out, made much of, as soon as his identity was known, but he had never relinquished the motley he'd once assumed, thirty-five years before, to disguise an adolescent's paralyzing shyness. In fact, the performance was now garnished with snippets from all the ham actors he had known. One of the lesser advantages of not being married to Owen was that you could be amused by these mannerisms instead of suffering the exasperation of living with them.

Always, when they met in public these days (though they had talked on the phone a score of times this past week), he greeted Amelia like a long-lost relative: say a backward younger sister he had mislaid some dozen years ago. As he made his way in her direction, he cried out several of those Darlings without which the theatrical world would have perished overnight, and when he reached her he gave her several of those great smacking busses which he knew annoyed her intensely but which were intended to remind everyone within earshot that here was one ex-marriage where the partners still remained good friends. In the face of such treatment it was a tribute to her patience and Owen's charm that she still remained very fond of him.

"You can relax," she said. "Everyone is now convinced that you're the guest of honor."

"I can't afford to be blasé," he said. "You have two more of these festivities to look forward to. I have to make the most of this one."

"That depends on how much Roger takes after you, doesn't it?"

He grinned reprovingly and moved along, gradually directing himself, she noticed, towards the young people's corner, where all the beauty was. Amelia hoped he would enjoy himself while he could. Later in the evening she would have a serious talk with him, if the opportunity occurred, and that he would *not* enjoy.

Owen's irruption had shaken Stephen out of his sociable phase:

he was beginning to take on that prowly expression of the sardonic onlooker. She cast about for someone who might stop her husband from relinquishing his fellowship and was pleased to see that Charles Fortescue was at loose ends for the moment. As yet the two men had exchanged little more than the barest civilities, and Amelia knew that she had been saving up for just this moment a common association that could start them towards a more familiar footing. . . . Oh, yes —South America, Peru. Fortescue was a tall, spare man with a long-jawed, ascetic face, a look of impatient self-assurance. He had dark bushy eyebrows, scarcely grey at all, but his hair—and he still had most of it—was nearly white. Amelia put him quite a bit older than his wife, in his early sixties probably. He looked more intelligent than most businessmen (her brother Douglas, for example, already gave one the impression that he would distrust any idea he hadn't heard of back in college), but that might be deceptive: leanness in a man of sixty often gave a spurious suggestion of intellect. Still, it seemed reasonable to hope that he could keep Stephen interested for a while.

5

Someday, doubtless (reflected Charles Fortescue as he manfully supported his share of the limping conversation), he and Professor Booth would get together, when that domineering woman wasn't about, and learn to enjoy one another's company. For the moment they were doomed. Because they had been told to talk about Peru, like obedient children they went on talking about Peru—perhaps they had been assigned this topic for some good reason, perhaps any deviation might lead them into unseasonable controversy. In their mutual ignorance they had no idea where else to go.

Yet Peru was a mistake. It appeared that a quarter of a century ago Stephen Booth had spent his field year there, but with one of the jungle Indian tribes on the other side of the Andes; whereas business trips had taken Charles up into the Andes, deep down inside them, but never beyond them. So after a few reminiscences of that improbable cross-mountain railroad which reaches such altitudes that oxygen tanks are standard equipment for the passenger cars, the two men had to compromise on Lima. Here Stephen had paused to inspect the archeological museum and the Library and to pay his respects to the resident scholars at the University; here, as a subordinate executive, Charles had kicked his heels waiting to cope with the quirks of the Peruvian government in those days, which was forever seeking new ways to surtax the Company; for instance, by claiming that some tailings dam had leaked into a nice pure river. But these two aspects of Lima really had very little in common, and after agreeing that the bar at the Hotel Bolivar served the best Pisco Sours in town, they found remarkably little to say. In despair, Booth had fallen back on anecdotes of 'his' jungle tribe, anecdotes which had been recounted so often to uncaring listeners that they had become perfunctory and juiceless. Charles took his cue from this. "Will you do me a great favor?" he broke in, offering a charming smile as indemnity for the interruption. "Will you come and talk anthropology with my father-in-law for a while? The youngsters are all terrified of him, and their parents not much less so, so he tends to be rather neglected at gatherings like this."

"Is Mr. Zimmerman particularly interested in anthropology?" asked Professor Booth, not suspiciously but with an innocent wonder.

"I know he'll be delighted to have an anthropologist to talk with," Charles said, "and I'm quite sure you'll not be bored." And he led Professor Booth to the chair beside the one where Jacob beamed out at the party with patriarchal and fraudulent benignancy.

There was a little harmless malice in this, since Jacob would doubtless try to convert Professor Booth to the theory that anthropology was merely licensed gossip-mongering, or something of the sort, but there was evidence that Booth could look after himself. For all his apparent gentleness, was he not thriving and contented looking after years of marriage to old Hilary Langstaff's daughter?

Stories were still told of old Hilary and the irony of them was that they were all stories Hilary had told himself to illustrate how rapidly the world was going to hell; nowadays they reappeared in some old-timer's after-banquet speech to illustrate how truly god-awful the 'good old days' had been. Hilary had been the last of a line of gentlemen bankers old enough to look on all other bankers as upstarts; he knew little about finance and not much more about banking, but he was an aristocrat to the polished soles of his English boots, with an aristocrat's innate conviction that his instinct was just a shade better than any textbook knowledge. Fortunately he had little to do with the running of the family bank, so there was still something to merge when it was absorbed by one of the larger, more efficient upstarts. Instead, he had devoted himself to what he referred to as public service: the true Langstaff forte was meddling in other people's business.

His children took after him, both of them. Oh, they had shed the overweening mannerisms, as had everybody today who lived in the world and not in one of the social reservations, but they had that same bland way of knowing what was best for other people. Douglas, now. Charles had not met Douglas Langstaff before, but had known vaguely he was down on Wall Street with one of those fancy firms that made out they were a cut above stockbrokers. It would have been natural for Douglas to want to make a good impression, to establish some sort of rapport towards the future. And in a way that was just what he'd tried to do. But he couldn't help himself. Within ten minutes he had been rattling on about some program whereby when an employee of a company gave money to his college's Alumni Fund, the company matched the donation—a splendid method for industry to support the higher education that supplied its technicians and executives. Matching Gifts, the plan was called, and why wasn't Andean C & Z taking part? Cerro de Pasco had been participating for some years now. . . .

And Amelia Booth had even bigger ideas: she was quite prepared to tell the entire world how to behave, always in the news with her League for International Disarmament. Yes, she was a chip off the old block for all that she had started off as the family rebel. There had been a minor scandal when she had insisted on marrying Owen Hilliard, a penniless scribbler as he was then. Old Hilary had been too unselfconscious an aristocrat to confine his outrages to the family circle: the thought of surrendering his daughter to bohemianism had brought on a very public attack of apoplexy, which carried him off a few days later. Undismayed even by this extreme form of moral suasion, Amelia went right ahead with the marriage. Back in the Twenties and Thirties a number of the more strongheaded society girls had had their fling at marrying artists of one sort or another, because they fancied themselves as inspiring genius or perhaps because they believed that artists were more tractable than ordinary men. Whatever the illusion, it rarely survived for very long.

Yet even old Hilary could not have sniffed at the success the scribbler had finally made of himself, for these days Owen Hilliard was one of the biggest names on Broadway. He was not a playwright exactly, since his plays were never originals but adaptations of other men's novels. But Hilliard got the credit for them, and he'd had four of the biggest hits of the past five or six seasons, sometimes two or three of them running at the same time. The latest, *The Cascade*, looked as if it might last out the century: they were already (as was becoming commoner every year) selling tickets so far in advance that a person over sixty-five consulted his heart specialist before purchasing them.

And for Charles Fortescue there was something distinctly intriguing about gaining as a member of the family someone from that alien world on the other side of the footlights. This was the more unexpected, since as a general rule Charles shied away from artists, not out of snobbery but from a feeling that he wouldn't have anything to say to them. He wasn't a great reader; he hadn't the time for novels, except the detective fiction that he read for frankly soporific purposes. He moderately enjoyed the occasional concert Ruth coerced him into attending, but nobody on earth (not even Madge, in Madge's heyday) could have dragged him into an art gallery. Poets and painters and people like that were from another life.

But a playwright was somehow different, just as Broadway itself was different. Broadway had its special glamour, but it was a familiar glamour; all his life Charles had been going to the theatre whenever he had the chance, he was never too tired for that. And then, too, Broadway wasn't just long-haired artiness, but something which overlapped with the business world: Charles had several acquaintances who invested in plays and even (sometimes) showed a profit on their investments. An actor might have dismayed him. But Owen had just the right blend of substance and strangeness, respectability and exoticism. Instead of waiting for the party to throw them together again, Charles went to rescue him from Vickie's prattle.

Not that Owen showed any anxiety to be rescued. He was smiling down at Vickie, talking away with mouth and eyes and hands. From across the room he seemed surprisingly youthful, with a tall and well-kept body that he still carried buoyantly, and a sort of rakish good looks. As a young man Hilliard must have enjoyed a clean-cut handsomeness. His nose was long and straight, his chin firm, his mouth thin but not unsensuous. Time had etched a few lines here and there without much affecting the outline. His dark hair, nearly black, still remained, though probably higher above the forehead than formerly. It was only close up that you noticed the eyes that gave him away: heavy-lidded above, pouched below. Cynical eyes, Charles decided, dissipated eyes—and then, chancing to catch sight of himself in a mirror and realizing that his own eyes could be described as heavy-lidded and pouchy, wondered to what extent he was influenced by the man's reputation.

"Of course," Owen was saying with great earnestness, "you still have ample time to rectify your mistake."

"Wouldn't I seem rather fickle?" Vickie asked, laughing up at him.

"Just sensible," Owen insisted. "A woman always has the right to be sensible."

"What's all this?" Charles asked.

"He's trying to persuade me I've caught the wrong Hilliard," Vickie said. "I'm not convinced. Wouldn't I be smart to hold onto the one who still has some illusions left?"

"The illusions of innocence," Owen argued. "Flimsy stuff, cold comfort. But think of the illusions of middle age, which have had time to take on richness and texture. You can wrap yourself in them like a thick, warm cloak."

"A little the worse for wear by now, isn't it?"

"Vickie, honestly!" Charles protested automatically, though supposing that such impertinence would offend an artist less than another man.

"Oh, there's no future in a flirtation when Daddy comes along," Vickie said, smiling at them both, and took her high spirits off to another corner of the room.

"Sometimes," said Charles, "you wonder what became of all the effort you put into good manners."

"Vickie's instinct is right, you know," Owen said. "One divorce is taken for granted, a second is a misfortune. But the third marks you down as an emotional lightweight, not to be taken seriously."

However accurate, this had to be denied. "That's not how she thinks of you," Charles said. "From what I gather at the dinner table, you're the last word in sophistication."

"The brutal admiration of the very young," Owen murmured. Charles could see what he meant, but also (though he would not have admitted it) he saw what Vickie meant: Owen's reputation as a Don Juan was a part of the man's fascination. Not merely that he had shed three wives with offhand aplomb but that he could still, at his age, have his pick of the beauties. Since last autumn, and particularly since Christmastime when Vickie's every second word had been 'Roger,' the Fortescues had been attuned to the name of Hilliard. Ruth kept coming upon mentions of him in the gossip columns, often with photographs. Owen Hilliard lunches at '21' with Gloria de Kay. Owen Hilliard supping at El Morocco with Denise

Durrell, whose sensational performance in *The Cascade* promises an early stardom. Gorgeous young creatures, not more than a few years older than Vickie, fresh and firm and vital. And all of them anxious to captivate the man who held the keys to success and fame and fortune. . . .

Charles cleared his throat. "We finally got to *The Cascade* last week," he said. It was the gambit he had brought with him, propitiatory and flattering.

"Enjoyed it, I hope," Owen said politely.

"Very much indeed," said Charles, who had come prepared to explain just how and why, at some length, in a manner which would show that he was *not* the typical businessman to be diverted by musical comedies: for him, every time, a drama that could take him out of himself for an hour or two. However, he was soon aware of a falling off of Owen's attention, and it came to him vaguely that a professional writer might grow bored with amateur raptures. Having nothing to offer but uncritical enthusiasm he cut himself short, floundered for a more promising topic and asked if Owen was already at work on another play.

"Not yet. I'm still recuperating."

"This is your vacation, then?"

"More or less. Not entirely. They send me books from time to time, but nothing that's appealed to me so far."

"You work at home, I suppose." Charles had been struck by a sudden vision of Owen stretched out on a sofa, reading a novel and calling it work.

"Mostly," said Owen. "Until rehearsals start, anyway."

"An odd life, not having an office to go to," Charles said reflectively.

"Not as odd as you'd imagine."

"I expect it's all a question of what one is used to."

"In the end it comes to much the same thing. Whether you cross the city or just walk into the next room."

"But you roll out of bed and you're right there," said Charles, on whom the idea had been working powerfully. "No, it's completely different. You don't have other people to face. My God, you don't even have to shave till you feel like it!"

Owen hooted with laughter. "I thought I'd heard all the reasons for thinking writers have a carefree time of it."

"I've a tough beard," Charles complained, fingering his chin. "An electric shave doesn't last me till noon. So I start every day in a foul mood from scraping at my face before I'm properly awake. Then I get indignant at the day's news, spill my coffee, and have to change my necktie. It's a lucky man who doesn't have to rush off looking his best every morning."

"I'll grant you the shaving," Owen said. "Someday I'll list the drawbacks for you."

"I'd be curious to hear what they are," Charles said, just as a couple of culture-hungry Zimmermans came up to pay their respects to the playwright. It amused him to find that all men, however untrammeled their lives, believed that theirs was a difficult lot. He liked the picture he had conjured up of an Owen whose life was untouched by any of those rules or disciplines that hedged the ordinary man. He liked to think of Owen sleeping till noon whenever he chose—then awakening, sometimes uncertain of which woman's body lay curled beside him, but oftener in splendid solitude, with nobody around to fuss at him before he was ready to face the new day. Lounging around, fixing himself a meal that had nothing to do with any other person's tastes or schedule. Letting his day's program be determined by whether or not he felt in the *mood* for working. Nobody to demand decisions from him, no accumulation of drudging details, no clashing of personalities to deal with—nothing to stop him from fixing a long drink, putting up his feet and watching television all day if that's what he felt like doing. And in the evening, parties and plays and night clubs to go to while he was still feeling fresh and alert, choosing his companion from an assortment of pretty and complaisant young actresses. . . .

It was not that Charles was envious, exactly (or so he insisted to himself); he indulged in no goatish daydreams of changing places with Owen. He was simply fascinated, as another man might be fascinated by the exoticism of a matador or a racing driver: someone utterly outside the bounds of a settled and orderly life. He intended to *collect* Owen Hilliard, as the conversation piece in his scheme of ulterior decoration.

6

Dinner had already started—a buffet dinner, inevitably, with so many people—when Dr. Morris Zimmerman finally arrived. Ruth and Vickie hurried to greet him at the door. Jacob put aside his plate and his argument with Professor Booth for the duty of inspecting his son.

Morris was trying to be gay and apologetic, but with half an eye you could see he was exhausted. So much grey putty, that's what he looked like. A fine doctor, Morris, and so, naturally, the wrong temperament. He took things too personally, which was fine for the patients, maybe, but not so fine for Morris. He wouldn't live to see sixty if he went on like this, if he didn't take more vacations. Jacob was always telling him: Go to Europe, Morris, go to California, go any place you like just so it isn't a medical convention. When did he ever pay any attention?

"So," he greeted his son disgustedly. "Even as a small boy you could never get anywhere on time."

"Good evening, Father," Morris said. "One of those things, I'm afraid. Thank you, Vickie, you're an angel—I need this." He took the cocktail from his niece and drank half of it off at a swallow.

"Professor Booth, this is my son, Morris," said Jacob. "This morning he was a doctor. From the look of him he has spent the afternoon killing off his last patient."

Morris shook hands. "No, not quite," he said. "Technically it was a good day. In six months or so the patient won't be at all grateful, but we're not supposed to think about that." He looked at them blindly, not yet escaped from whatever struggle had been engaging him for the past hours. "It would be nice if so many of our successes didn't end up seeming like officious meddling," he added quietly.

"Doctors should not be allowed to think at all," said Jacob. "It's no part of their profession, and they haven't the training for it. You need a vacation, Morris."

"I know."

"In the winter you know, and in the summer you find excuses. How is Susan?"

"Oh, she's fine." Morris's face lit up a little at the thought of his daughter. "You should be a great-grandfather by Thursday or so. Sue would have been here regardless, but Dan had visions of her delivering on the train and put his foot down: a typical first father in spite of having the benefit of all my lectures. But Tommy ought to be here somewhere . . . yes, there he is. I don't think he's speaking to me this evening. I am thwarting a promising career by declining to agree that a mid-town apartment is the ideal place to practice his music."

"What's wrong with practicing?" Jacob demanded.

"The jazz clarinet," said Morris.

"Thwart him, frustrate him, inhibit him," said Jacob. "Better a harmless neurotic than a monster in the family."

35

"I was thinking of the neighbors."

"When it's real music neighbors don't exist," Jacob said. Morris's color was beginning to come back. "Now go and have some dinner. You need food more than you need that pansy cocktail. Besides, you interrupt. I was explaining to Professor Booth how modern anthropology went astray."

"You have no respect for a man's lifework," Morris said. "Dr. Ritter's practice has been going downhill since you convinced him that psychiatry is an undiscovered science."

"Go away," said Jacob. He impaled a shrimp, waved it sternly at his son. "Professor Booth thinks I am a comical old man, too. He hasn't noticed yet that I am backing him gradually into a corner."

7

During dinner the children's corner included a scattering of adults. At the very center of the group Owen Hilliard sat boyishly on the carpet at Vickie's feet, eating from a plate in his lap. There had been protests at this; Roger had looked as though his own dignity were being undermined; chairs had been proffered, but Owen had insisted that he *liked* to sit on the floor, and on the floor he sat. This was not entirely an affectation of youthfulness. He had found that at any higher elevation his glance had a tendency to skid down the front of Vickie's low-cut dress: a meaningless and involuntary reflex which under the circumstances he felt was unseemly. From down below, out of temptation's way, he could effortlessly indulge Vickie in the mock-flirtatious banter which she had settled on as the proper tone with a father-in-law to be.

Up to a point he liked Vickie, but he was well aware that this meant no more and no less than that he found her attractive. She was gay, she was amusing, she was pretty, she had a delicious little figure. He had been unable to refrain from speculating whether she was a virgin, whether she and Roger had slept together, what she would be like in bed—unseemly territory again, but speculations that probably were succumbed to by every prospective father-in-law who had not yet abdicated his manhood, though most would deny it righteously.

But, leaving aside the matter of attractiveness, was Vickie likely to make Roger a good wife?

This was a more responsible form of speculation, for it was even conceivable that a father of Owen's experience could give his son a few constructive hints on how to deal with the particular young lady he had chosen. The difficulty was that on the evidence of her public behavior Vickie had no more character than the qualities which went to make up her attractiveness: she was wholly adorable and only rudimentarily a person. Presumably there was a latent personality under the surface, waiting to emerge, and presumably Roger had glimpsed it. But it was impossible to imagine what Roger had glimpsed, for the picture Vickie offered the rest of the world was a pleasing collection of negatives: she did not seem spoiled, she did not seem stupid, she did not seem ill-bred or humorless or flighty.

The only positive impression she gave, however, was the most treacherous of the lot: she showed every sign of being thoroughly in love with Roger. Charming to see, but not at all reassuring; it could mean a great deal or worse than nothing—pure trouble. At her age, love for a young man could so easily be an expression of some other yearning: to escape from her family, to have a home of her own, to be recognized officially as part of the adult community. She might love Roger for representing satisfaction for one or all of these cravings, but after the cravings were satisfied, perhaps long afterwards, there would be hell to pay unless she also loved Roger because he was Roger. Doubtless she believed she did, and maybe she was right. At this stage nobody could tell. But such evidence as there was, was alarming, to say the least. You had only to look at the girl's mother. A terrifying woman. Pernicious.

Not intentionally, of course. Oh, no. As sweet and well meaning a woman as you could find, with no malice in her make-up. Pernicious by innocence—as certain amiable cats, arching on your knee, will dig in their claws from utter ignorance that under the trouser fabric there is tender living flesh.

"May I get you some more to eat?" Vickie suggested prettily. "I'm going myself, anyway."

"Let Roger take care of both of us," Owen said. "Then we can discuss him behind his back. You can tell me what you see in him— the minor things you like and the major things you are planning to improve."

Badinage was no way to learn anything, yet this was the real enigma: whether Vickie *could* see his son, see him as a distinct individual. Her mother never would. Owen was all too familiar with the Ruth Fortescues of this world. By an unholy irony, though the two women were unalike in most ways, in this one respect Ruth Fortescue and Amelia's mother were identical: they hadn't a trace of self-consciousness. Unable to perceive themselves, they never noticed the need to distinguish between other people, whom they regarded as so many extensions of themselves. As a result, they were capable of infinite generosity and not a particle of personal considerateness. Owen still quailed at the memory of those ghastly weeks after Roger was born, when Mrs. Langstaff had been in and out of their apartment all the time. She adored him, when he gave her the chance. She had been a wonder of helpfulness, enchanted with her first grandchild—and she had very nearly driven Owen to the verge of hysteria. She had (among other things) expected Owen to respond to the baby as a father, precisely as she responded as a grandmother, and had been bewildered by his perversity when he would not. Owen had wanted to shout and throw things and had never got beyond composing imaginary monologues. "Look, dammit, I am not a middle-aged, middle-class, infant-smitten grandmother—I am *me*. In the first place I'm a man, which seems to have escaped your attention. In the second place I think of myself as an artist; whether I'm justified in that remains to be seen, but it's the most important single thing in my life. So part of me is overjoyed at having a son, and part of me is terrified of the responsibility. In one sense I'm bound to see little Roger as a menace, whose presence will be a complication to my work and whose very existence may make a mess of the career I want by forcing me to get out and scramble to support him and educate him decently. These problems will sort themselves out. I'm a normal, healthy man; I'm not especially neurotic. If you'll just give me a chance to learn to love Roger in my own fashion, at my own pace, everything will work out nicely. But you won't. You mean well, but since Roger was born every word you've uttered has added to my feeling of entrapment. The idea would horrify you, but you've done your unconscious best to make me dislike my own son. Now for God's sake get out before you succeed!"

He had never spoken a word of this. Partly because a reasonably well brought up young man simply did not talk to his mother-in-law that way, especially when the mother-in-law's allowance to her daughter was a major factor in keeping the household afloat. But mostly because he had known that Mrs. Langstaff would understand not a word of it; he would have hurt her feelings to no effect. She would have said, "But Owen dear, of *course* I know you're a man. . . . I'm sure you're going to be a *splendid* writer," and for the rest she would have been as astonished as someone suddenly slapped in the face by his own right hand.

Ruth Fortescue was another such, and if Owen had had any illusions about his son's sensitivity, he would have been upset. But Roger was a sturdy young man, almost tiresome in his normality. Possibly he would never notice that *his* mother-in-law hadn't the least comprehension of him as a person, and if he noticed he probably would not be perturbed. But what was acceptable in a mother-in-law could be intolerable in a wife, so the vital question was how much of this characteristic Vickie might have inherited from her mother.

He could only go on the analogy of Amelia (who had now come to have her dessert in the children's corner). She had taken much more after the Langstaff side of her family, but even so there had been distinct traces of her mother. In the first months of their marriage he had been baffled and then infuriated by the times when it had simply not occurred to her that there was any point of view to be considered but her own; if she dropped a milk bottle on his toe, she was convinced that the pain went away as soon as she explained that she hadn't *intended* to drop it. He had thought of this as youthfulness, he had thought of it as selfishness, and only later, some time later, had he realized it was neither: she had simply never been given any reason to understand that in an intimate relationship there was need for an intimate form of that public virtue called tact—a running awareness of how the other person was likely to be thinking. But, unlike her mother, Amelia was no fool. Once she had recognized there was some value to understanding how his mind worked, she had learned fast. A couple of years later she had been understanding him all too outspokenly for his own comfort.

Poor, darling Amelia: she was a perfect instance of a woman's ability to be practical without surrendering her illusions. She loved to think of herself as the black sheep, the Langstaff rebel; she talked of it constantly to this day. Yet she had never noticed that her rebellion was an exquisitely Langstaff rebellion; the blackness of the sheep hinted at a fashionable dye job. She had married Owen to defy her heritage, and in no time at all she had been trying to turn him into the Langstaff conception of what an artist should be. (The understanding he had demanded had led her all the quicker to an appreciation of how far he fell short of the mark.) When Owen proved too lazy to dominate and too elusive to be dominated, she divorced him, and then—having forsworn the family arrogance—looked around for new worlds to conquer. The academic world, offshoot of the servant class, was nearly as reprehensible as the artistic: she had married Stephen Booth and promptly set him to turning out anthropological best sellers. Despising her mother's salon of social-register chitchat, Amelia had founded a salon where the chitchat was little more profound for being academic and intellectual, and where (defiantly) an occasional Negro was welcome if he had a sufficiency of initials after his name. Loathing the traditional female Langstaff role of benevolent patroness, Amelia had become the despotic chairlady of a succession of progressive causes. Yet, "It is only out of respect for my mother," Amelia delighted in saying, "that I'm able to believe there's a drop of Langstaff blood in my veins."

So the emancipated Amelia had marched across the room (after making sure that Joan was getting a fortifying, nonalcoholic meal, and checking to see that Douglas and Stephen were still effectively deployed) and bestowed herself on the children's corner for no better reason than a sense of duty. For a moment she talked with the young man whose seat she had graciously accepted, but that she wasn't paying him the least attention became apparent when, as soon as she had picked up the drift of the exchange between Vickie and Owen, she interrupted herself to wag a roguish finger at Vickie. "Watch out for that man, my dear!" she cried archly; "he's been practicing that line for thirty years." Amid the prevailing foolery it was a hopelessly false note, like using an anthropometrical photograph of a dwarf to illustrate a fairy tale. But knowing that Amelia meant nothing, was merely trying to join in the fun, Owen felt sorry for her.

Presumably if you aged in daily intimacy with a woman, you never entirely lost sight of the girl you had originally fallen in love with; the alterations came so imperceptibly that there was an unbroken sense of continuity back to the first fine rapture. But the day-to-day intimacy must be an essential. Owen had never lost touch with Amelia. Except for the last two years of the war, he had seen her at least five or six times a year and usually much oftener: apart from the conferences about Roger they had numerous friends in common who knew it was no solecism to invite them both to the same party. Yet for some time now, though the habit of his affection had not suffered, he had found it quite impossible to discover in this trim and handsome matron any trace of the girl he had so adored. It was quite disconcerting to look at her across a room and know that at one time *this* had represented all the bliss there was in life, that he had dangled on her words and shifted from elation to despair with her moods, that he had thought her the most enchanting, amusing, exciting creature in the world and had positively ached to go to bed with her. Eerie, and no less eerie for knowing it must be, in these days of frequent divorce, a fairly common experience: people must always be running into former wives or husbands and wondering what lunacy had once possessed them. You didn't react so strongly on meeting the partner of some brief long-ago love affair, even if she had grown gross and blowsy in the interval: the mind was satisfied by the body's explanation: What a sexy little piece she used to be—what a pity! Only when you had lived with someone for a period of years was there the wish to protest at this middle-aged disguise and the wonder if perhaps it was really you who had changed so much.

For twenty years had not dealt harshly with Amelia. She had kept her figure. She was still handsome, and she had never been beautiful: her stubborn jaw and her too-pointed Langstaff nose might have been less sharply defined once upon a time, but they were not unattractive now. Her large grey eyes had always been her best feature, and they still were; the few wrinkles were more than off-set by a little make-up and the splendid carriage of her head. Her hair was a more becoming shade of reddish gold than ever, but even at her most bohemian she had never regressed to her natural color, which was probably a mousy blonde. No, Amelia was still in business as a woman (unlike Ruth Fortescue, for example, who had relaxed into plump housewifery), and it stood to reason that the fault was in him if he couldn't see a maturer version of his erstwhile beloved. He couldn't, not a trace of it.

In a sense, of course, she had never existed. All his precious insight deserted him when he fell in love; his understanding became a device to rationalize his optimism. What young man could help falling in love with a girl who was vivacious, idealistic, sensitive and passionate? As it happened, Amelia was none of those things precisely —nor had she practiced to deceive: she had simply offered the raw material for self-deception. Restlessness is not *quite* the same thing as vivacity, and rebellion needn't be idealism, but sometimes it takes a great deal of detachment to notice the difference. With no motive more selfish than a desire to please, a quick-witted girl can give a splendid impersonation of sensitivity. And far more experienced men than Owen had been have mistaken healthy sensuality for a grand passion.

There was no harm in the reality. Owen might have learned to be perfectly content with a restless, quick-witted, sensual rebel for a wife if alongside his own disillusionment had not marched in step Amelia's discovery that her husband was *not*, as she had believed, dynamic, masterful, excitingly eccentric, hugely talented and likely to set the world ablaze before he was thirty. Lord, how young they had been! How sweetly, flounderingly, pathetically *young*. Yet not so young, he realized with sudden dismay, as Roger and Vickie were. . . .

"Owen, Owen," Amelia said chidingly. "Have you forgotten the importance of being the life of the party?"

8

Following Charles Fortescue down the hallway (the two of them suggesting some new Aesopian fable about a stork and a hedgehog), Morris Zimmerman wondered what the trouble was this time. He had discounted his brother-in-law's assurances that this wasn't personal. Charles was a hypochondriac. Not the usual semihysterical variety, inventing ailments to make up for the inadequacies of life— Charles had what Morris privately called Samuel Johnson's disease: a morbid preoccupation with death. Although an uncommonly healthy man for his age, he found fatality in the most trivial of symptoms. If he woke up with a stiff neck, he saw himself a belated victim of poliomyelitis; if he discovered a pimple in his armpit, he knew that the bubonic plague had returned.

"The day after Vickie moves out," Charles said, "I'm having her room turned into a study. I need a study. I thought I had one when we moved into this apartment. But Ruth had other ideas and I ended up with an armchair in the guest room—which is a real economy of inconvenience: when there are guests I have no place to escape to, and when there are no guests I have no space to spread out."

They went into the guest room, and Charles carefully shut the door behind them. Here there was peace. The party was only a distant murmur, and even the occasional shrieks of young laughter were muffled. "Large parties should never go on for more than two hours," Charles said. "By then a man's supply of public courtesy is wearing thin. You take the armchair."

This display of manners was a bad sign; Morris began reviewing all he could remember of the rarer tropical diseases.

"I need your help," Charles announced.

"Yes, I gathered that. You look fine."

Charles glowered indignantly. "I'm getting tired of this attitude,

I really am. I *said* nothing was wrong with me. Do I come running to you with every little headache? Be fair."

"No, you don't," Morris said. "You brood about it until Ruth calls me up and tells me you've gallantly gone off to the office despite a brain tumor."

"Oh, for God's sake! See if you're still laughing when you're my age. Anyway, I'm fine. So is Ruth, so are the kids. All clear?"

"Not very," Morris said. "I don't suppose you want my opinion on how to invest your money."

"That reminds me," Charles said. "You couldn't go wrong getting friendly with that Langstaff fellow. It's his line of country, he seems nice, he'll more or less be a member of the family. He'd be bound to give you the best brand of advice."

"It wouldn't help," Morris said. "The money knows where it comes from. Whenever a company finds out that Dr. Morris Zimmerman has become a stockholder, it loses all confidence and begins to consult the bankruptcy laws."

Charles wasn't listening. From a drawer in the small desk that was the room's only concession to his need for a study he produced a couple of cigars, handed one to Morris, lit them both. Then he sat down on the foot of one of the twin beds. "Look, I need some straight answers, and they're notoriously difficult to come by from you people," he said. "I've come to you because I don't want to run up against a plea of medical ethics—which nine times out of ten is just a doctor's way of avoiding responsibility."

This was even worse, far worse. Morris went headlong to the conclusion that Charles had got his girl friend pregnant and needed an illicit recommendation. As a doctor the idea did not offend him: he considered the present abortion laws a striking example of man's inhumanity to woman. But as Ruth's brother he was outraged. His immediate impulse was to warn Charles not to make a fool of himself, and just in time he remembered that officially he wasn't supposed to know that Charles kept a mistress.

That was Gert's discovery. One didn't think of bridge players—the serious ones, anyway—as especially gossipy folk, yet Gert kept turning up with odd information about the unlikeliest people, and she had no life of her own apart from the family and bridge. At first Morris had doubted this story, but the evidence was too circumstantial. Someone at Gert's club was also a member of The Darkroom and knew of the dodge Charles worked there; someone else who worked at Andean C & Z had several times seen Charles dining at a *west* side restaurant with a lady who was certainly not Ruth. Gert, whose taste in fiction left much to be desired, was willing to toy with the possibility that Charles kept these elaborately concealed assignations with a fallen cousin, so disreputable (in some unspecified way) that she could not be introduced to the family circle. Morris was not. If you stopped to consider Charles's character (which was quite beyond Gert; since he didn't play cards it had never occurred to her that he *had* a character), it was obvious that Charles was capable of a mistress, but a clandestine cousin, never.

In some respects New York was a remarkably small town. The occasional indiscretion passed unnoticed in the city's bustle, but a long-sustained liaison inevitably, sooner or later, was noted and commented upon. It was upon this reasoning that Morris assumed an established ladylove rather than an impulsive evening on the tiles from time to time.

But what to do with the knowledge? Clearly, nothing. It was a galling bit of information to sit upon; curiously galling, since Morris knew plenty of married men who tom-catted about, and he had never given a thought to their wives except to suspect they probably deserved it. There was a difference, evidently, when the wife in question was your own sister. Yet Ruth's feelings were the only ones to be consulted, and on close inspection she seemed perfectly contented. If that contentment was based on ignorance, it would be gratuitous cruelty to enlighten her; if on philosophy, she would not be grateful for having her nose rubbed in a situation which she had consigned to oblivion. Morris had said nothing. Beyond that, since it was obvious that he would have to go on regarding Charles with exactly the same degree of family congeniality as heretofore, he had had to flatten his knowledge into just another trivial detail concerning his brother-in-law: Charles dabbled in photography, was allergic to shell fish, had a curious reluctance to speak of his schooldays, liked Irish whisky and kept a girl friend hidden away on the west side. So successful had been this policy that now Morris would be miserable at having to exhume emotions which had been so tidily buried. If Charles showed any sign of being too frank, Morris was prepared to cut him off sharply, refuse to listen any further.

"How well do you know Dr. Jeremy Wales?" Charles asked.

Morris examined this question suspiciously from all angles and could find no sin in it. "I've met him a few times. Worked with him once. I don't know him personally."

"Professionally, I mean. By reputation."

"Well enough, I suppose."

"There it is, then," said Charles. "How good a man *is* Wales? That's what I have to know."

Though not entirely reassured, Morris was beginning to think that his first supposition had been wide of the mark. "How did you get tangled up with Wales?" he enquired.

Charles batted at a plume of smoke. "There you go again," he complained. "I'm not tangled up with Wales. This is business."

"Oh?" said Morris.

"Wales ran into old Clarence Barbour somewhere," Charles went on grudgingly. "Biarritz, it must have been."

"Wales's mother is French," Morris said. "He visits there a lot, I know."

"Anyway, he sold Clarence on the idea that he could do a fancy job of medical research for the company. So the orders came down from on high. Now he's had eighteen months to play with the problem."

"The altitude sickness?"

"That's right."

"Has he come up with any answers?"

"Oddly enough, that depends."

"And oddly enough," said Morris, "this is exactly where there's a good deal to be said for medical ethics. You, as a layman, are preparing to pass—"

"I'm sick to death of that argument," Charles interrupted. "Like it or not, laymen have to pass judgment on you boys all the time, and all your ethics accomplish is to make sure we do it in a state of total ignorance. We have to pick our own doctors, and what's to prevent us from picking the semicompetent or the crook? Not your ethics, Morris. I've listened to you and your cronies talking, don't forget. What about that plastic surgeon who boasted that he'd been 'performing' operations until twenty-four hours before he went into the hospital himself for cataracts on both eyes? Which meant that after the patients were anesthetized, he stood aside and let some pupil do the work, but the patients got charged at his scale. You're ethical yourself, Morris, but did you rush to report your friend? The hell you did. No, your ethics are there to protect the profession, and the customer has to look out for himself as best he can. All right. This is a case where the responsibility is all mine. And I'm doing my best. I'm trying to get professional advice, and from someone who is usually less mealymouthed than most doctors. Don't pick this moment to go stuffy on me, Morris. Is Jeremy Wales a first-rate man or isn't he?"

"It's not that simple," Morris said. "Quite a few people like to pass judgment on Dr. Wales, only they get to different conclusions. I can give you two opinions. He's brilliant, and he's a crank."

"Well, old Clarence wouldn't have been hooked by anybody who was merely sensible," Charles said. "Can you break that down a bit?"

Morris snuggled more comfortably into the armchair and for the first time really began to enjoy his cigar. "Wales is the son of one of the four or five best surgeons of his day," he said thoughtfully. "I don't know why, but the children of top-flight surgeons don't often go into medicine, and when they do they are frequently the radicals of the profession, the eccentrics—which isn't to suggest that they aren't sometimes entirely in the right. And then, as I say, Wales is half French. He did some of his growing up in France, he speaks the language like a native, he goes back when he can, and he's more familiar with the fringe medicines in Europe than most of us. They are more tolerant over there than we are; they play about with home-opathy and acupuncture and I don't know what all, and the practitioners claim some pretty impressive results. All anathema to our Medical Association, of course, which everyone knows is the most exquisitely conservative in the world. Our official position is that it's better for a hundred people to die by orthodoxy than one to be cured by heresy, and you'll never get a lay person to understand that there's a good deal to be said for that point of view. There's also something to be said against it, and Wales is one of the most vocal. Nobody has ever caught him supporting one of the heresies, at least not in public, but at the drop of a hat he'll read you a lecture on how unscientific it is to assume that allopathy has *all* the answers while refusing to test the claims of anything else. He insists that we are becoming insular and timid, that our whole system is geared to the protection of the least-competent practitioner (here he's entirely correct), and that we're pushing all original thinking back into the laboratories. I'd say that he was a man who naturally bubbled with ideas, somewhat frustrated in a profession which tends to regard ideas with deep and well-justified suspicion. We need to have a few men like that about, but we'd spoil their value if we made life too easy for them. Does that help you?"

"I'm not sure," said Charles. "I don't think I care about how much of a crank Wales is. All I'm interested in is results. I know a man out in Akron who keeps two dowsers on his payroll; he knows as well as you do that there's no such thing as a dowser, but the men do the work he pays them for and he can't see that it's any problem of his that what they're doing is impossible, as long as it works. A crackpot can be a genius, or he can be a moron. Which is Wales likely to be?"

"In his own way he's a brilliant man," Morris said. "He might ride a hobbyhorse to death, but he'd have tried to be sure he was on to something in the first place. He'd never be guilty of sheer stupidity."

"That's better," Charles said. "A businessman would have said that twenty minutes ago."

9

At ten o'clock a New York party is at its prime. The initial uncertainties have long since faded, the duty conversations are all disposed of, and everyone but the confirmed misanthrope will have found a congenial soul or two to chat with. Another half hour will pass before the suburbanites start peeking at their wristwatches. The guests who went at the cocktails too enthusiastically have been succored by dinner, and dinner is not yet far enough behind for there to be any harm in those who are going too enthusiastically at the highballs. It is the mellowest part of the evening, the time to decide whether a flirtation is leading anywhere, the time to cement friendships, the time when the least expenditure of affability brings the greatest sense of social well-being.

It was also the time when Stephen could be relied on to come drifting by to inquire, from the corner of his mouth, when they could reasonably make their escape.

"Not yet," said Amelia. "You looked as if you were having a fine time with old Mr. Zimmerman."

"I tired him out finally," Stephen said. "He's an amusing old devil. I assume he lives at the Public Library; he seems to have read everything in print, and disagreed with most of it. He was having at me on anthropology, but I gathered he could have done equally well if I'd been an archeologist or an historian. Eventually I broke down and asked him what he'd taught. It turned out that until he retired, some twenty years ago, he was a cellist with the New York Philharmonic."

"I could have told you that much," Amelia said.

"I'm glad you didn't," her husband replied. "I'd never have discovered the rest. Look, we're not going to wait around for Roger, are we?"

"Heavens, no. He'll be here till Vickie pushes him out, I expect. But I want to have a talk with Owen."

"About the honeymoon?"

Amelia nodded.

Over her shoulder Stephen looked at the corner where earlier on Vickie had held court and where now Owen was the center of attraction. The groupings had changed. Roger and Vickie and a few other youngsters were still there, but now there were just as many of their elders, including Charles Fortescue, all of them listening with delight as Owen made hilarity from the vicissitudes of getting a show to Broadway. "The evening we opened in Boston," he was saying, "hurricane Clotilda was due in for a one-night stand . . ." and as he talked all the anxieties of the time were artfully turned to the diversion of the moment.

"It seems a pity," Stephen said. "He's having such a good time." And he drifted away again.

That Stephen should ungrudgingly admire Owen's enjoyment was typical of Stephen; that Amelia should promptly question it was, she supposed, typical of her. But she knew her ex-husband better. She knew that Owen could not help responding almost voluptuously to any role that was assigned to him. If people wanted to lionize a successful dramatist, he would give them a successful dramatist to lionize—even if the success which they paid homage to represented failure to him.

She wasn't sure that it did, of course; she only knew that once he would have despised the work he was doing now. He had thought of himself as an artist; he had taken himself very seriously as an artist. If he had been lionized for his novels, he would have been the happiest of men, but it hadn't worked out that way. Of his four books only one had been even a moderate success: the war novel, written just after he got out of the Army when there had been a ready market for war novels. Then, later, beguiled by a certain natural facility for dialogue, he had turned to playwriting—and if he had been lionized for his own plays, he would have been content. But it hadn't worked out that way either: a couple of mild critical successes off Broadway and then a succession of near flops on Broadway. Owen was widely liked and widely respected as a craftsman; for fifteen years he had been a 'coming' man, everyone expecting that next time, next time he would surely hit the jackpot—but in his own right he never had.

It was only in his new guise as a pure craftsman, a superb re-scorer of other men's artistry, that he had finally arrived.

And how did he really feel about this belated, secondhand triumph? No one knew, for sure. It was not a question one could decently ask, however circumspect or flippant the wording: Are you still doing any serious work, Owen, or have you learned to be content with income-tax problems? Nor was Owen one to volunteer his opinion of the irony; he absorbed himself wholly in whatever he was doing, and not for him was the self-solacing evasion: when this bit of hackwork is out of the way I'll get back to *my* project. He had always been a hard worker, between recuperative intervals of bone laziness, and these days he was busier than ever. He would be busy writing at a play, then busy with the casting and staging of what he had written, and long before this was done with—success breeding success—producers would be urging him to read this book or that as a possibility for adaptation. Perhaps Owen simply kept himself so busy that he had no time to remember his earlier dreams. Perhaps. Men had a way of finding cause for self-congratulation in the most accidental prosperity. But Amelia was inclined to suspect that there was a strong flavor of rue in Owen's taste of success and that his party impersonation of an exuberant master-dramatist was not really so pleasurable as he made it seem.

Feeling that way, Amelia also felt less guilty at the thought of interrupting his fun.

She was selfish in insisting on raising money matters at a party, but she was doing it out of self-defense. As a rule, when faced with unforeseen expenses, Owen raised the roof. He bellowed. It was a conditioned reflex: he stormed and bellowed to give himself time to figure out where the money was coming from, and when he couldn't he was able to go right on bellowing without having revealed any momentary weakness or uncertainty. The bellowing hurt Amelia's ears, which were very sensitive, and she knew very well that *this* time there would be an inordinate amount of bellowing if she didn't seize the chance to tackle him when he was absolutely obliged to behave himself.

So she delayed till he had finished the latest sequence of anecdotes and conversation had become more general again for the moment, caught his eye and wigwagged her wish to speak to him. Then she retreated to a more secluded corner and waited for him to join her.

He came eventually to settle in the companion chair, still in the beamish glow of playing fortune's favorite. "This was a good idea, this party," he said. "Quite to my surprise I find myself liking Charles Fortescue. Not as dry a stick as I'd expected."

"A pity Mother couldn't be here," Amelia said.

"Where is she now?"

"Taormina, at last report. She'll be back in May, and then we'll have this to do all over again, with the youngsters left out and some miscellaneous society thrown in."

"Is she stopping off at Monte Carlo this trip? Maybe she won't be able to afford a party."

"She is, and that reminds me," Amelia said, feeling there had been enough small talk. "This has all happened so hurriedly that no one has had a chance to think of the practical considerations."

"Now there I can't agree with you," Owen said. Quite suddenly he had lost his beamish mood. "I would say there has already been too much dealing with the practical considerations, and too hastily."

A digression, and how to keep from getting trapped in that argument? "I know you disapprove, Owen," she said soothingly, "but it was very decent of Mr. Fortescue to offer Roger—"

"It's no concern of mine to approve or disapprove of what Fortescue does. What I disapprove of is Roger's accepting. That's not my notion of how a man gets his first job."

"If he quits after a year, he'll have some experience behind him," Amelia said reasonably. "From all one hears, advertising is not an easy field to break into, and I can't see the harm of his starting right off learning something instead of wasting his first six months or so as a mail boy. But don't argue with *me*. Argue with Roger."

"A complete waste of time," he said. "Roger can't think of anything but getting to bed with that girl."

"Precisely what I'm getting at. There are some practical problems that come first."

"I trust that Roger can cope with them."

"Owen, have you given a thought to their honeymoon?"

"Not really. I'm not ashamed of my prurient imagination, but there are limits."

"I suspected you hadn't," Amelia said. "And there's the apartment, too, but we'll take things one at a time. Vickie wants a full church wedding."

"My God! Where?"

"No, she's Episcopalian—that's all right. But it will be big, undoubtedly, and the reception afterwards won't be much smaller.

That's the Fortescues' affair, and I promise you it will cost them a tidy fortune. The honeymoon is our headache."

"No headache at all," Owen said comfortably. "They can run off to Atlantic City for a weekend. We did."

"That's—"

"It was fun. I remember."

"Behave yourself," she said, fighting down the smile he was angling for. "I don't suppose I can expect you to see it in a social sense: that we simply cannot allow the Fortescues to spend several thousand dollars on their daughter's wedding and then have our son take her off on a fifty dollar honeymoon. No, forget that—I knew it would offend your principles. But you can't compare Roger and Vickie to us, you simply can't. We weren't such children. You'd left home years before, you'd come to New York, you had an apartment of your own. My father had only just died, and we couldn't have had a proper wedding if we'd wanted one, which we didn't. You were working to meet a deadline on something or other and didn't think you could get away for more than a weekend. And on top of everything, we hadn't a penny to our names."

"I still haven't," Owen said firmly.

"Whereas Roger and Vickie are a pair of babies, even if they don't know it," she went on. "They've both of them been about as sheltered as young people can be nowadays; they've never lived on their own for a day except off at school, and that doesn't count. Now they're stepping out into the adult world *and* getting married on the same day. They think it's all love and happiness after June, but we ought to know better. A honeymoon isn't just sex, Owen. Those kids need three or four weeks off somewhere peaceful and pleasant where they don't have anything to think about except getting their relationship on some sort of even keel before they have to face the workaday world again."

Owen was getting the look of a frustrated bellower. "Your eloquence has an expensive ring to it," he remarked. "I'm broke."

"Molly Jordan was telling me of a perfectly enchanting place down in the Islands. Jamaica, Antigua, I don't remember which. They would have a little cottage to themselves and a lovely beach that would be virtually their own. The food is extremely good, she says, and the servants are adorable: they know just when you want something and when you want to be left alone. She knows the woman who runs the place, and she's positive she can get us a decent rate—under fifty a day, anyway."

"Plus the plane fares, plus drinks—" he began, and at a glare from her he modulated his voice—"plus little excursions here and there, plus tipping, plus extras, plus I don't know what all. That's way over two thousand before they buy a souvenir. Amelia, do you realize that in exactly thirteen days I have to settle this year's taxes, and I'm still in debt for last year and the year before that?"

"And then there's the apartment," she went on remorselessly, sure that it was kinder that he appreciate as soon as possible where he stood. It took him a while to get used to these things. She had tried to warn him before, over the phone, but he had been too excited over Roger's engagement, or some girl had been at the apartment, or he had been furious about Roger's job, or he had been in a rush. "I daresay Mother will help there. She has some lovely old things in storage that she never uses; and if Vickie likes antiques, that's a beginning. Of course Vickie will bring silver and linens and china, and there will be a host of wedding presents, some of them useful—oh, that's another little item: Roger's wedding present to his bride. But it will still mean furnishing an apartment virtually from scratch—carpeting and curtains, beds, lamps, all the upholstered furniture. I'll help with the work of getting it, naturally, but you'll be writing all the checks."

"Look, this is just a pair of kids," Owen said with dazed horror. "They don't have to start out with the most elegant apartment in New York City. Roger has some perfectly good furniture down at college."

"No," said Amelia. "No, dear."

"That's good stuff! I paid enough for it."

"Four years ago. And four years of campus living does something very strange to furniture. I've seen it. I doubt if a junk dealer would give you—"

"Then the wedding is off," Owen said wildly. "I'm broke. It may sound cockeyed, but I'm dead broke."

"Poor darling," she sympathized. "I know it's a shock. Of course, you *have* spent the last several hours convincing everybody that you're the greatest success since George Bernard Shaw. But if you want to get up and make a public pronouncement to the effect that you're dead broke, go right ahead."

10

Even on normal evenings, when she had spent the day in shoes with medium stacked heels, there came a time when Ruth Fortescue was grateful to get out of her shoes and change into soft, fur-lined slippers. Tonight she had been wearing unaccustomed spikes since the first ring of the doorbell at a quarter to seven. By nine o'clock (she had had a busy day on her feet even before the party) she had been thinking longingly of her slippers; by ten thirty she had been in misery. Now, at nearly midnight, she had resigned herself to being crippled for life. But she would not take off her shoes, nor even ease them off her heels—though this was less a matter of principle than fear of being unable to get them on again. Ruth had very punctilious standards of etiquette about when she could be informal and comfortable. All outsiders had to be gone, naturally, except for youngsters —she didn't care how many of Peter's or Vickie's friends were around. With the family, distinctions were more subtle. Father didn't matter, of course, or Morris or Gert. Of her numerous other relatives, there were some with whom she always felt at home and some with whom her conduct varied according to the mood of the moment. There were a few, though, and Cousin Evelyn was the outstanding example, with whom Ruth could never feel sufficiently relaxed. Though professing the most radical opinions (to Ruth's way of thinking she might just as well have been a Communist), Evelyn had twenty-five years before made an unforgivable remark about Ruth's marrying a goy, and since that day Ruth had never been able to think of her as a true friend. It was silly, she knew, to hold a grudge for so long, but that was how it was. Evelyn had obviously long since forgotten the incident; she dearly loved a family gossip—though you'd have thought it beneath her high-minded ideals—and could be counted on to come first to any party and stay till the bitter end, to make sure that everybody had a fair share of her views. So Ruth kept on her shoes and suffered.

The other guests, the older ones, had all left. Most of the young people remained, with an air that the true party was finally getting started. Her father had begun the procession; he had become overstimulated and tired, and Gert had taken him home. Promptly the Long Island contingent fell to consulting their time tables. The thinning-out ritual began, the neatly spaced departures. It always happened that way, people were such sheep; one left and a party was doomed.

On the whole it had been a good party, unmarred by any unpleasantness, except for that one curious episode towards the end. Many of the others had already left when Joan Langstaff's voice, suddenly strident, cut through the room. She had been glaring venomously at her husband. "If I wait till two minutes before we leave to drink a toast to Roger and Vickie, you ought to be *delighted*," she had shrilled, and the word "delighted" had probably never been made to sound so menacing. But there had been only that one sentence. A few minutes later she had been all smiles and sweetness as the Langstaffs said good night, praising the party, remarking on what a lucky young man Roger was, and volunteering to help in any way she could with the preparations for the wedding.

In one respect only was Ruth left with a vague sense of dissatisfaction: she had wanted another few minutes of private conversation with Amelia Booth, and somehow she hadn't managed it. She had wanted to be quite sure that she hadn't committed herself too far on that question of Roger's little half sister acting as Vickie's flower girl; really, nothing like that could be settled without consulting Vickie. Perhaps the safest thing would have been to speak to Vickie right then, and if she disapproved of the idea *she* could have spoken to Amelia. But it seemed a shame to worry Vickie about anything so trivial on one of the happiest evenings of her life, and Ruth had felt sure she could attend to the matter herself. Her method of looking around hopefully whenever she was free had been ineffective with so dynamic a guest as Amelia, always in private colloquy with somebody or in the midst of a whole group, telling them about the League for International Disarmament. Ruth did not feel that she was particularly old-fashioned: she thoroughly approved of girls taking jobs until they got married, and if they never got married it was splendid if they went on to become executives or senators. But it seemed odd that a perfectly attractive woman like Amelia, with a home of her own and children to look after, should worry so much about disarmament—which, when you came right down to it, was the government's problem. And it was very difficult, when people were talking away about nuclear bombs, to break in with a flower girl. So nothing had been accomplished.

Last of the outsiders to leave—in fact, one of the very last of all—had been Owen Hilliard. This had seemed a charming compliment from such a witty, clever man, until she realized that he no doubt had a midnight appointment somewhere and didn't want to be too early. For theatrical people, she supposed, midnight was like high noon to the rest of the world: a topsy-turvy life. Still, when finally he had stood up to leave, he had appeared strangely reluctant to go, extending his farewells with much teasing of Vickie and his son, making plans to get together with Charles at some unspecified time in the future, and then going off with none of the gay vitality which had marked his arrival.

She was glad, if surprised, that Charles had taken such a liking to him. Charles didn't take to people easily; he had few intimates, most of them conservative business acquaintances as old as himself or older. Owen was the last person she would have expected to attract Charles, yet rarely had Charles gone to such lengths to be gracious and affable with a strange guest. Well, it was nice that he'd had some fun out of the party, since he certainly wasn't enjoying himself now. One of Peter's friends, with notions of becoming a mining engineer, was trying to use Charles as a fount of wisdom and benevolent advice, unaware of Charles's conviction, after thirty-five years of dealing with the breed, that mining engineers were the most exasperating form of subhuman life.

Meanwhile, Cousin Evelyn rattled relentlessly along. Having touched on each member of the family in turn, having dwelt at length on the splendid performance put on by Alison and Ben this evening considering that everyone knew they hadn't exchanged a civil word in private for months, she had finally arrived at one of her favorite themes: that Morris ought to remarry. It was fine that he had been so devoted to Reba, but she had been dead six years now, and it wasn't natural for a man to live by himself.

"Yes," Ruth said curtly. "He says he can't have dinner at your place without some dolled-up widow dropping in by accident." Without caring what was natural or not natural, Ruth felt there was something very beautiful about her brother's loyalty to Reba. Perhaps her mild brusqueness (for Ruth could never bring herself to be openly rude) got under Evelyn's skin for once; she suddenly allowed herself to discover how late it was and bustled through her adieux and her encomiums on the party.

Ruth hobbled to the door with her (letting Evelyn forage for her own coat), and as soon as the door was closed again, pulled off her shoes and hobbled on aching stockinged feet down to the bedroom. She got out her slippers, intending to go straight back and rescue Charles from the importunate young man, but then couldn't resist sitting down on the end of a bed for a moment, trying to knead some blood back into her toes. It was selfish, of course, and she was punished: in her one brief absence from the living room there was trouble.

"No!" came Charles's outraged roar. "No, Peter will *not* run down to the corner. The Sunday papers will be delivered at the normal time tomorrow morning. For God's sake, Vickie, won't you feel properly engaged until you see it in the *Times?*"

Ruth hurried into her slippers and back down the hall.

PART TWO

1

It was quite unthinkable, of course, that that peculiar amalgam of a parochial newspaper and a national archives, *The New York Times*, should fail to rise to the occasion. Prominent among the pages devoted to such matters, next day, was a photograph of Vickie looking thirty years old and distinctly homely, together with the explanation that 'Mr. and Mrs. Charles Mallory Fortescue announce the engagement of their daughter Victoria Emily. . . .' This intelligence was duly distributed throughout the country, for all who cared to look.

Some cared more than others. One, turning to that page first of all and catching sight of the photograph, caused her father to declare that just because a girl was engaged to be married didn't mean she couldn't still have her mouth washed out with soap. Less impatient souls made sure of glancing at that page as they worked methodically through the paper, either for the obscure pride of seeing a family name in print or to make sure that the names were spelled correctly.

Other friends and acquaintances came upon the item by accident, for the engagement had come about so precipitately that the news had had little chance to spread. There are people, women mostly, who never fail to skim through the society pages in hopes of coming upon some familiar name and, depending on the extent of their sociality, are more or less frequently rewarded. Thus, a young lady attending Sarah Lawrence read the paragraph with wonder and a toss of the head. The wonder resulted from the fact that last spring she had been madly in love with Roger Hilliard, had gone down to houseparties at Princeton determined at any cost to extract a proposal, and now could not imagine what lengths this hag had gone to that *she* had overlooked. The toss of the head was to remind herself that this was ancient history and that now she was madly in love with quite another young man; in fact, two.

While in New York City a second young lady, Joyce Neilson—who had never met Vickie and thought of Roger only as her employer's rather callow stepson—saw the announcement and astonished both herself and her widowed mother by bursting into uncontrollable sobbing.

Further from home, naturally, this fragment of news had less personal effect, usually none, yet for all that, it did not go unread. For, just as some men get a mysterious satisfaction from reading the obituaries of total strangers, some women are fascinated by betrothals and marriages almost in the abstract, albeit the parties involved are generally quite outside their ken. Up in Actonsville, Connecticut, for example, a middle-aged woman, wife to the local jeweler, was indulging in her weekly quota of this harmless amusement.

"Mr. & Mrs. Charles Mallory Fortescue," she read aloud in surprise. "Why, isn't that . . . ?" And wished that she had held her tongue. There was something suddenly grim about her gentle and reflective husband as he crossed the room and took the paper from her to see for himself. "I'm sorry, Louis," she said unhappily. "You have to learn to forget."

So does news, even the most insignificant, spread outward, having its various effects, under the remarkable aegis of *The New York Times*—a crumpled portion of one copy of which lay in one corner of the apartment on 55th Street, hurled there in a moment of pique by Jacob Zimmerman. "By now you'd think we'd know how to reproduce photographs," he growled. "The good European papers do it. Why can't we?"

Patiently Gert retrieved the offending pages and smoothed them out again. "This wasn't a decent likeness anyway," she said. "There wasn't time to have new pictures taken; this was left over from the batch Vickie had done last year for her Year Book."

There had been no photograph printed with the announcement of Gert's own engagement, though she had sent one in. Perhaps the *Times* had felt that a six-line notice was ample for socially invisible

Gertrude Zimmerman and Bernard Tepper; perhaps there simply hadn't been room for anything more. This was in 1942, and a few days after the party Bernie had gone back—not to college but to his army camp, to be sent overseas a few months later. In those days Gert had been working as a dental assistant for Dr. Baer, but her mother was still alive, looking after Father and the house; and she had known her evenings and weekends would yawn until Bernie came back, so she had taken up bridge, just to fill the time. It was still filling the time most successfully: she was one of the half-dozen ranking women players in the country. A full-time occupation now, she had quit work as soon as she was sure that the money she made playing cards, however erratically it came and went, averaged out at more than she was earning. These days her income was more stable: she took a few pupils, and aspiring players paid handsomely for the privilege of being her partner in club duplicates and minor tournaments. This was why she had been less than delighted to find that Douglas Langstaff would be, in a sense, a member of the family. For years he had been one of her favorite 'pigeons' at the rubber bridge table: an earnest and unimaginative player who had been carefully trained to regard her as kindly but infallible, he could be counted on to play his best when she was his partner and like a doomed man when she was an opponent—the ideal arrangement. Now he would grow familiar and unreliable and expect her to play with him for the fun of it in the Wednesday night duplicates.

By some chain of logic satisfactory in her own mind, she struck out: "It's going to cost a fortune to get this carpet properly cleaned. If they can *ever* get shoe polish out."

Her father paid no attention. Their conversation was often like that, strophe and antistrophe without a speaking acquaintance of each other. "It's very strange," he said. "Principles I have plenty of, and in principle I've no use for this race nonsense. People are people. Yet I can't help wishing that Vickie was getting married to a good Jewish boy."

Gert pricked up her ears at this, for it sounded as if it might be directed at her sister's husband. Jacob had never completely accepted Charles Fortescue, had always felt there was something wrong there. Ever since Gert had learned that Charles was keeping a young woman, she had been assiduous in his defense. Her father was too sharp; any faltering on her part and he might sense there was some justification for his suspicions. "That's ridiculous," she said firmly. "Don't be stupid."

59

"Ridiculous, yes," he agreed. "There's nothing to be done about it. But stupid? I'm not so sure."

"Roger is a nice boy."

"Who's denying it?" demanded her father. "But what are these nice boys thinking of when they get married? All the things you're not supposed to know about, all right, that goes without saying. And how much else? With a Jewish boy you know he's thinking ahead to the family he wants to have; even if he finds out he doesn't like his wife, he'll treat her decently, the mother of his children. They make better husbands."

"Alison and Ben," she threw at him. "There's a good Jewish boy for you!"

"You women!" he jeered. "Because Alison is your niece, then Ben must be to blame. I don't believe it. That girl doesn't fool me, I watched her grow up while you were playing cards. It was a pity Ann couldn't have any more children: she and Phil spoiled their baby rotten. And after Ann died, there was no stopping Phil: he let Alison walk all over him. Good husbands, yes, but good fathers? I didn't say so. Phil was a fool."

Adoring both her brothers, and especially the elder, Gert still felt queasy when she thought of his death in an airplane crash three years ago. "Your own son," she protested.

"That did not stop him from being a fool."

"Well, you needn't speak ill of the dead."

"Why not?" asked Jacob, instantly contentious. "What is this 'We shouldn't speak ill of the dead?' We should, it's a public duty. Who else is responsible for most of the trouble in the world?"

2

A young man proffers an engagement ring and goes back to college, blithely unaware of the drudgeries, exasperations and anxieties he has left behind for others to attend to. A train of action has been set moving. For the next several months the lives of some half dozen people will be discomposed; whatever their daily concerns and obligations, they will have to devote some part of their attention to the approaching wedding.

Least affected of the households involved, for the time being anyway, was that of the Stephen Booths. Amelia had a brisk dispatch with mere family matters, while Stephen, who had never spent much energy on his position as stepfather, went back to his normal routine: lectures and classes at the University, and the far more remunerative hours he spent each day in his study on the top floor of their house in Jefferson Mews.

Originally this floor had been partitioned into horrid little cubicles for servants; the dividing walls had long since vanished leaving one great, irregularly shaped room, dimly lit along its length by unevenly spaced dormer windows. In some stage of the building's evolution from Victorian times the room had been used as an artist's studio, for a large trapezoidal window had been let into the north wall; it was here that Stephen had his desk. Merely by swiveling in his chair he could look down on the little private gated alley, still lit at night by gas lamps—the gas provided by the adjacent householder. Each of the eight houses along the alley was of a period, each was owned or rented outright as a house: there was no letting of furnished rooms in Jefferson Mews. This was one of the quietest, most charming, most 'unspoiled' sections of Greenwich Village. It was also damnably expensive.

On an evening several days after the engagement party Stephen Booth sat staring down on this exclusive scrap of view, although strictly speaking his day's work was not yet done. At the far corner of the room Joyce Neilson typed away with halting industry, a reminder that he should get on with the revisions of Chapter Five if she was to have work to do tomorrow. The enthusiasm was hard to come by; in fact, it would be more accurate to say that the enthusiasm was all gone; what kept him writing was the need of money, nothing else. The day old Mrs. Langstaff died (it was quite dreadful how long this moral cancer had been growing in his mind), he would quit this nonsense right in the middle of a sentence. And then go back to writing the book he had started out to write, had always meant to write. If he was still capable of it. And if he was, he would probably have to publish under a different name to get himself taken seriously.

Stephen Booth was a man with a mission. He believed that the only value of anthropology lay in the light that primitive customs could throw on human behavior generally, and the light was wasted if it illuminated the minds of only a few other anthropologists. This was not in the least an original idea, of course, but very little that was worthwhile had been done with it. The best exception was still probably Frazer, for all that he was riddled with minor errors; a man with some knowledge of history could go to *The Golden Bough* and come away with a real understanding of the evolution of the priest-king which had such an impact on all cultures, down to the modern dictatorships. And Boas had done good work, and Ruth Benedict. But most of the other writing that had not been specialist calling to specialist had either dwelt so on the odd customs that readers said 'My, how quaint!' and missed the point, or been such clever, arrogant strutting of the ego that readers said, 'My, what an opinionated woman she is!' and discounted the point. It had seemed to Stephen that from the rich variety of societies the American Indian had created, he could build a telling (and reasonably popular) commentary on our contemporary civilization; and when his marriage to Amelia had settled into peace of a sort, this was the book he had set out to write.

Amelia had taken a Langstaffian interest in the project and made suggestions; before the book was a third done, she had found him a publisher, and the publisher made suggestions—for Stephen's benefit, of course: he wanted the book to reach the public, didn't he, and who knew more than a publisher about that? Then it seemed that the finished work was much too long, and the editor took charge of the cutting; somehow all the quaint folkways and the charming anecdotes stayed in and all the trenchant commentary was watered down or disappeared. But, under the editor's lamentable title *Our Brothers, the Amerinds*, the book was a success. A devastating success, the sort of success that drags other successes relentlessly in its trail, so at two- or three-year intervals there had followed *Our Brothers, the Samoans*; *Our Brothers, the Eskimo*, and others, till now he was charmingly and quaintly drudging out *Our Brothers, the Bushmen* without a spark of fraternal feeling for the Bushmen or anyone else left in his system. The book clubs found a specious prestige in giving sets of him away as dividends, and behind his back his colleagues sneered and called him Our Brethren Booth.

Dusk had fallen on Jefferson Mews, the puddles of lamplight stood out sharply now, and in one of them stood the woman from Number Four, out with her three toy poodles for their evening airing. Stephen felt in need of a drink and hadn't the will power to struggle against the temptation. He'd get some work done tomorrow between classes, or he could set Joyce to deciphering his notes towards the bibliography. "Well, I'm quitting," he said. "Would you like to come down for a glass of sherry?"

The typing went on for a word or two, then stopped. "No, I think not today," Joyce said in her precise, colorless voice. The missing 'Thank you' stood out, not because Joyce was a particularly gracious girl—she was too nervous for that—but because she was usually pathetically grateful for any gesture that treated her as a member of the family instead of hired help. As he crossed the long room, dark now except for Joyce's desk lamp, he glanced at her wastebasket: it was two-thirds full of crumpled paper. Never an efficient typist at best, on her bad days Joyce had to retype every second page.

"Oh, come on down; it will do you good!" he urged heartily—Joyce had a way of driving him into excessive avuncularity. "Eliot will be dropping in; he'll cheer you up."

"No, I'd better not. Thank you." She was a tall thin girl, with mouse-brown hair and a long, bony face which could express innumerable shadings of discontent. "I'll just finish up these few pages, and then I really ought to be getting home."

"Don't work too long," Stephen said, hesitating. Obviously she was punishing herself for something or other, but efforts to help Joyce could easily make her weepy or resentful. "Is Arthur still out of town?" he asked with off-hand caution.

"I haven't the faintest idea," she said primly, and turned back to her machine.

Stephen shrugged and started down the stairs; there were limits to what he could do. Joyce was the only child of an older beloved colleague who had died several years back after an illness too protracted and expensive to be more than partially covered by hospitalization; by the time he was dead, his savings and insurance had been wiped out, and Mrs. Neilson and her daughter had to live on a scrap of pension and whatever Joyce could earn. To make things jollier and quite like a radio drama, nursing her husband had left Mrs. Neilson a neurasthenic invalid, so Joyce could not have taken a regular job even if she had been trained for anything, which, of course, she had not been. She had stumbled through the beginnings of a secretarial course, and then in a moment of compassion, which he had regretted ever since, Stephen had taken her on as his part-time secretary. It was not the quality of her work he objected to—she was slow, obsessively conscientious and meticulous—but the responsibility: he had quickly realized that he would never get her off his hands unless some man married her away, and this was most unlikely since she rarely met any men.

A few weeks ago he had hoped that Arthur Vaughan was taking a serious interest in Joyce. Arthur was the paid secretary-treasurer of Amelia's League for International Disarmament, a modern type of saint, the realist-idealist, eager to impale himself on the thorniest

63

facts. For a while it looked as if he might impale himself on Joyce. Certainly she had gone out with him a number of times, abandoning her mother—and this was the sort of miracle with which a modern saint had to content himself. Joyce had taken some pains with her hair and make-up, for several weeks had seemed softer and prettier, and had even showed traces of an incipient gaiety. But now she had relapsed to her normal disconsolate angularity and had no idea whether Arthur was still out of town, so apparently nothing had come of it. A great pity. Stephen saw himself tottering into old age still playing father-surrogate to his secretary.

He went down past the floor of the children's bedrooms to the main floor, which consisted of the master bedroom in back and the long living room in front—the dining room and kitchen were still a flight further down, partly below street level. Stephen paused in the bedroom a moment to get a clean handkerchief and to listen for voices from the front room: the cocktail hour could be approached in a more tranquil frame of mind if there were a third person present. Relieved to hear that Eliot had already arrived, he stepped into the other room.

"Oh, splendid!" said Eliot. "You're just in time."

"Good evening, dear," said Amelia. "Had you a good day's work?" This was one of the advantages to an outsider: Amelia knew and scorned his disenchantment with the Bushmen and would have found a more cutting form of inquiry if they had been alone.

"Fine, fine," Stephen said. "What am I just in time for?"

"I hate repeating myself," Eliot said. "I was about to tell Amelia— I'm embarking on a new career."

"High time, I would think," Stephen said, sinking into the room's only comfortable chair; Amelia's decor was aimed at accommodating as many people as possible without crowding the room with furniture, but this meant that only one person could put his feet up. "Fix me a scotch on ice, will you, Eliot? Just a little water."

"I didn't say you'd find this any more respectable," Eliot replied, moving gracefully to the fitted bar. Eliot Clay was Stephen's half brother, his junior by eleven years, the sole offspring of his mother's remarriage to an aging syndicated sports columnist. Eliot's father had turned to journalism, if the inventive euphuisms of sports reporting could be called journalism, after a knee mangled during a football game had ended his dreams of playing professional baseball. By the time he married, years of grinding out his daily column from behind an alcoholic fog had made him seem more in need of a nurse than a wife, but the birth of a son aroused him from reminiscing about his widely admired feat of covering the 1920 Olympics without stirring from the hotel bar: he was determined that Eliot should take up that promising career which had been mangled along with his knee. He lived just long enough to leave Eliot with an abiding contempt for all forms of athletics and most other conventional manifestations of virility as well.

Released from his father's regime of push-ups and bar bells, given a chance to expand in the warmth of his mother's adoration, Eliot proved a charming, languid, witty young man, deplorably handsome, with a flair for improvising at the piano and another for composing satiric light verse. Those two minor talents, ripened in the acidulous brine of the homosexual life, formed the basis of his career: he wrote songs. Not popular ballads, the clever 'speciality' songs—sometimes topical, sometimes mildly bawdy—used by night-club singers with a comedic turn. On the proceeds of these songs, which were purchased outright by the singer, plus his mother's money (she had apologetically left her entire nest egg to Eliot), plus occasional 'loans' from his half brother, Eliot managed to sustain the odd nomadic life that appealed to him. He was always exquisitely dressed; he lived in a bewildering succession of elegantly appointed apartments borrowed from friends who were away vacationing or who spent part of each year in Europe or on the Coast; and he was rarely to be found at any of them unless it chanced to contain a piano. Eliot's constant quest for an available piano was the source of his adventure, his entertainment, and presumably a good part of his love life.

"I've decided it's time to be on my own Pygmalion," Eliot announced. "Don't take that too literally, will you; the only designs I'll have on my Galatea will be commercial. But I'm bored with the present crop of singers. Either they have such a highly developed style that any song ends up sounding like every other song, or they have so little style that they feel obliged to underline each nuance and then pause for the laughter. Sometimes I can't sleep at night after attending the execution of one of my pets. So I've decided to create my own singer—from the ground up." He brought Stephen his drink and then returned to his seat; his movements were trim and feline, not effeminate.

"You mean you'll be managing the girl?" Stephen asked. My brother Eliot? Oh, an entrepreneur of sorts. It sounded better.

"Well, I suppose it will amount to that," Eliot said, "though I refuse to wear suspenders or to smoke cigars. I've been keeping back my choicest numbers, so I can start the girl off with a complete act, all original and nicely balanced, even encores. Now I'm looking for the girl. For six weeks I've been looking for the girl. I didn't expect it to be easy, but I hadn't bargained for so much suffering. I feel as if I'd spent the time scavenging in garbage cans. You simply cannot imagine what is trying to break into show business in this town."

"The poor things," said Amelia.

"Your sympathy would shatter against their brazen effrontery," Eliot said. "I'm looking for a girl who knows she still has lots to learn, and that's just what I can't find. Every busty one of them is sure that all she needs is a lucky break. After all, she has been to a voice coach who has carefully extinguished the spark of natural ability that brought her there and substituted a set of vocal tricks: 'Anybody can sing a melody, honey; what counts these days is the liberties you take.' Then she's been to a dramatic coach who says 'The voice is all right, honey; what you need now is a personality,' and, no argument, he's correct. But where God has failed, he doesn't improve matters by turning out one more synthetic sexy hoyden whose idea of a delivery is to waggle her breasts and suggest that she is under the influence of some powerful aphrodisiac. What I need is a nice homely, flat-chested girl with a good sense of humor and an inferiority complex."

Joyce's high heels clicked down the stairs, and they fell silent with the guilty courtesy of people who are having a good time while the toiling class walks by. Then Eliot's face lit up, and he pointed at the hallway. "Can she sing?" he whispered.

"Only the blues, I'm afraid," Stephen said. The front door sighed and closed.

"What a shame," said Eliot. "Her figure's perfect, and that face would set a room giggling before she opened her mouth."

"Eliot, really!" said Amelia. "Anyway, why are you so set on finding a girl? Maybe you'd have better luck finding a man singer of the sort you want."

"Out of the question," said Eliot. "About half the stuff I do turns out more or less off color, and except at a show an audience will not sit still to hear a man singing bawdy unless he's a flagrant queen. I don't know why, but there it is. And a queen should never do business with other queens if he can possibly help it; the double-entry bookkeeping becomes too complicated. No, in the end I'll find my girl, and if she's tractable enough I'll grow sleek and rich on her earnings, but in the meanwhile the anguish is not to be believed. The

66

little dears all have agents, you know, and the agents are mostly pimps by vocation and can't imagine how to curry *my* indulgence. Since their usual merchandise won't do, they keep calling for another round of cheap whiskey. My liver is pleading for mercy."

He stayed for a while longer, talking almost constantly and almost constantly about himself. Usually Amelia was amused, but this evening as soon as Eliot left, after borrowing twenty dollars towards the overhead expenses of girl hunting, she decided to take offense.

"Really, he gets more outrageous every day," she complained.

"He seemed in fine fettle to me," Stephen demurred. "I like this new idea of his; it might be just what he needs to steady him a little."

"Before you came down, I mean. All he could spare for Roger's engagement was one fast flippancy."

"Oh, come! For the past ten years you've been grateful that he *hasn't* paid any attention to Roger. Why should he develop an interest now?"

"Yet he'd be offended if he weren't invited to the reception," Amelia said.

"I expect he would . . . and so would I."

"It seems a waste, really. One place where a pansy is out of place is at a wedding."

"Let me see," said Stephen. "Say there are three hundred people at the reception, half of them men—that makes a minimum of fifteen homosexuals there, some of them avowed and some camouflaged by their wives. I doubt if Eliot will stand out. Your mother will certainly insist on Freddie Ames being invited, and he's twenty times as flamboyant about it as Eliot."

"That's not true," Amelia snapped. "Freddie knows how to behave himself. Whereas if Eliot has too much to drink, there's simply no telling what he'll be up to."

"An argument that will keep our list to a skimpy handful. I wonder how they'll word the invitation to your brother, asking him to leave Joan at home."

"Don't be absurd. There's no comparison."

"If there's one person sure to get drunk—"

"Joan gets vaguer and vaguer until she passes out," Amelia said. "That's quite different from having Eliot chasing the ushers around the room."

"Vaguer and vaguer? What about the time—?"

"That was exceptional, and you know it. Anyway, I never suggested that Eliot wouldn't be invited. I only said that it seemed a waste."

They looked at one another with comfortable, homely hostility. With the children back at school and the need for putting a pleasant face on things in abeyance for the time being, the Booth household had resumed its normal atmosphere. The prospect of a wedding was just another source of friction.

3

At the Fortescues', on the other hand, where preparations were already in full swing, there was an air of pleasurable yet feverish excitement. Normally the tidiest of women, Ruth Fortescue these days always brought with her a suggestion of disorder: the harried look of a woman with too many things to remember and a suspicion that most of them would go wrong.

First thing on Monday morning Ruth and Vickie had gone over to Tiffany's to settle on the style of script they liked and to place the order for wedding invitations, the separate cards of invitations to the reception, and the wedding announcements for third-class relatives and friends who wouldn't be invited to anything. They had had to order many more of each than would possibly be used. Everything was happening in such a rush that it hadn't been feasible to calculate with any accuracy the lists of names that would be coming from the Booths, from Owen Hilliard, and eventually from Roger's grandmother, Mrs. Langstaff.

Later on Monday Ruth had telephoned Amelia to remind her to write to her mother immediately, so that Mrs. Langstaff's invitations could be sent off with the others, before the beginning of May. That telephone call had proved to be a decided mistake: Amelia had seized the opportunity to throw out, ever so casually, the spatter of misery which had been corroding Ruth's happy industry ever since. Franny was ecstatic at the thought of being flower girl. Sooner or later Vickie would have to learn of this, and almost certainly Vickie would not be pleased, and that might mean a scene. Vickie was not bad tempered, not her Vickie, but she did have spirit: when she didn't get her own way, she had quite a *lot* of spirit—possibly more than Roger suspected, but marriage would steady her down.

The trouble was that Ruth hated scenes more than anything in life: they upset her, and she never knew how to end one once it had started. So she had been procrastinating, waiting for a propitious moment, and now she knew she would never have a more propitious moment than this morning. In the first place they were busy. Family address books had been assembled, and they were making up lists: one for announcements and another for wedding invitations, with a capital R before the name if a card for the reception was to be enclosed. And then Alison was there, having come ostensibly to help but probably to complain of Ben's latest misdemeanors. And, finally, there was good news to gladden their hearts: at four-thirty that morning up in Boston her niece Susan, Morris's daughter, had given birth to a fine seven-pound girl who would be named Naomi. Under cover of this happy event Ruth hoped that the little matter of Vickie's flower girl might slip by virtually unremarked. She was mistaken.

Vickie's heart ungladdened itself in a trice. She hurled her pen against the wall opposite; fortunately it was a ball point and couldn't splash. "Mummy, you couldn't have!" she wailed. "You hadn't the right!"

"Amelia must have misunderstood," Ruth said. "I'm positive that I didn't say much more than that I'd think it over."

"Much more!"

"Well, certainly nothing to make her go home and tell the child it was all settled."

Vickie moaned and drummed her heels on the floor.

"Oh, come now," said Alison, "what's so tragic? Naomi won't be old enough by June, and there's no one else in the immediate family."

"You haven't seen the girl," said Vickie. "Have *you*, Mummy? Have you seen dear little Franny?"

"Why, no. She was out the afternoon that I—"

"I'll bet she was!" said Vickie. "And I'll bet I can imagine just how you picture her, too." When Vickie was furious, her voice could take on a cold and steely ring quite like her father's, which Ruth had always found so unnerving. "You picture an adorable little blonde angel toddling down the aisle. Don't you?"

"Well . . ." said Ruth.

"Well, she's almost twelve years old and stretched out like a bean pole," Vickie said, jumping up, her voice rising steadily. "She's damn near as tall as I am. Her face is spotty, and she has a mouthful of braces that will blind you at twenty feet. And she's got a great mop of carroty hair that would be a *calamity* with the rose-lavender dresses I want for the bridesmaids!"

"Oh, dear," said Ruth.

"I'd be a laughingstock, that's what I'd be," Vickie said, quieter but grim. "And I'm not going to stand for it."

"If that's the worst you ever have to stand for . . ." Alison said darkly.

"But I don't," said Vickie. "I don't have to have a flower girl at all. Practically nobody has flower girls nowadays. I just thought it would be nice to have the full do, and Cousin Bea's brat would have looked darling in a little tiny rose-lavender dress, but if we can't do it right, we'll just cancel the whole damn lousy idea."

"Language, dear," Ruth said from force of habit.

"I said damn and I meant damn," Vickie snarled. "Damn, damn, damn, *damn*." She fled the room, her bedroom door slammed violently, and she was face down on the bed weeping at the idea of the mess they were trying to make of her beautiful wedding.

After amused glances Ruth and her niece quietly resumed work. "What about the Richardsons?" Alison asked, and "Just an announcement," Ruth decided. She was oppressed now by the thought of relaying Vickie's decision back to Amelia, who would have a great deal to say about her daughter's broken heart.

"It seems silly to get *quite* so wrapped up in a wedding," Alison remarked.

"You were the same way, dear."

"Oh, I know; the more fool I," said Alison with a bitter little laugh. "At the time it seems like the most important day in your life, and every single detail is a crisis—and a few years later you've forgotten all the details, and the day itself seems like a great mistake. I'm just about fed up, Aunt Ruth; I really am. It's a shame to bring it up at a time like this, but I don't think I can stand much more. Do you know what Ben pulled yesterday?"

Ruth was resigned to listening, but privately she was convinced that Ben's only real crime of yesterday was that he hadn't got Alison pregnant—and that probably wasn't his fault but something Alison had inherited from her mother. Ann had had a hard time conceiving; there had been a couple of miscarriages before Alison and then a terrible labor, and afterwards she couldn't have any more children. And now after five years of marriage Alison was childless, and you needn't look any further for the source of all the trouble. If a woman had a baby or two underfoot, she hadn't the time or the energy to worry about every little quirk of her husband's behavior—and this, in Ruth's opinion, was happiness.

4

For Owen Hilliard the prospect of his son's marriage had reduced itself to a question of money; questions of money set him brooding, and brooding invariably set him to framing imaginary speeches. It was one of his bad habits that showed no sign of improvement with age: in times of stress he composed monologues of irresistible eloquence which generally never got spoken. Occasionally they did, of course, in which case his listener never remained stunned and passive, as Owen had imagined, but insisted on interrupting, arguing, muddling the flow of eloquence. This had no effect on the habit. Of their own volition strands of reasoning braided themselves into cables of logic; effective phrases came popping into his mind, striking metaphors arrived and insidious analogies—till it seemed obvious that nobody in his right mind could fail to be overwhelmed by the force of his argument.

In this manner a magnificent monologue against Amelia had been constructing itself ever since last Saturday, and finally the time came when the structure would permit of no more embellishment. The moment was inconvenient, of course, but Tony Elmendorf could be relied on to be late for any engagement, and Owen knew that unless he unburdened himself at the peak of his fervor, he would be fidgety and frustrated all evening. So he lit a fresh cigarette as he dialed the Booth number, and when Amelia was on the phone and it had been established that everyone was well and there were no distractions in the way of guests, he began.

With well-rehearsed phrases he described the pathos of his financial position: a money-lender's heart would have softened. Magnanimously he conceded that an apartment was better for having some furniture in it, while urging that this could be accomplished piecemeal—after all, Roger and Vickie wouldn't suffer if the wall-to-wall carpeting didn't arrive until the autumn: they'd be better off without it during the hot summer. However, presumably he could go still further into debt for some furniture. But this fancy honeymoon Amelia had in mind was different. Unless she could help with the costs—

"Who do you suppose paid for Vickie's engagement ring?" Amelia asked.

"What?" said Owen stupidly. There were another five or six hundred well-chosen words to go before he had allowed for the first interruption.

"I did," Amelia said. "And Roger's clothes are in shocking condition; he needs almost a complete new wardrobe. I'm attending to all that—though, believe me, it was a struggle to get him away from Vickie long enough to be measured by the tailor. But with two other children at school, that's the absolute limit to what I can do."

This was what always happened: unforeseeable detours like engagement rings and wardrobes came along, and a man's momentum was ruined. "Cash," he said, abandoning the rhetoric but clinging to the crucial truth. "Airplane tickets and hotel bills call for cash in hand. And cash is exactly what I don't have, and will have still less of in June."

"Save your pennies," Amelia suggested. "Think of it as insurance, Owen. A successful honeymoon now, however expensive, is cheaper than a divorce later."

"A lot you know," he said. "I took Barbara-the-Bitch to Venice for a month and not a penny of it was deducted from the alimony."

"Venice for you," she mused, "and Atlantic City for your son. . . ."

The unfairness of this took his breath away. "It's *because* I took Barbara to Venice that I can't afford anything fancy for Roger," he said. "You know that perfectly well. Oh, damn!" The doorbell had rung; for once in his life Tony was ahead of schedule. "Look, I have to run," he said. "I'll have to call you back. You still don't take me seriously; you're still convinced there's blood somewhere in the turnip. And there isn't."

"If you skip a couple of alimony payments and go to jail, it will be in a good cause," she replied cheerfully. "That place is in Jamaica, by the way, and I've already written for reservations."

Unable to think of anything to say but the childish 'Reservations can always be canceled,' he simply hung up the receiver with a feeling of complete futility. For once he hadn't been exaggerating his poverty: he was in debt up to his teeth. His income sounded impressive, but every spare cent for months ahead was already earmarked for taxes, back taxes, more back taxes, alimony installments, long overdue bills including a number of Roger's from college, life insurance, and payments to the bank on past loans. But it was the fashion today to plead broke, everybody did it and nobody believed it; the assumption was that you were bluffing just a little and could always find the odd thousand for an emergency. And so he could, in a pinch, but the four or five or six thousand that Amelia was expecting of him was hopeless. So hopeless that the only sensible thing was to shut it away in one of the convenient mental cupboards which made modern living endurable.

Owen grabbed up his hat and topcoat, switched off the lights, and walked down the two flights of stairs; the slow and tiny self-service elevator was for when he came home drunk or had a girl. He threaded between a couple of parked cars and climbed into the scarlet Volkswagen that served Tony as an emblem. Who else had a scarlet Volkswagen?—and the cops were so familiar with it that Tony could leave it almost anywhere except directly in front of a fire hydrant.

"You look bowed by the prospect of approaching grandfatherhood," Tony remarked, starting up the engine. Evidently the cupboard door was still ajar.

"It's getting that far that worries me," Owen said. "What are the chances of successfully robbing a bank?"

"Be grateful you didn't have a girl. I hear that's when it really hurts."

"Propaganda," Owen said. "With a daughter there's always a way out: you object to the marriage and then bribe her to elope." He forced himself to think only of the evening ahead. "Aren't we going to be a bit early?" he asked. Usually they timed it to get to the gallery just a few minutes before closing time, a token courtesy before the party at Katya's studio which would run into the small hours.

"Half an hour," Tony said. "There's a girl . . . I think she needs to be impressed by my knowing appreciation of abstract art."

Owen grinned. Tony Elmendorf, short, stout, jolly and invincibly cynical, was his oldest and closest friend. There had been lacunae in the friendship, for Carol had found him frivolous and Barbara had sensed that he detested her, but the bond had never weakened. And an essential part of that bond was that Tony was not an artist, nor had more than a passive audience interest in any of the arts.

When he had first come to New York, Owen had instinctively drifted into a circle of similar young people: aspiring actors and writers and dancers and painters. This had seemed so natural at the time, so inevitable, that it hadn't been till much later, some time after the war actually, that he came to see it as an act of folly. In the first place he didn't want to *write* about these people, whose lives were spent in a private backwater, off the mainstream of American life. In the second place, though their company was amusing and even stimulating on occasion, he found more and more that his best friends came from outside, from the real world. This was not without logic. There was something incestuous about intimacy with other writers, quite apart from their egocentricity making them deadly repetitive. Dancers and musicians both seemed unaware that there *was* a world outside, while actors were the most delightful of the lot and the least enduring: after all, if you stopped to think of it, there had to be something fundamental lacking in people who were so eager to repeat the same words and gestures for two and a half hours, eight times a week, for month after month after month.

Painters were different, and it was easy to see why. With no publisher or producer or conductor standing between them and their audience, with no need to please more than a single customer for each work, they had a more relaxed attitude towards their art, were freer to expand as human beings. Usually they were quite mad, but even their madness was something grander than an accumulation of affectations. Occasionally they were frighteningly sane and merely played at being mad. Katya Woikoveč was such a one, and a darling.

They left the car parked illegally on 57th Street, right in front of the gallery; took the elevator to the fourth floor, hearing the din before they passed the third. The little suite of rooms was blue with cigarette smoke and jammed with people all talking at the top of their lungs, rarely pausing to look at the huge unframed canvases on the walls. Katya, who always kept her eye on the door, spied them at once and flung herself at them: an elongated elf of a woman with enormous eyes, a mop of grey-black hair, and enough energy for three. She kissed them both, and Tony with the greater warmth because long ago she had very briefly been in love with him, and he with her, but at different times—so that nothing had come of it, and no doubt that was why the friendship had lasted so well. "Now my triumph is complete!" she said. "What would it be without Tony and Owen to make the nasty comments to my face? Behind my back the comments are intelligent with jealousy, because everything is sold this year, every one, all to museums. This is the year to collect Woikovečs, and you are too late, but you will help me celebrate without knowing why, and that is all that matters."

Only museums would have dared undertake these paintings: there were fewer than a dozen on display, and the smallest must have been five feet by seven. To Owen's uninformed eye they looked much like last year's collection, except that then the predominant color had been mud brown whereas this time it was blue. Stalks of sapphire picketed midnight, aquamarine amoebas recoiled from cerulean swoops, and here and there a grace note of turquoise decoyed the eye to a fresh area of incomprehensibility. While Tony had found his intense and leggy blonde and was making a fool of himself with mystical grunts of appreciation, Owen stared at one of the paintings and hoped, as he had hoped so many times, that a flash of enlightenment would be granted him. It never was. And with Katya's work he was always a trifle unsure how seriously she herself regarded it.

He had seen her early work, when she first came to America, and he knew she could paint. Her oils had been strong, vivid, groping—her vision was her own but her style not yet. This was at the beginning of the war, however, and Katya was a refugee without money or friends; she had to find a job. After a few false starts she had sold herself to Bel-Lady Cosmetics as a packaging designer, and as Bel-Lady moved to the forefront of the dime-store and cheap pharmacy market Katya moved right along: today she was an executive of the company with a salary to match. In time she went back to painting on the side. But in the interim she had had ten years to look around, see which way the fashion was moving, notice what caught the fancy of the more influential critics. It was a new Katya that emerged from the chrysalis: a Katya whose paint cavorted in color-of-the-year conundrums. She had caught the fashion, she caught the critics—but was this new style a belated flowering of genius, as her admirers claimed, or a creation of sheer cynicism? Tony characteristically assumed the latter and admired her for it; Owen, more humbly, remained uncertain.

Around him the crowd screeched and chattered and, failing to identify him, stared through him contemptuously in the manner of such crowds. Their talk of what a well-deserved flop Edward McNair's last exhibit had been, and was it true that Katya was sleeping with Gavin now, bored him to solitude. These were the social drifters and the hangers-on—whereas the people he wanted to see, would see soon at Katya's, had been in earlier in the day, at lunch hour or at their convenience during the afternoon. He was glad when Tony came along, with the leggy blonde in tow, and declared they must have a decent dinner before going on to Katya's.

"I simply cannot enjoy a sandwich there any more," Tony declared as they piled into the Volkswagen. "Not with all those hungry eyes resenting every mouthful." Katya always provided a monstrous buffet for these celebrations, and the place would be crowded with the artistic lame dogs she collected, who despised her salary, envied her success, and loved her dearly for the meal she provided and the leftover food she encouraged them to take home.

They went to Camillo's and over cutlets *Milanese* Tony tried to explain to the blonde, whose gods appeared to be Kafka, Camus, Alban Berg and Katya, exactly how he happened to find himself in the company of a slick hackwriter like Owen Hilliard. For all her intensity she was a pleasant child, with a prettier face and better figure than most girls who believed that commercial success was the stigma of the second-rate. She reminded him of Carol just a little. Tony would probably be good for her; when he was well enough fixed in her favor, he would abandon this farcical pose and encourage her in his belief that life could be enjoyed as well as disapproved of.

Tony called himself an Existentialist because he liked the modern sound of the term, but the more old-fashioned word hedonist would have done as well. He was a lawyer quite without ambition; the ambition had all been his father's, a Brooklyn building contractor who regarded the Law as a political escalator. Perversely, Tony had found a cosy niche in the District Attorney's office, undisturbed by the fluctuations of politics, and there he stayed. A brief and wretched marriage just after the war had had the sole virtue of ending inexpensively; since then his salary and his patrimony—one Brooklyn apartment house free of mortgage—had enabled him to play the field with verve and a certain elegance. "I'm a new type of man," Tony declared, "the working-class playboy." He was the sort of wolf Owen occasionally longed to be: too bitter at heart to let his emotions ever again be deeply touched, but with so much easy surface affection and good nature that his former girl friends greeted him with amused regret or amusing sarcasm, but never with rancor. To another man he was the best of friends, giving more of himself in warmth and loyalty because it was quite safe. And he had that most delightful virtue of friendship: a willingness to listen to your working woes and a reticence about boring you with his own. Except when Owen needed some legal wrinkle resolved for a plot line, they rarely spoke of Tony's work, yet Tony was always happy to provide comfort while Owen ranted on about the intransigence of directors or the paranoia of producers—only demanding in return, when he needed to overwhelm some new girl, an occasional pair of fourth-row-center tickets to the town's latest smash hit.

When he was on the trail of a new quarry, however, he had to be watched for a certain selfish perfidy, and Owen was prepared when Tony, over the coffee, started talking about the existentialism of progressive jazz, and wondered whether it might be a good idea to skip Katya's and go on to The Embers.

"And miss all the fun?" Owen asked. "Why, Henry Miller may be there, and Jack Kerouac and Dylan Thomas—"

"Dylan Thomas is dead," the girl said, mourning a personal loss.

"I meant Simone de Beauvoir," Owen said. "And Tennessee Williams and—"

"You're lying in your teeth," Tony said, but the girl's expression showed that she had been reminded of her duty to her intellect, and they drove down to Katya's.

Her duplex studio apartment in Chelsea owed more to Bel-Lady than to the sale of her paintings. The studio alone occupied half the depth of the building, an enormous room one end of which was furnished as a living room, the other end left bare for Katya's work. But now the easels and other paraphernalia were pushed out of sight, the great window draped over, the furniture backed against the walls, and the whole given over to Katya's annual celebration. Owen's list of guests might have been a complete fabrication, but an earnest searcher would have needed twenty minutes of elbowing and craning to make sure that any given celebrity was not there. Katya adored people and collected them greedily from all walks of New York life. Year by year her parties had grown until now there was a sporting chance of finding almost anybody there, except the other executives of Bel-Lady.

Owen looked around for the people he hoped to see. There were Audrey and Jay; he would get to them later, but it was Jim he particularly wanted to talk with. Finally he spotted Jim in a far corner and began working his way in that direction. As it happened, he never arrived there.

First there was a long detour to pay his respects afresh to Katya and to offer some rude comment on her paintings—it was an annual game—to show that he remained unconverted. She delighted in these outrages and quoted them about the room, probably to stir up controversy or compliments. "The only one I liked was the still life," he informed her gravely, and she squealed with pleasure. Retreating, he caught sight of the clever, sensitive black face of André Berthier and summoned up his high-school French. "*Bonsoir*, André!"

"Ah, O'en, *bonsoir*," said André. "*J'ai vu La Cascade; c'est assez drôle à condition de pouvoir admirer les putains au grand coeur.*" At this hour of the evening André spoke only French; if the party thinned out and he left convivial, he might switch over to slow but flawless English. He was a Haitian poet working at the legation in Washington, where he had learned that talking French kept him a person, whereas a lapse into English could reduce him to a nigger.

While Owen was still trying to puzzle out whether he had been flattered or not, an eddy in the party took him off to the left by the buffet. For a time he was trapped among the hangers-on, who kept a proprietary eye on the food while they talked of the impertinence of the public in having opinions about art: a true artist painted for other artists, and the public's place was to peek over artistic shoulders and keep a respectful silence. Owen escaped by a few feet into a wholly different world. "Cash is obsolete!" one impassioned crew-cut-and-horn-rimmed-spectacled account executive of fifty was saying to another. "I'm not exaggerating, George. Money has become an economic anachronism. In another ten years we'll pay for *everything* by credit card. Cab fares, candy bars, even call girls."

It was then that he saw Carol.

For a moment Owen stared at her blankly, still dizzy with the thought of all those credit cards. She was sitting part way up the stairs to Katya's living quarters, chatting with a young actor he knew slightly: they were absorbed, tranquil, aloof from the hubbub of the room. It was just four years since he had seen her; the last time had been here at Katya's too, and Carol had been pregnant. He remembered that her second husband (Bailey? Daley?) had not been pleased by the enthusiasm with which they had greeted one another and wondered if that was why they had not come in subsequent years. Childish.

Carol hadn't changed at all, but then she never did. How old was she now? Thirty-six, and he would swear she didn't look a day older than when he married her. She was a large girl, not heavy, but built to a big frame. Her features were in proportion: her dark wide-set eyes, the firm nose and generous mouth, had given her this same touch of matronly beauty even when she was much younger. She was tall and sturdy with a deceptive figure: on the street her body would provoke no whistles, but in bed it proved unexpectedly soft and feminine. But the most attractive thing about her was the impression she gave of easy, humorous warmth—here at last was somebody uncomplicated and at peace with the world. This impression was somewhat deceptive also, as no one knew better than Owen, but the attraction called to him even now, and he looked for an excuse to break in on her tête-à-tête. From her fingertips dangled a paper cup, evidently empty, and he turned back to the bar end of the buffet.

The rule at Katya's on these evenings was highballs in paper cups; a vile custom, but she claimed that after one of the earlier parties she had swept up the shatterings of several dozen glasses. He fixed a bourbon for Carol, assuming that her tastes had not improved, and a scotch for himself, and edged his way back to the foot of the stairs. The young actor had discovered his duty and was just starting down with empty cups; Owen groped for his name, came up with it, indicated to the lad that his place was about to be usurped, but sent him off with the compensation of having been recognized by Owen Hilliard. Carol had been talking through the balusters to somebody below and apparently missed this byplay, yet when she turned back and found Owen sitting beside her, she showed no sign of surprise. Her face lit up in simple pleasure.

"I thought you might turn up," she said, kissing him warmly and accepting the drink as if she had sent him for it. "You're looking wonderful, Owen! Success must be a tonic."

"And you're looking exactly the same." With Carol there was no wondering (as with Amelia) why he had been so in love with her; the temptation was to deny the bad memories and wonder why he had stopped. "It's funny, I was thinking of you earlier, at dinner."

"Why?"

For a moment he had forgotten; he had thought it an amiable coincidence and spoken on impulse, and now he remembered that it was Carol's dark side that he had been reminded of. "Coincidence," he said. "Is your husband here this evening? I haven't seen him."

"No. . . . Andrew died last September," she said quietly.

"Oh, good Lord!" Angrily—for why had nobody told him? But last September he had been caught up in rehearsals of *Cascade*: whole scenes had had to be chopped apart and rewritten, and for weeks on end he had seen nobody except the other people involved in the play. By the time he reappeared, the news had grown stale, everyone assuming he must have heard it from someone else. "I'm very sorry. I hadn't known."

"No, there were no headlines," she said with her own inverted pride. Andrew (whatever his last name) had been a sculptor, quarrying the same artistic vein as Katya's, but with no recognition. Other men's marble snow women and grotesques of ill-soldered metals might stir the critics to raptures, but for some reason his never had. And this to Carol would have been the ultimate proof of his genius.

"I was horribly busy," Owen said, "and no one told me. You know I'd have sent a note."

"I'm glad you didn't," she replied affectionately. "The letters were difficult to deal with. Everybody seemed expecting me to be prostrated, and I couldn't be. We'd expected it for too long."

"He was so ill?"

"Oh, no; it was quite sudden, but we'd always known it would be. Andrew had rheumatic fever as a boy, and it left him with a tricky heart that kept getting weaker."

"You knew this when you married him?"

"Of course I did. Really, Owen! One simply lives day by day. If you aren't morbid about it, it can be quite . . . exhilarating."

"Yet you went ahead and had a child!" Owen said accusingly.

"Yes—Lois is nearly three and a half now, and a sweetheart. You'll have to meet her."

He was outraged by the whole story. Andrew hadn't a cent; he'd clerked at Brentano's to support his sculpting, and with a heart like that he couldn't get insurance. Yet knowing he was likely to die at any time, he'd let Carol go ahead and have a baby. It was unspeakable and it was typical. "How are you getting by?" he demanded harshly, aware that he was merely exposing that bourgeois streak she'd accused him of so often and that she would despise him for the question. A dedicated artist would never trouble himself about the welfare of his own wife and child, much less that of an ex-wife. Carol had been brought up by her father, a widower, an artist *manqué*, an architect. In his own profession Henry Forbes had not got beyond designing suburban developments: he had a flair for planning houses that were essentially all the same house but looked pleasingly dissimilar from the outside. In his spare time he wrote art criticism and book reviews for the minor magazines. For the genius which had eluded him, he had a humble and inexhaustible adoration and had passed this on to his daughter, perhaps forgetting that a man may give his heart to an ideal whereas a woman is likelier to give hers to a man. Genius, creative genius and most particularly artistic genius, was the touchstone of humanity, the one sign of man's climb from barbarism, the one promise of man's claim to divinity. And the way to recognize an artistic genius, evidently, was by his barbarous dedication and his lack of recognition. "How are you getting by?" Owen demanded, expecting to be jeered at.

But this was a gentler Carol than he had known. "I'm all right, Owen," she said reassuringly. "Truly I am."

"You can't have gone back to the *Quarterly* after all this time," he persisted.

"No, naturally not. Remember Nora Saunders, with the antique shop on Greenwich Avenue? She's taken me in as a sort of partner. I'm not one really, but that's the way she treats me. There's space in back, so I can have Lois with me when she's not at nursery school. And I've turned one corner into a little gallery for the pieces Andrew left. Some of the other artists are becoming interested—we may end up with the place half antiques and half gallery. It's rather fun, and I get by. Dad helps out a little."

Owen grunted. Nora Saunders was a dyke but a decent soul—and her tastes ran to piquant little dance students. She would be no trouble to Carol, but her friends would be tramping in and out of the place and they would not all be so scrupulous. Carol was no child, of course; she could look after herself. But it seemed a pathetic destiny: fending off lesbians in a Village antique shop, peddling Village art to gawking tourists, and no place to practice all her dreams and her ideals except upon her unsuspecting daughter.

There was nothing to be said, however, for Carol would never acknowledge the pathos: whatever road she chose she pursued with all her heart and soul until she felt that one or the other had been betrayed. So he inquired after Nora, and then other common friends he had more or less lost track of in recent years—and they sat in peace above the swirling buzzing crowd, chatting contentedly of secondhand tragedies and triumphs. Eventually, because Myra was working at CBS and Dan was doing the sets for a new Broadway show, the talk moved uptown, came around to Owen's work. Again Carol was unexpectedly tender with him. She had seen all his plays and thought them excellent—for what they were.

What pleased her most was that he was making a really big name for himself, and she assumed this was all he had been aiming at. Carol could accept self-advertisement; it was part of the game as she understood it. Since talent was one thing and recognition was quite another, an artist was entitled to get himself known in any way he could—and she had never lost faith in him as an artist. When they were married, she had grown bitterly impatient with him, felt that he was wasting himself, frittering away his genius. But he was her first discovery, a part of her dream, and her faith held on. Now she took it for granted, calmly, trustingly, that when he had consolidated his name he would go back to his own serious work, sure now of an audience for whatever he did. And since Owen himself couldn't tell whether this was true or not, he was content to let her believe it.

Below them the party constantly rearranged itself, like a bad modern ballet as seen from the mezzanine. From time to time strangers to Owen would stop at the foot of the stairs to call greetings or questions up to Carol, glancing at him with incurious eyes. She never introduced him, for that would have been an invitation for the strangers to join them; while she affectionately kept them at a distance, he sometimes took the opportunity to drop down to refill their cups. Afterwards, conforming to some private etiquette of her own, she always identified the person she had spoken to: He's the man who carves those attenuated figurines that are so successful.

Then some new pattern brought Audrey and Jay to the foot of the stairs, to beam up at them with bright, identical smiles. They were astonishingly alike, as though double first cousins had married, yet they came from opposite ends of the country and were in no way related.

"Well, well: quite like old times," Jay remarked, sucking on the pipe no one had ever known to be lit.

"Hi, Carol," Audrey said. "Owen, duck, pass on our congratulations to Roger, will you? We spotted it in the papers." Jay held up an inverted cup, panting piteously, and they moved along towards the liquor.

"Oh, Owen, how will you forgive me?" Carol said contritely. "I started to ask after Roger, truly I did, but you distracted me. He graduates this year, doesn't he?"

"If he can keep his mind on what he's doing."

"But what did Audrey see in the papers?"

"A very small headline in a section you never read," Owen replied. "Roger got himself engaged last Saturday."

"He didn't!" she exclaimed with delight. "Oh, this is so ridiculous! I know he's about to graduate, I just said so, but I can't help thinking of him as still sixteen. I missed him, you know. If Andrew hadn't been so possessive—and he couldn't be blamed for it, poor dear—I'd have been seeing you both, mainly to keep track of how Roger was coming along. I kept wondering how he was turning out. How has he, Owen?"

"I'm not the one to ask," he said. "I love the boy and I do my best not to feel disappointed." It was wonderfully comfortable talking to Carol about something like this, without pretenses: for Roger had been part of her life, too, and she had shared in the hopes and anxieties and regrets. "He hasn't really changed at all that I can see, he's simply moved on to the twenty-two-year-old version. Sweeter than most, brighter than some. But very, very ordinary."

"So Amelia made a Langstaff of him, after all."

"I don't know if that's fair. I may have played more of a part than I recognize. My father was a gentle and ordinary man, thoroughly happy with his hardware, and expected me to be the same. I rebelled, and then I assumed that Roger would rebel onward and upward from me. But maybe the trick to rebellion is that it always takes the direction you least expect. At times Roger reminds me quite a lot of my father."

Carol shrugged; she was committed to a modern disbelief in heredity. "If he hasn't a talent, all that matters is what sort of a man he turns out to be, and that will take a lot longer to show. In the end he may prove to be very far from ordinary. Who is his girl, and what is she like?"

"Vickie Fortescue," he said. "Her father is the executive mastermind of something called Andean Copper and Zinc, and her mother is Jewish."

"Oh, lovely!" said Carol, giggling softly. "That will send old Mrs. Langstaff right through the ceiling, won't it?"

"Perhaps. I think there's a scheme to dodge the issue as long as possible, keeping the old lady's attention fixed on the Episcopalian wedding. If she becomes sufficiently attached to Vickie before she finds out, she'll decide that nobody much cares what your grandmother's maiden name may have been."

"Is she likely to, though? What is Vickie like?"

"She's nineteen years old," said Owen as if that covered the whole subject.

"Don't be tiresome. Is she nice?"

"Apparently. Aren't most nineteen-year-old girls nice when they're in love and everything is going smoothly?"

"But she's definitely in love with Roger?"

"She's definitely in love with *something*, yes. It might be Roger."

"You don't especially like Vickie, do you?"

He roared with laughter, booming forth so that several people down below turned to stare at the novelty—somebody laughing from sheer lighthearted pleasure. "Lord, I'd forgotten how feminine you

83

are! Because I answer several questions with the accuracy of ignorance, because I don't go maudlin and invest her with all the virtues I could only guess at, you decide I don't like her. So much for intuition. You've seen these bright, shiny youngsters on their best behavior when older people are around. Can you tell what they're really like?"

"I can guess," she said calmly. "If it were my son getting engaged, I'd damn well make enough of a guess either to make myself enthusiastic or miserable; I couldn't help it. And I don't believe you're that Olympian. You don't think much of Vickie—or else you're getting to be like Tony Elmendorf."

"All sanity isn't cynicism," he said. "Anyway, you're wrong. I could truthfully say that Vickie *seems* like a perfect darling, but anything more would be fatuous. This happened pretty suddenly; I should have explained that."

"That Barbara creature gave you a pretty hard time, didn't she? I heard rumors."

It took him a moment to realize that she was pursuing the source of his 'cynicism.' "Indeed she did," he said, "but I don't think she left lasting scars on anything but my self-esteem and my bank account." This was one episode of his life which Owen was reluctant to discuss; the pain went too deep for him to make an amusing story of it, and without humor he could not see the profit in exposing how entirely and systematically he had made an idiot of himself. To begin with, despite all his experience he had virtually hurtled into the marriage. Not in terms of objective time: there had been a decent interval between the broaching of the idea and the ceremony. But all through that period he had been working like fury on casting, revisions and rehearsals for *The Delectable Mountains*, which meant that he saw Barbara only in moments of hectic relaxation, when he was keyed-up, self-absorbed and grateful for any distraction. He had never had a chance for a calm, appraising look at her. And then he had married her in the celebratory week after the play opened on Broadway, his second smashing success.

This time his illusions had not even survived the honeymoon. Barbara enjoyed going to bed with him; when sufficiently indulged she could be amusing company, and she was pleased with the glamour and income of being wife to a successful playwright—and those were her most generous attributes. For the rest she was a self-centered and ruthlessly selfish little bitch. But Owen had simply not been able to believe that he had made so drastic a mistake, especially the third time around; the shock to his self-respect was too great. Besides, he knew that by temperament he was a domestic man and was determined to achieve domesticity. Barbara was young, not yet thirty, and could change if she wanted to. . . . He set out patiently to provide her with the incentives. It was no part of his philosophy that there were some people who regarded kindliness as weakness—it sounded an out-dated rationale for certain colonial policies—but Barbara proved him mistaken. Her philosophy was much simpler; the more he gave, the more she took, while any suggestion that she might give in return verged upon mental cruelty. She was infinitely tougher than he, and eventually the explosion came.

But by then the marriage had lasted long enough that Barbara had no difficulty in finding a lawyer who agreed that she had been wretchedly treated and deserved substantial compensation. He pitched his claims exorbitantly high so that his own fees would rise with the labor of being bargained down. This was a lengthy process, and in the midst of it Owen committed the ultimate idiocy of failing to notice that there were private detectives on his tail. After that, the majestic vindictiveness of the law was all on Barbara's side. In Tony's inelegant phrase, a man should expect to pay through the nose for a mistake of the heart.

"It would be a poor man who turned cynical on Barbara's account," Owen said. "My susceptibility may not stretch to the inscrutably virginal like Vickie, but I'm the same old romantic idealist I always was."

"I can't say you sound happy about it," Carol said reflectively. "It's funny. You *look* wonderful, but you don't seem especially pleased with life."

"I've been rattling around too much and too long. It keeps me young, but it's really not very satisfactory." Because he could make an entertaining story of his inadequacies and misadventures as a heart-free Casanova, he told her about them and made her laugh. He knew it was dangerous in a sense to speak of an unsatisfactory love life to any attractive and unattached woman, and he himself was never very safe except when an existing infatuation was already at the reins, whipping along his glands and his optimism in tandem— yet with Carol he felt curiously innocent and safe. They knew one another so well: too well for any poses or pretenses to make any difference. They knew each other's best and worst, and the affection that was left to them as residue of a once considerable love was a homely and comfortable warmth. It was good to relax.

85

And then Tony came along to find them laughing contentedly together, and it was obvious—at least to Owen—that the sight displeased him. "I was coming to invite you to find your own taxi home," he told Owen. "But is it safe to leave you here with a designing widow?"

"Hello, Tony," Carol said happily. "It's been a long time."

"Four or five frivolous years," he agreed.

"It was sweet of you to write when Andrew died," she said, and Owen was startled.

"I was laying a lay analyst about then," Tony said lightly, "and she insisted that having a lot of letters to answer was the best distraction."

"Perhaps she was right. But I was very touched."

"Yes, I always get more credit for a decency than worthy people do," Tony said. "Owen, we'll be stopping off at The Embers for a while first. Do you want to come?"

"No, you go ahead," Owen said. Tony shrugged and pushed his way back through the crowd. Owen was annoyed at him, for the breaking of a mood and especially for the way he had treated Carol. She had gone out of her way to be friendly, to suggest that the past was forgotten and she wanted to meet him on a new footing—and Tony would have none of it. His manner had been amiable, but every remark was edged, and the final invitation to Owen was an open slap. This was Tony's form of loyalty: he didn't believe that people changed, except possibly for the worse; he thought Carol had been a bad wife for Owen and was glad when they split up; and now it made him nervous to see them being so companionable again, even if just for a few moments at a party.

Yet Carol *had* changed: her sweetness with Tony was just one more sign of her new tolerance. She was easier with life, less prickly, much gentler. What had pleased Owen particularly was her defense of Roger: all that matters now is what sort of person he turns out to be, and only time will tell. This was the way Owen wanted to feel, though at times it seemed too much of a platitude and at times too indulgent. On both counts Carol would have shuddered away from the remark five years ago. Now it came affectionately.

So he stayed on to make amends for Tony's hostile behavior, though in truth Carol didn't seem to have noticed it, and the mood wasn't broken at all. Owen enjoyed the evening more than any in some time. When finally they came down, they were both stiff from sitting so long on a narrow stair, but they had made a date to have dinner the Tuesday following.

5

The new offices of Andean Copper and Zinc occupied half of one floor midway up one of those modernistic abominations on Park Avenue, seemingly constructed mostly of greenish glass, and looking like nothing so much as an oblong bar of green soap perched on end. The building was a triumph of artificiality. The city was shut out, sound and soot; elevators rose too silently and smoothly to be elevators; every cubic inch of air had been purified and processed until it smelled like some scientifically improved substitute. In a sense this was a fitting setting for Andean C & Z. Except for a few samples of ore tastefully arranged and labeled in a glass cabinet in the lobby, nothing suggested that these offices were concerned with so messy and noisy and dangerous a business as the extraction of minerals from the bowels of mountains thousands of miles away.

There was a lavishly appointed board room, rarely used. There was a splendid hierarchy of executive offices ranging from six windows down to one—window being understood to mean a stretch of transparency giving on the outside, rather than a contraption that opened and shut. There was Bruce Bigelow's miniature advertising department, where Roger Hilliard would be instructed in the mysteries of his chosen profession—the natural goal nowadays for young men who had nothing to show for their education but a B.A. in English. There were rooms for clerks who were mere adjuncts to walls of filing cabinets; there were rooms of third-rate mathematicians in attendance on first-rate mathematical machines. And, inevitably, there was the feminine pyramid of industry, typists, stenographers and secretaries, all of them aware that they did the work that mattered and secretly convinced that they could do it rather better if their bosses weren't underfoot so much. At the head of this pyramid was Charles Fortescue's secretary, Mrs. Peabody, the syntactical terror of Andean C & Z. Before her widowhood and return to work she had taught in a business school, where she fell in love with the niceties of language; now, as a tyrannical *doyenne*, she tried to insist on perfection in this respect throughout what she considered as *her* domain. It sometimes happened that when one of her disciples attempted to untangle dangling participles and split infinitives, the point of a letter would get lost and the whole thing would have to be dictated again, but nobody below the vice-presidential level dared complain of Mrs. Peabody.

The six-window office stood unoccupied most of the year, waiting the rare presence of Clarence Barbour III—unless, as Mrs. Peabody hinted darkly, it was occasionally used for amorous trysts.

In the five-window office Charles Fortescue sat at his desk. It was eleven o'clock on a lovely April morning, and Charles was methodically scanning Mrs. Peabody's flawlessly typed letters before scrawling his signature. In the morning's mail there had been one item which called for no reply. It lay now in thirty-two scraps in Charles's wastebasket: the annual reminder of a time better forgotten. Charles had learned to forget efficiently; after the brief nervous spasm which let him tear the pasteboard card into so many tiny pieces he had put the matter from his mind and settled to his work, as oblivious of the past as he was of the promises of spring outside. Now, as he came to the last letter of the pile, he buzzed Mrs. Peabody and asked her to put through the call to Owen Hilliard he had been contemplating for some days. He was surprised to find he had been inconsiderate. "I hope I didn't awaken you," he said, concealing his disapproval.

"That's quite all right," said Owen, his voice still thick with sleep. "In seventeen years I've never been able to train my agent to call me at a decent hour. It's not absent-mindedness, though; it's sadism. You characters who've been at your offices for hours can't bear the thought of anybody sleeping while you work—though you don't mind sleeping while *we* work. Sometime I'll call up all my conventional friends just when I'm quitting work at four in the morning and see how they like it."

Charles laughed with false heartiness. "I'm afraid I don't know many people who keep your hours," he said, but remembered now that he had envied Owen just this emancipation and wondered whether the telephone had aroused Owen alone. "I'll try to remember next time," he promised. "I was just calling to ask if we could get together for lunch one day, without a crowd around. If you eat lunch, that is."

"I don't know what the meal should be called, but I eat it."

"How about the day after tomorrow?"

"At one o'clock," said Owen firmly.

"The Four Seasons?"

"Not if we're splitting the check."

Somewhat taken aback Charles insisted that the pleasure would be all his. He hung up a moment later, but had no chance to dwell on the implications of his call before Mrs. Peabody followed her inaudible knock into the office. She was carrying a colorful leaflet folded letter size. "The June brochure, with Mr. Bigelow's compliments," she said brightly, and put the offensive thing on his desk.

These 'brochures,' as Bigelow insisted on miscalling them, were the main justification for the existence of the advertising department. Andean C & Z had little need for advertising. Periodically they took space in various technical publications to remind young engineers of the tax advantages of working outside the country for a paternalistic company like Andean. From time to time they had an arty industrial page in such journals as *Scientific American*, for no better reason than that everybody else did it. The 'brochures' were one of Clarence Barbour III's inspirations. His great bugaboo was socialism; ever since Franklin D. Roosevelt's second term he had been positive that socialism was creeping up on him. It might postpone the day, he felt, if all the stockholders across the country could be induced to take a friendly, personal interest in Andean C & Z. To that end, with each quarterly dividend went out one of these intricately folded glossy pages, rich with photographs of mines and men and Andes, statistics, human-interest anecdotes and general capitalistic uplift. The whole scheme was tax deductible.

But each new edition had to be approved, through all its phases, by Charles himself. Several years before, Barbour had chanced on the proof of a brochure wherein Bigelow had thought to reassure the stockholders with the information that no native Peruvian could rise above a grade-3 job with the company unless he held a diploma from a United States university. Though perfectly accurate, this was the sort of datum which some woolly-minded self-righteous do-gooder could turn into propaganda for socialism. Since then, in Barbour's absence, Charles was held responsible for making sure the stockholders were exposed only to the more seemly facts.

After depositing the leaflet on his desk and collecting the signed letters, Mrs. Peabody had not retreated; Charles looked up enquiringly.

"I thought this would amuse you," she said. "As I was going out last night, I couldn't help hearing one of the new typists on the telephone—a personal call, I assume, but after hours. She was absolutely furious about something. 'How *dare* them!' she kept saying, 'How *dare* them!'"

Charles smiled appreciatively, and she trundled away pleased with herself—a good secretary tries to bring a little sunshine into her boss's life each day. He tried to go back to what he had been working on before, and then decided he might as well get Bigelow's pride and joy out of the way at once, rather than have it hanging over him for the remainder of the day. He had already approved the copy, but Barbour was convinced that left-wing printers liked to slip in subversive misprints at the last moment.

The inane triviality of the job offended his sense of dignity and position: this was one of the penalties of Barbour's antiquated conviction that a good executive delegated no more responsibility than he had to. Since there was no convenient way to pass his resentment on to Barbour, Charles expended it in disliking the brochures. Though as a rule he had no morbid veneration for the truth, he despised Bigelow's unctuous and hypocritical prose and despised even more the photographs which were supposed to show you what things were *really* like, and which were twenty times as dishonest as the prose. Not that the photographs were faked in any way; they didn't need to be. A camera could not help lying.

Here was a picture of a llama; Charles had taken it himself some years ago. (Bigelow was fond of using Charles's pictures; it cut expenses and flattered the boss.) Llamas turned up in every second or third issue of the brochure: they were photogenic; they were local color. A shot of a cute little baby llama was just the thing to stir loyalty in the heart of a sentimental stockholder. There was nothing in the photographs to show that llamas were infested with vermin, that they stank with a stomach-turning rancid smell, and that they had a malevolent habit of spitting with diabolic aim. The local Indians had a convenient superstition that llama spittle on the skin was what caused syphilis.

Here were pictures of the new club house just completed by the company for the camp at Oñate. How attractive it was! How handsomely the men were treated! How happy they must be! Nothing in the photographs showed that the camp stood at an elevation of slightly over fourteen thousand feet above sea level.

Some sort of invisible dividing line existed at around twelve thousand feet: below that point a healthy man could be comfortable, but above, inevitably, there was *soroche*—the altitude sickness. And all five of the Andean C & Z mines were at thirteen thousand or higher. Charles had made it his duty to visit the mines every year or two, until five years ago when he caught himself developing psychosomatic ailments a week ahead of time, to avert the nightmare of the trip. He had then pushed that assignment off onto a younger man.

When first you went up to a mine, if you were a newcomer, you wondered what all the fuss was about. You felt fine—wonderful, in fact. The old-timers merely smiled and waited. It took four hours or so before the body realized that it was actually going to *stay* in this frightful place. Then it protested. Violently. Headaches the like of which he had never imagined, endless, excruciating. They had a great white pill, of a size appropriate for horses, which they let you choke down, and that helped somewhat but not enough, and they wouldn't give you another till four hours later.

And on top of that you felt a hundred and fifty years old. Despite the thinness of the air you were not conscious of being short of breath; there was no instinct to pant. You simply felt old, incredibly old and frail. A walk of fifty yards on level ground and you had to stop to rest for a while. The first time he had been up to Oñate thirty-five years ago he'd had to be shown over the concentrator the night of his arrival; the concentrator was due for its annual shutdown that same midnight. A concentrator, the mill where mined rock is crushed to dust and then the minerals floated off in a sequence of chemical baths, is most efficiently built lying against the steep slope of a hill so that gravity does all the work of carrying pulped ore from one stage to another. This means that there is virtually no level ground in the building, and a tour of inspection means one set of stairs after another. Charles had been in his twenties then, playing tennis and golf at every opportunity, as fit as could be. And he found he could take just six or eight steps at a time before he had to pause for a minute or two to recuperate.

Of course, in time you acclimatized. After a week or two the headaches went away . . . almost, and you reverted to feeling your normal age . . . almost. That was the best you could hope for. As one of the old-timers had put it: "We never feel completely comfortable, we just get used to feeling slightly uncomfortable all the time."

And these were the men who *could* adjust to the altitude. Some simply could not, though the company hired only young men in the best of physical condition for the camps. Cerro de Pasco retained a special doctor to check their personnel; Andean C & Z found they got about the same results going by the insurance medical reports. About ten percent of the men sent down from the States failed to acclimatize themselves.

This was a ferocious expense to the company. One man in every ten to be transported down to Peru and up into the hills with all his possessions, there to idle about one of the camps till it was clear he couldn't adjust, and then to be brought back bag and baggage, paid for his time and discharged—a total loss. A sheer waste of money which had to be budgeted for each year. No wonder Barbour had been tempted when Dr. Jeremy Wales came along with his glowing promises that this expense could be cut in half.

It had been understood that a couple of years would probably be needed to test out Wales's theories. After all, it was meaningless if out of any given ten men two came back or none, and men were not sent down every day or even every month. But the turnover recently had been high: several men had retired, several others had quit for other jobs, and one of the camps was being expanded. In the past eighteen months, under Wales's supervision, twenty-seven men had been sent down. As of the day Charles had talked to Morris, four had washed out. Fourteen point eight percent; not a conclusive figure, but one to make Charles restless. And yesterday morning word had come that one of the last batch, a mining engineer who had been reported fit, had actually been faking for the sake of a job he liked the looks of and had finally collapsed under the strain. Five out of twenty-seven. Eighteen point five percent. It was too much. Charles wasn't prepared to wait any longer.

But there was still the problem of what line to take with Wales. Charles had been hesitating, because this was not necessarily as obvious as it appeared. Now, finally, he thought he'd found the answers; he pushed aside Bigelow's brochure and pressed the switch on the intercom.

"Mrs. Peabody, would you ring Dr. Jeremy Wales for me, please?"

6

The house in Jefferson Mews was an inconvenient distance from the mid-town office of the League of International Disarmament, but this was an inconvenience which troubled Amelia Booth very little. She sat in her living room, comparing herself favorably to the fashionable patronesses of other days, and let the professional staff waste time bringing reports to her. She looked down her pointed nose, convinced of her visionary superiority, convinced that no mere professional could match her industrious idealism. "This was only in Washington?" she inquired briskly.

"Only in Washington," said Arthur Vaughan; he was practiced in concealing his impatience, even from himself. "The other chapters are making an excellent showing. I was very favorably impressed." The League was planning to hold its first national convention in Madison Square Garden at the end of July, a tremendous bid for publicity and recognition as a force that might have to be reckoned with politically. As Secretary, Arthur had been off on a tour of the major East Coast chapters, from Boston to Charleston, making fund-raising speeches and seeing at first hand how well the collection of pledges was shaping up. It would be better to postpone the convention for a year, forfeiting the deposits, rather than have an unspectacular turnout. But the enthusiasm he had met with had been most gratifying. "Boston is up in arms," he said, making a small joke.

"Boston is Martha McGuire," Amelia said, nodding. "She's a good worker."

She was indeed, and so was Amelia, and this was why he had to put up with these women, study to get along with them, cater to their sense of self-importance. With rare exceptions it was impossible to get American men to do any work for a cause, however worthy they might concede it to be. Men lent their names to letterheads, made out an occasional check, went to a meeting if it promised to be entertaining, but for the day-to-day routine you had to rely on women. It was absurd: the country was overflowing with retired businessmen complaining of having nothing to do, and if you offered them something to do, they promptly wanted to be made chairman of the committee. After a lifetime of striving for a position where other people attended to all the drudgery, the habit persisted.

The women, however, even the best-intentioned of them, were really bent on proving to themselves and the world that God had meant them for something nobler than mere housewives. Amelia was no exception. She was an ordinary woman with the ordinary woman's extraordinary conviction of her own superiority: an undefined, undemonstrable, unappreciated but deeply felt superiority. She was dissatisfied with her husband because he failed to acknowledge this superiority; she was dissatisfied with her home and children because (the servant problem being what it was) they demanded too much of her; and these very dissatisfactions were added evidence that she was intended for loftier purposes.

Yet the impetus which had driven Amelia from cause to cause was really nothing more than a misdirected maternal impatience with that wayward, wrong-headed child, the world. She wanted to scold and bustle it into minding its manners. She was constantly irritated by its reluctance to appreciate that Mother Knows Best.

As a consequence, she was much less effective as an evangelist than she might have been, for she had little tolerance for the slow necessities of persuasion. She was a headlong crusader, convinced that righteousness had no need of tact or strategy, and could be relied upon, nine times out of ten, to turn a seminar on Peace into a flaming, embittered battle. And still, at the same time, she was invaluable. As a Langstaff Amelia had access to the social world, as wife of Professor Booth she had access to the academic world; she could extract money from the most unlikely sources; she was a tireless and dedicated worker. However much she exasperated him, he had to get along with her.

In point of fact, Arthur Vaughan had been getting along with Amelias for much of his adult life.

Arthur was the son of an Episcopalian minister who had, part way through his brief tenure in Minneapolis, perhaps coincidentally, developed grave theological doubts about St. Paul. After a long period of study, brooding and prayer for guidance, he arrived at the conclusion that Saul of Tarsus had been the true Anti-Christ—not an open opponent but a subtle and devious corrupter. "No wonder Paul suffered fools gladly," he announced to his family; "nobody else would stomach such perversion of Christ's teachings." Dr. Vaughan was no sectarian by temperament; he never preached this heresy in public. He merely, thenceforward, chose all his texts from the Gospels of Matthew, Mark and John (Luke was suspect of the Pauline taint) and as a consequence of preaching pure Christianity rapidly got himself known as a radical. His bishop was unimpressed by his explanations, and Dr. Vaughan was hastily transferred to the midst of a Quaker stronghold in Pennsylvania and forgotten by his superiors.

As a boy Arthur had suffered passionately for his father's views, as an adolescent he felt himself humiliated by them, but he came away from both of these phases with a curious respect for the older man. He recognized that as a result of believing intensely in *something*, his father got rather more excitement and amusement out of life than did other people. Most people these days (and especially Episcopalians) didn't seem to believe strongly in much of anything; they had carried tolerance to the point of moral lethargy, and, lacking some little spark of fervor, their lives were drab.

The difficulty for an intelligent man was to find a belief which didn't entail the possible discomforts of martyrdom; as was natural for the son of a clergyman he felt no calling to the ministry. At college he had begun by specializing in sociology, under the mistaken impression that it was a social science. Halfway through he had glimpsed his destiny as through a glass darkly and crammed in as many courses in business administration as he could manage. He had some vague idea of fitting himself for the administrative end of one of the welfare services, but the war arriving just as he graduated altered that plan as so many others. Arthur's foot disqualified him from any military service, but there were any number of worthwhile causes to be served, each needing a core of trained, paid personnel —and this was the start of Arthur's career. He rose from Bundles for Britain, refugee organizations, CARE, fund-raising committees of a hundred kinds, campaigns against racial discrimination and cerebral palsy. Enthusiasm was no substitute for the professional touch, and for twenty years Arthur had been supplying that touch to innumerable different causes, sometimes a dozen or more at the same time, always looking for the one Cause he could dedicate himself to without stint or reservation. For a time he had thought the United World Federalists might be it—a noble idea, but too rational to have dramatic appeal, and after a time its partisans had argued themselves into futility.

But in the meantime Arthur had switched allegiance and had found peace. The concept of international disarmament was an ideal cause: utterly essential, utterly unfeasible. Practical men laughed at the League as a collection of old women and cranks, thought of the League as a great joke, and so it was. But it was a joke on the side of the angels, a joke that more and more people could be persuaded to take seriously, a joke that might end—as some other historic jokes had done—in changing the thinking of the entire world. And the League was Arthur. He had nursed it from loosely connected gaggles of amateurs who sat around pointlessly agreeing on the horrors of war to a taut national association of proselytizers. He had given it everything from a vulgar, catchy slogan (Support the L.I.D. and Help Put the LID on War!) to a dedicated recognition that the League would cease to be a joke the day it had recruited enough members to make the politicians sit up and take notice. But it was slow, exhausting, exasperating work, since everything he accomplished had to be accomplished through the medium of women like Amelia Booth.

"How was Charleston?" Amelia asked skeptically; she had a small feud with the chairwoman there.

"Coming along splendidly," he said. "But I gather we mustn't expect too much from any place further south, except Florida. They are more concerned with the color of their skins than with keeping them whole."

"And then you got to Washington," Amelia prompted.

"Yes, it was very strange. I'm going back there next weekend; it just so happened that both of my best personal contacts were out of town."

"Perhaps we shouldn't be surprised if the chapter there seemed a bit disorganized," Amelia said thoughtfully. "I've always felt the Orchard woman was a bit . . . lightweight for her post."

"No, no, she's very dedicated," said Arthur, who always defended his lieutenants to each other, whatever he might think of them. "Anyway, disorganized isn't quite the right word. It was a sort of unease I couldn't pin down. I couldn't help being reminded that everybody in Washington keeps one ear to the political ground; they may not know anything specific, but they're remarkably sensitive to atmospheres. And when I tried to make my appointment with Senator Browning, and couldn't—"

There was a knock at the hall door; Amelia excused herself and called "Come in."

It was Joyce Neilson, embarrassed, as always, out of all proportion to the intrusion. "I'm sorry, Mrs. Booth . . ." she began, and then stopped with a little gasp as she caught sight of Arthur Vaughan. "Oh . . . I had no idea. . . ."

"Hello, Joyce," Arthur said, calmly and just a shade reproachfully.

"Good afternoon." She refused to meet his eyes, and an angry pink mottling had appeared at each cheekbone. Arthur was disconcerted to see that Amelia was watching with the raised eyebrows of amused malice.

"Is your mother well?" he asked.

"She's all right," Joyce said flatly, too awkward to make even the slightest effort to smooth over the moment with courtesies. "I'm sorry to interrupt, but Professor Booth said he left a book. . . ."

"Let me see," said Amelia. "He was reading by the window. Would that be it over there?"

Obliged to go the length of the room under the silent observation of two people who wished her out of there, herself desperately eager to be gone, Joyce made the passage in an ungainly rush, like some great bird unaccustomed to walking. She snatched up the book, scarcely pausing to verify the title, and fled, gasping out thanks and apologies as she went. She slowed long enough to shut the door silently behind her, but then her heels clattered up the stairs as if she were pursued.

Amelia seemed ready to make some caustic comment, but Arthur intercepted her. "Poor child," he sighed. "It's a cruel thing to say, but if her mother doesn't die soon, Joyce won't have a chance of making some sort of life for herself." But in actuality Arthur was aware that it was already too late.

He had misjudged Joyce badly, he who considered himself an expert at calculating the neuroticism of homely women. As a young man, discouraged by several rebuffs, he had come to feel that his looks and his foot repelled women, and for quite a time he turned in upon himself. He was almost thirty before he made two electrifying discoveries: that these disadvantages, if properly employed, could actually be turned to advantage if he was willing to content himself with the rejects, the natural spinsters; and, secondly, that such women tended to be eagerly grateful for a little romantic attention and often had unexpected reservoirs of pent-up sensuality. Since then Arthur's life had been much richer, and also greatly varied—for not least of the charms of unattractive women was that they could easily be put aside, before they grew tiresome, once he had acquired the proper technique. He had never, since first he learned his lesson, been the one to weary of an affair. This led to railing and recrimination. Instead, he allowed himself to be bitterly hurt by the way the lady treated him. In her insecurity she was likely to be possessive, and Arthur was reproachfully eloquent about the cruelty of possessiveness to a manly soul. Occasionally she was too clever to be possessive, but in that case she was sure to be proud of her cleverness, and sooner or later this would give deep offense to a sensitive man. Always he was the sufferer, the victim, driven from a fine love by a woman's lack of insight or understanding. With a little encouragement they were quick to feel guilty for this was a natural emotion to them: they might be no plainer than countless women who had married happily, but they had accepted plainness as a punishment and half expected it to spoil everything, so they were guilty. No tedious recriminations. Promises to reform, pleas for a second chance—but these could be handled in a variety of ways. Arthur had reached the point where he derived nearly as much gratification from the elegance of his retreats as from the adroitness and speed of his conquests.

The one hazard was that all these women were neurotic to some degree, and the degree could not always be assessed accurately in advance. With Joyce he had foolishly violated one of his own maxims, which was to steer clear of girls who were the sole comfort of an invalid mother or father; the long-compressed emotions were likely to come out with something like an explosion. It was a mistake he would never make again. He had hurriedly begun paving his avenue of retreat even before the conquest was complete, but nevertheless there had been several scenes of most unpleasant intensity (on her part) before he finally managed to make his escape behind a heavy smoke screen of hurt feelings. It was the sort of episode that left him, most unjustly, feeling like a hypocrite.

"She should go to a psychiatrist," he said, and remembered too late that Amelia was currently doing precisely that herself.

"A marriage broker might be more to the point," Amelia said drily. "It's a pity they've gone out of style. Well, to get back to Senator Browning. I've never seen him as one of our more ardent converts."

"Possibly not," Arthur agreed. "But have you ever heard of a Senator who could resist a captive audience of eighteen thousand people?"

"Well, what do you think it is, then?" she demanded.

"I'm not sure. As I said, I'm going back next weekend. I have two friends I can trust who are right in the middle of things on the Hill. But I have a hunch we may be in for an investigation."

"That's preposterous!" said Amelia, snorting with indignation.

Arthur smiled at her innocence. He had been expecting something of the sort for several months now and was almost looking forward to it.

7

After some consideration Owen had decided against any of the Village restaurants which he and Carol had frequented in the old days. At first he had thought that a touch of nostalgia might be pleasant, but then realized that Carol now had five years of Village associations in which he had played no part, and any place he chose might prove to be haunted not by himself but by Andrew. So he turned his mind uptown and finally settled on the *Licorne*, a French restaurant on East 55th of subdued elegance and calculated intimacy in the evening, after doing a roaring business at lunch time. The prices were quite outrageous, for Léon was convinced that this was the New Yorker's only way of judging values, but the food was truly superb—*if* you remained in a condition to appreciate it. Léon had some devious method of keeping in contact with the kitchen. When a patron ordered his third cocktail, the chef learned that he needn't exert himself over that order, while the Madison Avenue five-martini type was likely to be served a dish that had been rejected by some other customer. But if you contented yourself with a single cocktail and then ordered a bottle of good wine, you could expect as fine a dinner as might be found anywhere in the city.

And Léon's oleaginous delight in greeting a customer by name, his lordly manner of leading the way to a table and sending minions flying in every direction, all of which could make too much of a special occasion of the simple act of dining out, yet lent a festive air when the occasion *was* somewhat special. Carol had treated it as such. Her dark hair was piled high in the fashion most becoming to her, and she wore what was doubtless her best black dress with a fribble of gold at the throat—Owen thought he remembered the pin as one he had given her, but was not sure enough to comment on it. She sparkled with touching gaiety, eager to be delighted by anything and everything, reminding him of how long it must have been since she was out on the town like this. "You must come here quite a lot," she said, gravely amused by Léon's antics.

"Perhaps half a dozen times a year," he said. "Léon doesn't understand that his performance loses some of its impact when you see it repeated for everyone who comes after."

"He's impressive with names, though. Remember how Giovanni insisted on calling you Mr. Heel?" So, easily and naturally, the reminiscent mood came anyway; in these uptown surroundings with no intrusive ghosts to jar them, they picked their way among the best of old times out together. Sunday brunches under the skylight of The Jumble Shop, dining out at Emma's when they were broke and at Luchow's or The Penguin when they were flush, after-theatre hamburger sandwiches at Julius's.

"I have a story for you," Owen said impulsively. Though he could only tell her a little bit of the story, the least interesting part, he had abruptly realized that Carol was one of the few people who would appreciate that little bit. "It's a coincidence that wasn't a coincidence at all. Not long before I came out this evening, the telephone rang. It was a person-to-person call from somewhere up in Connecticut, and I remember noticing that somebody had waited ten minutes to be quite sure of getting the evening rates. Then a man's voice came on the wire, an ordinary voice, rather deep, and I couldn't tell whether I recognized it or not. 'Mr. Hilliard? You will have no idea who I am, but my name is Melmoth.'"

He paused. For a moment Carol's face was blank, then she broke into a wide grin. "Lord! that does bring back old times, doesn't it?" she said. "Who could it have been? Bill? But he's supposed to be out in Arizona, someplace. I've completely lost track of Al Gross, but somehow that doesn't sound like Al. Who was it, Owen?"

He had reacted the same way, assuming his caller was a practical joker from out of his past, from one particular sliver of his past, the first couple of years with Carol. By then the post-war craze for parlor games was subsiding, but in certain company there would still be the occasional evening devoted to *The* Game, or to Pedantry, and once in a session of the latter somebody discovered that Owen prided himself on his knowledge of pen names. It was a harmless vanity; he had noticed one time that people found it disproportionately amusing if a professional writer could not instantly produce the proper name behind Stendhal or Currer Bell and afterwards had made a minor hobby of collecting literary pseudonyms. When his secret was discovered, it became, for the better part of a year, a running joke to try to catch him out. At any party somebody was sure to be ready with a new challenge or two: who was Fiona McLeod, or Corno di Bassetto, or Smectimnuus? The game had died dismally one evening when a young intellectual fresh from Harvard took a hand by inviting Owen to identify Themistogenes, loftily insisted that the author's work would be on anybody's list of the great classics, and then wandered off before he had answered his own riddle. Ordinary reference books gave no help, and it was not until a week later that some scholarly friend unearthed the esoteric fact that this was the name under which Xenophon had originally written *The Anabasis*.

But it was to this period that Owen automatically harked back when his caller on the telephone produced that remarkable surname.

"So I said, 'Sebastian Melmoth, I presume,' " Owen continued, for this was the pseudonym which Oscar Wilde had adopted for a time after his release from prison. "There was a sort of puzzled silence. And then the man said, 'No, there is some mistake. My name is Louis. Louis Melmoth.' " He ended triumphantly, but Carol's face, which had been half smiling in anticipation, reshaped itself to bewilderment.

"I don't think I understand," she said.

"I warned you the coincidence wasn't a coincidence at all," he said, feeling let down, realizing that this confusion which had seemed so comical to him, perhaps because of the subsequent melodrama, had fallen very flat as a story. "I was looking forward to this evening with you, and when someone said Melmoth I assumed a joker from our Christopher Street days. But it was a real, live Louis Melmoth."

"Yes, I see that," she said, producing a consolation smile, "but who *was* he?"

"Oh, just a crackpot," Owen said, rather unfairly, since Melmoth had done his best to avert just that accusation. 'I hope you won't think of me as a crackpot, Mr. Hilliard.' However, though he had a reasonable respect for Carol's discretion, he did not intend to tell her the rest of the story. New Yorkers had a way of forgetting how intricately interlinked were the myriad coteries of metropolitan life. A good anecdote was irresistible conversation fodder, and it seemed no betrayal of a confidence when you felt sure the person you repeated it to had no contact with the victim—yet if the anecdote were sensational enough it traveled on and on. "Somebody who is going to be in town next weekend and wanted to meet me."

"One of the penalties of success?" she jeered unsuspiciously.

"You could look at it that way," he said. "There are times when it seems that the penalties are many and the privileges remarkably few."

"That's a bad sign," she told him. "They come back to Village parties, from time to time, the ones who have finally made the grade uptown, and sit around sentimentalizing about the happy, uncomplicated days when they worried where the next bottle of gin was coming from. And we always know it means they've gone completely commercial. Have you already forgotten, Owen?"

"No, but it was a form of snobbery that never much appealed to me," Owen said, responding seriously to the voice of the old Carol before he realized that now she was merely teasing him. "Oh, hell, it's easy to get defensive when you spent as long as I did on the outside looking in. And people do tend to think a few successful shows mean all sorts of things that they don't really mean at all."

"I know you must get impatient with the sort of work you've been doing," she said sympathetically.

"There's a lot of satisfaction in it, too," he said; he would apologize only so far and no farther. "I've learned a lot. I can see now that my main weakness was getting too absorbed in the ideas that interested me, forgetting that it's the emotional movement of the characters that keeps a play alive, or a novel for that matter. So I pick books with a strong emotional line of their own, and that gives me a discipline to work within—but there's been enough of me in each play so far that I can't complain too much of frustration."

"What then?" Carol asked. "I know you have a low opinion of

theatrical people, but if you insist on writing plays, you can't complain if a great deal of your time is spent with them."

"You'll laugh, but in the old days it was easier to be sure where the next bottle of gin was coming from."

"I shan't laugh if I mustn't, but I'll point out wistfully that in all the time we were married I was exposed to very few menus like this with a bottle of St. Something '52 on the side."

"Four years ago my tax man made an error," Owen explained readily, finances having engrossed his thoughts these last few days, "or at least he took a position that seemed reasonable at the time, but a couple of years later the government ruled that he hadn't appreciated the full ingenuity of their fine print and wanted all the money back. Only by then Barbara-the-Bitch had made off with it, as well as a generous chunk of my income until the day she decides she can afford to remarry."

"I won't have any dessert," Carol volunteered.

"No, that's the point I'm making," he said. "When you have thirty-five dollars in the bank and nothing more coming in till a week from Friday, you act accordingly. But when your bank account is like a high-speed revolving door, with thousands of dollars flying in and out every month, it becomes obvious that the odd taxi fare or the occasional splurge are quite irrelevant. Even when you add them all up they can't have any appreciable effect. Yet since money never *stays* in the account for more than a few days at a time, I must be as broke as the man with thirty-five dollars to his name."

"I'm sure there's a flaw there somewhere," Carol said, "but high finance has never been one of my strong points."

"And the worst of it is the way Hollywood keeps popping out from the wings offering to solve all my tax problems and provide me with a few new ones."

"Well, you won't go out there, anyway," she said comfortably.

"I'm not so sure," he said with deep gloom. "Now they want me to do the film treatment of *Cascade*. Unless I do it I don't quite see how Roger's going to get married."

"You're not serious?"

"No, of course I'm not," Owen said, for this was not part of Carol's idealism but his own point of honor. He had no snobbish disdain for Hollywood. It was a hard working, overglamorized place where they turned out a lot of remarkably good films, but it was sheer death on writers. When a man went there he was finished, as far as ever after writing anything first-rate was concerned, because his respect for his own work was shattered. When a play of Owen's was in rehearsal, he rewrote and rewrote, and expected to. If an actress couldn't speak a certain line, he tinkered with it until both she and he were satisfied. But when the curtain went up on opening night, every word spoken on that stage was his—and this was his self-respect. In Hollywood a man had no control over his own words. They would be revised by other writers, altered at the whim of producer, director or star, or the most significant of them vanish forever in the cutting room. Yet none of this affected his weekly pay check; he was better paid than ever in his life for writing what he might not recognize in the finished work. Something happened to his belief in himself, or his self-respect as an artist. Every writer who went out there, even on a 'Just this once' basis, came back a lesser man. Seeing this in action all his working life, seeing what had become of so many once-promising men, Owen had early vowed that this was one temptation to which he could never succumb. "But I wish they weren't so damned seductive about it!" he grumbled petulantly.

"I don't understand about Roger's getting married," Carol said.

"Oh, that. It's a headache." Owen wanted sympathy, but wasn't sure that on this score he'd get any from Carol. Even in her new tolerance she was likely to be impatient with any suggestion that a pair of youngsters *needed* to start off with a fancy honeymoon and an extravagantly furnished apartment. She would say this was more of Amelia's Langstaff foolishness, and to an extent she'd be right. Yet in a sense, which he wouldn't have wanted to try to defend, Owen knew that he too was in favor of giving Roger a 'proper' send-off in this marriage—probably it was a residue of the guilt he had always felt for marring Roger's childhood. "It's one of those things that just get rolling. The Fortescues are throwing a big wedding and a lavish reception as their share; they simply took that for granted. We're expected to provide a honeymoon to scale and do something about outfitting the kids' apartment. And as things stand, 'we' means my checkbook."

"Yes," Carol said thoughtfully. This conversation had gone on intermittently, between mouthfuls, but now it was time for cigarettes and the last of the wine. "Well, it explains your preoccupation with money. Perhaps you're exaggerating; you rather tend that way. How much of a honeymoon do Roger and Vickie really expect?"

"Look, with love's young dream rattling around in his head, Roger has all he can do to keep from flunking out at the last moment. He can't coast; his grades aren't good enough. So we had to encourage him to leave all the practical details to us, not to worry. Without entirely realizing what I was doing, I committed myself to arrangements that won't humiliate Roger in front of his bride."

"Then Roger's expectations really depend on Vickie's," Carol said. "If *she* decided that a week on Nantucket would be dandy, then he couldn't feel humiliated, could he?"

"I suppose not. But I suspect that Vickie has a more prosperous imagination than that."

"Her parents could probably help you there if they wanted to. What are the Fortescues like?"

"That's quite a good question." Despite all experience, the mind was so tidy about pushing people into pigeonholes. He had taken a dislike to Ruth for no very good reason, since her inadequacies could be of no concern to him, who would never be on an intimate footing with her. She appeared to be sweet, well-meaning, not very intelligent; probably she had few interests outside her home and family. He had labeled her Typical Housewife and filed her away. Charles was much more of a person, though some of the enigmas about him vanished on closer acquaintance. Always prone to speculate about the people he met, Owen had thought it rather adventurous for an executive on the way up, as Charles must have been twenty-five years ago, to marry a Jewish girl. But during lunch the other day, expansive after several concoctions of bouillon and vodka, Charles had said something to suggest that he was distantly related to one of the families that held a controlling interest in Andean C & Z, so perhaps his career had been too clearly marked out to be jarred by such trivialities. He was amusing, intelligent, well-informed, conservative, introverted without being intellectual (a combination Owen was unaccustomed to), and had the most preposterous notions of what a writer's life was like—which was normal. Owen quite liked him, and not least for being the contented domestic man Owen had always longed to be. A conventional businessman with a certain private individuality; this was how Owen had filed *him* away.

And then up in Connecticut this afternoon Mr. Louis Melmoth had got on the wire. A deep, calm, reasonable voice. "I hope you won't think of me as a crackpot, Mr. Hilliard. I'll be in New York next weekend, and I'd like to see you for half an hour, if that's possible. You should be interested in learning that your son is engaged to the daughter of a murderer."

It was meant to be frightfully shocking, of course.

Someone truly debonair would have answered, 'My dear chap, as long as Vickie wasn't involved, I don't care how many people her parents have killed,' which was about the way Owen felt when he thought it over. But at the time he was too startled to find the retort. When Melmoth had declined to say anything further over the telephone, Owen had made an appointment with him for Saturday afternoon, and by then it was mainly out of curiosity to meet someone who was capable of such restrained melodrama. For melodrama it surely was. Melmoth might be no crackpot most of the time, but he was certainly someone with one special bee in his bonnet; it was absurd to think of either Fortescue as ever having poisoned Uncle Walter's coffee. Had Ruth, at the wheel of a too-powerful car, killed some unfortunate child? To the child's father this might seem like murder, and in a way he would be right, but there were many such 'murderers' at large and righteous in the land. Had Charles once been responsible for an order that led a man to death in a mining disaster? It was tragic yet meaningless episodes like these, brooded over too long, that could lead a close relative of the victim to make such a charge. Owen was sure that Melmoth's story would prove to be something of the sort.

Or at least he was *almost* sure. No matter how promptly and glibly you rationalized an accusation like that, it seemed to leave an insidious uncertainty in the mind. If he really believed in these plausible explanations, why did he keep adding new ones to the list?

And what did it do to his neat, superficial portraits of the Fortescues? Presumably one of them had been the cause of another person's death, fortuitously no doubt, but directly enough to attract the blame. Wouldn't this affect anyone's character, probably deeply? Would even a Ruth Fortescue ever be able to absolve herself for the death of a child—although the child had been at fault, darting out from behind a parked car. Wouldn't she always be haunted by the memory of that crumpled little body? The mere innocence of intention could never entirely erase the guilt of circumstances. There would be an unassuageable remorse, shut away by time and all the defenses of the ego but nevertheless there, forming a part of one of the natures he had characterized as 'typical' and 'conventional.' But he, *he*, should never have needed such a sensational reminder that the faces people offered to the world were more of a convenience than a reality and that the ordinary person might contain as much anguish or loneliness as the exquisitely sensitive, although bearing with it more sturdily.

"I've only met them a couple of times," he said. "Just enough to know I'll like him and try to avoid her. They seem good, solid, Republican, backbone of the nation. Probably a crawling mass of complexes when you know them better. Who can tell?"

"If you get along with Mr. Fortescue, why don't you explain the situation to him?" Carol asked earnestly, but Owen pictured himself blackmailing Charles on the subject of honeymoons with the knowledge that his wife was a murderer, and the lunacy of it made him laugh aloud. "What's so funny?"

"Me," he said. "I'm funny. Here you are, clerking in a dusty antique store with a little girl to support, and I've devoted the whole of dinner to complaining about my finances, making you sympathize. The masculine ego is not a lovable thing. How about some dessert?"

"If we can afford it, I'd like a demitasse," she said. "But I'm serious about talking to Fortescue. A businessman would understand your problems, and he could get Vickie to be reasonable."

"Well, perhaps," said Owen, whose pride was revolted by the suggestion. "And that is absolutely enough about me for one session."

"I doubt it, somehow."

"Don't be rude," he said, and ordered coffee for both of them. "I'm the one who needs to be brought up to date. This job of yours with Nora. I can see its advantages—it's close to home, and it solves the problem of what to do with the kid after school. But apart from that isn't it pretty deadly?"

"No, not really. Oh, you'd go mad, I expect. But I always manage to enjoy myself."

"You *have* changed."

"I don't think I have," she said, frowning.

"Lots," he insisted. "Maybe you aren't aware of it. This day-to-day philosophy, look on the bright side and enjoy yourself—all of that is new since my day."

"Because I nagged at you? Owen, you're an idiot. I'm a woman, I'm no more talented than Roger is, but I'm a woman, so my ambitions are bound to be at second hand. I nagged you in the same spirit that I sewed buttons on your shirts. Somebody had to push you into fighting for yourself, somebody had to protect you from your idiotic loyalty to people who were willing to see you throw yourself away if there was money to be made by it. Are you *still* with Polly Spurgeon?"

"Oh, Lord!" Owen moaned.

"It must be nearly twenty years now, and what has she ever done but try to make a commercial hack of you?"

"Darling, will you never understand that an agent doesn't collect ten percent for encouraging one to be an undiscovered genius?"

"Well, but Polly's supposed to be a good friend of yours, too. At least you always say so. She ought to know you by now. And I'll bet she's still not satisfied. I'll bet she's been pushing Hollywood at you."

"You can't blame her for trying."

"I do blame her!" Carol said fiercely. "And when you were still writing novels for Quillow's it was that Jeff Aronson. A great editor and a great friend, you insisted. Always trying to wheedle a best seller out of you. 'Can't we get just a bit more sex into this section, Owen?'"

"He never said anything remotely like that."

"Didn't he tell you your attitude towards sex was too healthy for the popular taste?"

"That was just a joke."

"I don't believe it," Carol said. "He was trying very hard to make a success of you—*his* kind of success. He wanted a best seller, but he never had any difficulty convincing you that he was a dedicated seeker after the great American novel. You're a sucker for being liked, Owen. It doesn't occur to you to protect yourself from people who are fond of you, even when they're trying to turn you into somebody else. Of course I got impatient with you, and I guess I was disgustingly tiresome about it. But all I wanted was to see you dig in your heels and fight to be your own man with your own talent."

"It didn't take long to get back to me, did it?"

"Oh, I was just proving that I haven't changed at all," she said with a great beaming grin.

Probably nobody liked to have it argued that he had altered appreciably; it was pleasanter to reshape the memories a little and believe that one had all along been one's present sensible self. Yet Carol was mistaken. This view of their quarrels was appealing but distorted, a rationalized view, the view of someone grown more relaxed with life who looks back to find excuses for past intolerance. And later in the evening he had an even more striking evidence of the change.

They went back to her place for a while, to release the baby sitter. The apartment was small but more attractively arranged, and tidier, than he had expected; apart from a tortured bronze on the mantelpiece there was no trace of her late husband. They played records and talked of this and that, rediscovering one another. It was some remark of Carol's about her father that led Owen to ask politely how

Henry was: a cautious inquiry, since Carol could be brutally impatient on the subject of her parent, whom she adored grudgingly through a fog of principled disapproval.

"Dad's the same as always," she said, and then her mouth quirked. "No, that's not quite accurate. After all these years he's actually thinking of getting married again."

"Not seriously!" said Owen, unable to associate romance with that prim fastidiousness: the earnest owlish face, the manicured white hands, the vest pocketful of mechanical pencils.

"I don't know if anything will come of it. He's bothered by the morality of marrying someone two years younger than I am. Since he's always sneered at such marriages, it's a struggle."

"How do you feel about it?"

"All in favor," Carol said. "Enid's a sweet girl, and very dependent. She'll give Dad someone to worry about besides me."

"But how on earth did he *meet* her?" Owen asked.

"She's the daughter of a client, one of those suburban development promoters, who was so pleased with some plans Dad did for him that he wouldn't have anyone else for the designs of his own home. You can imagine—Dad's first private job for years and years! He was giddy with it for a while. Visions of Frank Lloyd Wright danced in his head. But Enid's father had some firm ideas of his own, and in the end it was just another split-level ranch-type house, a little more elegant than most."

But all this was told affectionately, without sarcasm, as if she had finally accepted the fact that there was room in the world for the second best, as if at long last she had forgiven her father for the compromises which had enabled her to go (resentfully) to Putney and Sarah Lawrence. She was satisfied to think of her father's happiness as an end in itself, without quibblings of principle, and this lent a new generosity to her intelligence. For she was intelligent, quick and understanding, with an oblique insight which could give unexpected meanings to the commonplace. After years of women who had no opinions worth listening to on any subject but themselves, Owen reawakened to the delight of a woman who was no less feminine for having a brain of her own.

Otherwise, a quiet, uneventful evening, notable only in that when they harked back to the old days, as they did from time to time, it was with a growing note of regret, as if they both recognized that they had let something good go to waste. Only that, but it seemed promising. Owen left with an invitation to have dinner there on Saturday, so he could meet Lois. But in the taxi going home his mind was only half on the pleasure of this prospect, and half on his other Saturday engagement, the exasperating, inscrutable mystery of Louis Melmoth.

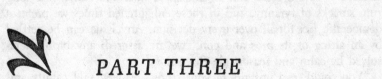

PART THREE

1

On a fixed evening each week the officers of the Manhattan chapter of the L.I.D., perhaps with a few influential converts in attendance, met for a council of war at Amelia Booth's. Two years ago the fixing of this evening had been the occasion of a dispute between Amelia and Stephen which he regarded as anthropologically instructive.

"Mondays would be best," Amelia had declared. "That's the one evening people are almost always free."

"Anything *but* Monday," said Stephen. "That's when they have the rapid-transit tournaments at the club." His usual place of refuge was the Marshall Chess Club on 10th Street, but each Monday evening there they held a tournament wherein games were played at the dizzy speed of ten seconds a move. Of course some tables were not occupied by the tournament, and he could generally find an opponent, but the atmosphere of frantic tension, with pieces being slammed about and the clock chiming out six times a minute, was not appropriate to the sort of tranquil, placidly analytical chess game he enjoyed.

But be it noted that there were valid reasons on both sides. In many marital differences neither party feels strongly enough to argue; in many others one person feels less strongly than the other and increases his moral credit rating by giving in gracefully. There are times, however, when both sides feel the importance of the matter, when both sides can lay claim to necessity and logic, when there is no available solution by compromise, and somebody has to yield. These are the moments that test a marriage. In the bad old days a husband merely laid down the law, and it is rumored that in some households he still does. But this method, though it might be claimed to save a good deal of emotional wear and tear in the long run, smacks of tyranny, and in these enlightened times we prefer a democratic free-for-all over every decision. Any issue can be settled by an airing of its pros and cons, we are assured; any problem resolved by calm and reasonable discussion.

"You could read upstairs in your study," Amelia said calmly and reasonably.

"After working up there all afternoon," Stephen replied in the same spirit, "my one idea is to escape."

"Tuesday evenings are out because of the Opera," she went on, "and later in the week people always have other engagements."

"I see the problem," he conceded, "but I'm not in favor of solving it for you by spending Monday evenings for the next year or two in the bar around the corner."

When reason fails, as it invariably does, there comes the appeal to the other person's better nature.

"You're out visiting friends that often anyway," Amelia said. "You could easily plan your visits for Monday. It seems a small sacrifice."

"I visit friends at their convenience, not mine," he said, "and in any case I prefer to sacrifice to my own gods. It would be more fitting if your ardent colleagues sacrificed some of their social life later in the week."

The democratic process founders here on the difficulty of taking a majority vote when there are but two voters. The ideal of an untroubled collaboration foundered long ago on the dichotomy of sexual temperaments. Tyranny, then, had been replaced by a less obvious struggle for supremacy, and a 'happy marriage' was one where that struggle had been won with a minimum of fuss. In American 'happy marriages' the winner was generally the wife: she expected to win (although vehemently protesting to the contrary), she was better equipped for the war of nerves, and her husband (having been brought up by another such woman) was usually willing to settle for peace at home and take his revenge in infidelity. It was when the contenders were evenly matched that there was the devil to pay.

Amelia's masculine streak was nicely balanced by a feminine streak in Stephen—he was perfectly aware of this—and from the first their marriage had suffered from a hideous equilibrium. Outsiders thought them uncommonly well mated. Both were strong-minded, articulate and independent, each was quick to resent an injustice, particularly to himself, and neither could be accused of an excess of unselfishness. Accordingly it had proved quite impossible to devise any formula for resolving the head-on clashes of exigency or opinion that arose from time to time. Every collision became an all-out battle of wills, with victory going to the person who was willing to suffer more for his cause.

"At times you seem to forget this is also my house," Amelia said, alluding delicately to her mother's contribution towards the purchase price. But this was a makeshift argument, calling for no reply.

"Why don't we farm out your mother's opera tickets, and then you'd have Tuesdays," Stephen said equally impractically. "At your age you can scarcely care whether you see still another *Traviata*."

"Three or four times a season there's something I really do want to see," she said. "No, Monday is the only practical day, and you're just being obstructive. What do you want? I'll agree to Mexico for the summer if you'll be reasonable about this."

"We'll discuss Mexico some other time," Stephen said, feeling strong. "I don't see that it has much in common with this other idea."

"What *do* you want, then?"

"Peace in my own home."

"Don't be difficult, Stephen. I'm trying to be friendly about this."

"You're also trying to push me out of the house on the most inconvenient night of the week. I don't intend to be pushed."

"I'm *trying* to be friendly," she repeated warningly.

"And you'll stop trying," he replied, "as soon as you find it's not getting you your own way."

"If you want to be like that, all right," she said, as if the road ahead was now clear. "There's no question of pushing you out of the house, but you can't deny me the use of one room one evening a week. I'm sorry if it's inconvenient, but I have to put up with a few inconveniences myself, as well as a great deal of unnecessary rudeness. It's a pity we can't sometimes settle a question like this without it becoming unpleasant, but I'm sending out notices fixing the day as Monday, and that's that. You can go where you like."

"Oh, I shan't go anywhere," Stephen said. "It's not easy to banish a man from his own living room. I'll be right here Monday evenings, talking on interminably about my brothers the Bushmen. They're a peace-loving people, too, so the subject won't be inappropriate." In this fashion it was determined that the officers of the Manhattan chapter of the L.I.D. meet at Amelia Booth's each Wednesday evening, and some weeks Stephen visited friends, and others he enjoyed himself at the Club.

On this particular Wednesday evening Stephen went to the Club and was pleased to find one of his favorite opponents, Mr. Rivkin, eager for a game. Although the two men had not met in some weeks, they wasted little time in salutations, but sought out a quiet table where Mr. Rivkin drew the white pieces for the first game, made his usual joke about a surprise opening, and as always pushed forward his king's pawn. He was a burly middle-aged man with a bland, benign, heavy-featured face and neat grey hair which would be in shocking state before the first game was done: it was Mr. Rivkin's habit, when thinking hard, to seize upon a clump of hair and twist it endlessly about one finger, till after a while the top of his head was covered by a random arrangement of these small grey horns. His style of play was more adventurous than Stephen's though not quite so sound; their games were leisurely of pace, fiercely contested and utterly silent. While setting up the pieces afresh one or the other of them might comment on the game just finished: "A wild one to come out of a Ruy Lopez," but otherwise the hours went by without a word being spoken.

This evening the honors were perfectly even: Mr. Rivkin won the first game, Stephen the second, and the third was a hard-fought draw that continued to be exciting to the very end. Both men were pleased with themselves, and after several hours of silent concentration felt more disposed to be sociable. At Mr. Rivkin's suggestion they strolled over to a bar on Sixth Avenue for a drink.

In a booth at the back as far from the jukebox as they could get, they continued for a while to argue the merits of the French Defense, to which Stephen was devoted and which Mr. Rivkin considered too delicate for amateurs like themselves. Then, suddenly, Mr. Rivkin smote himself on the brow. "I forgot!" he exclaimed. "Only at dinner I was reminding myself if I ran into Professor Booth this evening to congratulate him. And I forgot."

There was something faintly exaggerated about this performance, and Stephen was confused. "Congratulate me on what?" he asked.

"Your son getting married," said Mr. Rivkin. "My wife spotted it in the papers."

"My stepson," Stephen corrected.

"It's the same thing," said Mr. Rivkin. "This silly game is to blame: I forget the other players are real people with lives of their own. To me you're Professor Booth who plays the French and who has a weakness for holding on to the bishop pair if you possibly can. You must forgive me."

"Nothing at all," muttered Stephen, who was passably fond of Roger but was not so rich in family feeling that he could see the marriage of a stepson as a landmark in his life.

"Oh, there's more in this than meets the eye. We better drink to it." Their glasses were almost empty. Imperiously Mr. Rivkin summoned another round, and when the whisky came insisted on solemnly drinking a toast to the happiness of the young couple. "Charles Fortescue's daughter," he added musingly. "There's the coincidence, and that's the name my wife spotted in the papers."

"You know Charles Fortescue, then?"

"Never met him in my life," said Mr. Rivkin. "But I do a good bit of work for his company."

It was Stephen's turn to be conscious of the inhumanity of chess, for though he had known Rivkin for a number of years he had not the least notion of what the man's line of work might be. Nor had Rivkin ever stopped to wonder, he was sure, what Professor Booth might be a professor of. The atmosphere of the club was friendly enough, but for the most part it was the impersonal friendliness of collective monomania.

"Or you might put it," Mr. Rivkin said, "that I do a good bit of swindling of Charles Fortescue's company."

And finally Stephen realized that this whole performance had been planned in advance—the suggestion that they have a drink together, the belated remembering of Roger's engagement, had all been Mr. Rivkin's way of leading up to some undesired confidence or confession. "Why tell me about it?" Stephen asked ungraciously.

"Because you might be able to help," said Mr. Rivkin. "I'm not happy about the way things are; I've never been happy about them. Mind you, I don't pretend to be a remarkably ethical man. I wouldn't want to answer to God for my income tax returns, and if anybody offers to fix a parking ticket for me, I don't argue. But I like to run as honest a business as possible. It's more satisfactory that way, and it's better business in the long run. Yet it isn't always easy these days."

"I have to admit I don't even know what your business is," Stephen said.

"Printing," said Mr. Rivkin. "All sorts of plain and fancy printing, preferably in big lots—and this job for Andean C & Z is one of my biggest. Four times a year, nearly a hundred thousand copies at a time. It's a propaganda throw-away they send out to the stockholders. Lots of companies do, and this is a nice one: plenty of photographs and a three-color type job. The man in charge of it is called Bigelow, Bruce Bigelow. He brought me in the copy five-six years ago and asked if I could handle it and how much? I ran him up a neat proof and sent that to him with the estimate. A few days later he came in again. He liked the work, he said, but he wasn't too happy about the price. I said it was as low as I could get it, prepared to bargain a little if I had to, but that wasn't the point at all. He wanted me to raise the price."

"In matters of business I'm a child, Mr. Rivkin," Stephen said. "You'll have to explain."

"It's always kickbacks, these days," said Mr. Rivkin. "His idea was that I bill the company for four hundred dollars more than my price every quarter. Bigelow okays the bill, and when I get paid I send the four hundred in cash around to his apartment or give it to him the next time he comes in. Simple? As a matter of fact, Bigelow was generous: he said if I wanted to add in an extra hundred for myself he wouldn't object. And he thought I was an idiot when I turned that part down."

"But why didn't you take this story to Mr. Fortescue or one of the other officers of the company?" Stephen asked.

"All right, supposing I did," said Mr. Rivkin. "Who am I? A guy with a small printing business; there are others just as good and perhaps a few better. And who is Bruce Bigelow? I haven't any idea, if you know what I mean. Maybe he's Mr. Fortescue's brother-in-law, maybe he's the nephew of the biggest stockholder. So they say Now, now, Brucie-boy, you shouldn't do that sort of thing, and he says Rivkin is a dirty liar, and what proof can I show? I've lost the job and I've earned me an enemy who maybe can pass the word to his friends that Rivkin is the lowest heel in town."

"Oh, dear," said Stephen.

"Let's have another drink," said Mr. Rivkin, waving. "These glasses get smaller every year. Now, just for the fun of it suppose Bigelow isn't anybody special, and suppose Mr. Fortescue believes my story, and suppose Bigelow gets fired. Then what happens? When the next fellow comes in does Mr. Fortescue say to him: 'Now be sure to send all our printing to nice Mr. Rivkin; he's an honest man and if you try any hanky-panky he'll report it right back to me.' I ask you."

"Um," said Stephen. "If you needed the job, I can see why you felt it was safer to go along with this arrangement, but—"

"But is it really safer?" Mr. Rivkin put in helpfully. "You're right with me, Professor. Sooner or later Mr. Bigelow will stub his toe or move along to another job, and a new man will take over. And there I'll be, down on the books as charging four hundred a quarter more than the job is worth. It makes *me* look like the crook."

"Does this Bigelow have something to do with the advertising department?" asked Stephen, who had taken little part in the recent discussions about Roger's future, but who had been becoming increasingly convinced that Bigelow's name was somehow familiar.

"He *is* the advertising department," said Mr. Rivkin. "They're the real kickback artists."

"This is getting involved," Stephen said. "He's the man my stepson will be working under after he gets married."

"There you are, then!" Mr. Rivkin said triumphantly, as if he had neatly shifted all the responsibility from his shoulders to Stephen's. "You don't want your boy picking up tricks like that in his first job."

"I suppose I could pass this story on to Fortescue," Stephen said doubtfully, "but I don't see what good it will do you."

"Look, you're an intelligent man, Professor," said Mr. Rivkin slowly, spinning at a lock of hair. "You can talk to Mr. Fortescue socially, and that makes all the difference. You can find out first if Bigelow is related to anybody, because if he is there's nothing to be done. As for the rest, I don't want to lose the job, but if I have to. . . . Well, I can afford it better now than I could a few years ago. Frankly, I'm thinking of my reputation, and I'm fed up. A little graft here and there I can stomach, but sixteen hundred dollars a year is plain stealing."

"I'll do what I can," Stephen promised unhappily, and Mr. Rivkin insisted on drinking to this. "Tell me," continued Stephen, whose mind always shifted as quickly as possible from the uncomfortable particular to the intriguing abstract, "you say that a lot of this . . . um . . . kicking back goes on?"

"All the time," said Mr. Rivkin. "There's nothing original about Bigelow; it's just that his job allows him to be greedier than most.

Usually it's fifty dollars here, a hundred there. The ones who prefer to think they're honest let drop how fond they are of Haig & Haig Pinchbottle and leave it to me to decide whether the job is worth a couple of bottles or a whole case. I don't think I do a dozen jobs a year where somebody doesn't get paid off."

"It hasn't always been like that, has it?"

"Not to hear my father. He was still around during the depression, when there wasn't too much work going and a man expected a little something for pushing it your way. From the way he carried on I'd guess it was just getting started then. Oh, there've always been chiselers, but that's when decent people got into the act. Times were tough, and you couldn't really blame them, though my father did. God knows what he'd think now, since the second war. Times are good, and *everybody* has his hand out."

"Yes, that's what I'd gathered," Stephen said. "The standards have completely changed."

"You can say that again," said Mr. Rivkin, looking around for the waitress.

It had long been a belief of Stephen's that matters like ethics got scant inspection in our society. Ministers beat their monotonous drum of disapproval, columnists moralized from time to time, philosophers speculated about the future, and nobody paid much heed to any of them. Scientific observation of the trends of current morality there was virtually none, and it seemed fit work for such anthropologists as were willing to regard all contemporary cultures as primitive. For his *magnum opus* he had dreamt of a splendid chapter to be called The Evolution of Ethics; this was one of the ideas dropped by the wayside as unnecessarily controversial. But he was still in love with the idea; it called to him periodically, and rarely so strongly as this evening with a sympathetic audience right at hand. "Take the Indians, for example," he began.

"What Indians?" asked Mr. Rivkin, startled.

Stephen looked at his companion and realized that Mr. Rivkin had had too much to drink, and it was too late in the evening to start with the Indians and work forward. "Forget the Indians," he said broadmindedly. "We'll stick to the modern concepts of honor. Have you read Conrad's *Lord Jim?*"

"Of course!" Mr. Rivkin said with indignation. "You professors always think a businessman is illiterate."

"All right, then—"

"I wouldn't guarantee I remember the story off-hand. There's a jungle, isn't there?"

"That comes later on. At least I'm not sure, but the real story begins on a ship."

"I expect you fellows have to reread these books every year or so."

"I don't teach English Literature," Stephen said. "I'm an anthropologist."

"Aha!" cried Mr. Rivkin, welcoming enlightenment. "Indians!"

"No, people," said Stephen, tired of that distinction. "Civilization shouldn't be measured by television sets. Do you think we're so much less primitive than the average Samoan? Believe me, by most rational standards the Samoan could beat us hands down."

"Good for him," said Mr. Rivkin amiably. "I'm a bit confused; does *Lord Jim* take place in Samoa?"

"No," said Stephen, wondering if he himself had taken a drink too many. "It was the story of a man who failed himself. He had a duty, a responsibility, and in a moment of crisis he panicked. No great harm resulted, though it might have. But that didn't matter. He had betrayed his sense of honor. He knew it, other people knew it. That one loss of honor shattered his life, made an outcast of him, eventually destroyed him. Remember now?"

"Sort of," said Mr. Rivkin.

"That book was published early in this century, not long before I was born," Stephen said. "It was a serious book and people took it seriously. Nobody seemed to find it remarkable that an ordinary man should react in such a way—evidently in those days a man's honor was a very important thing. But now, only fifty-some years later? People of perfectly respectable background rehearse their cheating for the television quiz programs, college basketball games are at the disposal of professional gamblers, business is conducted by price-fixing and kickbacks."

"I'm with you again," said Mr. Rivkin happily. "Yes, things are certainly going to hell."

"But that isn't my point at all," Stephen said. Mr. Rivkin's face fell. "Well, perhaps it is in a way," Stephen corrected himself, finally acknowledging the liquor and despairing of making Mr. Rivkin understand why he regarded all moralizing as a waste of time. Standards of behavior were subject to the democratic process like everything else; whatever enough people did was the true ethic of the period, and no amount of righteous preaching would alter that scientific fact. When enough people disapproved of a law, as had happened during

Prohibition, then it became, empirically, perfectly ethical behavior to flout that law. As enough people came around to diddling their income tax, or having traffic violations set aside by favor, or expecting kickbacks, these would become part of the accepted, or true, morality. Already it was noticeable that people who maintained high standards of conduct themselves had lost much of their capacity for disapproval when others were caught out in a fall from grace: sociological and psychological explanations were searched for, and genuine indignation was left to the very naive. Honor was a private virtue, not yet shameful, but not to be credited automatically to anybody outside the immediate family circle. "But doesn't it strike you as having happened surprisingly *quickly?*" Stephen asked.

"Oh, I don't know," Mr. Rivkin said judiciously. "Just about everything is going so much faster these days."

"Perhaps you're right," said Stephen. "It isn't always easy to recognize progress."

2

At about five o'clock the following afternoon, towards the end of a routine day, untroubled by any suspicion of his advertising manager's defalcations, Charles Fortescue had Mrs. Peabody ring his apartment, feeling it was about time to report that he wouldn't be home for dinner. Since he had been planning this move all day, it might seem that his delay in calling was a discourtesy; actually it was an act of consideration. He had learned that it was a mistake to call earlier: with Peter off at college Ruth would simply put together a makeshift dinner of leftovers from the refrigerator as adequate for Vickie and herself. Whereas by five o'clock or so dinner had taken on an impetus of its own: even if Ruth had not begun preparations, she was so used to the idea of the scheduled meal that she would cook it anyway, and Charles's conscience was just that trifle easier for knowing his wife and daughter were enjoying a proper meal.

"Hello, hon," he said, when Mrs. Peabody had assured him that Mrs. Fortescue was on the line. "I'm very sorry, but I warned you this might happen. Harry's flown in and he's in a stew about that conference with the Grace people, so the only thing to do is take him out to dinner and soothe him down." None of this made the least sense, but he knew from old that Ruth never paid any attention when he talked of office matters.

"Oh, dear," said Ruth. "Well, perhaps it's just as well. We've been going through all Vickie's clothes to find out exactly what she needs, and the place is still a mess."

"No rush about straightening up," Charles said cheerfully. "Since I'll be in mid-town anyway, if I get free from Harry early enough I'll probably stop by The Darkroom for a while."

"All right, dear. Is Harry someone I should send my regards to?"

"No, no. He's from the Lima office. You haven't met him."

"I wasn't sure. Don't be *too* late, dear."

Half an hour later Charles left his office building and strolled westward. It was a pleasant evening and he enjoyed walking, and also The Darkroom lay directly on his route. There was no real need to stop by there in person, a telephone call would have sufficed, but Charles's conscience was an intricate and nervous mechanism. He had a superstitious conviction that if one day he didn't stop by, the building across the street would burn down, or the bank next door would be held up, and his ignorance of the occurrence would give him away.

On the surface The Darkroom was a thoroughly legitimate enterprise, catering with uncommon elegance to the needs of camera enthusiasts. There were three small but very well equipped darkrooms, the use of which was included in the annual fee. There was a fair-sized studio (an extra, rented by the hour) equipped with well-kept backdrops and every variety of lighting including stroboscopic. The halls were hung with a permanent exhibit of members' work (one of Charles's llamas was there), and twice a year the studio was cleared out, hung with the members' latest efforts, and a cocktail party given for friends, relatives and critics. To top it all, George Nicolaides, the proprietor and manager, was an expert repairman, able to make the most recalcitrant camera behave.

Yet the remarkable popularity and financial success of The Darkroom derived less from any of these assets than from George Nicolaides's recognition that in New York City there was a crying need for a place where a domesticated man could reasonably profess to be of an evening, yet where he could not readily be reached by telephone. New York was not a town of lodge meetings or bowling societies; the excuses that could take a man out of reach of a telephone were very few, and could not be repeated too often. The Darkroom provided a solution. "I'm afraid Mr. Walters is in one of the darkrooms at the moment," George would say. "I'm sorry, Mrs. Walters, we have a strict rule. You see, if I called him out, it would destroy whatever he's working on. Is the matter urgent?" Usually it was not urgent, and the message could be passed on when Mr. Walters called in later that evening. But if there was even a hint of real emergency, George made an excuse to hang up: "There's another call coming in; I'll have him call you back immediately," and then promptly rang Mr. Walters at a number which was recorded in code in well-locked files. This arrangement was expensive—as George put it: "The privilege of not using the darkrooms is slightly dearer than the privilege of using them"—but was widely appreciated. On a busy evening the three small darkrooms might ostensibly be occupied by upwards of two hundred and fifty men.

George Nicolaides, slender, bald and urbane, considered that his club performed a valuable public service. When he could be induced to discuss the matter at all, with an old and valued patron, he was quick to point out that by no means all of his patrons, perhaps not even a majority, employed his offices in the pursuit of adultery. There was a large body of young men (and in this case 'young' extended well into the thirties) who used the Darkroom as a refuge from over-possessive mothers, nothing in mind but freedom from surveillance. In at least three cases that George knew of the stolen hours had been spent in respectable and successful courtships which would have been rendered awkward and miserable, at the very least, if the mothers had known what was going on. And then there were a number of older men, George had no idea how many, with an irresistible passion for some activity hotly disapproved of by their wives, such as poker or the trotting races—and peace in the home was maintained by The Darkroom. George was a confirmed believer in peace. "If a man keeps calling home with an unconvincing excuse," he would say, "his wife suffers. It adds insult to injury. Give her something she can believe in, even if she knows it's a lot of nonsense, and she's happy."

Not all women, unfortunately, lived up to George's opinion of their credulity. The occasional wife, suspicious of her husband's sudden enthusiasm for photography, might set private detectives to work and glimpse the truth. But when caught in a hopeless position, a man generally preferred the comparative dignity of paying for a Reno divorce, without scandal, and the public reputation of The Darkroom had never suffered.

A red light over a door showed that one of the darkrooms was legitimately in use, but otherwise, as was customary at this hour of the evening, there was nobody about. Charles paused at the bulletin board to make sure there were no close acquaintances on the list of recent applications for membership—another good reason for looking in periodically. He poked his head into George's closet-sized office to say that he could be reached at the usual number, and then resumed his stroll northwestward.

Everybody else seemed in a great hurry to get somewhere, thrusting along the sidewalks, vacant-eyed, impatient. Charles had no such sense of urgency; he could scarcely remember it. His anticipations were quiet ones: for the moment he looked forward to boasting a little, and to a better dinner than he ever got at home. And there were anxieties as well. Madge had been touchy recently, and especially these last few weeks. During their previous meeting she had flared up at him for no apparent reason at all. Of course, by nature she was a far more temperamental woman than Ruth. In the beginning this very unpredictability had been a great part of Madge's charm for him: there was nothing placid about her; she was volatile, intense, always interested and gifted with a wonderful, infectious gaiety. But she had her periods of depression as well, and since her illness these had grown more frequent; at times she seemed to take a perverse pleasure in making him work and work to cheer her up. Those were the moods that Charles particularly dreaded and had come to think of as the most exhausting of his responsibilities.

Madge lived on the seventh floor of an apartment building of decayed respectability just off Central Park West. Once there had been uniformed doormen and elevator men; now there was an invisible alcoholic superintendent and the elevators were self-service—an arrangement which suited Charles Fortescue if nobody else. He let himself in the front door, went up in the elevator, but rang the bell at Madge's door. Although he had a key he punctiliously never used it except when Madge was out.

She let him in quietly (there was a snoopy neighbor down the hall), closed the door behind him before she came into his arms; he had time to see the strain underlying her cheerfulness. After a flare-up she tended to brood despondently, he knew, and torment herself with the possibility that one day he simply wouldn't show up. Nothing he said did any good: since her illness she had lost her self-confidence as a woman. He hugged her closely, trying wordlessly to give her reassurance, kissing her—and thinking wryly what an unromantic spectacle they must present.

Several times this past year Gert Zimmerman had dropped pointed generalizations about the nastiness of old men who kept young mistresses; it was evident that she had stumbled on some clue to Madge's existence and had assumed (in her spinsterish way) that Madge must be an abandoned, gold-digging hoyden. The salacious imagination would have been disappointed in Madge. She was in her middle fifties, and just in the last few years had come to look her age. When Charles first knew her, she was a handsome, exquisitely tended woman with the fine wrinkles of vivacity and a slender, youthful figure. Time and illness had made her gaunt. Broad daylight was now a haggard-making cruelty, but with soft lighting and painstaking make-up she could still produce an illusion of handsomeness, though her beautifully coiffured pale gold hair was now more of a defiance than an ornament. Loving her with the quiet habit of nearly twelve years, Charles still found her attractive, but both of them knew he was the last man who ever would . . . her anxiety, his responsibility.

"You seem upset," he said finally, for she clung to him more than was usual in her greeting, and he had learned with her (the very opposite of dealing with Ruth, who shied away from any discussion of emotional problems) that it was best to get a misery into the open and argue it away.

"I'm sorry," she said. "I didn't mean it to show."

"Never mind that. Have I done something?"

"Of course not. Poor Charles!" She broke away, bright and smiling. "Come and sit down. I have the cocktails chilling." From the kitchenette she added: "It's just that I had another letter from Gretchen today."

Relieved that it was only this old, recurrent vexation, Charles settled in the armchair established by custom as his own. The rest of the furniture was antiques, inherited from her mother, either perilously fragile or, for one of Charles's proportions, uncomfortable. The room was nocturnal, heavily draped against daylight, fussy and cluttered with mementoes of Europe and South America, photographs of Gretchen and half-forgotten friends, presents that Charles had given her; a room where things accreted, never to be discarded. Near the kitchenette now stood a card table, but a card table disguised by the yellow white of old linen reaching nearly to the floor, glinting with silver, sparkling with crystal wine glasses, promising a dinner that had been lovingly composed and created. "How is Gretchen?" he inquired politely.

"Just as always." Her daughter's tireless, brutal good health was a grievance. Madge brought in a tray: a pitcher of martinis, frosted glasses that had spent all day in the freezing compartment, fragments of toast spread with caviar. "But they're definitely moving, and Gretchen talks on and on about the lovely room they'll have, all for me. She's nagging again." Madge's only daughter was married with three children, living in Chicago. When Gretchen was small, she and her mother had been close, but not for many years, and Madge saw her daughter's constant invitations to come to live there as efforts to acquire an unpaid cook and baby sitter. Besides, she detested Chicago and despised her son-in-law. Not one decent restaurant in the whole city—it was that barbarous—and her son-in-law and his friends sat around longing for another great Depression so that labor would get put back in its place. Yet much of the time in New York she was lonely, at loose ends. Before she fell sick, she had done a great deal of volunteer work for one of the hospitals, but now she hadn't the energy for that, nor even, evidently, to make new friends. From time to time she tormented both of them with the thought that perhaps she should go.

"I would say you'd mastered the technique of putting them off," Charles said.

"They keep finding new ways to pin me down. This time they don't want to furnish a guest room if there is any chance of my bringing my own things."

"You'd have to give up three-quarters of what you have," he said, and then realized that this sort of logic wasn't at all what she wanted from him. "You won't go," he added flatly, though for some time he had felt that life, if it lost much of its savor, would be a great deal less troublesome if she went. "You know you won't."

"Of course not," she agreed. She had poured the cocktails; now she sat down gracefully, opposite him. These days she wore long-sleeved flowing house robes which she made herself and which concealed the spareness of her figure. "But it gets harder and harder to invent new excuses."

"I can imagine." He had met Gretchen a number of times, and they had not taken to one another. She knew, or at least suspected, his place in her mother's life, and disapproved. Madge charged her with a hard young incredulity for the emotions of anyone past forty-five, but Charles thought it was rather worse than that: he saw Gretchen as a cold and pragmatic woman—the Scots blood coming out in her, perhaps—who conventionally 'adored' her husband for providing children and paying the bills, and simply couldn't understand the utility of a man in any other capacity. "Yet she knows you can't stand Chicago."

"The grandchildren are supposed to make up for that. They are sweet, but oh! the noise they make. After three days I begin longing for the peace and quiet of this apartment."

"It's quite absurd," Charles said. He knew the very thought of grandmotherhood discouraged her (whereas Ruth, who preferred babies to children, was already looking forward to it), and he sought for a way to change the subject without sounding too unsympathetic. "Why should both of us be wretched?" he asked. "It's quite absurd, Madge darling, and you've promised not to tease me like this."

"Oh, I know, I know. They make me feel guilty and then you make me feel guilty for feeling guilty." But she was smiling, and Charles sipped contentedly at his martini, satisfied that he had done his part. And sure enough, for it was a point of honor with her never to displease him, except when she could not help herself, a moment or two later she was asking what had been happening at the office: "You sounded very smug about something the other morning."

It was not an inquiry of courtesy; she was sincerely interested— knowing in some respects even more about the company than he did —and in a sense this had been the origin of their affair.

Virgil Blair had been Superintendent of the mill at Oñate, regarded by the company as a more reliable man than most simply because he was married; most of the engineers were too much delayed adolescents to think of marrying, even if they could find women willing to endure the altitude. But Blair had disillusioned them by getting himself killed in a peculiarly harum-scarum manner: driving drunkenly off the road (a fatal mistake in the Andes) on his way back from an unsanctioned hunting trip which amounted to a dereliction of duty. This had created a dilemma for the company. On the one hand they had their reputation as a paternalistic organization to consider, on the other it seemed excessive to award a full pension to the widow of a man who had died in such an irresponsible way.

The matter was still under consideration when one day Mrs. Peabody informed Charles that Blair's widow was in New York and anxious for an appointment. The prospect appalled him—he expected some weeping, whining, greedy, tiresome female, there for the purpose of working on his sympathy—but there was no decent way he could refuse to see her. He was pleasantly relieved to find that Madge Blair was a trim and attractive woman, seemingly undismayed by her sudden widowhood. Her request, for which she had asked this meeting, was matter of fact and modest. Their only child, Gretchen, was due to start college next fall at the University of Illinois in Urbana, where Virgil's parents lived; they had no money to speak of, and the immediate problem was the cost of Gretchen's schooling. Beyond that, if the company chose to give her a small pension it would help, but she admitted frankly that she had inherited a small competence from her father, enough to get by on if Gretchen's education was taken care of. All this was explained calmly and even humorously, in a faintly accented voice which Charles found captivating. It was only later, and very gradually, that he had built up a picture of her background.

She was the daughter of a Scots mining engineer and a Danish mother, and except for her schooling in England she had lived all her life in South America—Chile, Bolivia, Peru, wherever her father happened to be working. For a while he was with Cerro de Pasco, and it was during this period, at one of the famous New Year's Eve parties at Oroya, that she met Virgil Blair, just down from the States for Andean C & Z and invited over by a college classmate.

Of the private side of her marriage Madge said little, and this was quite in character. If she had been superbly happy, she would have considered it poor form to dwell on that happiness to a subsequent lover, but Charles suspected that she had not been very happy. Her father evidently had been a robust romantic but a mature man, sensible and humorous and wise. Doubtless Madge had looked for those same qualities in her husband, and the probability was that she had not found them. The men sent down by the company were highly able men technically, but most who sought after such jobs were psychopaths in the pleasantest sense of the term: emotionally backward, underadaptable, overmasculine, with the manners and motives of so many schoolboys. It had often been plausibly argued that such psychopaths were the salt of the earth, the pioneers, the adventurers, the men who did the dirty but essential jobs. Perhaps, but they were damnably exasperating people to deal with in a business sense. (For the bachelor engineers' annual three-week holiday the company rented one floor of a hotel in Lima and each year had to budget an extra *twenty thousand dollars* for high-spirited damage done to the hotel.) It seemed to Charles that a man of this stamp would be equally exasperating for an adult woman to live with in intimacy, but Madge's loyalty permitted of no complaints. The probability that Virgil had merely been 'one of the boys' had to be pieced together from her occasional mention of nonstop, high-stake poker sessions and anecdotes turning on the adolescent antics of one or another of Virgil's closest friends—but then it became impossible to see Madge as contented in such an atmosphere. She was a woman, meant to be cherished and appreciated as a woman: not serve as playmate to an overgrown schoolboy.

When Charles, already half captivated, got her a far better settlement from Andean C & Z than she expected, he took her out to dinner to celebrate. He told himself it was a gesture of kindly benevolence to an unfortunate, and he knew he lied. But his downfall came about in a most unexpected fashion: he discovered the seductive joy of talking shop to an attractive and knowledgeable woman.

This discovery was an ironic unfairness to Ruth, whom he had loved, and still loved, for very different reasons. For herself, of course, and she had been a lovely girl, and for her amusing, close-knit, proliferating family—something he had always missed. But a considerable part of Ruth's charm for him (thirty-six he had been, nearly fifteen years the elder) had been an atmosphere about her, a promise that she would create a tranquil, domestic citadel of a home, a refuge from the world outside. She had kept that promise to perfection, and without effort, for apart from music she had only the most absent-minded interest in the world outside. While no man married a girl with the intention of boring her with his workaday problems, there came a time, especially if he achieved an executive level where he was generally obliged to keep his own council, when he would have liked an admiring or sympathetic audience at home. Ruth spoke of Andean C & Z as 'our company,' and she made a decent pretense of listening to Charles's woes and triumphs, but it invariably became obvious that she had all along been thinking of the children or tomorrow night's dinner or last Sunday's concert. "Of course I'm interested, dear; you *know* I am. It's just that I got distracted for the moment." After a few of these experiments some five years after they were married, when he was on the verge of vice-presidency, he gave up talking about the office except in the most superficial terms, and Ruth never noticed the difference. He had no grounds for complaint. If this was a flaw in his paradise, it was a flaw which he himself had written into the specifications.

So accustomed did Charles become to keeping his working life in a soundproof compartment of his mind that no woman could have interested him merely by a willingness to listen intelligently and make appropriate comments. Madge's fascination lay in her unexpectedly intimate knowledge of the company. He had taken it for granted that she would be thoroughly familiar with the Peruvian end of things and had even (as part of the elaborate justification for taking her out to dinner) solemnly assured himself that he should take advantage of this opportunity to acquire insights not usually divulged to a top-level executive. These insights were there for the asking, but what astonished him was the degree to which the Peruvian personnel was conversant with what went on in New York. The authorities and rivalries of the different operational executives were well known, and even when the men rarely got down to Peru in person, their characters were shrewdly assessed; Charles himself was considered coldly efficient (why coldly?), but scrupulously fair and nobody's fool. The balance of power was accurately comprehended, and as evidence of this the blame for the historic assaying-decision fiasco of '51 had been assigned with remarkable accuracy, considering that it could have been based on nothing but guesswork.

Talking shop with Madge, therefore, was not just a ventilating of his mind but a stimulating, two-sided discussion in which he often gained as much as he had imparted. She could tell him, for example, how the engineers were really likely to react to certain decisions, whereas his subordinates had a fondness for telling him either what showed them up well or what they believed he wanted to hear.

Yet it would be the merest rationalization to pretend that their love affair had rested on office gossip; it was only that something like this enchanting companionability had been needed to jar him into noticing what an attractive woman she was. A contentedly domestic man, he had lost the habit of looking for temptation in women; unlike many men he had not been on the lookout for opportunities of infidelity. He had blundered into one. And Madge had blundered too, in a different sense, for she was fundamentally a man's woman, a one-man woman, and could never have wished for a situation which allowed her only a partial lien on her man.

Once begun, however, there it was, and apart from pious regrets little to be done about it. If Madge was not by temperament a mistress, she made a splendid one by disposition, and Charles knew he had far and away the better of the bargain. Although she was no more passionate than Ruth, and perhaps rather less so, she brought an imaginative seductivity to their love making that Ruth in her matter-of-fact, no-nonsense approach to the facts of life would never have dreamt of. And there were other little things, absurd perhaps, which Charles found very endearing. Madge's instinct was to cater to a man. After years of a home diet which was at least partly regulated by Ruth's notions of what the children ought to eat, he was charmed by dinners that were designed and slaved over for himself alone.

But while most other pleasures grow routine with time, it was unquestionably the joy of having a knowledgeable confidante which kept Charles faithful through the years while the love affair was drifting from an infatuation to a habit to a responsibility. A conflict of personalities at the office was less irksome for knowing that Madge would sympathize; the smallest success was more gratifying for knowing there was somebody to appreciate and applaud.

"Yes, I was feeling rather pleased with myself yesterday," he admitted, settling back to tell the story.

"Have you talked with the Grace people already?"

"No, that's not till next week. This is something quite different. Trivial in a way, yet maybe not. Do you remember my telling you, about a year and a half ago, of a certain Dr. Jeremy Wales?"

"Yes, of course," Madge said. "He's the one who is going to solve the *soroche* problem. Barbour discovered him, didn't he?"

"That's right." What he told her she remembered, and the rest she knew for herself: having spent much of her life above twelve thousand feet, she was no stranger to the problem. He never needed to embark on long-winded explanations which quite overpowered the effect of some petty triumph.

"Are you inviting Barbour to the wedding?" she asked.

It jarred him: her interruptions were almost never so far afield. "The Barbours and the Haxtons," he said. "It will mean extra loot for Vickie, but I doubt if they'll put in an appearance."

"What about people at the office?" she asked.

He supposed he must make allowances for women's preoccupation with these functions. "The other senior vice-presidents as a matter of courtesy," he said. "And Bruce Bigelow because he'll be Roger's direct boss: I thought it might start them off on a more cordial footing."

"How about old Dougherty?"

"Not much point in it. Since his retirement he's been living in Santa Barbara, and with that son of his in and out of institutions all the time he hasn't the money to throw away on presents. Why?"

"I was just wondering," she said. "I'm sorry. Of course I remember about Dr. Wales."

He lit a fresh cigarette to compose himself, find his stride again. This was an incident he was rather proud of, and he intended to make the most of it. Methodically he reminded her of the origin of the experiment, elaborating it now with the description of Wales's background and medical idiosyncrasies as he had gleaned them from Morris. Then he told of the gathering signs that the experiment wasn't working out well, as man after man failed to acclimate himself to the altitude: three rejects out of nineteen sent down, four out of twenty-six, finally five out of twenty-seven, the last straw, prompting him to have a showdown with Wales.

"The evening before I spoke to you," he went on, "I had an afterhours appointment with Dr. Wales at his offices. Very plush offices, with original oil paintings in the waiting room. Wales himself is a tall and extremely ugly man, froglike, but with a great deal of charm. So much charm, in fact, that it put me off him at first." No need to explain to Madge that he regarded charm as an enervating quality in men, encouraging them to be slipshod in their intelligence and industry. "He has an insinuating way about him—the French side coming out, I suppose. Before I said a thing he managed to suggest that he couldn't imagine why I was there, since the experiment had another six months to run—while implying that a visit from me was the one thing needed to make his day a success. And he served tea, which I haven't seen in a New York office since I was in my twenties. I let him fuss with the sugar and cream, and then I pointed out that in the past eighteen months we'd sent down more new men than we normally send down in a couple of years, and it seemed time to look at the record—five rejects out of twenty-seven: eighteen and a half percent. Just as I had expected he tried to argue that these figures were too small to be significant. I agreed with him. But I added that, if the figures continued to lean in this same direction, by the time they became scientifically significant Andean C & Z would be bankrupt, which wasn't really the idea behind the experiment. That slipped past his charm. He gave me a haughty look and asked if I was prepared to discard the experiment as a failure."

At this point Charles suddenly realized that Madge was looking not at him but just past his right ear, and her eyes were distinctly glassy. "You aren't even listening," he said in astonished accusation.

"Charles, of course I am! You were saying how charming Dr. Wales was."

"That was quite a way back."

"Yes, and he served tea and didn't think your figures were significant. And when you said the company couldn't afford to wait for them to become significant, he asked if you considered the experiment a failure."

But Charles had played this trick many times himself: at board meetings his mind frequently went off on tangents of its own, but if necessary he could call on the tape-recorder part of his memory to parrot off the gist of what had been said during his inattention—proof that he had been hearing if not listening. "That's all very well," he said, "but there's something else on your mind. I can tell."

"Please go on with your story, Charles," Madge begged, distressed. "I'm very interested."

He was annoyed by the unreason of his own reaction. Surely in a dozen years a woman was entitled to one lapse of concentration, yet he felt outrageously betrayed, as though at a wilful breach of contract, and disliked himself for feeling so. "I'm not annoyed," he said. "The story can wait; it's of no consequence, but you'll enjoy it better if you aren't distracted. I'd much rather know what's troubling you. Still Gretchen?"

"No," she said, and looked at him uncertainly for a second. "Promise you'll finish the story afterwards?" she asked, and he promised. "Well, it was selfish of me, but I couldn't help thinking. You know, except for you, old Mr. Dougherty was the only executive at the company who ever saw me in person."

"Perhaps so," said Charles in complete bewilderment.

"Well, don't you see?" she said eagerly. "If he's out in Santa Barbara, there won't be a single person at the reception who would have the faintest notion who I am."

"Oh, no!" exclaimed Charles in sharp dismay. "Madge, this is most unfair of you. I said there'd be no harm in your coming to the wedding, if you wanted to come, but I took it for granted you'd see that the reception was out of the question."

"It's not out of the question at all," she replied, on her feet now, pacing. "You've just not thought about it. You know perfectly well that for years I've been dying to meet Peter and Vickie, but of course it hasn't been possible. Your children, Charles—it's a very natural impulse, you know. And you've never stopped to think that this reception is probably the one chance I'll ever have to meet them, talk to them, get to know them just a little—all in complete safety."

"You have rather remarkable notions of what constitutes complete safety."

"I mean it," she insisted, heedless of his disapproval. "Charles, you're the sort of man who avoids wedding receptions if he possibly can, and on the rare occasions that you go I'm sure you've not noticed how they are conducted. Now just listen to me for a moment, and try to be fair." It seemed to Charles that since her adoption of these long trailing robes Madge had grown more histrionic; she had always been restless, but her pacing had never been so dramatic as in this new costume, and she was aware of it. "Remember," she said, "there's nobody at the door checking off names against a list of invitations. There's no need. As a rule nobody crashes a wedding reception except by mistake, and the mistake gets shown up on the receiving line. But not this time. Don't forget, you've already said you'd have no part of the receiving line, so Owen Hilliard won't either. The receiving line will be Ruth and Vickie, her maid of honor, Amelia Booth, Roger, and the bridesmaids. And that's all. Now I expect Ruth will have a bit of a struggle keeping your business associates straight."

"She'll know them by name, anyway," Charles said grimly.

"Right, and Amelia will do as well for her husband's colleagues and friends. But—don't you see?—there will be nobody on the line to identify the people that Roger's father has invited! They'll simply have to introduce themselves: quite a few do that anyway as a courtesy unless they're confident of being recognized. 'Such a charming wedding; I'm Mrs. Whortleberry,'" she brayed, playing the hearty guest, and then, switching over to the gracious but weary hostess, drawled: "'So delighted that you could be here.' But who the devil is Mrs. Whortleberry? If Ruth can't place the name, and Amelia Booth doesn't claim her, it will simply be assumed she's a friend of Owen Hilliard's. There will be at least a dozen guests coming through the line like that, and one more won't make the slightest difference. Once I'm in the main room I'll be invisible. Don't you realize that including old Mrs. Langstaff's friends there will be seven or eight factions that have nothing in common? The Andean people don't know Ruth's relatives or Owen Hilliard's theatrical set or the academic crowd, and so on. I'd always be taken for belonging to one of the other groups."

"But you'd be all by yourself; you wouldn't know anybody," Charles said desperately. "That would make you noticeable."

"No, it wouldn't. Don't underestimate me, Charles. There will be lots of women my age there, abandoned by husbands who are off in a corner talking shop or exchanging bawdy wedding stories; the wives will be only too happy to have another old crone to chat with sentimentally about what a lovely bride Vickie is, but how weddings just aren't as impressive as they used to be. I'll talk with the wives of your other vice-presidents, and they'll think I'm a retired actress friend of Hilliard's; I'll talk with the wives of Professor Booth's colleagues and leave them thinking I have some connection with Andean C & Z. It's perfectly safe: nobody compares notes at a party like that; and if one of them does, I'll have been so vague she'll think she must have misunderstood me. And between times I'll be able to eavesdrop on Vickie and Peter, exchange a word in passing, watch them dancing . . . have a few memories to go with the photographs you've given me."

It was extremely upsetting for Charles, who believed in the invincibility of intelligence, to have someone he was fond of make such a reasonable and logical defense of a course of action which he disapproved of on purely emotional grounds. Probably Madge was right, and she could come in absolute safety. He could conceive of no way in which her identity as his mistress could be disclosed. But if by a miracle it should be, her presence at the reception would be an insupportable insult to Ruth, and that knowledge was stronger than any logic.

He had no idea whether Ruth had any suspicion of Madge's existence. He had covered his tracks as well as he possibly could. The exigencies of his job demanded a good deal of traveling, not merely to Peru and Washington and Palm Beach (where the Haxtons lived), but to various kinds of conferences all over the country, and he had trained Ruth to the idea that he disliked being seen off or being met. Thus, by leaving a few days later than Ruth believed, or returning a few days earlier, he had often been able to steal a weekend with Madge. A judicious mixture of business banquets (he had not actually attended one in years) and visits to The Darkroom accounted for his evenings out. Still and all, though Ruth was the least possessive of wives, comfortably engrossed in her music and hobbies and domesticity, it seemed quite incredible that in all these years she shouldn't have guessed. They said that women always sensed these things—but, on the other hand, 'they' said a wife was always the last to know. Certainly Ruth had never given a sign of knowing. (Gert's hints were an irrelevancy; he knew the Zimmermans well enough by now to know they would never meddle in the well-being of any member of the clan until she turned to them for help.) The likelihood was that Ruth had suspected now and again but had simply and sensibly declined to entertain the suspicion, as something that could only make for misery. This was as much as any man could reasonably expect of his wife. And it left him with the responsibility of seeing to it that her own good sense and good manners were never betrayed. It would be utterly unpardonable if, even by the most implausible concatenation of coincidences, Ruth's suppressed suspicions were turned to reality on Vickie's wedding day.

Charles poured himself another cocktail.

"I'm sorry, Madge," he said unhappily, groping for some cogency to support a visceral argument. "I daresay you're right, and that it would be safe. The chances are thousands to one, I admit. But you do have friends of your own, and we haven't always been entirely discreet in front of them—and we simply cannot tell who the Booths and Owen Hilliard may be inviting. The damnedest coincidences can happen in this town. Even if the chance were one in millions, I couldn't let you take it. The trouble is that there isn't the slightest excuse for your being at the reception except by *my* connivance. I couldn't disown your presence, nobody would believe me if I tried—and the insult to Ruth would seem deliberate." At last he had found the emotional appeal to match his own obduracy: "Madge, don't you realize that I'd be wretched every second of the time for fear something would go wrong?"

She had stopped pacing, to lean against the back of a chair, and for an instant the desiccated figure seemed to contract still further within the softly flowing robe. "I was afraid you'd say that."

"Madge, darling, I'm terribly sorry."

"Well, it was just an idea." She strained at a bright smile.

"You know I'm right," he pleaded.

"Of course you are," she agreed. "It was naughty of me to want to come—I'm perfectly aware of that. But . . . well, let's just say I'm a foolish and sentimental woman and leave it at that, shall we?" She came back and sat down, took a long swallow of her martini, lit a cigarette; her hands were very shaky but that need not be the stress of the moment. Since her illness she was often like that.

Nevertheless Charles felt like a monster. "I wish—" he began, with no clear idea of what he intended to say.

"No, I should be the one to apologize," she said briskly. "I mean it, Charles. It was an impossible suggestion and bound to upset you— I see that now. I expect I'm alone too much these days, and I get silly ideas."

"You ought to get out more," he said, foolish with the inadequacy of the suggestion.

"I know I should; I intend to," she said. "Now forgive me, Charles. It was an unfortunate outburst: I'm afraid you just have to expect them from time to time. Please go on with your story."

For a moment Charles had no idea what she meant. Then the

thought of continuing the description of his encounter with Dr. Wales seemed to him the dreariest of punishments. It was the thing to do, he supposed: pick up the conversation just where it had been interrupted, pretend that nothing had happened. But to recapture the mood of modest triumph, without which the anecdote was meaningless, was quite impossible.

"Dr. Wales was asking if you were prepared to discount the experiment as a failure," she prompted him.

"I replied that, on the contrary, I thought it a remarkable success," Charles said mechanically. "He thought I was being sarcastic."

"And weren't you?" Madge asked, throwing herself wholeheartedly into the new humor.

"Certainly not," said Charles, who earlier had looked forward to the disclosure of this paradox but now was irritated by Madge's lack of comprehension. "Wales is a good doctor: it had to be assumed that the men he sent down were in perfect health. If a disproportionate number of them washed out, it had to mean that Wales was on to something, even if he had it backwards. When I suggested this he said it was quite impossible, but I asked him to think it over. I pointed out that he must have begun with a theory as to what made some men more adaptable than others to high altitudes and then looked for certain physiological tendencies to match. Low blood pressure, high basal metabolism, hyper-activity of certain glands—*I* had no idea. But a theory was only a theory, however inviting, and the evidence so far was that he had been right but upside down. I gave him a list of the men who had been sent back and asked him to check his records; if my hunch was right, these would have been his likeliest candidates to survive, while the men he'd rejected would probably have come through with flying colors. Well, he did think it over, muttering to himself all the while; he turned over the list and did some calculations on the back. Finally he went off with the list to another room, and when he came back he was looking sheepish. 'It still seems crazy,' he said, 'but it checks out. Those were just the men I felt surest of: like a fool I didn't think to check the *names* as they came in. But I'll confess I never expected to take a lesson in flexibility of thinking from a businessman.'"

"What an odd but delightful compliment!" exclaimed Madge.

Charles had thought so too, at the time, but in his general disappointment now, his mood that life was turning against him, this little triumph of acumen seemed hollow and dusty. Dr. Wales was a very charming man. In exchange for that inexpensive compliment, the experiment, and Dr. Wales's retainer, had been extended for another two years.

3

In the elevator going up to the fifth floor Vickie said, with the nervous defiance of one who has saved bad news till the last possible moment, "Mummy, *please* don't let yourself be offended by Mrs. Godolphin."

"Why on earth would a saleslady want to offend me?" Ruth asked, already exasperated by all this nonsense. To her way of thinking, when a girl wanted a wedding dress she and her mother simply walked into Bergdorf Goodman's, for example; and if they didn't find just what they liked, they went on to Henri Bendel's, Gray and Arbuckle's, Saks Fifth Avenue, and so on, until they found what they did like. But no, apparently not. That was the shop girl way of doing it. A girl in the know—said Vickie, as if she belonged to some select and fashionable set—went to Mrs. Godolphin (by appointment only, thank you) at Gray and Arbuckle's. Mrs. Godolphin turned you out as the bride you had always imagined yourself. Presumably if you relied on your mother and your own taste, you would end up looking like a scarecrow.

"That's just it, she isn't a saleslady at all," Vickie whispered rapidly. "She's head of the department and very special; she's English and aristocratic and a good deal of a character from all I've heard. And in stores you *do* sometimes get huffy and embarrassing if people don't kowtow to you enough."

"Rubbish!" said Ruth firmly, so that people turned to stare at them as they stepped out of the elevator. She was annoyed by this description of her behavior, she who knew herself to be too gentle natured for her own good. But Vickie had the usual adolescent's terror of public scenes and would meekly suffer any degree of insolence or impertinence rather than protest.

"*Please*, Mummy?" Vickie persisted, as they made their way to the Bridal Department.

"This is your wedding dress, dear," Ruth said evasively. "I didn't come along to spoil the fun."

They sat in silent discomfort on the small love seat in the vestibule waiting room, while Ruth summoned her patience to deal with the presumptive arrogance of this Mrs. Godolphin: she would not look for trouble, but neither would she suffer her daughter to be trampled on, even aristocratically. A salesgirl on the fly accepted the information that they had an appointment with Mrs. Godolphin, and then for a long while they waited alone—till Ruth, glancing irritably at her watch, discovered that the hour of their appointment was just arriving: Vickie had brought them there well beforehand.

On the stroke of eleven Mrs. Godolphin appeared in the door opposite them: a large, portly woman in a dull black, man-tailored suit with odd streaks of whitish powdering down the bosom. Her iron-grey hair was cropped short and brushed straight back; her chin was too heavy, her mouth too small, her nose too beaky, and on the last sat a pair of uncompromising circular horn-rimmed spectacles—yet the effect, though startling, was kindly clever rather than formidable. Her voice was harsh and very, very clipped. "Mrs. Foscue, Miss Foscue?" she said, introducing herself in a manner brisk and forthright. "I find the best way to begin one of these sessions is with a good talk: ten minutes' conversation is worth half an hour in the fitting room, but I *cannot* talk without a cigarette and the only refuge from insurance-company spies is my office. All right?" She led the way down a narrow, behind-the-scenes hallway to an office just large enough for her desk and a few straight chairs for visitors. Ruth had expected the room to be hung with a display of autographed bridal portraits intended to impress, but she was cheated of her contempt. There was one large photograph, a hazy distant shot of an outdoor wedding, taken from back among the trees so that only the bridal pair could be seen through the foliage, and the bridegroom was just a looming manly figure in the background. It was the bride who stood out; although her features were not distinct, nor the details of her costume, she was the quintessence of all the loveliness of a bride. A bold stroke of sentimentality, but so beautifully executed, and so unexpected, that Ruth felt the tears start to her eyes.

"Yes, Gruber did that for me," said Mrs. Godolphin, leading Ruth to a seat but then taking Vickie lightly by one elbow, preventing her from sitting down. "It's a pity that more weddings can't be held out of doors; the atmosphere is so much holier than in most churches. Personally, I've never been able to imagine God as the indoor type —but that is precisely the sort of remark that sends the more pious clients running to Henri Bendel's. I don't know why I can't control my tongue." All the while (behind the horn-rimmed spectacles her eyes were shrewd and appraising) she had been studying Vickie as though she was a side of doubtful beef. "Are you an especially pious type, my dear?"

"No, I don't think so," Vickie said, giggling nervously.

"Well, precisely the question is to determine what type you are," said Mrs. Godolphin. She released Vickie's arm and produced a compartmented box of cigarettes which she offered; then she retreated behind her desk. Her own cigarette remained in the corner of her mouth, waggling madly as she talked, and occasionally dribbling unnoticed ash down the front of her suit. "I have fifty or sixty different styles of gown out in the stockroom, and with a little imagination we should eliminate all but a handful before we get started. How formal a wedding are you planning, my dear, and just when is it?"

"Moderately formal," Vickie said. "June seventeenth."

"A full-length gown, then?"

"Yes, definitely."

"With a train? Medium length, I should say; you really haven't the height for anything longer. All right? And for that time of year, peau de soie, definitely. Well, that's a beginning, anyway. I must say it's a comfort not to have to worry how to create the illusion that you have a figga of sorts—that leaves us with more room for choice. Too much room, in a sense. It brings us back to the question of how you picture yourself. Not as a nun, we've established that, though you'd be surprised at the girls who do. As a femme fatale, then? As a gamine? As the sophisticated type or the demure and maidenly?"

"I don't think of myself as a type at all," Vickie said stoutly, and Ruth wanted to cheer.

"Of course not, my dear; none of us does," said Mrs. Godolphin. "But we all have one or two illusions, and a wedding is a splendid time to cater to them. Understand me, Miss Foscue. You are an attractive girl with an attractive figga: you would look quite lovely in any of a dozen different gowns. Presumably you came to me because I'm supposed to have a flair for helping a girl pick out the gown which suits her best. Well, I can do that. It's my business, and I'm good at it. But selling you the dress is a very different matter. If in secret you have a high opinion of your modesty, I could alienate your interest by stressing how well a gown showed off your bosom; or if you pride yourself on your sophistication, I might easily put you off by using too many coy adjectives."

Ruth (who had placed 'Mrs. Godolphin' as Whitechapel Jewish with diction lessons) thought this as outrageous a speech as she had ever heard: the woman was virtually declaring that *she* would pick out the dress and then cozen Vickie into buying it. But Vickie seemed relaxed, enchanted and amused.

"I suppose I like to think of myself as sophisticated," she said, "but I'm not too confident."

"Let me guess," said Mrs. Godolphin. "You sometimes enjoy a sentimental movie because it makes you cry, but you wouldn't admit this to a soul."

"Not even to you," said Vickie delightedly.

"Well, I think we understand each other well enough to get on." There was a knock at the door, which opened a few inches, and somebody outside spoke inaudibly. "That's fine, Miss Davies," said Mrs. Godolphin, "we'll be along in about two minutes." The door closed again. "There's one more question, since at this season two months doesn't give us any too much time. Is there a veil in the family?"

"No," said Ruth, trying to compress all her disapproval into a single word.

"Well, we all know that I have a personal interest in trying to sell you a veil here in the store," Mrs. Godolphin said cheerfully. "Also, we all know that the antique lace you can find in the shops is lovelier, apart from the snob appeal. The question, really, is whether it's a thousand dollars lovelier. Some people think so. Some girls would prefer to have the difference in cash, and I'm inclined to agree with them, but that may just be my private, pecuniary prejudice. Well, well, quite so. I'll show you what we have, and you'll decide, but I must ask that your decision be quick. Before you leave, if possible; by tomorrow at the latest. If we're going to make up a veil for you, the order should go out immediately. All right?" Mrs. Godolphin beamed and stood up briskly, brushing ashes from her bosom, and led the way to the fitting room. Ruth was growing ever more irritated by her cool assumption that a wedding gown would be selected and ordered before they left the store.

The fitting room was blind and mirrored, with straight pins and threads on the carpet, a rack, a love seat for display, and a couple of straight armchairs which, however, when Ruth sat down in one, proved unexpectedly comfortable. Waiting for them there was a slim and smiling young woman whom Mrs. Godolphin introduced: "This is Miss Davies, the best assistant I've ever had—and next week she's going off to get married herself. And after four years in the Bridal Department she's getting married at City Hall!" Hooting with hoarse laughter, Mrs. Godolphin went off to the stockroom with her assistant.

Ruth leaned forward to deliver a trenchant opinion of the woman, but Vickie, already unbuttoning the jacket of her suit, was ahead of her. "Isn't she *wonderful?*" she whispered. "She's exactly like Miss Finley." Ruth sat back. In Vickie's last year at school Miss Finley had been her housemistress, English teacher and hockey coach, a lady famed for her acid but presumably affectionate sarcasms, the object of an adoration on Vickie's part which, though somewhat late in the day, could only be described as a crush. It occurred to Ruth that Mrs. Godolphin's success at dealing with girls Vickie's age lay partly in her generic resemblance to the sort of schoolmistress girls fell for, her possession of that same quality of clever, forthright rudeness which made the girls feel they were being treated as intelligent intimates. Having learned that a mother was no match for an infatuation, Ruth held her tongue.

And went on holding it for the most part during the subsequent hour, while the ivory gowns were brought out one by one, draped over the love seat and discussed, then lifted over Vickie's head by Mrs. Godolphin and Miss Davies and pinned by the latter into an illusion of perfect fit. Mrs. Godolphin's running commentary was more outrageous than ever but seemed to keep Vickie fascinated; and it was obvious that the woman not only knew her job but took a perverse delight in it.

". . . Now this is partly for my own pleasure. It's a copy of a Dior based on the Goya portrait of that simpering Infanta whose name I never remember, and just for a change I'd like to see it on someone whose figga can carry it off. On your mark, Miss Davies. You'll think it too radical, I fancy, and for a girl your age you'll probably be right. But the effect we're aiming at is one of extreme simplicity, and you'll appreciate it all the better when I've tired you with a few exoticisms. . . ."

"I don't know that I'd have the nerve, frankly," said Vickie. "What do you think, Mummy?"

". . . The high neck here may appeal to your sense of sophistication. It's a possibility, I'll grant you. But I'm afraid we'll find that you're a little bit too busty for it. The penalty of being well-built is that you have to steel yourself against clothes that are cunningly designed to conceal the inadequacies of the less fortunate. . . ."

"Do you think it makes me look too busty, Mummy?" Vickie asked, and Ruth was not appeased by recognizing that Vickie had lost the slightest interest in what Mummy might think.

". . . The sash waist puts this one quite out of the question. But we're narrowing down to the princess style, whether you realize it or not, and the gown I'll be showing you has a portrait neck. Either God or your parents saw to it that you don't need a portrait neck, and this one is exactly what I have in mind. Heave ho, Miss Davies. Now, don't worry about the line of the bodice my dear; it's only the neckline I want you to remember. . . ."

In the end Vickie settled on the gown which Mrs. Godolphin had evidently had in mind from the beginning—a gown that existed at this point only *in* Mrs. Godolphin's mind. As best Ruth could visualize it, she grudgingly had to admit it should be stunning. And with a mantilla of Chantilly lace reaching just below the fingertips—but here Ruth dug in her heels, in restrained fury. She had not, she declared loftily, decided whether they might not prefer antique lace after all; she would have to discuss the matter with her husband.

It was an idle gesture, without a doubt. When Vickie had conveyed Mrs. Godolphin's financial arguments to her father (and a conspiratorial glance from Vickie to Mrs. Godolphin assured this), Ruth would be outvoted. No matter: Vickie could phone in the surrender tomorrow. At the moment, Ruth needed some recompense for a useless and harassing morning; she could not have endured that odious woman's victory to be complete *and* immediate.

Now that everything was effectively settled, Ruth's overstrained patience gave out. She was on the verge of tears of frustration, yet somehow she would have to find the self-control to keep from flying into a rage at Mrs. Godolphin as soon as they left. She could hardly wait to get out of there, yet she had to wait. Vickie, exhausted now, had to put on her street clothes and repair her make-up. Vickie had to make an appointment with Mrs. Godolphin for later in the week to look at bridesmaids' dresses. Vickie had to find words for her undying gratitude to Mrs. Godolphin.

Ruth fretted openly, kept glancing at her watch, edged towards the door.

Finally they arrived there.

"Well, good-bye, Mrs. Foscue; it's been a pleasure," rasped Mrs. Godolphin heartily, and this was the final straw.

"*Fortescue!!*" Ruth exploded.

"God bless you," said Mrs. Godolphin.

4

The only thing remarkable about Louis Melmoth was his poise.

Although he had a big man's voice, deep and resonant, he was short and frail looking; a grey-haired, grey-moustached little man in his mid fifties, dressed in a neat and inexpensive grey suit with a straight edge of white handkerchief in the breast pocket. He was the sort of man you passed a dozen times in a city block without noticing. Yet his self-assurance was most impressive. Come on an errand of pure melodrama, his manner was neither nervous and high strung nor apologetic; he might have been paying a courteous visit on somebody newly arrived in the neighborhood. "It was good of you to see me, Mr. Hilliard."

"Your method of inviting yourself was quite irresistible," Owen said drily.

"I suppose that is so," agreed Melmoth, unperturbed. He looked around with mild curiosity, took the chair that Owen indicated, declined a drink and accepted a cigarette, all with the air of somebody fulfilling an old-fashioned ritual of civility. "Yes, I'm bound to admit that I forced myself on you," he went on. "And now that I am here, I feel certain that I will make a mess of what I want to say." But there was no real embarrassment in this utterance: the kindly visitor was unsure whether it was too soon to ask the newcomer to contribute to a local charity. "Do you believe in God, Mr. Hilliard?"

Owen flinched.

"There, that is exactly what I mean," said Melmoth. "I am particularly anxious that you do not think of me as a crank, and already I have half convinced you that I am a religious fanatic. I am not. On the contrary, I am an atheist, and that is directly related to my reason for being here today. But I have no wish to offend any religious convictions of your own, which is why I asked that question."

Melmoth was calmly, and quite humorlessly, sincere, and Owen felt he began to understand his visitor. That astonishing poise was probably not poise at all but the blind self-absorption of the amateur intellectual, too earnestly engrossed in his own ideas to notice that he might be making a donkey of himself.

"I would like to believe in God," Owen replied. "At my age it would be comforting to feel that my death would not mean the end of the universe as far as I was concerned. But as yet I haven't been able to work up the necessary credulity. Will that do?"

"I must say I'm greatly relieved," said Melmoth, settling back even more comfortably than before. "It makes everything a great deal simpler. Frankly, if you had been a religious man I should have been tempted to play on your prejudices—as a substitute for any meeting of the minds. But as an atheist yourself you will have no difficulty understanding me."

"I think I'd rather describe myself as an agnostic," Owen said solemnly.

"An agnostic is merely an atheist who leaves a loophole for his cowardice," said Melmoth in a grave voice, quite unaware of the possibility that anybody might find this an offensive observation. "I'm not at all sure I would be here this afternoon if I were an agnostic. On the whole, I think not. Once you allow for the possibility of God, the possibility of an immortal soul, then laziness and selfishness set in. We're all lazy and selfish by nature, and a little faith reassures us that there's really nothing to worry about except the salvation of our own souls. Never mind about injustice; God is attending to that. Don't pay any attention to all the meaningless tragedies; God is working in a mysterious way. And above all don't give a thought to the victims; they're much happier in Heaven anyway. No, if I believed these things, if I thought them even remotely conceivable, I probably shouldn't be here."

It began to appear that Melmoth was prepared to discuss the philosophic justification of his visit for hours, without coming any nearer to the point. "I'm afraid I'm still not very clear as to why you *are* here," Owen prompted.

"You may think of me as a busybody," Melmoth said. "If you were a religious man, you would be bound to think of me as a busybody, although I might be able to persuade you to see me as an instrument of God. A little farfetched, perhaps, yet no more so than many of the things they swallow with unimpaired digestions. As an agnostic you will probably appreciate my motives for coming, but won't be able to understand why I bothered."

"Why not let me decide for myself, Mr. Melmoth?" Owen suggested gently. "As nearly as I could make out from your telephone call, you consider either Mr. or Mrs. Fortescue responsible for the death of somebody—presumably a close relative. Is that correct?"

For the first time Melmoth showed some trace of emotion. "I am sorry to have left you with that ambiguity," he said. "I can see that it might have distressed you. The possibility never occurred to me. So far as I know the girl's mother has led a blameless life. These things aren't hereditary, of course, yet just the same the thought would have been unnerving. I am very sorry."

"Then Charles Fortescue—"

"Charles Fortescue killed my sister," Melmoth said quietly.

"An accident of some sort."

"No, Mr. Hilliard, no. Your agnostic dislike of discomfort cannot be satisfied this time. There was no accident." Melmoth reached to his inside breast pocket, but then his hand came away empty. "I'd better tell you the story from the beginning," he said. "There are a few newspaper clippings I can let you see, but for reasons you'll eventually understand they don't amount to very much. By any chance do you happen to be familiar with Actonsville?"

Except in that he had a calm unhurried approach to his narrative, Louis Melmoth was not a born storyteller. He seemed to have little notion of what was relevant and what was not, he digressed, he became annoyed with himself for his inability to remember the year his father had installed a new clock in the Town Hall. Yet gradually, maddeningly yet vividly, the place and the people and the story emerged.

Actonsville, Connecticut, was a small, quiet, not untypical New England town, just far enough upcountry to be out of reach of even the most hardened commuters. There were two mills and several small factories, but primarily the town served as a market town to the surrounding countryside of small farms and orchards. And it was the site, of course, of the Courtney Preparatory School for Boys.

A watchmaker by trade, Melmoth's father had settled here at the turn of the century, first as a repairman working in the window of a gift and novelty shop, eventually with a small shop of his own. He was a stern, gentle, orthodox, hard-working man, unusually clever with his hands and indefatigable in adding to his skills. To repair the mangled trinkets that were brought him from time to time, he learned to cast the pieces that were past mending, and from there went on to making simple jewelry of his own design. He offered a price that barely covered his own expenses and acquired the concession for making class pins, school rings and the like for Courtney, arguing that in this fashion he would soon have all the schoolboys coming to his store as a matter of course for watch repairs and tie clasps and charms for their girl friends' bracelets. The scheme was a success financially, but it was thus that his daughter Sophie had met young Charles Fortescue.

Owen had been drifting with the story, assuming that it would connect up with Peter Fortescue's prep school; now he awoke to a distinct recollection that Roger's roommate had gone to Hotchkiss. "Do you mean to say this all dates back to *Charles* Fortescue's schooldays?" he asked.

"That's right," said Melmoth.

"Oh," Owen said, nonplussed. "Pretty ancient history, isn't it?"

"That depends on the point of view," said Melmoth, pleased to turn from the strains of narrative to the delights of philosophic inquiry, yet with a trace of sternness in his manner. "I told you this was an atheist's errand, Mr. Hilliard. Sophie was my older sister; she has been dead now for just over forty-five years. Not enjoying herself in Heaven, mind you; just dead. No one can say whether those years would have been happy or unhappy, of course, since she was robbed of the chance to find out. But I can see no reason why as the number of years grows greater the sense of injustice should diminish."

"Perhaps you're right," Owen said. "Excuse me."

Sophie had been a lovely girl but too shy and gentle for the town boys, a spinner of dreams, a writer of poetry, someone who expected glory of the world. She was just sixteen, Charles Fortescue a few months older. A wonderfully handsome boy, but at school he was considered sullen, withdrawn, unpopular. He was an only child. His father was first or second cousin to half the socially most prominent families of New York and was a neurasthenic despotic weakling; when Charles's mother ran off with a Belgian hairdresser, he placed the boy in school at the earliest possible moment and settled down to drinking away whatever of his inheritance wasn't in trust. Charles had been off at one boarding school or another since before he was seven. An unfortunate upbringing, doubtless, but one to which most boys would sooner or later have learned to adjust; Charles had stayed fixed in a habit of moody rebelliousness—too superior to conform, too superior as a rule even to disclose the source of that superiority. He had disclosed it to Sophie, though. She had spoken with awe of his ideas for improving the world: this was someone who would leave his mark, either in politics or in philosophy, it was hard to say which.

"Have you ever met Charles Fortescue—since he was a boy, I mean?" Owen asked gently, and Melmoth shook his head, surprised at the question. "He's changed considerably, you know." But Mel-

moth was not interested in that. It was odd, the photographic intimacy that tragedy could leave behind, so that Melmoth could produce this detailed and not unsympathetic portrait of a long-ago
Charles Fortescue—a sea horse preserved down the years in transparent plastic—as far removed from the reality as were most tormented adolescents from the adults they painfully became. "It's not
easy to see him as a sensitive boy, caught up in his first love."

"One tends to forget the intensity of emotions at that age," Melmoth said. He was unhappy, speaking of feelings rather than ideas.
He wanted to say that Charles and Sophie had both been lonely
youngsters in their different ways and had fallen head over heels in
love, each finding the other the answer to all misunderstandings.
But the crudity of unphilosophic emotions embarrassed Melmoth; he
picked his way gingerly among the words for passion until Owen
felt obliged to come to his rescue.

"It's a hell of an age," he said reminiscently. "Glorious and agoniz-
ing. A time when you know you're ready for love, and society chuck-
les indulgently and knows you aren't."

"Nobody chuckled," said Melmoth. "Our father had his own
standards and couldn't imagine anyone departing from them. I'm
not denying his share of the blame. Either he raged or he refused to
treat the matter seriously. Sophie learned to hide the way she felt."

"And Charles couldn't expect any sympathy at home, either,"
Owen said. "Where would he turn?"

"There was no place else to turn, he'd seen to that," said Melmoth. "It had to be his father. So at Easter vacation that year
Charles made his appeal. You are a father, Mr. Hilliard. What
would you have done?"

"Played for time," Owen said promptly. "A youngster can usually
be persuaded that his grand passion will survive till his schooling is
done. When it doesn't, you can argue that the flaw was in the grand
passion."

"Charles's father was a different man," said Melmoth. "For one
thing he was probably two-thirds drunk. For another, he went berserk at the very idea of his son being involved with the daughter of a
cheap little Jewish tradesman." There was only a remote, rarefied
bitterness at this description of his father; it was a reality that people thought this way, and he had accepted reality. "He made a scene
of quite remarkable ugliness. And the next day he began preparations
to send the boy West for the summer and to a different school in the
autumn."

"Idiot!" said Owen.

"There are other terms for it," Melmoth said. "When Charles went back to Courtney, he took with him the revolver he had pilfered from his father's desk. . . ."

The story was one, Owen realized, anticipating the remainder, that appeared with distressing frequency in fragmented form in the daily newspapers: the adolescent suicide pact with one survivor. And almost always, or so it seemed, the survivor was the boy. There it was from time to time, one more item in the day's quota of sensation, the bare bones of a tragedy. A second-act-curtain situation to wring the heart, as one thought of the boy's anguish when he found he'd destroyed his love and failed his manhood. But never a first act, for the parents weren't going to boast of the lack of empathy which had brought their children to such a plight; and never a third act, for after that one day's titillation the newspapers always dropped the story into oblivion. From their point of view the drama was over: nobody had the time to worry about aftermaths. Even Owen, unimaginatively, had never stopped to wonder what became of such a boy in later life, and if he had wondered he would not have conjured up Charles Fortescue. "Poor wretch," he murmured. "I expect he lost his nerve?"

"He lost his nerve," Melmoth agreed. "That is the one fact that was never in dispute."

"I don't follow you."

"When Charles went out that afternoon," Melmoth said heavily, "he intended suicide. He left a note for his roommate to find. My parents were never permitted to see it, but there was a note. Sophie left no note."

"Yes, I see," Owen said. "That doesn't really prove anything."

"No, it doesn't. It raises the intangible of what sort of girl Sophie was. I myself was only ten at the time, so my testimony wouldn't be worth very much. If my father and mother always swore that Sophie wasn't a girl to do that without leaving a note, if they swore that she went out that day in her usual spirits, you can reply that they'd already shown they didn't understand her too well. So there it is. Perhaps there was a pact. Perhaps there had been talk of a pact and Sophie decided against it, went off that afternoon expecting to argue him around and he proved the more persuasive arguer. And perhaps he never consulted her at all—just took the unhappy situation into his own hands and then lost enthusiasm half way through. They're all possibilities."

"But there must have been an inquiry," Owen protested.

"Of sorts, of sorts," said Melmoth. "The school was right in there immediately, of course, fighting against scandal. Charles was rushed off to a hospital, suffering from extreme shock, so they said, and it was some time before he could be questioned. The school carries a good deal of weight locally, as you can imagine, and the Fortescue relations were busy pulling strings and hiring the local legal talent. And nobody much wants to persecute a miserable sixteen-year-old boy when there's a plausible story to be told for him, especially when the influence is on his side."

"None of that would slow down the newspapers," Owen said.

Again Melmoth reached to the inside pocket of his jacket, this time to bring out an envelope from which he produced several yellowed clippings. He handed these across; Owen scarcely glanced at them. There were only four, and none was longer than a couple of inches. "There must have been more," he said. "With a big New York name involved the metropolitan papers would have been onto the story in a flash. I hope you aren't going to suggest that influence kept all the papers muzzled. It just doesn't work that way."

"Look at the date," Melmoth said. "This was April of 1917. The papers had more news than they could handle."

"Oh, yes, naturally," muttered Owen, feeling foolish, wondering why his instinct was to quibble with Melmoth's story every step of the way. The clippings were all from local papers. He read the longest, from the Actonsville *Courier* of April 19, 1917. The story was a model of tact, if of neither logic nor journalism. A suicide pact was hinted at obliquely. Charles Fortescue was identified as 'attending a nearby preparatory school.' The young lady had shot herself fatally, 'perhaps by accident.' A Mr. Abel Wilcox working not far away, investigated the shot and 'arrived at the scene in time to dissuade the young man from pursuing the same unfortunate course.'

"Horrible," he said. "But I can't see that it makes much difference which of your various alternatives was closer to the truth."

"I have no doubt that was the argument they used with my parents," said Melmoth. "I don't know, of course; a ten-year-old boy isn't called into conference at such a time. But they were coming and going every day, solid substantial people with walking sticks and spats, and I can almost hear them pointing out that nothing could bring Sophie back to life, and that what was important was that there mustn't be any more unnecessary suffering. A very hush-hush hearing, not a trial, was held in front of a judge, and I learned much later that my father appeared there to say that he blamed himself more than anybody and hoped Charles would not be punished more than he had no doubt already punished himself. And that was the end. Sophie was dead and buried. My father went back to making school rings for Courtney. And three years later there was a full scholarship for me there. They told me at the time I had won it by my grades, and I was very proud of myself."

"Perhaps it was true," Owen said.

"Perhaps the Virgin Birth was true," replied Melmoth contemptuously. "But in one respect, when you say it doesn't make much difference which was the correct story of that afternoon, you are absolutely right, Mr. Hilliard. Whichever way you look at it, the blame is still all Charles's. Say it was a suicide pact, pure and simple. Where did the idea of suicide come from in the first place? Not from Sophie, I assure you. She was a girl, dreamy and poetical if you like, but perfectly normal and healthy, looking forward to having babies of her own more than anything in the world. And that's not a person who spontaneously thinks of suicide."

"By any chance—?" Owen asked.

"Was she pregnant?" Melmoth nodded tight-lipped, not in answer to the question but in acknowledgment of its justice. "It's terrible to think that giving life can be such a calamity when there are couples like my wife and myself who have always wanted children and without success. But no, Sophie wasn't pregnant. It wasn't that sort of panic. It was adolescent panic; life wasn't worth living if they couldn't be together, something like that. I don't pretend to know what went on in their minds. I don't have a fanciful imagination; I try to keep to the facts. It was Charles who had never adjusted to the world he had to live in. It was Charles who brought the pistol back to school with him, days beforehand. It was Charles who left behind a suicide note when he went out that afternoon. He was responsible. I don't think that can reasonably be disputed."

"Probably you're right," said Owen, who was much less interested in the rights and wrongs of the tragedy than in what it had done to the men who had had to live with it, in their separate ways, for so many years. "Tell me, is this the first time you've . . . done anything about it?"

"Gracious, no, of course not." Melmoth was distinctly offended by the suggestion. "This isn't a senile morbidity which has overtaken me, I assure you. A great many years ago—it was almost precisely the twentieth anniversary of Sophie's death—I paid a similar visit to a

Mr. Jacob Zimmerman of this city. Is he still alive? An irascible and unsympathetic individual I found him, disposed to inform me that each atom of the body replaces itself every seven years so that whatever happened to a man twenty years ago had really happened to a distant relative. But he listened, and that was all that mattered. After that I had some cards printed up: simply *In Memoriam* and the date, and I've sent one to Charles each anniversary since. No name, you notice, so if somebody else opens the envelope he can explain it away as he likes. Now I've spoken to you. And in a few years the Fortescue boy will most likely get himself engaged, and presumably there will be another father for me to call upon."

"Only fathers?" Owen inquired. "I was wondering if you planned to call on Roger's mother, as well."

"No, I don't," said Melmoth. "Call it cowardly. Men are generally rational about other people's tragedies, but there's simply no telling how a woman will react. I have a terror of emotional scenes. Although there's no question but that talking to the women might serve my purpose much better."

"Your purpose," Owen repeated. "I admit that still escapes me."

"Is it really so subtle?" asked his visitor. "I remember now that Mr. Zimmerman also had the greatest difficulty understanding that. He felt I must be trying to discourage or embarrass his daughter's marriage to Charles Fortescue. When I assured him this was not so at all, I think he decided I was slightly out of my head. An intelligent man, was my impression, but grown intolerant of people—especially non-Zimmermans."

Owen smiled at the unconscious humor. He was trying to make sense of Melmoth's preliminary justification for his visit: 'an atheist's errand' he had called it. "In some fashion you are playing the God you believe Charles Fortescue will never have to meet."

"Yes, we are supposed to be ashamed of any taint of arrogance," Melmoth said, replying to the intonation which Owen had tried to avoid. "Yet I cannot think of myself as arrogant. As much as anything I am simply trying to keep Sophie's memory alive. And I can't help feeling that Charles Fortescue escaped too easily, too completely. A boy of that class doesn't even go to jail for a few days to have that to look back on: he stayed in the hospital until he was released in the custody of his father. A World War confined the scandal to a few local newspapers; off at school and college in a different part of the country he probably never again heard an echo of the story. I don't doubt that he was a most unhappy boy for a time—but would you say that he was a man troubled by an uneasy conscience?"

"Our acquaintance is still slight," Owen apologized. "Superficially, no."

"I shouldn't think so. He's really a very lucky man. In a few weeks he'll be marrying off a daughter, a happy occasion which my father never experienced. He can look forward to dying surrounded by his grandchildren; my father was cheated of even that semblance of immortality. Of course Fortescue is scarcely to blame if my wife and I were unable to have children, but how very different *our* lives might have been if we'd had nephews and nieces to keep us from subsiding into middle-age selfishness. There it is, Mr. Hilliard. Forty-five years ago my sister and Charles Fortescue fell in love—and look at the consequences. Sophie was killed. My mother died a few years later; I shan't say of a broken heart but she died unhappy. My father lived long enough to know that I was the dead end of all he had struggled and worked for. And I live out my life lopsided for a part of me that isn't there. While for Charles Fortescue, unless you rely on a God who evens these things out, nothing but a faded memory of an adolescent escapade. I ask you. I'm not a vengeful man, but I find the injustice upsetting. I can't help feeling that Fortescue's present contentment was in a sense bought and paid for by Sophie all those years ago, and it isn't right that she should be forgotten. So, annually I remind him of the debt. And I see to it that a few of the people close around him know the story. You'll find it sticks in the mind, Mr. Hilliard. Whenever you see Charles Fortescue from now on, you are going to remember Sophie Melmoth. It will affect your attitude towards him just a little. Perhaps one evening you'll have a cocktail too many and let drop a hint that you know. Sooner or later you are bound to confide the story to your son, I should think. Yes, that is probably what appeals to me most. I should like to believe that Sophie will be remembered even when I am no longer here to miss her."

Melmoth stopped as calmly as he had begun, looked about him with refreshed interest, lit a cigarette, said that now he would like a drink if the offer was still going, remarked that he understood Owen was a playwright by profession. Owen had no idea what to make of his visitor. Apart from a certain wistful tenderness in his voice whenever he spoke of his sister, Melmoth had told his tragedy with remarkable dispassion, objectively and analytically. It was as if decades of intellectualizing his sorrow had twisted every emotion into an exercise in dialectics, yet his visit today, this quiet round-about persecution of Charles Fortescue, was the action of a driven man.

It was impossible to say whether Melmoth had achieved an eccentric form of refined sanity or was as mad as the proverbial hatter. But already Owen was feeling an exultant, exuberant pity for this man who thought he could use Owen Hilliard as a cat's paw in his campaign against Fortescue. Unless Owen's instinct was much mistaken, he would never, never drop the slightest hint of knowing about this curiously dramatic episode in Fortescue's past.

Having asked for his drink to be made very light, Melmoth drank it off thirstily. Although his poise remained unshaken, now that his task was done he seemed placidly at a loss: making small talk out of some sense of courtesy or because he wanted to prove that he was an ordinary social being. After a few minutes, thanking Owen for having heard him out, he stood up to leave. At the doorway Owen suddenly remembered his second curiosity.

"That's an unusual name you have," he said. "It startled me on the phone the other day."

"Oh, that," said Melmoth. "It's a common story. My father had one of those unpronounceable Polish-Jewish names, and an impatient immigration officer made what sense he could of the first couple of syllables. It's bothered me occasionally, sounding as though we'd changed it, as some do. But it scarcely matters, does it, since I'm the last of the species?" Smiling for the first time, an oddly shy smile, he settled his grey hat on his head and stepped through the door, a quiet, colorless, anonymous, haunted little man, no instrument of destiny, perhaps, but a messenger from the only gods Owen truly acknowledged.

5

The repetitive drudgeries of domesticity had never been a strong point of Carol's, with the result that until recently any hospitable occasion produced a nightmare of last-minute misgivings. Had she dusted in all the likely places? Would anyone peek into the bedroom and discover the chaos there? Did she *have* any clean towels to put on display? For the first half hour or so, until cocktails established the mood of the evening, Carol had been a highly self-conscious hostess.

No longer. Having a three-and-a-half-year-old child concentrated one's anxieties wonderfully. This evening she had made a casual effort to tidy up and a not-so-casual effort with her appearance, but beyond that she didn't seem to care. She couldn't worry about how the casserole would turn out or whether Owen would notice the sorry condition of the curtains. It was quite enough to worry about how Lois would behave.

Alone with her mother Lois was generally a sweetheart, if not overtired, but socially she was unpredictable. She was of an age for positive and capricious likes and dislikes, and not of an age to conceal them. By a miracle she worshipped Nora Saunders, who was gruff, impatient and wholly antimaternal, while some of Nora's friends who professed to adore little children sent Lois into outrages of sulkiness. There was no telling, and it was worse than useless to try to enlist Lois's sympathies in advance; Carol had learned that lesson the hard way. So she had simply explained informatively that Owen was an old and dear friend she hadn't seen in quite some time and hoped for the best. Lois's observant little eyes had doubtless noticed that her mother was taking more pains with her person than she took when Nora came to dinner, but Carol also dressed up for Martin Antinori, and despite all Martin's exertions Lois had decided that he was 'silly' and could scarcely be troubled to be polite to him. It was his own fault, of course: he tried much too hard. But she liked Martin and found Lois's behavior embarrassing.

By accident Owen handled her perfectly, arriving in one of his states of ebullient self-absorption. His greetings were boisterous; he was courteous with Lois, amusing, but it was perfectly evident that his mind was miles away, where little girls scarcely existed. He had learned that morning that there were backstage fireworks among the cast of *Cascade*, and just before he'd left his apartment, somebody had called to ask if he could give a course in playwriting at some summer session; while he made cocktails Owen chattered on about these. Nothing could have been better. Finding herself virtually overlooked by this large, attractive, adult male was a challenge to all Lois's innate femininity—and it is deplorable how feminine a three-and-a-half-year-old can be. Lois knew better than to make any obstreperous effort to attract attention: she simply flirted with Owen, daintily but shamelessly, until she had captured a fair share of his interest, and thereafter was delighted with him and herself. The extent of Owen's conquest was not revealed, however, till Lois's bedtime, when she bade him goodnight tenderly and marched off to bed with a look of guileless virtue which declared to all the saints that she *never* made an unladylike fuss about bedtimes.

"Cute little monster," he said, when finally Carol returned to the living room. "No wonder men never have a sporting chance—the girls start practicing so much earlier."

"She's a bit starved for victims. Sometimes I worry that one day I'll catch her practicing on one of Nora's pals for lack of anyone better."

"I shouldn't," he said vaguely, his mind already wandering. He was good with children, but his interest grew with their personalities; at this stage he could be intrigued by Lois while she was around, but she was not yet a fruitful topic of discussion, whereas Carol, fascinated by the month-to-month transformations, could have talked about her for hours. "What would you say if I told you I was taking this idea seriously?" he asked.

"Which idea?"

"The teaching thing in New Hampshire, this summer. Their getting on to me this late certainly means that somebody else failed them at the last moment, but I don't think I should let pride stand in my way."

"Can you afford to do it?"

"The appeal to the ego is simply tremendous," he said, bypassing the practicalities. "All those young talents still in the plastic state, eager to learn from you if you have anything real to say to them. And I think I do. There are so many phoney theories about, so much cheap psychology and pansy criticism. I'd like to try carrying the banner for old-fashioned craftsmanship. Put over the quaint idea that an artist is still only a third of an artist till he's learned his craft. Professionalism. Lord, you can scarcely find a young actor these days who can come on stage up center and cross down left to answer a telephone without his first having to wrestle with his psyche to find the right approach. And the writers are just as bad: there's no shortage of talent, but they don't want to work; they don't want to write books or plays, they want to expose their unconsciousness. It's not their fault, it's what they've picked up. . . ."

She loved his gift for enthusiasm. This project had arisen an hour ago; by tomorrow it might be discarded as unfeasible, but this evening he was enamored of a vision of himself holding a clutch of aspiring writers in thrall, animating them, provoking them, goading them on. With most men this would have been a febrile enthusiasm of the moment only, a fugitive daydream of glory, but not with

Owen. If the opportunity passed, he would turn without much regret and with equal verve to something else, but if the plan came true, if he went to New Hampshire, this evening's vision would somehow survive the summer in the face of all discouragements. Finding that talent was less prevalent than he had believed would not daunt him; he would discover the stirrings of genius if he had to invent them himself, and he would set off to each class with renewed conviction that today he would surely strike off a spark of inspiration.

For this ability to give himself with equal unreserve to any conception that caught his fancy, briefly or enduringly, was constitutional with Owen, was merely a symptom of that quality of vitality which made him so attractive to Carol—that quality, in fact, which was her primary touchstone for the attractiveness of men in general.

She did not know how other women picked their men; often the process baffled her. The marriage of some of her friends, women she considered smarter than herself, to amiable and earnest husbands, excellent providers and fathers no doubt, but with sluggish minds that moved only from one unalterably fixed opinion to another— these marriages were incomprehensible to her. However charming such men might be, however attractive physically, they seemed less than half alive. She had no inflated regard for her own intelligence; she was not predisposed towards intellectuals, most of whom struck her (probably unjustly) as mere dialectic gymnasts. What appealed to her was simply vitality, the mental vigor and restlessness that played tiddlywinks with the self-evident, that embraced every new idea with ardent skepticism, that was always ready for a new optimism, that was constantly spring cleaning among old conclusions and flinging out the threadbare, that was neither ashamed nor proud of being out of step with the whole army of sheep.

It was a masculine vitality: unrealistic, romantic (immature?) and infinitely appealing. Her father had it in a way, for all that he had frittered it on jerry-built homes for the jerry-built lower middle class. Owen had it to a marked degree, which was why she had never entirely fallen out of love with him. Andrew had had it, exaggerated and distorted by his inescapable awareness of living on borrowed time. In him it had taken a self-conscious shape, a part of the philosophy that served him in place of any religious faith. With the physique and energy of a young athlete he had had to adapt himself to the life of a semi-invalid, schooling himself to calm and unhurried movement, avoiding any strain or sudden exertion. Even his love making was leisurely and tranquil, and indeed he had died in the doze following one session, leaving Carol with the guilty feeling that he had been overexpending himself on her behalf, out of some proud, wrong-headed fear of frustrating her. That would have been like Andrew. But all the vitality curbed by his physical circumspection came bursting out through his imagination. He was fascinated by everything, incapable of boredom even for a minute—overturning the dreariness of the dreariest visitor and by sheer force of energy eliciting the suppressed unique or the forgotten remarkable. His own death entertained him, not as a morbidity but as a topic for ingenious rationalizations. "Every terror displaces another," he would say; "the man in danger of drowning forgets that he's three months behind in his alimony. For me, the worst thing on earth would be to reach a point where the prospect of so much pain drove me to the bottle of sleeping pills, knowing that by my own action I was obliterating tomorrow. That is real misery—by contrast it's a comfort to know that it will be quick, painless and wholly unexpected. In fact, you're the one who'll be left with the misery, and if there were a bit more of the saint in me, I'd feel sorry for you instead." Not so much by temperament as by effort of will he found exhilaration rather than panic in the knowledge that he had no time to waste; out of superstition he would never lay plans even a day ahead, feeling this might attract the notice of Atropos, but made of each day a new and delightful adventure. Only in retrospect did the years with Andrew seem to have been lived under a shadow; at the time she had been swept along almost heedlessly by the strength of his vitality, which to her was so akin to life itself that she had never completely believed that between one moment and the next it could be extinguished.

It was a masculine vitality, but it didn't necessarily have anything to do with the rest of masculinity. Martin Antinori had it too, and she was not much more convinced of his innate virility than, in moments of depression, was he. Martin was not overtly queer—she was sure of that—but he had his doubts. At present he was in love with her, or in love with the idea of being in love with her. He brought her his poetry, fine poetry, possibly first-rate; he stayed talking till the small hours; and in five months he had never once made a move towards taking her to bed—as, unless she mistook the signs, Owen would certainly do before the evening was over. Martin was frightened (she had no need to be told this) that if he made the attempt and it proved a fiasco, what little remained of his confidence would be destroyed. It was a worrying relationship. She was very fond of Martin, and at times she felt positive that if she helped him over this hurdle, he would prove as much of a man as any, at least with her. But she also suspected that by helping him she would be committing herself to more of a responsibility than she was yet sure she wanted to undertake. Martin was an odd young man—several years younger than she, in fact—with some money of his own and no discernible interest in life but writing poetry. Among other things Carol was uncertain whether his poetry would survive the discovery that he could be a normal contented male, and she didn't want Lois to grow up with an idle drifter for a stepfather.

"Oh, do be sensible, Owen," she said, breaking in as he was being given a testimonial dinner by all the great young dramatists twenty years hence, as the major inspirational force in their careers. "This is all very well, but they can't be offering more than a token salary, and the last I heard, you couldn't afford to throw your summer away so lightly."

"I wouldn't be throwing it away," he said, coming back to earth with a grin of mysterious smugness. "On the contrary. The teaching part shouldn't take more than a couple of hours a day, and I'd have the rest of the time for my own work. And away from all the interruptions of New York life, away from all my dear friends who throw too damn many parties, I'd probably get more and better work done in less time."

"Perhaps," she said. "These summer retreats from the madding crowd seldom turn out to be as productive as people expect."

"How about that summer on the Vineyard?" he reminded her. "Even with Roger underfoot I got three quarters of *The Huddling Place* written."

"The weakest of your novels," she reminded him.

"Oh, I don't know," he demurred, with an author's intransigent fondness for his backward children. "Some people thought it was my best. In any case, I don't think the Vineyard enfeebled me. You forget I'm a country boy at heart. And since I saw you last, a new project has come up, which might very well profit by a break in my routine."

"Tell me about it later," she said, getting up. "It's time I did things about dinner." She assumed (knowing how slowly and laboriously his original ideas evolved) that when he spoke of a new project he meant that he had found another novel he wanted to adapt for the stage—and the thought offended her. To a degree she sympathized with his desire to give Roger and Vickie the appropriate honeymoon, but also she saw this as an excuse. When once a man had found a formula for success, there would always be excuses for repeating that formula instead of striking off into new and dangerous territory: each success made it that much more difficult to risk the possibility of failure. She was afraid that unless Owen made the break from this hackwork soon, he never might or might leave it till too late and find that he had spent his talent in the service of other men.

But if she was going to be offended, she wanted it to be later in the evening, when she suspected she would need all her defenses. She knew her own frailties, and Owen had access to all of them. In so many ways he was exactly the man she wanted from life—for herself, and now for Lois as well. Physically there had always been a great attraction between them, and that evening at Katya's they had both recognized it still existed. Well, there was no harm in that. Except for one brief hiatus she had been well married for the better part of ten years. The past nine months of celibacy hadn't left her feeling frustrated, precisely—women didn't react that way, or at least she didn't—but she couldn't deny that part of her was favorably disposed towards the way this evening was tending. Still, if she went to bed with Owen, she wanted to go as a free woman, uncommitted. She didn't want the needs of her body jostling aside the old reservations, prompting her to depths of emotion she was by no means prepared to concede so readily again, if only because this time she had Lois to think of as well. In her susceptible condition (which she hoped was not too obvious) the more reasons for disapproving of Owen the better.

He had brought a bottle of wine with him, the casserole was a success, and dinner was festive, reminiscent and obliquely flirtatious —they knew each other far too well for any of the standard routines of seduction. Owen was the one who had changed in the past several years: the last of his boyishness had become stylized; he had grown more poised, positive, perhaps a little harder. It was the maturity of age, all to the good, and somewhat the maturity of success—but the latter was kept in perspective by his vitality: he was still too restless to look backward, smugly. He annoyed her a little (excellent!) by his typical male egoism, his attitude that she must be available for his wooing if he decided to take pity on her, his inability to conceive of another man in the background with superior claims. Arrogance of a sort, but she couldn't make too much of it, knowing that over-nice scruples on his part would have pleased her even less. Since

Martin Antinori's shortcomings as a rival were not in evidence, she contrived to introduce his name into the conversation often enough to unsettle some of Owen's complacency.

She cleared off the table, declining help, implying that the dishes would somehow wash themselves in the morning though she would have to do them herself that night however late he left. The living room became a living room again. She produced coffee and a bottle of armagnac hoarded since Christmas and piled the record changer with The Well-Tempered Clavier, which was as delightful to talk against as to listen to. Feeling that perhaps she had set the stage too romantically, she inquired what novel he was planning to adapt next.

"No, no," he said. "It's not an adaptation at all. It looks very much as if it's going to shape into my first original play in—what is it, now? —over six years, anyway."

"So suddenly?" she asked, thinking that anything that came to him impulsively, when he was under a pressure such as Roger's engagement, couldn't possibly be right for him.

"Quite suddenly," he agreed. "It's a miracle. There's still a devil of a lot of hard thinking to be done, but it *feels* right. As I've told you, and you probably knew it already, the hard thing for me is to find a story that interests me, yet with enough dramatic movement to keep me disciplined—well, this has everything. It's funny. We split up, you and I, just when they were dickering with me to do the dramatization of that book of Ivy's, and here we are again just as I'm getting back to my own work. Not that I'd ever again be such a fool as to let you get even a glimpse at a first draft."

"That's cruel."

"So was your own brand of constructive criticism. Except in bed."

"But how did you come on this idea out of the blue?" she asked, still distrustful, though his air of barely suppressed excitement delighted her.

"Aha! I said it was a miracle. It walked into the apartment this afternoon. On two feet."

"This afternoon? That man who insisted on seeing you?"

"He came to tell me a story."

"But you *hate* that sort of thing," Carol said in bewilderment, remembering how often Owen had complained that the curse of an author's life was the people who fell upon him with glee to recount either their lacklustre histories or else some true anecdote of staggering coincidence, 'which he was welcome to use if he liked,' but which was no more believable merely for being true.

"This was different," Owen said. "He had no idea he was telling me a story in my sense of the term; he was just a man with an itch that needed scratching. An old-fashioned *deus ex machina*, that's Mr. Melmoth, and we strike him out of the story altogether as a cheap device that would offend the more fastidious critics. There's no need for him, anyway, at least not as an active figure." For the moment, elbows on his knees, staring down at the carpet, he was off in his own vision, mumbling rather to himself than to her. "I'll be treating the story from a completely different point of view—part of it has to be brought up to date. Yes, and I think I already see how to handle it most effectively." He looked up at her again. "There's only one thing I find a bit worrying."

"What's that?" she said patiently, knowing better than to ask about the idea itself while it was still in the process of gestation.

"The story, which is fairly remarkable, concerns somebody . . . I know quite well."

"What difference does that make?"

"Oh, I know, I know," he said irritably. "You've always been the ruthless purist. What difference how many people get hurt or humiliated in the name of art? I wonder how you'd feel if you were the victim. If someone who'd known you and Andrew intimately built a play out of a crisis in a family which lived with the knowledge that the husband was liable to drop dead at any moment—and you saw Andrew and yourself upon that stage speaking lines you could remember. The author needn't even have heard you; if he knew his business, he'd write the dialogue you *must* have spoken."

Carol tried to be fair and think about it instead of answering on principle. "It truly wouldn't bother me at all," she said just the same. "At least not if the play was a good play."

"I'm not so sure I believe you."

"Maybe I'm kidding myself, and I'd hate it. Why is that so important? If it was a good play and all the other thousands of people got something valid from it, wouldn't one person's discomfort be irrelevant?"

"All right, that's the logic of it," Owen said. "But there's a bourgeois streak in me that won't let me accept that logic. Call it a failing. If the play would somehow get itself written, I might feel that way afterwards, but I get self-conscious writing. I know; I've tried. Tony Elmendorf's marriage would be the ideal subplot for a play I've been kicking around for years. He's talked about it often enough, it's alive in my mind—and I cannot make it go. The thought of Tony sitting there on opening night stops me cold. Probably *he* wouldn't care; he might even enjoy it. But the very thought of him inhibits me, turns the dialogue stilted and artificial. I don't know why. I don't have any particular sexual inhibitions, either, but I'm damned if I could make love in public. Something to do with my middle-class upbringing, I suppose."

"Then how are you going to solve it this time?" Carol asked.

"Where's the problem?" Owen said earnestly. "Lois is safely asleep in her room, and there aren't any other visitors coming."

"I mean with this new idea for a play," Carol said, angry at feeling herself blush.

"Oh, that. It's unnerving the way you keep changing the subject. Well, the story is one that's pretty effectively buried a long way in the past; under normal circumstances I never could have stumbled on it. I don't see that anyone can assume I'm wise, except one person who won't be talking. If I'd really helped my father burn down his hardware store for the insurance—we discussed it once back about '31, though not very seriously—and thirty years later a friend who couldn't possibly know of that episode writes a play about a kid who helps his dad with some profitable arson, I have to call it a coincidence. Even if the characters seem a bit familiar, I'll decide that maybe all us firebugs are somewhat alike. It's like that. As long as nobody knows I know, I feel comfortable. It's a rationalization, but if it works that's all that matters. And if you see a large flaw in it somewhere, don't tell me till after the first draft is finished, because after that I can be as ruthless as anyone."

"I shan't argue," she said. "As long as you get back to your own work, I don't care how you do it."

"Women are so wonderfully single-minded," he said. "There are times when I almost wish I were a woman: it would make life so much simpler. But there are other times when I don't wish anything of the sort."

6

It was just luck, bad luck, that Stephen happened to be in the living room when Arthur Vaughan arrived with his news. Stephen, of course, burst out laughing. Even in her consternation, even as she was quailing at the prospect of her mother's sarcastic vexation, Amelia had an emotional surplus to devote to annoyance at her husband's ill-timed hilarity. Dealing with Arthur Vaughan was a strain at the best of times. She detested the man; she had detested all the Arthur Vaughans she had dealt with in her day: men of professional dedication and grubby efficiency who used causes as stepping stones in their careers. However sincere they tried to be, they invariably brought the cynicism of personal ambition to the most selfless idealism—but there was no getting along without them.

"Your sources *must* be misinformed," Amelia said.

"I'm afraid not," Arthur replied, compassionate, exasperating. He was thin, morbidly thin, ugly, crippled, with a cultivated beauty of expression, the smile on the face of torment, the saintly resignation to an indiscernible martyrdom.

"But it's absolutely ridiculous!" she protested. "I suppose there could be a few Communists or ex-Communists among the rank-and-file members and the people who've signed L.I.D. petitions. That couldn't be helped. But there isn't a suspicion of one on the Executive Board or among the Regional Chairmen, or any of the people who matter. We've deliberately been cautious to the point of stuffiness."

"I thought at first we might have attracted the notice of our natural enemies," Arthur said. "After all, if we have our way, one day they'll be converting the Pentagon to a youth hostel. But the Pentagon doesn't seem frightened as yet. It's all a congressman named Updike. He faces a tough election this fall, he has to stand on his record, and he woke up one morning to realize that he has no record to stand on. They tell me he has nothing to show for the past eighteen months except getting his brother-in-law made a Postmaster. The only thing that can save him now is some splashy headlines. He's timing the hearings for mid-July, just a few days before our national convention at the Garden; that way he'll get the maximum of publicity."

"How did you learn all this?" Stephen asked.

"How shall I put it delicately? One of the things I'm paid for is having access to this sort of . . . freemasonry. But I don't think it's more than casually secret. Congress sees itself as an avalanche, with little need of the advantages of surprise."

"I wonder how he came to settle on you people," Stephen said with the annoyingly mild curiosity of trained objectivity.

"Apparently he read some article that said disarmament would be a blow to our national economy," Arthur replied. "I won't say this convinced him we must be part of the conspiracy, but he decided we could be made to *seem* like dupes of the Russians, and that was enough for his purposes."

"I never cease to marvel at the cynicism of the true idealist," Stephen remarked.

"I just try to be realistic," said Arthur humbly.

"And that means assuming hypocrisy on the part of anyone who opposes you," said Stephen. For some perverse reason of his own he chose to defend the possibility that this Updike creature was animated by the noblest patriotism. The two men bickered the question, manlike, and Amelia ceased to listen.

Her first reaction to Arthur's news had been to dread what her mother would say. Mrs. Langstaff would not wait to hear the rights and wrongs of the matter. She had always been contemptuous of her daughter's crusades—they seemed to involve one with such dubious people—and now she would feel justified in her disapproval. To Mrs. Langstaff's way of thinking, being publicly accused of something was infinitely worse than being guilty of it.

So the perfectly normal promptings of panic in Amelia's mind became terribly involved. Her impulse was to resign her chairmanship on the spot, nor did this impulse need to be the result of any moral cowardice. She honestly doubted her physical ability to withstand the imagined ordeals of the investigation; she could picture herself all too clearly prostrated by one of her headaches at the very moment when she most needed to be clearheaded and forceful. It might be better for the L.I.D. if someone sturdier were at the helm in such a crisis.

At the same time, however, she could hear her mother's clipped, dispassionate voice urging all the practical excuses for resigning—the ugliness of the publicity, the invasions of privacy, the embarrassment to Stephen and the children, the damage to the family name. And in any case there was so little dignity to carrying the banner of a lost cause while people shook their heads sagely and agreed that where there was smoke there must be fire.

In the upshot Amelia simply could not stomach the possibility that one of these pusillanimous practicalities was worming away at the back of her mind, the true reason hiding behind the convenient excuse of her uncertain health. There could be no question of resigning. She was obliged to nail her colors to the mast out of fear of being influenced by the thought of what her mother would say. Yet this decision made her position no less galling, for it merely emphasized to what extent she *was* still influenced by her mother, if only in the necessity for defiance. And Dr. Eckhardt would sit smugly at his mahogany desk arguing that if she had not outgrown her mother's dominion it was because she didn't want to.

As a release from these confused exasperations, Amelia lost patience with the academic squabbling of the men. "Oh, for heaven's sake!" she burst out. "What possible difference can it make whether the man is sincere or not? The point is that he's attacking us, and what are we going to do about it?"

"Fight," proclaimed Arthur Vaughan, with a gentle, agonized smile.

"Lose ungracefully," prophesied Stephen. "You never had a prayer of accomplishing anything, and now you'll be made to look sinister for having tried. You'll squirm and protest and whimper, but eventually the League will wither away like all the rest, and Arthur will be renting his experience to some other crusade. You've never had anything on your side except sanity, and according to one of my colleagues in the Psychology Department that is a quality which should be kept locked up for the protection of our society. But you won't believe me, of course, so I'll leave you to work out the details of your gallant but futile defiance." He beamed at them both impartially, gathered up his books and a moment later was trudging up the stairs to his study.

"Pay no attention to my husband," Amelia said. "He's professionally dedicated to the idea that we've civilized ourselves back behind barbarity." She smiled brightly from a sense of duty, but added a fresh tally to her grudge against Stephen for forcing her to find comradeship in men like Arthur Vaughan. "We'll fight, of course. But I don't really see what we can do."

"We have to meet the accusation more than halfway," he said briskly, and it offended her to recognize how much confidence she gained from his self-assurance, his appearance of looking forward to the struggle. "There will have to be a meeting of the executive board right away, and I'm counting on you to support my proposals. . . ." It was evident that Arthur had wasted no time on despair but had turned his attention immediately to considerations of strategy and tactics. He was filled with schemes to discredit Congressman Updike and display the League in the best possible light. Yet as he talked, it also became evident that his ardor was not so much for a principle as for the fight itself: his ego was committed to one side of a struggle, so he was determined that that side would win—for the greater glory of Arthur Vaughan. Nothing would ever disarm the souls of men, for they were born pugnacious in the best of causes, themselves. Amelia could sense that, win or lose, Congressman Updike would probably gain the publicity he wanted: win or lose, Arthur would emerge with a reputation as a pucky fighter which would lead him to a higher salary. She was realist enough to accept this. Woman's strength lay in turning men's vanities to worthy ends.

"One last thing for the moment," Vaughan said, "though I daresay others will occur to me. We should reconsider our list of guest speakers for the convention. They are all three distinguished men, true, and they seemed ideal choices at the time. But one is a poet, one a professor, the third a nuclear physicist—they're all handicapped by too much intelligence. The public has more confidence in the intuitive stupidity they call horse sense. I'm going to suggest we cut these three men down to five minutes apiece and balance out with a trio of good, solid businessmen."

"I don't like that," said Amelia; it was the last whimper of conscience. "It means coming down to their level."

"One way battles get lost," said martyred St. Clausewitz, "is by assuming you'll be allowed to fight them on your own terms."

"Perhaps you're right," she admitted, despising the masculine forms of expediency. "It won't be easy to find them."

"Oh, not too difficult, I shouldn't think. P. P. Cooper will do for one. This is his first cause, so he can't be dismissed as a chronic enthusiast—but he *has* been married four times, and that smacks of a share-the-wealth program. The other two will have to be as conventional and estimable as we can find."

"We only get their wives," Amelia said wistfully.

"Then we'll blackmail them through their wives." Vaughan's crippled vigor filled the room. "Do you know who would be a perfect prospect? Prominently Republican, not a blemish on his character. Roger's future father-in-law, Mr. Charles Fortescue."

PART FOUR

1

Living with women, working with women, required that a man learn to adapt himself to the emotional rhythms and inconsistencies which affected even the most intelligent. In theory Stephen Booth approved of this. In the classroom he spoke of it as one of the more revealing measurements of a civilization and pointed out that the upper-class British habit of sending women off to the drawing room by themselves while the men lingered over their port was clear evidence that that society was as adolescent as the Tchambuli or the Berber tribesmen.

At times, however, he privately suspected that the British (and the Berber tribesmen) were sensible. No matter how hard a man tried to prepare himself against a woman's vagaries, he was foredoomed to surprises; the most cunning defenses for his peace of mind would be overrun by assault from a completely unexpected quarter. In the years that Joyce Neilson had been serving as his part-time secretary, he had had ample time to learn her idiosyncrasies and how to cope with them. He never criticized her work but blamed himself whenever he found her in error. He asked each day about Mrs. Neilson's insomnia, because a particularly bad night left Joyce on the verge of hysteria—while with the turn of each new moon she was on the verge regardless. Above all he had learned that what sent her over the verge, she who claimed an uncommonly sensitive soul,

167

was any slight joggle in the routine of her drudgery. Familiar nuisances she would take in her stride, but a misplaced box of paper clips reduced her to tears. Stephen purchased tranquility by changing her typewriter ribbons himself, double checking the supply cabinet, and personally soaping the drawers of her desk so they would not stick.

Even so she outwitted him.

"I do my best, I really do, but it's simply no use," she sobbed at him as he trudged up the stairs, as soon as his head appeared above the level of the attic floor. He was not feeling at his best. He had stayed up too late the night before, squabbling with Amelia about the future of the League and drinking far too much, and this morning, as was always true when he faced them with a hangover, his students had been exceptionally trying. But he could never be humanly irritable with Joyce. It took her days to recover.

"What's the matter, Joyce?" he asked, wearily assuming the avuncular heartiness which seemed to soothe her.

Her face was mottled pink, and she had obviously been crying. "I can't go on like this," she wailed, "not if you won't even make an *effort*. Do you realize that I've been sitting here uselessly for the past two hours? Your handwriting is simply impossible!"

So it was. For the past four years his handwriting had been a standing joke between them. She had struggled with it gamely and finally come to be almost as adept as he at making it out; when he helped with a word it was usually because he remembered what he'd written and not any superiority at deciphering. Today the joke had abruptly ceased to be funny. And it appeared that instead of turning to any of the other tasks that needed attending to, as she would ordinarily have done, she had brooded over one illegible scrawl until she worked herself into a paroxysm of weeping.

"Well, well, let's see what crime I committed this time," he said jovially.

But she was not ready to let him off so easily. She had suffered, and he was to blame and must be made to appreciate her suffering. She made no effort to point out the offending scrawl; with childish petulance she covered the page with a half-sheet of carbon paper she kept for his office memos. "You'll simply have to print," she said in a rush: the speech she had been elaborating for the past hour coming out in an unbroken sentence, "it isn't so bad when it's a whole page of longhand you don't fuss with that but when you're revising you change words and then strike out the corrections and scribble something else on top it's enough to drive one mad and you'll have to print your corrections or I'll quit and this time I mean it and you'll never find anybody who'll put up with it for as long as I have."

"Now, Joyce, you wouldn't do that to me."

"You know I don't want to," she wailed, having worked herself back to the point of tears, "but you can't imagine the *strain* it is."

Although tiresomely in character this whole performance was yet subtly disconcerting: Joyce's threat to quit had come out sounding like the most recent in a long succession of such threats, yet it was nothing of the sort. Always before, this had been one of her heavy-handed forms of teasing; in her very best moods she took an arch delight in protesting that she wasn't appreciated, warning him of the difficulty he would find in replacing her—whereas in moments of agitation she would accuse him of wanting to be rid of her. Stephen was baffled. He had tried to elicit an atmosphere of comradeship for their working hours by sharing with her his opinions of whatever he was doing: she knew when he was enthusiastic about a student, she knew that his impatience with vulgarized Bushmen was excuse enough for his scribbles. He thought of reminding her of this, but something about the working of her mouth, the way her eyes were darting about without ever once meeting his, made him suspect that an effort to be reasonable could send her into hysterics. It was easier to promise to print his corrections, figuring that he could remember to keep that promise through the lunar phase, till this storm was forgotten.

After he had unriddled the illegible scrawl for her, acknowledging truthfully that nobody could have been expected to make sense of it, he stayed on at her desk for a few minutes trying to jolly her into a happier frame of mind, but she was not to be mollified. Normally she would have tittered and scolded at the description of his hung-over misfortunes. Today she sniffed. When he sensed that she was searching his words for fresh grievances, he gave up, went down the long, irregular, book-lined room to his own desk, wishing for the thousandth time that there were some hope of her getting married —but then, for a change, asking himself why (apart from selfish reasons) he wished anything so fatuous.

The reaction was human and instinctive, yet on the face of it pre-posterous. Joyce wasn't a child, filled with unguessable potential. She was a grown woman of proven inability to transcend her bad luck, highly strung and neurotic. It was all very well to think of the passing miracles that love could work, but what chance was there that somebody so maladroit at impersonal relationships would withstand all the stresses of an intimacy? Unless she were fantastically lucky in her choice of a man, finding someone with just the right blend of solidity, patience and strength, there was absolutely no chance at all. Her frantic needs for security, exacerbated beyond reason by all the wretched years, would claw any marriage to pieces, and she would end up unhappier than before. Only a hopeless sentimentalist could question that prognosis as long as most other people, infinitely more stable than Joyce, were making such sorry work of their private lives. Yet without exception, everyone encountering her reacted in just the same way: if only she could find a husband. It was a backhanded compliment, Stephen decided, to that unquenchable optimism which was so much more characteristic of *homo sapiens* than sapience.

2

Ruth Fortescue looked around her lovely, comfortable living room, which sometimes seemed the very symbol of her security, and found nothing to say. What did one say? The moment was outside her experience; she could not even be terribly sympathetic without feeling dishonest.

"It's the timing that's so unfortunate," Alison said brightly. "I feel badly about that. Of course, I shan't go out to Reno till after Vickie's wedding. I wouldn't miss that for anything."

"Oh, Alison!" The juxtaposition brought sudden tears to Ruth's eyes. After Ann's death Ruth had acted as substitute mother for Phil's child, and most especially at the time of Alison's wedding. She had coped with all the problems, she had gone with Alison to pick out a wedding gown—and without help from any Mrs. Godolphin, yet everybody agreed there had never been a lovelier bride—and she had served as hostess at the lavish reception Phil had given. Vickie had been one of Alison's bridesmaids. And now Phil was gone, too, and Alison would be at Vickie's wedding with her bags all packed for Reno. Ruth's tears, which she fought back, were of outrage as well as sentiment.

"Well, it can't be helped," Alison said, as if warding off the sympathy she wasn't going to get. "I just hope Vickie isn't too upset."

"Not Vickie," Ruth said callously, "she's too wrapped up in herself. She's just annoyed that Ben won't be at the reception. She adores dancing with him."

"Yes, I like dancing with him myself. I can scarcely remember the last time I had an opportunity."

"Alison, that's simply childish!" Ruth snapped, her impatience with her niece breaking loose. "Ben has a job that tires him out." He was assistant circulation manager for a weekly news magazine; she could never remember which, and had only the most general idea of what he did, but everyone agreed that he worked very hard and was doing phenomenally well for a man not yet thirty. "You can't expect him to go on courting you indefinitely."

"I don't—and it isn't childish, Aunt Ruth; it just sounds childish. You see these things from the outside. An attractive couple with a nice apartment, lots of friends, all the money they need . . . what can they find to be unhappy about? You're lucky, you have no idea what can go on inside a marriage like that."

"That's not from want of your telling me."

"But you never listened," Alison said. She sat with her feet tucked under her in one corner of the green sofa, a slender, black-haired, oval-faced girl, even more attractive now than when she had been married. She had lost the last of her childish softness; the beauty of her bone structure was clearer, and so (it appeared to Ruth) was the wilfulness of her spirit. "You just sat there waiting for a chance to say it would all straighten out when we had children, and for a while I believed you. Now it seems awfully, awfully lucky that we never did, because nothing would have straightened out. I doubt if it ever does, that way. Children just make it harder to break away."

"You had too much time on your hands."

"And whose fault was that? When Uncle Morris said I'd be likelier to get pregnant if I weren't working, Ben was the first to insist that I quit."

Ruth bit back the impulse to say that Ben probably hadn't needed to insist very hard. It was only at the prompting of the rest of the family that Phil had made her look for a job in the first place; he would have been content to let her go on lounging around the house all day. And then she had been hoity-toity about what she would do or wouldn't do; nothing suited her, till she ended up working as Morris's receptionist. Ruth had no doubt that her brother's advice was well-founded medically, but she knew he had been glad of the excuse to exchange Alison for someone who could be relied on to be on time in the mornings.

"Anyway," said Alison, "that free time just gave me a chance to see what the matter was and that I couldn't do anything about it however hard I tried. Ben doesn't want to be married at all."

"Rubbish," said Ruth.

"I mean it's not a wife he wants; it's a mother."

"That came as a surprise?"

"Honestly, Aunt Ruth, I'm not stupid—you mustn't keep hearing me in clichés. I don't mean the way they say that every man wants a bit of mothering. Except for half an hour two or three times a week, Ben doesn't want anything else. He has an honest-to-God mother fixation, he really does. It's no wonder Mrs. Levy goes around boasting what a wonderful son he is, since she's seen to it that he isn't much good for anything else."

"Most girls have a certain amount of difficulty with their mothers-in-law," Ruth said.

"There you go again!" said Alison. "I've never had any difficulty with Mother Levy; she's so conscientiously impartial it's funny. Any time she's around she takes my side in every other dispute. And that's Ben's ideal of womanhood. His mother doesn't have a brain in her head, so it upsets him when I have an opinion. His mother never notices when he's nasty and sarcastic. His mother was happy to wait on him hand and foot, and then called him the soul of consideration for bringing her a last-minute box of Loft's chocolates for her birthday, even though she's allergic to chocolate. His mother has persuaded him he's God's gift to the human race, so I must need a psychiatrist if I suggest ever so subtly there's room for improvement. I'm not joking, either. Last year he was all sold on my going to a psychiatrist, to straighten me out, as he put it. What he had in mind was brainwashing."

"I know, you told me at the time," Ruth said wearily. The news that Alison was alone in the apartment, that Ben had gone back to his mother's, and that both of them were talking seriously of lawyers and Reno had come over the weekend. Despite their history of discord, Ruth persisted in finding it a shock. Alison's dissatisfactions with her marriage had become a fixture, tiresome to listen to, but something that would work itself out sooner or later. Why she should have been so confident of this was hard to say. Half the people she knew had been divorced at least once, though never, as it happened, in her immediate family. She could scarcely have supposed Zimmermans miraculously immune, and in retrospect it seemed obvious that unless matters had somehow improved between Alison and Ben the marriage was bound to collapse altogether at some point. Nonetheless, it had come as a shock to all of them. She wasn't alone.

On Monday, Morris had spoken on the telephone with Ben: even *he* seemed a bit stunned by the suddenness of it all, but in no mood to talk of reconciliations. He had spoken darkly of his suspicion that Alison had fallen in love with somebody else.

There was no trace of this in Alison's discourse, but then there wouldn't have been unless she wanted to forfeit the last vestige of sympathy in Ruth. Whether in guilty self-justification or innocent self-pity, Alison confined herself to the old list of complaints against Ben, and these Ruth found quite exasperating enough. Despite Alison's constant attempts to insist that there were subtleties of cruelty, spitefulness and want of consideration in Ben's behavior which utterly eluded her, she could see only that her niece had undertaken the responsibilities of a wife and had acted the part of a spoiled child. Gert didn't agree with her; but though Gert was cleverer in a lot of ways, she'd never been married, she had a lot of romantic notions, and Alison had always been her particular pet. Gert was bound to put all the blame on Ben. Well, no doubt Ben had his defects. What man didn't? And if such a man came along, who (except Alison and Gert) would say that Alison deserved him? Both of them paid lip service to the possibility that Alison might have her drawbacks too, but these were made to seem virtually beside the point. All the stress was on Alison's deserts, and this was about as ridiculous an approach to marriage as Ruth could think of. However, it was no use trying to tell these young people that if you could just learn to relax and love your husband and concentrate on making him happy, quite enough happiness reflected back without your straining for it. They chattered about complexes and companionship, defensiveness and ego, and manic-depressive tendencies and took it for granted that you were being sanctimonious and glib.

It wasn't that Ruth believed her formula an easy one. It took time and patience and self-control to learn to relax with a husband and make the best of him, and loving him could make it just that much more difficult—and this was precisely why she found Alison's present behavior so incomprehensible. Throwing away a four year investment in a man! What could she imagine she was accomplishing? She wasn't going to find anyone more easygoing than Ben, that was for sure. She'd have all that period of adjustment to go through again, harder the second time since she'd probably have to unlearn all she'd learned with Ben, and with the knowledge hanging over her head that she already had one failure behind her.

For most of the past twenty-five years Ruth had lived her marriage without troubling to analyze what she was doing. It was only recently —with Peter and Vickie soon to leave home for good, with Charles's retirement looming ahead (although, thank God, that was still several years in the future), and perhaps with the constant buzzing of Alison's complaints—that Ruth had become self-conscious about marriage in general and especially about her own marriage. It had to be accounted a success, so she had every right to be contemptuous of far cleverer women who made a botch of what she had achieved by simple instinct; but the success seemed to be one of ever-decreasing satisfactions, and the injustice of this had set Ruth to brooding. It wasn't right that she should have worked so hard to reach a point where the years ahead appeared as a time of emptiness brightened by grandchildren, yet she could not see that she had in any way been to blame.

There had been plenty of people, years ago, to say that she was making a mistake in marrying Charles. From all directions it had been pointed out to her that he was fifteen years the older and a Gentile and that she was a fool to give up such a promising career. For the last, it was inconceivable in the Zimmerman home that she should have come out openly and said that she never wanted to touch the hateful violin again, yet that was how she had felt at the time. They would have thought her doubly a fool. She had been good, very good, well on the way to becoming first-rate; she had had everything that innate talent, a deep feeling for music, and incessant practice could give her, and she hadn't had even a flicker of the temperament. The 'promising career' had been foisted on her before she knew what was happening, and after that, all through her girlhood, it had seemed too much of a sin to throw away all those thousands of hours of practicing she had already put in. She had needed a better excuse than mere wilfulness.

As for the rest, once she had got over her surprise at his taking her so seriously, she was unaffectedly in love with Charles. His age she found an added attraction rather than otherwise; the acquired poise of so many recital halls was already making the young men of suitable years seem callow. The Jewish-Gentile side of it she simply couldn't bother about. They were neither of them in the least religious (*that* had cropped up in Peter and Vickie for some reason, perhaps as a reaction against their racial ambiguity), so there was no problem on her side; on his, she simply had to assume that he was old enough to know what he was doing. She had been a little apprehensive of the social side of his business life, but it turned out that he shunned this as much as possible, so there had been few embarrassments, or at least few that ever came to her notice.

Of course there were facets to Charles which she had never understood, but this had not seemed to her either unnatural or upsetting, unlike the girls of Alison's generation who viewed a difference of opinion about a movie or an election as the first symptom of irremediable incompatability. Alison's first disillusionment, recounted in tones of horror, had been the discovery that Ben thought John P. Marquand a bore and read science fiction on the sly. Shattered, then and there, were her hopes for a beautiful companionship.

This concept of marriage as a state where people lived in one another's mental pockets had never even occurred to Ruth; the idea rather repelled her, like sneaking a look at somebody else's correspondence. You married a person, which wasn't at all the same thing as marrying his opinions or his politics or his business life. She had tried on principle to show a proper interest in Charles's work—and had been discouraged for her pains—but she couldn't really see that the incomprehensible doings of Andean C & Z were any concern of hers, any more than the problems of the household ought to be a concern of Charles's. In matters of opinion it was instinctive with her to keep to areas where they were in accord and let the disagreements lie. What possible good did arguing ever do? She doubted if to this day Charles realized that she'd listened peacefully to all he had to say and then had gone out and voted for F.D.R. just the same. Suppose she had quarreled with him. He would have talked at her all the harder about how the country was being ruined, trying to make her understand things about economics and the like which she didn't even want to understand, and in the end it wouldn't have had the slightest effect on the fact that she *trusted* Mr. Roosevelt more than those other men, particularly Mr. Dewey who had to be photographed sitting on a New York City telephone directory. Charles would have felt thwarted and indignant, she would have felt ignorant and indignant, and how could any of that possibly make them more companionable?

She understood Charles quite well enough as a man, as a human being. She had learned his nature, mood by mood; she had studied his likes and dislikes; she knew what he wanted of his home life and for the most part she knew how to give it to him. He was not an easy man to satisfy. He had grown set in many of his ways before she married him. In a sense this made things easier—Ruth could not imagine how you went about adapting yourself to a man who didn't really know his own mind—but it also meant he had become fixed in the patterns of a private individual. He yearned for domesticity, yes, but not as something to which he surrendered himself: he expected the warmths and the comforts to be waiting when he wanted them but could see no reward in the concomitant exasperations. Well, it was a point of view, though she couldn't understand it. She felt he was missing a great deal, would have been happier if he could have treated their family life as a focus instead of as a peripheral retreat, but Charles wasn't like that at all, and perhaps few men were.

She knew by heart his preferences and prejudices, his quirks and crochets; on the whole they agreed about the people they knew, and they had learned to understand one another's responses to whatever they did together. It was mainly in the realm of ideas that she lost him, and this had never bothered her. She took it for granted that he was more intelligent than she (although no exception to her observation that intelligence was not necessarily very sensible) and found that a comfort. What seemed to her important was that in the past twenty years she and Charles had never once had a quarrel which could properly be called a quarrel, in contrast to most of the married couples she could think of.

Surely—when you assumed the endurance of their love, shaken down to the jog trot of familiar affection but still very much alive —surely this had to be considered a success.

Yet several years back, that first winter when *both* Peter and Vickie had been away at school and she had suddenly found time lying so heavily on her hands, she had been obliged to wonder what that success really added up to. She had had periods of feeling that the more you put into a marriage, the less you could expect to get out of it. In a sense it was true. The better you brought up your children, the less need they had of you as they grew older. The better you ran your home, the less it demanded of you. The happier you made your husband, the less real contact you had with him.

For the first time she had begun to think of the future in her own terms—instead, as she had been wont, by juvenile landmarks: when Peter graduates from Hotchkiss, when Vickie stops wearing those horrid braces—and was fearful of what she saw ahead. The children would leave home altogether and would belong primarily to other people. They would still love her, of course, but her relations with them would become self-conscious: she would have to learn to guard against making a nuisance of herself. No doubt she and Charles would move to a much smaller, even less demanding, apartment. And most frightening of all was the prospect of Charles's retirement.

Probably she was exaggerating. There was every reason to suppose that he would remain on the Board of Directors, and what with that and one thing and another he would have his own methods of keeping busy. There was no real justification for the picture that came to her mind: of the two of them sitting idly across from one another in a small and cluttered living room with nothing whatsoever to say. It was quite silly, they were neither of them like that, yet the fact that the picture haunted her meant something. Charles had always been *so* busy, and the higher he went the busier he became. Trips to South America, conferences here and conventions there, banquets and functions and what he called 'maneuvers around the martinis'—and with so much on his mind she could hardly begrudge him his photography. For stretches it was a rare week when he was home more than two or three evenings, a rare month when he wasn't away a weekend or two. And when he was home, he so obviously wanted only to relax.

At one point some years ago she had briefly wondered whether a part of all this activity might really be an excuse for seeing some other woman, and almost the worst of the humiliation (before she put the idea out of her mind forever) was the thought that another woman was hearing and enjoying a side of Charles that was closed to her. She knew he was impatient with her indifference to so many ideas that interested him. At home this scarcely mattered, because they had so much shared immediacy. But when they were thrown on their own resources, when they were off together on one of Charles's vacations with the household concerns forgotten and the children become remote, when, for example, they were trapped by a three day downpour in that little hotel in Copenhagen with no other guest who spoke English but an alcoholic and anti-Semitic British spinster, it became glaringly apparent that they really had little in common but a span of domesticity. Charles's retirement was that hotel bedroom in Copenhagen perpetuated indefinitely, the smell of stale cigar smoke, rain trickling down the windowpanes, Charles lying grumpily on one of the beds reading Penguin after Penguin, herself sitting at the little wooden desk filling sheets of tissue stationery with simulated vivacity.

The discovery that time could lie drearily on her hands had sent her scurrying for outside interests. Now it was far, far too late for second thoughts about the violin. There was a disadvantage in once having been very good: her ear had altered; she quailed physically at the sounds produced by the mediocre professional. Knowing the mountains of labor before she regained even a fraction of her former proficiency, the further mountains before she began to take any pleasure in what she was doing had simply been too discouraging—and she lamented her father's lifelong contempt for that bastard instrument, the piano.

A winter's art lessons had taught her that there was some irreparable failure in the circuit between her eyes and her hands. She had gone to a series of lectures on current events and a series of luncheons where you met people who had just published a book. She had dabbled at needlepoint and ceramics and japanning boxes and had driven Gert to a frenzy by an ill-advised attempt to learn bridge. On the theory that when Charles retired they would do a lot of traveling, she had brought home a couple of albums of phonograph records which were supposed to teach her French and Italian; but sitting in an empty room repeating after the dulcet-voiced man *"Buon giorno, vorrei cambiare venti dollari"* had quickly come to seem an unrewarding pastime, and until the day when Charles might be induced to study with her (assuming he altered his opinion that people everywhere spoke enough English for his purposes), the albums had been retired to the closet that housed the paraphernalia of so many abandoned hobbies. The only lasting enthusiasm she had found—one that shamed her by its futility—was for jigsaw puzzles. Whenever she saw three or four lonely evenings ahead, she would shield the dinner table with a great square of black felt (left over from an essay at making golliwogs) and tumble out the six-hundred-odd pieces of one of her favorites.

Ruth had come to conclude that this diminishing of her satisfactions was nobody's fault, was simply one of the dirty jokes that life played on you as you got older. You were used to the extent of your capacities, and just about the time you began to look around for some reward you were relegated to the scrap heap—exactly the way that in a few years, Charles, knowing more about the operation of Andean C & Z than any man alive, would be obliged by company policy to retire. That was the way it went, evidently, for women just as for men; and though she didn't *feel* so very much older than the day she was married (and in truth she was only forty-six), she had to get accustomed to the idea that the best of life was behind her. Whatever gratifications might lie ahead, she was sadly positive, would be trivial compared to marriage in its most active phase. Hectic, maddening, often seeming more than she could possibly cope with —learning every single little thing from scratch, since she'd been too busy being a prodigy ever to boil an egg—and Charles had times of being so incomprehensible—and then Peter coming, and Vickie, adding new dimensions to the confusion. She could remember the times of sitting down and crying from exhausted bewilderment. Yet never had she been so happy, never would she be so happy again. Then she was complete. She was doing exactly what she wanted to do, what she had always felt herself designed to do (let other women play at careers!), and she was doing it creatively: the contentment of her children and her husband, the feeling that existed within their home, was in no small measure of her manufacture; and she knew it. She could imagine no greater satisfaction. And this was why she felt so much pity for women, like poor Gert, who teased themselves with delusions of self-sufficiency, and so much impatience with a girl like Alison, who seemed bent on destroying her happiness for the sake of words like ego and compatibility and pride. It was the opportunities for spending yourself to the utmost that made you happiest, as you found out fast enough when nothing more was asked of you than your small change.

"There's one thing you may be sure of," Alison said, tossing her head. "I shan't be in any hurry to get married again."

"Don't be a fool," Ruth said angrily, angry with herself, with Alison, with the essential unfairness of life. "You've not yet been married at all."

3

Owen closed the street door silently behind him, stood for a moment on the little stoop, four brownstone steps above the level of the sidewalk. It was a lovely night, crisp and invigorating, without a trace of that intolerable humidity which in another month would turn New York into a subtropical city. He would have to think about giving Carol an air conditioner, for the bedroom at least. Was it a sign of age to be so conscious of the seasons? As a young man, living not far from here, he had slept through summer nights in a pool of his own sweat and wakened none the less refreshed. Now it would make a wreck of him.

Midnight was gone; the street appeared deserted except for the two lines of grimy, parked automobiles. As his senses adjusted, however, he realized that this appearance was deceptive. Someone was smoking a pipe in a doorway farther down. The faint clank of a garbage lid betrayed the presence of one of the night's scavengers at work in one of the shadowed areaways. A rustle became a tattoo, resolved itself into the brisk clicking of high heels long before the girl emerged into the puddle of lamplight to Owen's left. She looked up at him incuriously and passed on. Seventeen or thereabouts, vividly pretty in a black-haired, olive Puerto Rican style. She was so precisely the type he had in mind for his play that he was tempted to hurry after her, ask for her name. Foolish—she or another like her would not be hard to find when the time came. The town was full of them these days. He might be the making of a new star.

His mood was one of optimism. This pause was not from languor, but from sheer well-being: he felt stimulated, satisfied, unhurried, at peace with the night. There was work ahead, but his main problem was solved and first he had to digest the implications of his moment of insight.

Often it happened this way, sometimes to his embarrassment. Legend had it—and in matters of this sort he had nothing to go on but legend—that most men were enervated by sex, tending to flop right over and go to sleep. Not he. He was refreshed, animated, the tensions drained away. And when he was working, he was quite likely to revive from the little death, his mind bubbling over with ideas. Once in a while he would find that some work problem which had been nagging at him for days had somehow resolved itself, without any conscious effort on his part. It was a remarkable sensation, the closest he had ever come to that phenomenon which so fascinated the layman and amused the professional: inspiration. He would be lying there scarcely alive, suspended, a mere spark of sentience in the formless void. Then sluggishly, reluctantly, his mind would stir. The obsessive problem, whatever it might be, always poised to intrude itself whenever his mental defenses were down, would rush in upon him —and it wasn't a problem any longer! The solution was so obvious, and the solution, once recognized and appreciated, brought in its train a wealth of new and vital possibilities. Yes, if he did this, it would take care of that; he could drop the entire scene with the old lady which had never satisfied him, he could. . . .

And thus at the time of purest communion, as cramped limbs were straightening and disentangling, when a man might be expected to murmur an endearment or two, Owen was likely to say, "You know that muddle at the end of the second act? I think I've cracked it!" His mind was effervescent with the new inspiration, and his instinct was to talk about it.

Almost painfully he had learned to curb that instinct. He had tried to promote the idea that it was only natural that a rite which might create new life within a woman should also evoke the creativity in a man, but he had met with surprisingly little sympathy. Instead of basking in the implicit compliment, women complained of a certain lack of delicacy and romantic feeling. They were prepared to be an inspiration to him, but not in quite that way. At such moments his attention should be on them, and not on his plays.

Carol knew him far too well to be offended, of course; at one time she had been resigned to his bad manners. But in the intervening years he had acquired self-control—and this time, in any case, he didn't want to talk about his ideas. Don't move, he had murmured, and for a while longer they lay there peacefully. By the time they stirred, reached for cigarettes, began to talk about themselves, he had known it was all right.

His problem had been essentially technical: one of the age-old problems which arose in telling a tale entirely in terms of dialogue. Melmoth could hardly have been out of the apartment building that afternoon before Owen had scented the most dramatic way to handle the Charles Fortescue story: as a tragic situation that repeated itself a generation later, a new and slightly more melodramatic version of Maugham's *The Circle*. His pivotal character would be Charles, of course; in the play to be called by another name, but Owen couldn't help thinking of him as Charles. A Charles grown arrogant and conventional with success, a Charles as far removed as possible from the tormented, shaken adolescent who had so mangled that suicide pact. All his adult life he had been running from that suppressed, forgotten tragedy. The more successful he became, the more respectable, the better he justified his survival. Yet in his flight he had outrun all touch and sympathy with his own son, and now the lad had lost his idiot sixteen-year-old heart to a Puerto Rican girl—like the one who had just walked by.

There was the basic situation as Owen had conceived it. Yet obviously, for this situation to emerge on stage, there had to be another character besides Charles who knew of that ancient tragedy. And not an intrusive outsider like Louis Melmoth—he would have to be replaced by somebody in the family circle. But who? Not a doddering parent, certainly. In theory Charles might have a brother or sister, yet that abortive suicide pact, or whatever it had been, seemed peculiarly the action of an only child. Might Charles have once, in a moment of weakness, confided the story to his wife, to a close friend? Awkward and unconvincing.

In the meantime fragments of scenes had come crowding in upon him. Introductory scenes with still-shadowy minor characters establishing Charles's personality, scenes between Charles and the boy, the boy and the girl. Nothing to be done with them, however, beyond an occasional jotted note, for Owen knew that the whole tenor of the play would be altered by the solution, when it appeared, to his one basic dilemma.

How right he had been. And what a nasty problem. And how ridiculously easy the solution.

He came down the steps, turning his attention to the matter of getting home: gone were the days when you walked to the nearest corner and looked for a cab going in your direction. Eighth Avenue was closest, but not rich in taxis down here at this hour, as he remembered. Seventh Avenue, by courtesy of a government which could beneficially be replaced by the most inefficient of city managers, was one-way in the wrong direction. So it would have to be Sixth: you caught there the cabs returning from a late fare to Brooklyn. Thank heavens it was a pleasant night.

He went left, walking with easy, lounging strides, glad of the excuse for a little exercise. Uptown he detested walking. After a few indistinguishable blocks of anonymous grey apartment buildings he began to fear for his own identity. He was nowhere, obviously, and that tended to make him feel like nobody. Better to be transported as rapidly as possible from portal to portal; in between was a futuristic cemetery, all grass dispensed with.

For all its faults, the Village was a *place*. Not the place it had been in the Twenties, to be sure, but he had no memory of that. A place even more tawdry, what with sidewalk displays of paintings and homemade jewelry brought in by the truckload from Weehawken and points west and sold to the unwary tourists as samples of local manufacture. It was the natural habitat of the art phony and the art bum, the beatnik and the transvestite, as well as all the people, talented or not, who simply like the neighborhood of old houses and unexpected streets. And all of them added something to the character of the place, even the phoniest. There was still a vigor and a ferment here—and the fact that most of it was unproductive or even downright warped mattered less than that it was there. Uptown there was quite as much phoniness, but the dreary, flatulent sort that was measured by status symbols. Down here the competition was much keener: they measured by dreams.

Owen felt all this, yet he had no desire to return. His friends were mostly uptown; his life was there. He enjoyed the space and comfort and quiet of his apartment; actually less expensive than anything of the sort he could find down here. There were still the cheap little Village apartments to be had, if you hunted, but good places had been pushed sky high by the art bums. At this stage of his career for him to be living in the Village would have been something of an affectation.

Only on a chance evening like this, strolling through the quiet familiar streets in a mood of creative exaltation, as had happened so frequently and fruitlessly in earlier days, did he feel a surge of nostalgia for this locale of his young ambition and sense that his transition uptown had marked a turn, perhaps a decline, in his own vitality. Doubtless both feelings were equally perverse and illogical, a part of his masochistic probing for the day when he would finally have to acknowledge middle age. Or possibly it was just that any man walking in footsteps twenty years old was bound to notice, however far he had come, how far short he had fallen of his youthful dreams.

A quartet of young people, three men and a girl, overtook him and swept on, their harsh young voices clattering in the quiet street.

"Well, I'm tired of listening to her run on about Martha Graham."

"But to ask if she remembered Isadora. . . ."

"Do you suppose one day we'll talk of this as a golden age?"

Meaningless, juvenile. But uptown it might have been two men under a street lamp, their voices blurred by alcohol, agreeing that Bridges had made a mess of the Murphy account and it was a bleeding outrage that he should have been the one sent to Pittsburgh. There it was. With the two men he would forever be an alien; they might as well have jabbered in Hungarian. Whereas with the young dancers just vanishing around the corner, he had something in common. He would like them no better as people, probably less: nothing was so tedious as a roomful of dancers. But at least they talked a language he understood.

Seventh Avenue was quiet; he crossed without waiting for the lights to change, thinking it fitting and even auspicious that Michael had been conceived of in the Village. It was Michael who had come to him, full grown, Minervalike, in the silent semidark of Carol's bedroom, and Michael was a spiritual Villager, a native product.

There was one situation intrinsically even lonelier, unhappier, than that of an only child, however neglected. To be a child untidily left over from a previous, unfortunate marriage. To be the child of a selfish and heedless mother who rather resented being reminded of her first husband, who was wholly absorbed by her new husband and her new son. This was how Owen now saw the early background of his Charles. As a boy rejected, watching all the attention and affection he needed being lavished upon an envied and detested younger half brother—Michael. Being sent away early to boarding schools because that detestation showed itself too clearly. There were the origins of that long-ago adolescent tragedy.

And in the years since? Charles the contemptible, the disinherited, has grown ever more successful, prosperous and respectable. While the spoiled and charming Michael has become disreputable. Just which form of disreputability still remained to be determined. A bearded, beatnik artist, a bullfight tramp, a foreign correspondent, a drifter with a weakness for the odd corners of the world? Something of the sort. How I Buggered My Way Through Saudi Arabia—but that would have to be cleaned up for the matinée audiences. Well, the exact details would come later. But the point was that this established black sheep would turn up in New York periodically, sardonic, witty and flat broke; willing to put up with Charles's condescension and moral strictures in exchange for a loan to tide him over.

Anyway, whatever Michael's vocation or avocation, it was to this deplorable demiuncle that the boy, Charles's son, would turn for sympathy with his own ill-starred young love. And would find it, of course. This would have to be handled very carefully, or it would just be another story where smug respectability was the villain of the piece while the raffish outcast proved to have a heart of gold. No, no. Michael's sympathy could in part be genuine, a worldly impatience with provincial racialism. But it would also be cynical, frivolous, petty—a chance to strike back at Charles for all the holier-than-thou years. His sympathy would take a practical form that the boy could not have imagined: a callous dragging-up of Charles's long-buried tragedy.

CHARLES (outraged) *This was never to be mentioned!*

MICHAEL *Not even when you see your son following in your footsteps?*

Then would come the big scene between the half brothers. And a fragment of the conversation Owen had had with Melmoth could go onstage virtually unchanged. Right at the beginning, when the audience was just beginning to understand what was being disclosed.

CHARLES *I was sixteen and a fool. And I lost my nerve.*

MICHAEL *You lost your nerve, all right. That was about the only fact that was never in dispute.*

CHARLES *What the devil does that mean?*

MICHAEL *When you went out that afternoon, you intended suicide, agreed. You left a note for your roommate to find. But the girl didn't leave a note, did she?*

That should set the scene rolling. Charles protesting that Michael had just been an offensive little brat at the time and couldn't know what he was talking about; Michael proving that Charles's self-protective memory was at fault. Flashes of the childhood animosities and resentments revived. Just a hint that Michael had longed for the comradeship of his older brother and had been distrustfully rebuffed.

Yet it would be this well-intentioned, or partially well-intentioned, intervention from Michael that destroyed the last channels of communication between Charles and his son. From that moment on Charles would be consumed by this new outrage. His son had betrayed him by turning for comfort to this detested half brother who had spoiled his childhood, malshaped his whole life. His son had provided Michael the excuse for taunting him with the humiliation of his own adolescence. And in this mood of blind, resentful self-pity Charles would drive his son to . . . what? Repeating the tragedy? Very likely, but after a certain point this was what the audience would be expecting; and if it could be done without too great an anticlimax, it might be effective to outwit them. Michael might discover the boy late at night with one hand in a drawer of his father's desk—it having been established earlier that there was a revolver there. The pattern was repeating. But no, not at all. It was only the knowledge of Charles's early morbidity that had filled the atmosphere with suicide. The boy jeers coldly at the idea. His generation is tougher than that. He's never considered anything more drastic than running off with his girl and was looking to pinch some ready cash. The revolver is for his father, when he becomes lonely enough and learns that his grandchildren have been taught to think of him as already dead. And the boy accepts whatever money Michael has on him and goes off. . . .

Well, that was a possibility to keep in mind.

But the more natural ending was the discovery that the boy had gone out—leaving a note for his father. The housekeeper would bring it in, interrupting a quarrel between the half brothers. Charles reads the note; turns very slowly to look at the desk. The drawer stands open. He sinks into a chair. Michael takes the note from him.

CHARLES (dully) *We'll have to find them.*

MICHAEL *In this city? Don't be a fool.*

CHARLES *The police?*

MICHAEL *Do you even know the girl's name?*

CHARLES *Of course. Carmen, Carmen . . .* (He gropes helplessly for the remainder).

MICHAEL (savagely) *A girl named Carmen!*

CHARLES *What can we do?*

MICHAEL *We'll wait. We'll sit here and wait, Charles. Until somebody comes to tell us whether your son has turned out to be more of a man than you were. And you'd better start deciding which way you want it to be.*

(Curtain)

Yes, something on that order was much more probable. But he would have to wait to see how the body of the play developed. In thumbnail synopsis the story seemed on the melodramatic side, but this would thin down when stretched over a couple of hours, and everything would depend on how he handled it. Particularly how he treated the characters of the two half brothers. Michael was a natural for providing a constant strain of comic relief. Urbane, witty, self-mocking, something of a conscious comedian. Even in the more dramatic moments unable to resist a good wisecrack. An emotional lightweight, incapable of imagining the harm he was doing.

While Charles, apart from his obsessive ambition and his relationship with his son, should be as sympathetic a figure as possible. That wouldn't be so easy, but it could be done. It might be wise to weight the scales a little; have the boy given to some fuzzy, impractical idealism which would be bound to exasperate his father. So that Charles, a charming and highly intelligent man in his own way, could be shown as disappointed in a son who hadn't quite measured up to expectations. A fundamentally well-intentioned man, but impatient, self-absorbed and unimaginative. . . .

Gradually, it seemed, he was working his way back to the proto-type, the real Charles Fortescue (already growing more insubstantial in Owen's mind than the creature of his invention). Fundamentally well-intentioned, but impatient, self-absorbed and unimaginative—that description applied well enough to Fortescue. To be sure, Fortescue got along agreeably with his children without seeming especially interested in them, and his craving for success and status had

186

never become obsessive. On the surface he was less flamboyantly haunted by his old tragedy than his theatrical counterpart would be. Nevertheless, there was evidence of haunting. It couldn't just be a coincidence, that one unconventional action of his adult life, the taking of a Jewish wife; not when you remembered that Sophie Melmoth had been Jewish.

From the quiet and gloom of Christopher Street Owen emerged onto Sixth Avenue, bright with the neon of all-night coffee stalls. This was one of the corners of the city catering to people with topsy-turvy lives, who might need a full luncheon at three in the morning. Several of the places were almost full. Through one of the great plate-glass windows, he watched a burly character, cap pushed back on his head, wolfing at a plate of pale yellow fried potatoes. The sight made Owen realize that he was hungry. But food at this hour of the night left him dull and sleepy, and he wanted to get these first inchoate impressions down on paper for tomorrow's cooler, more critical consideration. With a sense of virtue he turned away. There was a north-bound cab paused at the red light, and Owen hurried across the street to catch it.

4

Amelia's headaches were not physical in cause, that much was certain. In time they would probably yield to Dr. Eckhardt's investigations of her childhood at forty dollars an hour. Meanwhile she had to get by with pills that did very little good, compresses that did none at all, and try to avoid periods of stress and anxiety. A headache could arrive at any time, completely out of the blue, but they came most often when she was upset. The moral was obvious. Doing something about it was another matter.

At the moment, quite apart from the worry the League was giving, she was deviled by the activity of Ruth Fortescue. Ruth was helpfully rushing about looking for an apartment for Roger and Vickie. So far she had found three, all within convenient walking distance of the Fortescues' on Sutton Place South. Ruth might lay claims to the best of intentions, might swear that she wouldn't dream of inflicting herself on the young people, but she wasn't to be trusted. She was a woman with no interests apart from her family, with an itch to be useful, and there was no stopping someone like that. She would be underfoot a dozen times a day, and that was no way to start off a marriage. Fortunately, all three places had been well beyond Roger's means. But Amelia lived in dread that Ruth might yet stumble on something unexceptionable before she herself could locate a truly suitable apartment at the far end of town—down near Jefferson Mews, for example.

And as if these troubles were not enough, for the past fortnight she had had hanging over her head the ordeal of meeting her mother at the ship. This was a duty which always devolved upon her—Doug was busy and Joan, thoroughly intimidated by her mother-in-law, either made excuses or got drunk—and Amelia hated it. At best it was a ghastly way to meet somebody: the huge, drafty, echoing dock littered with baggage and people, and L-for-Langstaff right in the heart of the turmoil. But her mother's arrivals were also exercises in humiliation for Amelia, against which the years had brought no defense. Mrs. Langstaff was a model of everything her daughter disapproved of. She was arrogant and ignorant, prejudiced, credulous, snobbish, opinionated and almost invariably in the wrong. Yet she still maintained, would maintain till her dying day, the moral whip of parental ascendancy. It took her half a minute to reduce Amelia to the status of a defensive twelve-year-old, quivering with impotent frustration. And she did it every time.

Headaches, therefore, had recently been frequent, and between two of them Amelia had welcomed Guy Abercrombie's offer to accompany her to the ship. Guy was a bore, but he had a car and chauffeur at his disposal, and for this a great deal could be forgiven him. She had known him all her life. He was the son of her father's closest friend, and for a while, till Owen came along, they had been informally engaged. Guy was a portly bachelor now, overrich and underoccupied, but a man of sentimental loyalty. Each year he reappeared at Mrs. Langstaff's parties and played with Amelia a ponderous game of pretending that they had been meant for one another, intended lovers parted by a capricious fate.

This tedium was a small price for being picked up at her door, carried smoothly across town with someone who might serve as a buffer against her mother. Less tolerable was another characteristic of Guy's, which Amelia forgot between encounters.

"I saw Sheila and Rodney the other evening," he remarked as they were starting up the ramp to the West Side Drive. He always brought her up to date on the people she had left far behind her.

"How are they?" she asked idly.

"Sheila's as mad as ever. Rodney is looking very fit, considering."

"Has he been sick?"

"I thought you would have heard. He had a slight coronary at Christmas." Long acquaintance with Guy was needed to recognize the undertone of complacency in this remark. There was a ghoulish side to Guy's loyalty: he might feast upon friendship, but he battened on the friends he outlived. He was the sort who went back to every school and college reunion, not merely to blow on the ashes of adolescent fellowship but to draw a sense of superiority from the thinning of the ranks.

As a rule, when Guy spoke of acquaintances she had known but slightly, Amelia could overlook this failing. But Rodney was different and she felt slightly sick; Rodney was a minor but unforgettable part of her own past. It was he, lean, dark, saturnine, more enterprising than Guy and less loyal, who had put an end to her virginal curiosities one night in the back seat of his father's Lincoln. Now he had had a slight coronary at Christmastime: that once vital, hard-muscled body was marked down for the scrap heap. Friends of her maturity had dropped dead, but the shock had somehow been less personally threatening than this. Those were acts of God. This was the word that she had reached an age where her true contemporaries, the friends of her childhood, were beginning to crumble.

To keep the headache at bay, she rejected the news outright, eschewing even the most perfunctory expression of regret. "I hope to God that Mother was at a dull table this time," she said at random. "The last crossing she had the Norwegian Ambassador at her left and spent the next six weeks being an authority on international affairs."

"She's a remarkable woman," Guy said fondly. "I just hope I have half that much energy when I'm her age."

Guy had obtained dock passes; they found Mrs. Langstaff already ensconced among her luggage, browbeating the customs official. "Don't argue with me, my good man. I bought that at Georg Jensen's three years ago (Hello, Amelia. Guy, how very sweet!), and I assume the price I paid included the duty." Few people, these days, would have tried to browbeat customs officials, but Mrs. Langstaff, who combined an indomitable will with an appearance of extreme fragility, divided the world into personal friends and servants and generally got away with it. The performance invariably unsettled Amelia: she envied the success of it and despised the fraudulence.

Mrs. Langstaff was obviously a born patrician; to look at her was to know that she had been issuing orders all her life—and to know this was to be quite mistaken. Her father had run the poor man's undertaking parlor in Schenectady, and that was the background from which she had escaped as soon as she was old enough. A few years later Mr. Langstaff discovered her dancing in the chorus line of something called 'The Madcaps of 1909.' Probably he had not been looking for a wife there, exactly, but those were the days when a girl could dream of graduating from the chorus line to the Social Register, and Amelia's mother must have been one of the more efficient dreamers. Yet she was not a gold digger in any ordinary sense of the term; there was reason to believe that all along she had deluded herself with the theory that she had been the victim of one of those maternity hospital mix-ups, switching her from her true upper-crust family to a home of what she later called upstate professional people. Her marriage was no leap upward, but just a return to her natural environment. She had always looked the part, and it had taken her no time to pick up the polish; practically from the start she had been twice as aristocratic as any of the young ladies Mr. Langstaff ought to have married.

"How was the crossing?" Guy inquired solicitously.

"Detestable," said Mrs. Langstaff.

"Wasn't the service good?"

"Excellent," she replied. "But it has reached the point where the stewards are better bred than the passengers. Another such trip and I shall be reconciled to socialism. That package is the Rosenthal piece listed in my declaration, and I won't have it pawed open unless you're prepared to wrap it up again just as neatly."

In Mrs. Langstaff's presence Amelia felt a flaw in her detestation of snobbery: she wished that she could disapprove of her mother solely on highminded principle, without forever being reminded of the undertaker's daughter.

"Guy," said Mrs. Langstaff commandingly, "go and see if you can help poor Vanessa. They've mislaid half her luggage just when she's in a particular rush to be out of here; Dodie's boy is in the hospital, you know." But that this was to some extent a manufactured errand became apparent the instant he was out of earshot, when she turned a forbidding glance on Amelia. "What is this I hear about Roger's fiancée being half Jewish?" she asked.

"Oh, God!" said Amelia. Prayers were never attended to.

"It's true, then," Mrs. Langstaff said, nodding. "I assumed it must be. Don't you think you or Douglas might have warned me?"

"There was nothing to *warn* you about," Amelia said as witheringly as possible.

"Wasn't there? It doesn't seem the sort of news that should reach me from the lips of a virtual stranger." There was always a virtual stranger. Mrs. Langstaff talked to everyone she met and straightaway set about determining whom they knew in common, with the result that she had a better international spy system than the government. When Douglas had been admitted to full partnership in his firm, she had been on a cruise, completely out of touch, yet a week later a congratulatory cable arrived from Athens. This time it had been a busybody in Monte Carlo whose husband was on the Board of Andean C & Z.

"Vickie is a perfectly nice girl in every way," Amelia said.

"Then I see no reason to have concealed her antecedents as though you were ashamed of them. It's the dishonesty that offends me," said Mrs. Langstaff, turning to the customs official to claim as a family heirloom a set of silver-backed brushes Amelia had never seen before. "As you should know by now," she resumed, "my prejudices are entirely practical. For some reason it offends you when I say that some of my best friends are Jewish; I can't think why, since it's perfectly true. They can be admirable people. But to marry one means a lifetime of small embarrassments. I'm afraid that you've fallen down on your responsibilities."

"At one time or another I've pushed Roger out with the granddaughter of every friend you have. It's not my fault if he found them an unprepossessing lot."

"There's no shortage of eligible girls in New York," said Mrs. Langstaff. "Part of the trouble is that neighborhood you live in."

"I wrote you that Vickie is the sister of Roger's roommate at Princeton," Amelia retorted. "What neighborhood is a safeguard against that sort of thing?"

"I've had my reservations about Princeton for some time," said Mrs. Langstaff. "It's not the place it was in your father's time. Why are you looking like that?"

"I have a headache," said Amelia.

"You don't get enough fresh air," said her mother unfeelingly. "Keep an eye on these things, will you, while I try to make these people see sense." She went off, accentuating her appearance of frailty by leaning heavily on her wholly unnecessary cane. When she returned, she was in a better humor. "Well, there's no use crying over spilt milk," she said, as though Amelia were the one in need of this homely wisdom. "All the way across I've been thinking about the best way to put a good face on it. I shall have to give a large party right away."

"You always do," said Amelia. Her mother never stayed for very long and found it expedient to begin her visits by having all her friends indebted to her at the start. Thereafter if a day passed without at least two engagements, she complained of neglect.

"See if you can tidy up some of the disorder that creature left in his wake," Mrs. Langstaff ordered, and obediently Amelia crouched over the open suitcases. The blood rushed to her head. It was through a haze of pain that she tried to smooth away the evidence of a hasty ransacking. Above her, her mother's harsh, clipped voice committed fresh outrages. "Most parties aren't such a strain as this one will be," she said. "I suppose the mother is quite presentable by now?"

"She's better mannered than half the people you'll invite," Amelia snapped, bristling in defense of her enemy.

"What is vulgarity in a Jew is eccentricity in a Gentile," Mrs. Langstaff said, "and we won't be able to alter the world by the end of next week. One or another of us will have to stay in the vicinity to change the conversation whenever it becomes dangerous."

"Why don't you invite some of those Jewish best friends you are always talking about?" Amelia asked. "If there are enough of them there, people will have to guard their tongues."

"I had thought of that, naturally," said Mrs. Langstaff, who recognized no sarcasms but her own.

Amelia snapped the suitcases shut regardless and stood up dizzily. In the distance they saw Guy Abercrombie returning, too late to be of the slightest assistance.

"I can't help remarking," said Mrs. Langstaff, "that none of this would have happened if you had married Guy."

"The one thing nobody tells a girl is how very little difference it makes which man she marries," Amelia said. "Three years later all she has left is a husband."

"Your mistake was in choosing sensitive men," said Mrs. Langstaff. "They are the sort that can't be managed. Now, Guy would never even have noticed."

"I don't recall your warning me that sensitivity was an affliction."

"Of course I did," said her mother. "But you knew better."

"I had no idea Dodie's lad was so ill," Guy said, rejoining them. "Vanessa tells me there is very little hope." His tone was sorrowful, but his stance was jaunty; nothing raised his spirits like the funeral of somebody much younger than he.

"Perhaps we were both wrong," Amelia moaned, and gave up the unequal struggle with her headache. In the end, she who had come to be helpful had to be assisted, blind with misery, back to the limousine.

5

Mrs. Langstaff's arrival was touched on when Charles and Owen met again for luncheon the next day, the third such luncheon in as many weeks. Charles had got the impression that Owen was rather lonely for anything that could be regarded as a family relationship.

"What is the old lady like, really?" he inquired. "Vickie has been taught to think of her as a dragon."

"At close range, Mrs. Langstaff is one of the world's menaces," Owen replied. "At a safe distance, and at long intervals, she can be quite entertaining."

"Oh? Well, I gather she's abroad most of the time."

"That's no guarantee of safety," Owen said. "She has a flair for ubiquity. The last time I was in London—and only for a week, mind you—I ran into her twice."

"It must be nice to get over to London whenever you like," Charles said wistfully.

"When I'm there it's generally for business."

"Yes, maybe. But it's marvelous what can be counted as business."

"Now that is just one crack too many!" Owen said with sudden annoyance.

"I didn't mean anything by it."

"It's the twentieth time you've implied that an author's life is one long romp. Apparently I'm going to have to hammer it into you that compared with us you businessmen are the ones who have an easy time of it." There was an interruption as their food arrived. As always, Henri bustled over to supervise, with his air of suggesting that nobody else on earth was competent to transfer a chop from the chafing dish to a plate. By the time they were left in peace again, most of Owen's heat had evaporated. "As a rule I don't care what people think," he said. "If they like to imagine a writer's life as glamorous, let them. But you're going to be a member of the family, so to speak, and inside the family an attitude like that can become damn tiresome after a while."

"Look, I don't doubt that you put in a great deal of hard work,"

Charles interjected hastily, perturbed to find that Owen was taking this more seriously, more defensively, than he had intended. "I'm sure you do. But don't exaggerate. Think of being able to work exactly when you feel like it!"

"Everyman's notion of freedom," Owen mumbled mockingly through a mouthful.

"Well, it would be freedom to the rest of us," Charles insisted. "You can't even dream what it's like to drag yourself down to an office morning after morning, regardless of how you feel or what the weather is like or what you'd rather be doing. And mind you, I love my work, just as presumably you love yours. But pulling myself out of bed on a sleety January morning, with a hangover or a cold coming on, and a day full of niggling decisions ahead—you don't know how lucky you are."

"The schoolboy view of his classroom," Owen remarked. For a moment he ate in silence. "All right, I'll carry your argument a step further for you. It would be fair to say that there's virtually no drudgery to what I do. As long as I can hire a girl to do my typing and a little correspondence, there's no mechanical routine for me. How does that sound?"

"Sheer bliss," said Charles. "And no dealing with people whose temperaments don't quite blend."

Owen's roar of laughter startled a nearby matinée goer into choking on her cocktail. "Never say that to a playwright. There are animated temperaments known as directors, producers, set designers, agents and, above all, actors."

"Sorry," Charles said, feeling that his ignorance was being imposed on. Surely when a playwright had finished a play, he went on vacation and let those people struggle with the problems of putting it on the stage.

"No, it's enough for your purposes that there's no routine to what I do, and I can work when I choose," Owen said. "According to you those should make for sheer bliss. Now let's look at the other side of those glories—remembering that I'm every bit as human as you, just as prone to hangovers, colds, spring fever, fits of indolence."

"I suppose it must take a fair amount of self-discipline," Charles conceded.

"You haven't even begun supposing," Owen replied. "I shan't labor the degree of self-discipline needed to keep my nose to the grindstone when there's nobody to give a damn if I read the paper instead. You could perfectly properly reply that if I'd not been capable of that I shouldn't have become a writer. And I shan't labor the equally obvious point that if I'm to get any work done, I have to 'choose' to work as methodically as anybody in an office, so that my glorious freedom reduces to the privilege of fixing my own hours. But it's worth noting that when *you* take a day off the company doesn't grind to a halt."

"In the past ten years I don't think I've missed a dozen days," Charles said proudly. Then he remembered the business trips that had been extended a day or so at one end or the other for Madge's sake, and added, "At least, not for reasons of health."

"A credit to your constitution," Owen said. "And every day that you're at the office are you earning your salary?"

"There might be some question whether I ever do that."

"I don't mean it that way. I mean those days you spoke of, when you drag yourself in with a hangover or the first stages of a cold."

"I'm just as busy as ever," Charles said. "I put off the more ticklish problems if I can, but there are always plenty of routine . . . oh, I see what you're getting at."

"Yes, a certain amount of routine has its advantages, hasn't it?" Owen asked. "But I can *never* simply muddle through a day, waiting for five-thirty to come around. I always have to be at my best, such as it is, or nothing at all gets done. So there goes your notion of the dissipated artist because I cannot afford to have hangovers. Some men may be able to do a good day's work on three or four hours sleep, but I can't, not any more, so there goes your notion of the free-wheeling playboy bohemian."

"You mean to say you work regular hours five days a week just like the rest of us?" Charles asked in dismay.

"Oh, no," Owen said with a wolfish grin. "Weekends are for businessmen. *Seven* days a week. You forget that all the momentum I have is what I create myself. When you go to your office on a Monday morning, you may find that half a dozen new problems have arisen and need dealing with, apart from those pending. I have nothing like that. If I took a weekend off, on Monday I'd just find a sheet of paper as I left it on Friday—except the ideas that were bubbling in my mind would be half-forgotten, the characters would have come to a standstill, the whole scene would have gone flat. It might take me hours of hard thinking just to regain the state of mind where I'd quit. That's too much waste. When I play, I play. And when I settle down to six months' work, that means that barring illness I'll be working for a hundred and eighty-some consecutive days."

"Oh, hell," said Charles.

"You're beginning to catch on," Owen said. "I'll give you a tip. I'm just now starting work on a new project, and if we meet at a cocktail party some weekend evening you can see for yourself the difference in our lives. You'll be sipping a highball, relaxing virtuously after a hard week's work. And if you look closely you'll notice that the amber liquid in my glass is ginger ale—because *after* the party is over I still have four or five hours work to do."

"That's right, you work at night, don't you," Charles said, still grasping for a straw of romance.

"The city is quiet then," Owen said with merciless pragmatism. "The telephone rarely rings. Not even the most pertinacious of door-to-door salesmen drop in at two in the morning."

Charles was deeply disappointed. He considered himself a realist; he was a great believer in looking a fact in the face, yet there were a few aspects of reality that left him feeling cheated. In contrast with the magnificence of a magician's illusion, for example, the explanation, thrust upon him by some young smart aleck, always seemed squalid and ignoble. It wasn't that he liked to believe that the lady had walked through a solid brick wall; it was the revelation of the mechanical simplicity by which he had been deceived that offended him. And in the same fashion he felt a sense of deprivation in the loss of his vision of Owen as a light-hearted rake who dashed off a play now and then between orgies. In his heart he must have known all along that this picture was dubious, that in actuality Owen must put in periods of sustained hard work. But the discovery that Owen grubbed away as methodically as any accountant somehow made what he did seem so much less . . . artistic.

As if sensing something of this reaction, Owen quietly said, "I'm sorry. You must recognize that it becomes very trying if people close to me treat me as a carefree dilettante."

"I suppose so," Charles conceded, deciding that Owen had grown defensive about the anarchy of his life, probably hankered after a bit of middle-class respectability, and no doubt had been exaggerating outrageously. "You're starting on a new project, are you?"

"Yes, I'm having a fling at a play of my own, for a change."

"Is that right? You may find this as simple as my other opinions, but I've always thought it wouldn't be so difficult to write a novel or a play once you'd thought of the idea. But how do you come by your ideas?"

Owen, who had not allowed the demands of conversation to interfere with his appetite, pushed aside his plate and lit a cigarette. "That's a professional secret," he said. "If we let that out, everybody would be writing plays and novels."

"All right, don't make fun of me," Charles said. "I'm sure it's hard work. But I've always wanted to ask a writer where his ideas came from."

"I'm not really making fun: it's an impossible question," Owen said. "Sometimes an idea rattles around in your head for years. Do you know the old legend of Persephone? Offhand I don't myself, except that she spent half of each year on Olympus and the other half in Hades. There's a lovely story there, and I happened to know the girl when she was a kid. Her parents had split up, and her mother remarried a man who had inherited a good deal of Standard Oil and lived down in Palm Beach. By terms of the divorce the girl spent six months down there and six with her father—of course it didn't quite work out like that because of her schooling, but near enough. Her father was a friend of mine, a fabulous man, a rotten painter and a fine *basso cantante*: he kept alive singing in the choruses at the Opera. But everybody adored him; he had a cold-water studio apartment just off Bleecker, and one reason that his painting never amounted to anything was you'd always find half a dozen people there, day or night, with a bottle of red wine and an argument going. The wine was dreadful, but the arguments were the best in town. This was fifteen years ago, and I'd bet that two-thirds of the people who've made the grade since showed up there at one time or another. For the kid, the contrast couldn't have been sharper: shuttling between the luxurious stagnation of her mother's life and the squalid stimulation of her father's. Only, which one was Hades? All I know is that when she arrived she always intended to stay on with her father forever, and when it came time for her to leave she could hardly wait to get back to Palm Beach. Whichever direction she was traveling was towards Olympus. If you handled it honestly, if you kept it from turning into a slick-magazine marshmallow, there's a good valid situation there. But you'd have to find a plot that would make it move."

"And is that what you're working on now?" Charles asked.

"No, I just gave you that as an example. Something you observe or hear about or even read in the papers will stick in your mind as a situation that appeals to you, although not enough by itself. Then maybe another idea comes along that ties in. Perhaps one day I'll get interested in doing a certain sort of crisis between a man and his mistress, say, and then I'll see that I can use my painter friend as the man and play the crisis out against the background of one of Persephone's visits."

"Yes, I see," Charles said. "Did your new play evolve that way— from something that happened to one of your friends?"

"Oh, no, no, good God, no. It almost never happens that way, so perhaps it wasn't a very good illustration. No, this is based on something I heard of that happened a long time ago . . . out in California. But I don't like to talk of what I'm working on. If you talk about something too much, it never gets written."

"Sorry," Charles said. "I didn't mean to be too inquisitive."

"Please don't apologize," said Owen. "How could you possibly know?"

6

It was Stephen Booth's habit, when writing the first draft of one of his Brethren books, to permit himself a free hand with the ideas that truly interested him. For the time being he was just as trenchant and outrageous as he pleased. His hope was that the enthusiasm he thus stirred up in himself might extend over into the sections of curious ritual and quaint folkways and make them more readable. Afterwards he could go back and cut out, or water down, the more offensive paragraphs.

Up to a point this plan worked fairly well. If it brought no remarkable vitality to the chapters that bored him, at least it kept him from quitting in disgust before the book was a third done. The first draft got written, almost painlessly. The pain came later, with the editing.

Yet he had to do this himself. He had learned that if he did the destruction ably enough, he was allowed to retain more of what was important to him than if he left the task to his editor. She was ruthless, especially if she first saw the manuscript in its original 'preachy' version. From then on she would be on the warpath. Whereas if she didn't see the book until he had deleted or tidied up the grosser outrages, she could generally be persuaded to accept the remainder.

The torture was exquisite. He was in the position of a man obliged to amputate seven-eighths of his soul to preserve the rest, yet never entirely sure which were the portions he must sacrifice. It would be a mistake to leave in a word too many, a tragedy to take one out unnecessarily. So he went through the book sentence by sentence holding long anguished imaginary colloquies with his editor, a terrible woman named Gail Galloway, evil with charm and candor and sweet, firm reasonableness.

For the past couple of days Stephen had been in this manner nibbling away at the indiscretions of Chapter Six, all the time skirting one pair of paragraphs smack in the middle which were the most indiscreet of the lot. He put them off and put them off, but in the end he had to face them. He was facing them now, and he was not happy—because the paragraphs pleased him. If there was one observation worth making in this trivial book, this was it. And he could not see it surviving Gail's determination to shield the public from an instant's discomforting thought.

Although frequently called a harmless or submissive people, the Bushmen are not by nature placid or easygoing. As we have already seen they are envious, prone to suspicion, quarrelsome. Yet it is true that these qualities never lead to strife. Instinctively the Bushman seeks to disarm suspicion. His response to a quarrel is to remove the causes. He will go to extraordinary lengths to avert envy, giving away freely any possessions which might arouse jealousy. There is no pugnacity in his make-up; it has been schooled away. In the Bushman folk legends the brave and noble lion is invariably outwitted, cuckolded, killed. It is the sly and shifty jackal who is the hero.

By sophisticated standards, such submissiveness would be taken as proof of weakness. Oddly enough, the reverse is true. The Bushman has learned that he is too strong to fight. He has only one real weapon in his armory, the poisoned arrow he uses for hunting game. This poison, made from the pupae of a certain beetle, is not rapid—a wounded animal may take several days to die—but it is invariably fatal, and there is no known antidote. A weapon, be it noted, quite as deadly in the hands of a child or an idiot as those of a skilled hunter. So any strife between Bushmen would be fatal, almost certainly to both sides. There is a clear choice between peace or death, and long ago the Bushman made his choice and learned to pay the price. He seems none the unhappier, but then his is a primitive people, barely civilized enough to shoulder the responsibility of a weapon for which there is no antidote.

Well, really now, Stephen. A little heavy-handed, don't you think? Yes, indeed. I meant it to be.

But what are you proposing, exactly? That the United States should give away everything it has, so nobody would envy us? A short-sighted policy, that. Nobody would be able to afford a copy of your next book.

Don't be childish. I daresay we're giving away enough right now, even though we're giving it in the wrong fashion and to the wrong people. But would you pretend that we're showing any sense of responsibility for what we've let loose on the world? The incessant propaganda of enmity. The belligerence of brinkmanship. Encouraging a bomb-shelter mentality. The—

Yes, I know. We have to think of these things every time we pick up a newspaper. But don't you suppose that when someone takes an hour or so off to read about the Bushmen, he's rather hoping to get away for the time being? He doesn't want nuclear horrors pouncing out at him from behind every baobab tree.

I don't give a damn what he wants.

I know that, too. It's precisely why I'm here. . . .

Oh God, oh God! He'd have to tone it down somehow or Gail would be onto all the other innuendoes in the book as well. That last sentence was the real offender; there must be some way to take the sting out of the sarcasm yet leave the implication intact. That would probably get by. Gail didn't mind an occasional idea creeping in as long as it was handled cosily, if you took the reader by the hand and led him gently through the horrid experience and out the other side. Now let's see. . . .

For several minutes Stephen had been vaguely conscious of a muffled, rhythmic whuffling sound. One pane of his great trapezoidal window was open on the fine early-May afternoon, and he had assumed that the noise was another of the many mysterious noises the city produced in its process of growth and self-repair. Now, as the sound grew louder, he realized it was in the room with him and put on his other glasses. Joyce was hunched over, her face in the typewriter, sobbing. He looked at this spectacle in dismay. As far as he was concerned, he had been through this scene already, earlier in the week, and was entitled to an interval of peace. Supposing he spoke of the Bushman's naive answer to a problem that still perplexed more civilized peoples . . . ?

On Joyce's desk the dictionary by her outflung hand was inching closer and closer to the edge; finally it toppled and fell to the floor with a thud. Purely accidental, of course. First her sobbing grew louder, then she pushed a book to the floor, but she would respond with paranoid indignation to any suggestion that she had deliberately sought his attention.

"Is it my handwriting, Joyce?" he called down the room. "I've been trying to be careful."

The buried head shook negatively, and that was all. She was like a small child, wanting to be coaxed for the source of her misery. Stephen marveled at his patience. How did a sensible man get himself into such situations? He was far less indulgent with his own daughter, but then, of course, he had high hopes for Fran while accepting Joyce as beyond optimism. Too much tolerance was a symptom of pity.

And of self-interest, sometimes. Right at the moment he couldn't afford to be harsh. The book was promised to his publishers for the end of the month, and he would need Joyce's untroubled industry to meet that deadline. He hauled himself to his feet, summoning his reserves of compassion. She was the victim, he reminded himself, of this new urban civilization that lived in little compartmented boxes, requiring that people find their contentment by ones and twos. Some simply weren't equipped for it, and Joyce was such a one. She was meant for the days of great sprawling families where a maiden aunt had been welcome for her utility; a frustrating life in some respects, yet far richer in vicarious satisfactions than anything Joyce had to look forward to. It wasn't her fault that she was born out of her time.

He perched on the edge of her desk, looked down distastefully at her shaking bony shoulders, the tangle of mousy hair, imagining her blotched face and reddened eyes: Joyce was not a girl who wept prettily. "What is it this time?" he asked. "Is it your mother, Joyce?"

Her head shook again. Then with a sudden movement she pushed away from her desk, spinning around on her swivel chair so that she faced away from him, looking out the little dormer window. "I'm sorry," she said in a thickened voice. "I thought I could get through the afternoon and then think about it at home. But it's too horrible."

"Nothing is ever that horrible," he said gently.

"Not to you, perhaps. We're all a lot of goldfish swimming around in a bowl for your entertainment."

"Come now, Joyce. Have you found me so inhuman?"

"Oh, you're *nice*," she said, as if this were an offense in itself. "But you don't really think much of people as people. You aren't comfortable until you can turn them into abstractions. And . . . and there's nothing abstract about the baby inside me!" she finished with a wail.

"Oh, dear God," Stephen muttered, appalled. Having successfully dragged someone else into the heart of her misery, Joyce huddled over again and went on with her weeping. It was precisely to the Joyces of this world that these things happened, he reflected. The casually promiscuous were too knowledgeable, the undersexed too cautious; the securely attractive girls could afford to wait in confidence. Only the homely and overanxious were the victims, fearful that they were being cheated by life—and this, doubtless, was what Joyce had meant by his turning people into abstractions. Belatedly he realized that she could scarcely have been alone in this enterprise. "I suppose it was Arthur Vaughan," he said uncertainly. "Would you like me to speak to him for you?"

She half turned, and for the first time looked at him for an instant. Her face was streaked and mottled, as he had expected—and contorted into a grimace of blazing hatred. "I never want to set eyes on that son of a bitch as long as I live!" she screamed at him.

Her intensity drove him from his perch; he took a bemused turn about the room, glancing covertly from time to time at the hunched figure by the window. Such violence was so utterly unlike the vaporish nerve storms he was accustomed to that he wondered if this latest misfortune had overturned her reason. But no, that couldn't be. She had been behaving perfectly sensibly till a few minutes ago. And that use of 'son of a bitch'—on Joyce's lips like a string of vile obscenities from anybody else—had had an artificial ring of melodrama about it, surely. No doubt she and Arthur had had some unpleasant quarrel, and Joyce was exactly the girl to barricade herself behind a hysterical pride. She would have to be coaxed into being sensible. But he felt singularly ill-equipped to deal with such a situation. He would have liked to call Amelia upstairs: a woman would take this sort of thing in her stride. However, he knew that Joyce felt uncomfortable with Amelia, believed that Amelia despised her, and believed correctly. He would have to cope as best he could himself.

Stephen paused before a whole shelf of *Our Brothers, the Samoans*: there had been an overprinting, and he had bought several dozen copies at a few cents apiece to give away as autographed gifts. The jacket designer had enjoyed himself with photographs of bare-bosomed nubility, even working one specimen onto the spine of the book, so that Stephen found himself regarded by the endlessly repeated image of a laughing-eyed, proud-breasted young lady who scoffed at any tragic consequences to sex. "I presume you have had some unfortunate misunderstanding with Arthur," he said slowly, fumbling for the appropriate eloquence. "Probably you feel that he has treated you abominably—"

"He has!"

"Nevertheless—"

"No, wait," she begged, and he waited to the sound of labored gasping as Joyce fought for a measure of self-control. Courteously he continued his inspection of the girl who would have regarded pregnancy as merely a tiresome interruption of her youthful promiscuity. And the remarkable thing was how very rarely they *did* get pregnant until they were ready to marry and settle down, usually in their late twenties. Rather as if they had achieved a state where conception, although unimpeded by drugs or rubber goods, waited upon the serenity of family love when children were truly wanted. What an extraordinary effect such an arrangement would have on the world that deemed itself civilized! The population explosion would be cut off overnight, the divorce rate would shrink to a trickle, psychiatrists would go hungry, children would grow up in security, the madhouses would empty out, and girls like Joyce would have nothing to be terrified of.

"I'm sorry," she said more steadily. Her mouth was trembling and she was pulling a limp scrap of handkerchief back and forth between her fingers, but she was sitting up; she had made some repairs to her face, she was much calmer. "I don't want to talk about Arthur, but there was no misunderstanding, except when I thought he was decent and wonderful. He isn't, he's a . . . monster. But it's quite humiliating, and I don't want to talk about him. Please."

It was hard to tell with Joyce: she could refuse to tell something because she wanted you to drag it from her under protest. But that final 'Please' had had a despairing ring to it, as if this were the *sine qua non* of her uncertain equilibrium. "Well, what are you going to do, then?" he asked irritably. "You have to be practical, Joyce. Would you think of having the baby anyway?"

She flushed but didn't turn away. "I wouldn't mind, myself, you know. It might be fun to have, and I wouldn't need to care who the father had been. But it's out of the question. It would kill Mother."

Stephen did not believe this for a minute. Mrs. Neilson invited that sort of remark; she was the sort of woman who liked the people around her to believe that the least shock was likely to carry her away. She was also the sort of woman who outlived all those who worried themselves to an early death shielding her. Much more to the point was that Mrs. Neilson was a ferociously conventional woman; the discovery that her daughter was going to have an illegitimate child might well lead her to excesses of righteous, maternal sadism. The months of Joyce's increasingly recognizable pregnancy, while friends and neighbors made comments, would be sheer hell for Joyce. Instead of expiring herself, Mrs. Neilson could easily drive her daughter to suicide.

"Yes, your mother has to be taken into account," he agreed.

"I knew you would understand," she said gratefully. "Some people would be shocked, and I'm not too happy myself, but the only thing is to get rid of it. I've already accepted that."

"I'm sure you're right," he said thankfully, beginning to think of the inconveniences this would mean to *him*. Twice already he had postponed the delivery date on the new book; the second time Gail had pinned him down and warned him she was announcing the *Bushmen* in the Winter catalogue—he could not fail her again. In a pinch he could get a typist through the University service, but of course she wouldn't make any sense of his handwriting. Thank heaven he'd begun to print his corrections, but even so. . . . "It isn't too late, is it?"

"Too late?"

"For an . . . to get rid of it."

"Oh, no."

"You're positive?" He couldn't be blamed for questioning her familiarity with the facts of life.

She blushed again and looked towards the window. "I'm horridly regular, you see. From what girl friends had said I wasn't too frightened at missing one period just then, but when I realized I was missing a second . . . well, I went straight to the hospital and gave a false name. That was the other day, when I got so upset over nothing. This morning they told me it was positive. But it can't be more than six or seven weeks along."

He grunted in relief. "That's all right, then." Apart from the problem of his manuscript, he was starting to feel more cheerful. All in all Joyce wasn't taking it too badly, and he thought he had discharged his avuncular responsibilities rather well. His avoidance of the brutal word 'abortion' had been a masterstroke of tact.

"Except . . ." she said hesitantly.

"Yes, I know. Properly it's Arthur Vaughan who should be footing the bill. But if you're absolutely adamant about my speaking to him, and I wouldn't mind that assignment at all, then I suppose I'll have to manage a loan for you. We can spread it out over your salary for the next year or two, so it won't hurt too much." There he went, committing himself to these exasperations forever.

"No, it isn't that," she said. "Oh, I'm terribly grateful, Professor Booth, honestly I am. I have a little money saved up, and of course I haven't any idea whether it will be enough, so I may have to call on you for help. But that isn't my main worry now. I simply haven't the slightest notion how to go about it."

"Ask around among your friends," he said easily. "Somebody always knows of somebody. You'll be surprised."

"That's just it," she said, looking as if she were about to start crying again. "I can't, I couldn't. I just don't *have* any friends like that. I'd never be able to look them in the face again."

The pathetic idiocy of this statement made Stephen blink. Unless her earlier remarks had been empty posturing, she had felt prepared to face up to her friends with a fatherless child; yet now she was ashamed to turn to them for help in procuring an abortion. Nor was she a Catholic. This contradiction had to mean, if it meant anything, that she had acquaintances she could have outfaced for the sake of a baby, and not a single real friend on whose loyalty and sophistication she could rely. The thought of such loneliness embarrassed Stephen and made him realize how very little notice he had taken of Joyce as a person. Her accusation, as it applied to herself, was absolutely true. She had been a collection of labels to him. Bob Neilson's daughter, neurotic spinster, proof of his benevolence, thorn in his flesh. A hook from which he could hang generalizations about modern urban society. . . .

To some extent this must be Joyce's fault. He did not treat most people like that, did he? Her very personality was angular and awkward, deficient in the qualities that inspire affection; hence her lack of friends, and hence his attitude. Yet it seemed there was something toughening about life in the invisible ghetto of the unlovable: this afternoon Joyce had shown, as he could see now, unexpected strengths of character. After her initial burst of weeping—and any girl would be excused a few tears at such a time—she had been astonishingly resolute in keeping herself under control. She had answered his questions frankly, at whatever cost in anguish to her prudish soul. In effect she had dumped her problem into the lap of the one person, probably, she completely trusted and done it with less fuss than she had often made over a sheet of carbon paper put in backwards. Perhaps one of the qualities of the unlovable was that they faced up better to a real crisis than people accustomed to trading on their charm.

"You know so many different people," she said.

Startled, he began harshly, "Well, it just happens that I don't know any—" and then cut himself off short. "Sorry, Joyce." She was looking at him with wide red eyes in frightened appeal. But it was no good getting impatient with her innocence. When you undertook a girl like Joyce, you had to expect this sort of thing. She hadn't the least notion what she was suggesting. If a single girl inquired about for an abortionist, that was one thing. She might be in trouble herself, which was her bad luck, or she might very reasonably be asking on behalf of a friend. But when a married man did the inquiring, especially a married man of his age and standing, nobody would dream of giving him the benefit of the doubt. Oh, no question of it, he knew people who would supply the information without a minute's hesitation. Paul Mason, over in Sociology, would probably offer him a choice of half a dozen addresses. Acquired, he would say with a wink and a smirk, strictly in the line of professional research. But Paul would feel that his intelligence was being insulted if Stephen tried to insist that this was an innocent favor he was doing someone else. Paul would hear out his explanations with indulgent contempt. Of course, Stephen, I quite understand. You don't have a thing to worry about. The secret is quite safe with me. And the story would be all over college the next day.

Yet knowing that the information was readily within his grasp, he hadn't the heart to send Joyce off to seek it on her own. Probably she was telling the literal truth: if she had the sort of friends who could put her on to an abortionist, she might not be in need of one today. He was trapped by his own concepts of decency. "Well, I suppose I can ask around," he grumbled unhappily.

With the realization that her chief anxiety had been lifted from her shoulders, Joyce's self-control gave way completely. She instantly went back to weeping, more noisily than ever, and at the same time trying to express the depth of her gratitude. It was a messy performance and one that brought Stephen, aware of the spirit in which he had made his noble offer, no sense of gratification whatsoever. He quickly became uncomfortable, his pity curdling. He had accepted with fair grace the expense, embarrassment and inconvenience of Joyce's plight, and his reward was to be subjected to this scene of damp, raw emotionalism which he could do nothing to stop. He gave her his handkerchief. He thumped her shoulder encouragingly and found that she tried to seize his hand and kiss it: probably the most harrowing moment of his entire life. He trotted downstairs to fetch her a glass of water. Nothing did any good.

His assurances grew more extravagant: he vowed to search out the safest practitioner in the city, she wouldn't have a thing to worry about, nobody would ever know. Here his own ravings gave him a clue, and he added a brutal qualification: unless, of course, Joyce's present carryings-on made it difficult to explain to Amelia what all the commotion had been about. This worked. Joyce gulped and gasped and turned to begging him in a hoarse imploring whisper on no account to say anything to Amelia, please, please, please, she couldn't stand that, she'd never have the courage to come face to face with her again. By contrast, this was much better. Stephen gave his promise, grasping the opportunity to introduce his own concerns. Amelia knew how determined he was to meet this deadline on the book; they would have to find a good excuse for Joyce's disappearance for several days at such a critical period. He explained that it might well take him a week or more to locate a suitable man, and Joyce swore that she would work overtime every day in the interim.

By the time they had settled these conspiratorial details she was a great deal calmer again and guiltily eager to get back to work. But Stephen had no faith in the permanence of this lull, and he felt that he had seen as much of her tear-ravaged face as he could stand for one day. He declared she was in no condition to work; the sensible thing for her was to get out into the fresh air, steady down with a brisk walk home, and have a stiff drink before she faced her mother. By tomorrow she would feel like a different woman—he promised it. With hearty little cries of comfort and exhortation, he managed finally to get her out of the attic, at least as far as the bathroom downstairs where she could perform a thorough overhaul before meeting the street.

Then Stephen sighed heavily and went back to his desk by the great window to look down at Jefferson Mews and consider the implications of what he had let himself in for.

Comfortably he had pitied Joyce for her lack of loyal and sophisticated friends, feeling himself secure. When he thought it over, he no longer felt so secure. There were three or four men who would probably give him the shirts from their backs, and that was the snare. For these same men who were hypothetically so generous with their wearing apparel were not necessarily noted for their discretion, and there was one temptation against which few masculine loyalties were proof: the temptation of a really clever quip. The witty possibilities of his predicament sprang all too easily to mind:

Hadn't you heard? Yes, Brethren Booth is extending his scope. He's working on a new book to be called *Our Sisters, the Cyprians.*

Just the flavor of erudite double entendre to be irresistible to the academic humorist. The sort of remark that would be thrown out in his presence, for *his* amusement, with the easy defense later that 'Oh, well, Fred couldn't have any idea what I was talking about.' But Fred could guess, Fred no doubt prided himself on the subtlety of his guesswork, and that was how stories got started. And there was always some kindly soul to contribute the suggestion that the girl in question might be one of his own students. A professor's bugaboo. Otherwise Stephen wouldn't have minded so much.

As he catalogued his friends, assessing their virtues, he realized that there was not a single one in whom he placed enough confidence for a matter of this sort—not one who would really *believe* in his innocence and respect the secret accordingly.

All of which would have been most unfortunate if Stephen had had no place else to turn. He would have felt almost as helpless as Joyce. But from the first he had sensed that the person to rescue him from this dilemma was his half brother, Eliot Clay. In matters disreputable, Eliot was his ace in the hole.

It might seem a fool's errand, in a sense, to look to a pansy for the latest word on abortionists, yet Stephen knew beyond a doubt that Eliot could have the information he needed within five minutes. The half world that Eliot inhabited socially was only exiguously homosexual. It was the party world, the playboy world of youngish and would-be-youngish people with more money and leisure than they knew what to do with, living from one amusement to the next. Its pseudopods reached into sports and show business, wherever ornaments could be collected, and a scattering of the cleverer and more talented homosexuals was very much a part of the decorative scheme. It was a world that lived by its own rules, where marijuana was a commonplace and heroin *declassé*, where an orgy could mean anything from a cocktail party to an orgy, where fidelity was a challenge and chastity a standing joke. Since sophistication tempered by alcohol was no proof against accidents, these people would have been no end inconvenienced if abortions could not be readily procured. Eliot might not know the answers himself, but he knew where to ask the questions.

And, partly because they lived in such different worlds, Stephen felt entirely secure with Eliot. It was an odd relationship they had formed, based on no common memories of boyhood. The gap in their ages was too great. After all, Eliot had been in training pants when Stephen set off to high school; the year of Stephen's field trip to Peru Eliot had just been entering on that adolescence from which, in a manner of speaking, he had never graduated. They had come together, finally, during the last illness of the sweet, foolish mother they shared. She had never acknowledged to herself the bent her younger son was following. To the very end, despite all the evidence that had been thrown in her teeth over the years, she was still talking of the sensible girl who would someday induce Eliot to settle down. Yet though she gave no name to her apprehensions, she evidently felt that in some fashion her spoiled ewe lamb was ill equipped to face the world on his own; she wanted Stephen to feel a fraternal responsibility for him and had done her bumbling best to bring the two men together. This might easily have had the opposite effect, but it hadn't. Since Stephen believed that sexuality was strictly a personal affair—better a contented homosexual any day than one more neurotic ego-questing heterosexual, was the way he looked at it—Eliot's defensiveness had quickly beat itself out against the air. A mutual bemused fondness sprang up. Eliot found a sense of security in having a foothold in the settled conventional world; he could know that he held some unspecified place in Stephen's affections and amused him by bringing stories of one of the more colorful North American tribes. Eliot joked at the bond between them, took outrageous advantage of it, yet in the end respected it.

So that was all very well, except for one small detail. Where *was* Eliot?

He had dropped by one day last week to complain that the Nicholsons were coming back unusually early this year, so he'd be moving out of their place in a day or two and as yet had not located his next residence. This was rarely a problem for long. Disorderly though the rest of his life might appear, he had a fussy, feminine tidiness about any place where he lived; people greatly preferred to leave an apartment in his care than have it standing empty.

As a rule Eliot rang up within a day or so to leave his new telephone number, but he was not meticulous about this; if he got sufficiently absorbed by something he might forget. Several times he had remained out of touch for weeks at a stretch. Since Stephen had never been able to conceive of a situation where anybody for any reason would have need of Eliot in great urgency, he had not complained. It seemed probable that Eliot would be even less conscientious if he felt a sense of obligation.

If Eliot had called in this time, Stephen hadn't heard of it. There was a chance that Amelia had simply made a note of the number and then forgotten to tell him; this was obviously the first thing to check on. By now Joyce had had plenty of time to get out of the house, so the coast should be clear. Abandoning any further thought of work until his mind was easier, he started down the stairs. Just what he was going to do if Amelia did *not* have the number he couldn't begin to imagine. Eliot's stories were filled with the names of people he knew, but he never gave the impression of intimate friendship with any of them except that fellow in the Diplomatic, currently enjoying life in Greece. Stephen could not picture himself blandly calling up this Hungarian professional divorcée or that polo player who also kept a stable of multicolored mistresses and inquiring if by chance they knew where Eliot was staying. Yet what else was he to do?

As he came down the last flight of stairs, he saw that Amelia was at the front door, saying good-bye to a woman he'd not seen before, tall and remarkably emaciated with a look of weary-eyed good humor. "That's absolutely splendid of you, Mrs. Blair," Amelia was saying warmly. "And I'll look forward to seeing you on Friday."

"Just one favor," said the stranger. "Call me Madge, won't you?" She gave an incongruously girlish flirt of the hand, turned and was gone. Amelia closed the door behind her and spun around gleefully. "There's a catch for the League!" she exclaimed. "I don't know when I've met with such enthusiasm, and she actually wants to *work*. Speaking of which, why are you down so early?"

"Do we have Eliot's new number?" Stephen asked.

"He hasn't called in. Why?"

"I suppose I must want to get in touch with him. It seems the likeliest explanation."

"Well, it's no use calling the Nicholsons," Amelia said, returning to the living room for a cigarette. "They'd like to know where he's gone, too. He left their place in such apple-pie order that they can't find anything."

"Damn!" said Stephen, staring down blindly at the remains of tea and cinnamon toast for two, a survival of Amelia's upbringing. "How did *you* happen to be trying to get hold of him?"

"You made it clear there'd be tantrums if he wasn't invited to the wedding, and it helps if an invitation has an address on it. I've finally had to invent an excuse and tell Ruth to send it care of us—mildly humiliating. I expect he'll reappear before then."

"Don't be silly," Stephen muttered. Eliot was bound to turn up well before the wedding, but possibly not for weeks and weeks: ample time for Joyce to grow frantic with worry. How the devil could he track him down? But before he could give the problem any coherent thought, he was distracted by an ugly suspicion. "You haven't by any chance invited that Arthur Vaughan, have you?"

"I felt obliged to," she said apologetically. "I know he won't be any addition, but we work so closely together, and he takes such a personal interest, that it would have seemed odd if I hadn't. He was already asking for suggestions for a wedding present."

"Oh, for God's sake!" Stephen snapped in outraged disgust. Amelia's eyebrows went up inquiringly, and he felt hamstrung by the promise of secrecy. "You raise objections to Eliot and then go and invite somebody who isn't fit to be seen in civilized company!"

"Why, Stephen!" she said with a mocking grin. "That's the first time I've ever heard you admit the rest of us were civilized."

7

Another of the weekly Thursday evening duplicate sessions at the Nottingham Bridge Club was finished. The casual players and the also-rans were already on their way home; the enthusiasts and the hopefuls were waiting around to post-mortem the results of the scoring. After several hours of huddled tension the great room was abuzz with relaxed conversation, though there were still a few friendly arguments in progress; it being understood that in bridge circles such a remark as 'That four diamond call of yours was probably the most fatheaded bid of the century,' delivered in full voice, is considered perfectly friendly.

Off in an alcove in the quietest corner of the room Gert Zimmerman and her favorite partner, Derek, were deep in a different sort of discussion. They were not particularly interested in the scores; this evening was not an end in itself but the first of a series of practice sessions in training for the major tournaments of the summer ahead. They knew they had played smoothly together, with few misunderstandings, and this was all that mattered. However, they had had some difficulty over the little card that traveled with them announcing the bidding conventions they employed.

This was not entirely their fault. In an access of patriotism or something of the sort, that august body, The American Contract Bridge League, had ruled it improper to play any of the European bidding systems which had so convincingly defeated American teams for most of a decade. The American systems may have been shown up as sadly inferior, but they were home grown, and that was what counted.

There was one way around this rule. You could not simply write on your convention card 'We play Acol' (for example), but you could, if your printing were fine enough, itemize the particulars of Acol and hope for the best. In effect this was what Gert and Derek had tried to do. But all evening long opponents had demanded more detailed explanations of the significance of one bid or another. In a relatively informal club tournament this didn't matter, but at the Summer Nationals it would bring the tournament director down on their necks. Now they were trying to improve on their wording. They had reached the point of wondering how to indicate that the jump raise of a partner's suit was a limited bid without inviting the query '*How* limited, dammit?' when Saul's harsh macaw's voice rose about the chatter of the room:

"Gert! Gert Zimmerman! Telephone!"

She hurried over to the phone on Saul's desk expecting to be told to stop at the delicatessen on her way home and pick up a hot pastrami sandwich; about twice a week her father developed a midnight hunger which the refrigerator would not satisfy. But it was Ruth on the wire, in tears, and Gert felt a surge of the long-suppressed panic. "Is it Father?" she asked, impatient to hear the worst.

Obviously it was, but Ruth could never confine herself to a bald unpleasantness. "Morris dropped by the apartment and couldn't get any response though he knew Dad must be there. So he got the janitor to let him in. And he was lying there on the living room floor."

"Is he dead?"

"Oh, no. The ambulance arrived while Morris was calling me. They've rushed him to the hospital. But Morris is afraid it's a stroke, and a bad one."

So there it was, and Please, God, let him die! thought Gert, remembering Uncle Abe lying in that little room for the better part of a year, his face in a fixed grimace, barely able to move one hand, a spark of mind trapped in the most unspeakable of dungeons.

"Oh Gert, it was so dreadful," Ruth went on. "Vickie was right here. And all she could say was 'Will it mean the wedding has to be postponed?'"

"Just be grateful you can't remember all the things you said at that age," Gert snapped. "I'll meet you at the hospital."

She explained quickly to Derek, collected her coat, and joined the knot of people in the hallway waiting for the elevator. She thought of the stairs, for privacy rather than urgency—there was no rush about waiting in the hospital lobby, perhaps for hours, until the verdict came down—but she had a horror of enclosed places, and there was no way out till you reached the bottom.

"Congratulations, Gert," said Ira.

"What?" she said stupidly.

"You and old Derry came in second. Are you getting too blasé to look? I told you we'd given you a cold top on that spade hand."

"Sorry, Ira; I've just heard my father's been taken to the hospital," she said, and by this rude shock of reality bought herself isolation. For years she had been bracing herself against this moment; she could never have been surprised into such an unself-conscious utterance as Vickie's. Yet in a way she sympathized with the child's reaction. Only someone like Ruth, secure, falsely secure, in her own tidy little life, could see this as a sentimental tragedy, quite unselfishly.

But if it was a stroke and he didn't die yet didn't recover, who would be the one to nurse Father through all those ghastly months? Whose life, such as it was, would be put into moth balls for the duration?

Down on the street Ira hailed a cab, helped her into it, murmuring the conventional regrets and encouragements. He was a decent soul, and unwittingly he contributed to Gert's feeling that she was a heartless wretch. Yet she loved her father deeply, she had always been closer to him than the other children, except perhaps her elder brother, Phil, Alison's father. She adored the dryness of his humor, the curious energy of his mind, his gentleness with young people and the solemn delight he took in small children, the impulsiveness of his generosity, the absurdity of his eccentric economies. . . . Oh, so many different things! But when you lived with somebody through his seventies and into his eighties, you lived with a gathering awareness that one day next month, next year, certainly within the next few years, the great upheaval was inevitable. You couldn't help it. Nor could you help thinking, while the guilt grew dull, of the changes it would mean in your own life.

Could she afford to keep on the apartment without the help of her father's pension, and even if she could, would she be able to abide living by herself?

She loved her father, and the thought of his dying sickened her. She gave him the benefit of all her own terrors of death and felt that her heart would stop with the agony of it. She thought of herself when her own time came, with the people she loved standing around looking down at her with hypocritical misery and thinking all the time of the dislocation this would mean in their petty lives—would the wedding have to be postponed? God, it was disgusting! Ruth was absolutely right. And he had been such a fine man, such a wonderful father.

But she'd hate sharing a place with another woman, and in the end that would mean moving in with Morris, keeping house for him. This had been *her* apartment, really; Father had been no trouble, lost in his books most of the time. Whereas Morris was a fussy man with his own ideas of how things should be—and there were all the agitations of a doctor's household.

Meanwhile Father was lying at the threshold of eternal oblivion, probably never again to shuffle across the living room in his disreputable grey bathrobe to peer out the window at a new morning, wondering aloud why anybody in his right mind would choose to spend a lifetime in such a misbegotten city.

By the time she paid off the driver and started up the hospital steps, she had achieved the appearance of a properly distraught daughter, weeping bitterly.

PART FIVE

1

It was the mark of Tony Elmendorf's loyalty that he became angry only with the people he was truly fond of; the rest of the world never troubled the surface of his flippancy. "You're really taking her seriously," he said crossly. "All over again. After three marriages and a reasonable number of affairs you still haven't the least understanding of women."

"Perhaps I don't want your sort of understanding," Owen said.

"Anything else is illusion, self-deception or romanticism."

"Rubbish," Owen said mildly, settling back. Ten years ago he would have been outraged by Tony's breezing in like this at the afternoon's end, just when his work was moving along smoothly, and for no better reason than that Tony had a couple of hours to kill before an uptown dinner engagement. Now—and Owen had no idea whether to ascribe the change to age or to an increase of confidence—he rather welcomed the interruption. He would give Tony a few cocktails, confining himself to a single bottle of beer; then fix himself a sandwich and return to work all the fresher for a little distraction. There was no longer the sense that some deathless phrase might elude him forever if he quit the typewriter before exhaustion set in. "Your trouble, Tony," he said, "is that you don't really like women."

"Well, don't spread the word around," Tony said. "I've kept those tendencies well hidden."

"I'm granting you sex. But what use would you have for women if you couldn't go to bed with them?"

"I'd have very little use for anything except a gun to shoot myself."

"You're so busy admiring your standing as a Don Juan that you haven't noticed I'm saying something," Owen said. "It's the major distinction between men, this, and you and I belong to opposite camps. You're with the majority, I think: the men who don't really like women as individuals. They're not all predators like you, either; most of them are married, more or less contentedly. They may love their wives and be fond of their children. But apart from sex and domesticity, they vastly prefer the company of other men. They put up with their friends' wives, but they haven't any women friends of their own. No more do you. Oh, Katya, I suppose, whom you see three or four times a year. And she's the complete list."

"All perfectly true," Tony agreed. "As we Existentialists put it: Most men recover from their mothers, but some don't."

"It's Liza you've never recovered from," Owen said. "And I doubt if Existentialists say anything of the sort."

"Then they should." Cocktail in hand, Tony was wandering along the built-in bookcase that filled one wall of Owen's living room, scanning the titles at eye level. From time to time he would borrow a few books of an improving nature with the laudable intention of reading them, but the books always came back a month or so later with a confession that he couldn't seem to find the time. "You're suggesting that to more perceptive souls like yourself women can be likeable quite apart from being desirable—and there has to be a good psychological reason behind any proposition as silly as that."

"How can you pretend to understand them if you don't even like them as people?"

"Because what I *do* understand is that they *aren't* people," Tony said. "That's the fundamental error all you romantics make. You like to think they're much the same as you are, with a few different mannerisms and more attractive packaging. And you're dead wrong. They have all the fascination of the alien, at their best they can be sensual little treasures, but they belong to a wholly distinct species. I'd as soon go mad all the way, like spinsters and Britishers, and choose my friends among cats or horses."

"You get worse year by year."

"I get smarter," Tony said gloomily, "but not smart enough to make you see what you don't want to see. You should spend some time down in my office. It's not all confidence men and petty racketeers. We had a woman there this afternoon, for example. She's as sane as any of them, but a squad of masculine psychiatrists will eventually decide that she's nuts: they won't be able to help themselves. She's divorced with a couple of cute kids, three and five. Last week she got picked up on a nasty morals charge. No great problem except for her: the father's remarried and was delighted to accept custody of the children. Except that last night she filled up the bathtub and held them under water until they were quite dead—and all afternoon she was trying to explain to us how she'd done the right thing."

"Yes, ghastly," Owen said. "It was in today's paper. Along with a young man who cut his girl friend's throat simply because she preferred to go to bed with somebody else. Is one so much worse than the other?"

"I'm not saying worse or better, just different," Tony replied. "Completely different. That young punk was in love with his girl. When she threw him over, his ego got a nasty kick in the groin and he went berserk. It's deplorable, it's barbarous, but at least it's comprehensible. And for what it's worth, at least he knew he'd done something wrong. But what that woman did isn't comprehensible in the same sense, and don't be glib about it, Owen. She's just an ignorant and rattle-brained little tramp. Nobody's ever given her a medal for bringing up children. The trouble she got into was strictly of her own making; she was asking for it. Yet she sat there insisting that if those kids couldn't have the benefit of *her* upbringing, then they were far better off dead. She believes it, too, and there's the point. Their minds are actually capable of working that way without blowing a fuse. . . . Should I read *Moby Dick?*"

"You should," Owen said. "There isn't a woman in it. But you won't." In the background of all Tony's generalizations was a girl named Liza Pond: black-haired, white-skinned, green-eyed—intelligent and passionate and schizophrenic. He had been twenty-five and in the army when he fell in love with her, and they hadn't known each other very long when Tony's outfit was sent off to the South Pacific. It was three years before he saw her again, but throughout all that hideous interim she remained constant, at least in the fashion which had then counted for most. Other men's wives wrote apologetically of divorce; other men's sweethearts wrote forswearing all vows or—perhaps less brutally, for a period of uncertainty could brace a man against despair—simply stopped writing altogether; but in every mail came letters from Liza, cheerful, humorous, affectionate. She wrote very well. (Seven years later she wrote a turgid, poetic and highly dishonest psychological novel based on their marriage.)

But in the hellish implausibility of living from Guadalcanal to Iwo Jima—Tony had been shipped home after that campaign, wounded but not seriously, just before the invasion of Okinawa— the letters from Liza had become the one fixed point of sanity in an insane world. Where sleep would have seemed impossible, he put himself to sleep on reveries of the tranquil, normal life they would share—if only he survived. She became the symbol of his survival: he grew superstitious about the day when mail would be distributed without a letter from her, and although that day never came, his courage ebbed and flowed with the anticipation. For the few days after mail call he would be bold with invulnerability, then caution would reassert itself, and eventually he would lapse towards cowardice while he waited to learn whether he still possessed his talisman.

He subsisted for so long on dreams of his homecoming and their marriage that it was impossible for him to appreciate, when he finally did come home, that things weren't precisely as he had imagined them. Liza didn't disagree with his eloquent descriptions of their great love, but she did have all sorts of reservations about marriage: she was doubtful of 'surrendering her freedom.' He rode over her objections—or, more accurately, he agreed to all her stipulations without really listening to them—and they were married. For three or four months the reality lived up to the expectation, and later on he would say that perhaps this was all any man had a right to expect.

Then one day Tony woke up to the realization that he had committed himself to a marriage wherein each partner was to be scrupulous of the other's freedom; each must feel able to go his own sweet way with no questions asked. He had paid no attention to this condition at the time it was raised. Perfectly aware of the obsessive quality of his own yearnings, he had thought it natural that any girl might feel a trifle apprehensive of being submerged by such possessive intensity. Those fears would vanish as he reverted to his normal, easygoing self. Now he learned that Liza's attitude had nothing to do with him personally, but was her considered response to the institution of marriage which, as customarily practiced, she regarded as degrading to the human spirit. Binding oneself to fidelity to one other person was primitive and unhealthy; unless one remained free to pursue self-expression in every direction, one's personality became warped. Evidently she had already begun to chafe under the yoke, for as soon as Tony endeavored to dispute the question as rationally as possible, she defended her independence by hurtling into bed with several of his closest friends. But this in no way, she solemnly insisted, reflected on her love for Tony.

At any other time of his life Tony would doubtless have come to his senses at this point and simply walked out, with no great damage done to anybody. He wanted to break away; he knew the situation could only get worse, but he found himself helpless. Despite himself, however unhappily, he was still in love with Liza. What was worse, he was still wretchedly dependent upon her simple physical presence: for instance, the thought of waking up from one of his frequent nightmares and not finding her there beside him was more than he could face. He had to try to make a go of it—and the months that followed were an ever-increasingly subtilized torment.

Liza soon came to feel that his own fidelity was a reproach, putting her into danger of feeling guilty. Since nothing was so corrupting to the psyche as a sense of guilt, he must (if he respected her) have love affairs too. When he showed a distressing lack of initiative in this respect, she went so far as to produce a selection of girl friends, each primed for the occasion with an indignant awareness of Liza's misbehavior and more or less willing to provide consolation.

Here was the 'tranquil, normal life' he had dreamt of, and each twist in the labyrinth of misery led inexorably to yet another. In her horror of inhibitions, Liza decided it was essential to regale him with the explicit details of each new sexual encounter, for otherwise would she not be exposing herself to the perils of repression? Somehow Tony adjusted even to this. But then, for Liza was not a selfish girl and was as solicitous for his mental health as for her own, she expected him to repay the compliment. When, to satisfy his wife's insatiable craving for forthrightness, Tony found himself describing vivid perversions committed on girls he had never even shaken hands with, he felt his own sanity slipping and found the resolution to call a halt.

(This was the tragicomic situation Owen had several times tried to work into a play, always to be defeated by self-consciousness at the thought of his friend's reactions.)

In one sense Tony had got out cheaply, because Liza was too high principled a woman to expect to profit—except in experience which might be turned to semifictional purposes—from a relationship which she had *warned* Tony was psychologically unnatural: they had meticulously divided the costs of her trip to Mexico for a divorce. In other respects the cost was high. Although soon able to talk with dry amusement of the human capacity for adapting to the most bizarre circumstances, he had suffered very real anguish at the time. The suffering was a direct result of his having given himself, emotionally, into another person's keeping, and this was a mistake he was determined never to make again.

But he would not admit that his opinions of women generally had been colored by this episode. He was the first to point out that Liza was a special case, that a man's chances of stumbling on a second Liza were slight indeed, and that therefore only a fool would let himself be biased by such an oddity. His jaundiced (or, as he preferred to put it, realistic) view of the sex was entirely the outcome of maturer observations. If he persisted in noticing the wilfulness beneath the vivacity, the vacuousness beneath the good nature, the selfishness beneath the generosity, this was from the record of other men's misadventures rather than his own. You could call him cynical if you liked; he didn't mind, but wasn't he usually proved right in the event? He might predict disillusionment and catastrophe for three marriages out of four, but over the years, in their circle of acquaintances in New York, how often had he been obliged to eat his words? Had his estimate of the character of Barbara-the-Bitch been correct, or had Owen's?

"But I like women in novels," Tony objected, replacing *Moby Dick* on the shelf. "I'm fascinated by the way the unscrupulous and sexually retarded heroine always nails her man while the warm-hearted divorcée goes down to ignominious defeat."

"Don't you find the happy endings depressing?"

"No, no, you misunderstand me," Tony said. "I'm the average, unintellectual reader: I'm cheering for the heroine every time. I even approve of her technique. If she's got this far in a state of innocence, she's probably better off remaining an unknown quantity and hoping she'll find her stride on the honeymoon, whereas a premature demonstration of her ineptitude might send the hero running for dear life. She's a smart girl, and I'm all on her side. She'll probably make the poor bastard miserable, but there's a chance that she won't: she has a fetching assortment of virtues, and presumably she's in love with the guy since she's pursued him with a ruthlessness that would do credit to an undernourished tigress. Perhaps she'll make a go of it. Whereas I'm every bit as suspicious of that easy-natured divorcée as I'm supposed to be. For one thing, I'm convinced that she has a child or two hidden away somewhere that the hero wouldn't learn about until he was helplessly entangled in her toils. And that means—"

"That means I've been ambushed," Owen said. "For divorcée read widow, and for widow read Carol. You're creeping up on me from the damnedest directions, these days. But I can't seem to identify the virgin huntress in your parable."

"How should I know?" Tony asked. "There was that cute little actress a couple of months back."

"Oh, dear God—Denise Durrell! No, thanks. She's not cut out for your heroine, Tony. She already has ambition, talent, an agent, a business manager, a poodle, a psychiatrist and two hundred and fifty dollars a week pocket money. A husband would be excess luggage."

"I only saw her that once," Tony said defensively. "I liked the way her behind twitched."

"An inadequate foundation—for matrimony."

"Don't try to be lofty with me. Not after the time you assured me I was nothing but a cynical misogynist and then married one of the hardest-boiled little trollops in New York City."

"All right, so I did. She put on a performance that was pretty impressive. You didn't happen to be taken in by it, but then it wasn't aimed at you."

"And what sort of performance is Carol putting on?" Tony asked with studied rudeness.

Owen refused to be offended. When, one day, he achieved the happiness Tony disbelieved in, there would be nothing but pity for his lonely friend. "But I *know* Carol," he said patiently. "There's no room for a performance. She's much the same person she always was, a little more tolerant of life."

"*And* a little older *and* a little poorer *and* just a teeny bit conscious that she has a kid to bring up," Tony snarled. "She isn't putting on an act, but all you've noticed is that she's a little more tolerant of life! Sweet Jesus, Owen!" Indignation drove him back to the pitcher for another cocktail. "I can understand it when the itch in his groin unsettles a man's wits, but you achieve the same result on the itch for domesticity. Haven't you even the sense to know that a woman is *never* the same woman when she's had a child?"

"That includes the possibility of a change for the better."

"I know that motherhood is supposed to do wonders for the character, but I can't say I've noticed it in practice. The boozers go right back to the bottle, the slobs have a new excuse for letting things slide, the whiners become giddy with the embarrassment of riches. The most I'll say is that some of the unlikeliest women turn out to be surprisingly good mothers. And this usually means that their husbands have to look elsewhere for a little home entertainment."

"You're getting warmer," Owen said. "Their possessiveness can take a new direction, as you describe it, but it can also become diffused a little, to everyone's benefit. Be fair, Tony. Apart from getting tired of being disapproved of for your frivolity, you were also convinced that Carol was the wrong wife for *me*—and that was largely my fault."

"You *are* in a bad way," Tony said mournfully, returning to his chair.

"I kept complaining to you of the way she meddled in my work, and Lord knows it was true. She couldn't help herself. She insisted on doing all my typing, but she could never get through half a page without discovering six reasons why the chapter should be rewritten from scratch to give it a profounder significance. And the next thing you'd know we'd be in a flaming row."

"If you're trying to remember those fights as friendly quarrels which were reconciled by a kiss, I'll be happy to disabuse you."

"No, they were hell, and I haven't forgotten," Owen said. "But such unnecessary hell. Carol is a big girl and she has an outsize in energy and possessiveness, and there was nowhere to spend them except on me. She got more obsessed by my alleged genius than I've ever been, at least since I was an adolescent. She was going to make another Proust of me if it killed us both. None of that would have happened if there had been a brat underfoot to occupy half her attention, but at the time we were broke and I was frightened of still another responsibility, and I never thought of the solution till afterwards. Well, she has a child now, and it's made a lot of difference, believe me. In that way she's . . . changed, and quite a bit." Arguing with Tony always led a man into sounding more ardent than he had intended. "I hope you realize this is all quite academic, though," he added. "I'm taking her seriously, yes, to the extent that I'm back in love again—which is where I like to be. My work goes better for my knowing I don't have to prowl the roof tops. But I'm a long way from finding the courage for a fourth shot at something permanent. And if I suggested it, I'm not at all sure that she'd be in favor of the idea."

"Now there is precisely where you make a damn fool of yourself," Tony said briskly. "She'd snap at the bait, and she wouldn't spend ten seconds worrying how bad the quarrels would be this time. That's what I was getting at earlier. When you tangle yourself with a novice —I don't mean a virgin but a girl who still hasn't turned professional —there's a sporting chance that you're what she's been looking for. She has some practical considerations in view, no question, but she also wants a *man*, some particular sort of man, and if you can help her persuade herself you're the man she's had in mind, she might even settle down to trying to make you the happiest guy in the county. I've known it to happen once or twice, and I've never figured out why those jokers deserved such luck. But when a woman has a child on her hands, she isn't thinking like that, no matter how beautiful her character has become under the uplifting influence of motherhood. Carol isn't looking for a man *as a man*. She's tired of worrying what will happen to the kid if she falls ill and can't provide an income. She's looking for someone to be a father to little Whosis. She wants to get the responsibilities off onto somebody else's shoulders, so she can go back to the uncomplicated and rewarding drudgeries of raising the child. That's what Carol is thinking, and don't fool yourself."

"And it all seems quite natural to me," Owen said.

"Oh, it's natural enough, but where does it leave you?" Tony asked ferociously. "You aren't a person at all; you're just a collection of advantages. And don't delude yourself on that score either. You may think of yourself as being broke, but these things are relative: you'll never worry where the next month's rent is coming from or whether you ought to find a less expensive dentist. I don't doubt that Carol has you taped as a man who gets a kick from playing father. And she has that quirk about the art world: she'll want the kid to grow up knowing the theatre and the art galleries and the neurotics who keep them filled, and nobbling you again will answer very nicely. She'd swallow you without a qualm. The most I'll say is that she'll think of your check book as dessert, whereas Barbara thought of it as the main course."

"Is that supposed to dismay me?" Owen asked. "Because it doesn't."

"No? You'd rather be a convenience than a human being?"

"Tony, you know perfectly well that two people getting married never make the *same* bargain with one another, whatever they pretend. They have different ends in view, and it's just as well: if they both expect to be indulged in the same fashion, someone is going to have to give way, and that's where trouble starts. Of course Carol has

Lois uppermost in her mind; I'd like her less if she didn't. All that concerns me is whether she has energy and affection left over to be a wife. And it's actually a relief to have a clear awareness of what she needs of me. With your virgin huntresses there's no telling what they expect from life. Parties, constant stimulation, babying, playing hostess, babies of their own. Who knows? I'm not exactly a youngster myself. I want somebody who has some understanding of the demands of my work. Who is friendly in bed. Who wants to devote a reasonable amount of attention to making me *comfortable*. And who can make me feel that I'm working for something besides Barbara-the-Bitch and the Collector of Internal Revenue."

"And it doesn't bother you at all to realize that Carol would drop you like a shot if you started blowing your money on the ponies or if little Whosis took a dislike to you or if you quit writing plays to become a used-car dealer in Peoria?"

"I'd not realized it before," Owen said, "but the shoe is on quite the wrong foot when you accuse *me* of being a romantic."

2

To Jacob Zimmerman's way of thinking the small semiprivate room was overcrowded with women. Perhaps Ruth sensed his feeling for she promptly turned to making conversation with his roommate, Mr. Ying, who was recovering from a gall-bladder operation. Mr. Ying was a pharmacist, a graduate of N.Y.U., and a lover of Italian opera; when the two men were alone they got along splendidly, for Mr. Ying reserved his deplorable humor for the nurses, doctors and Jacob's visitors. "Me velly much betta today, sank you," he was saying to Ruth. Since Mr. Ying had not the slightest talent for dialects, his Oriental features lent only a flimsy verisimilitude to this improbable accent.

The two girls were being tiresome in different ways. Vickie was frankly depressed by the hospital surroundings and tried to dispel them by chattering away brightly about all she'd been doing, the news from Roger, the unlikelihood of her surviving to the wedding day without landing in the hospital herself. Whereas Alison, harking back to her stint as Morris's receptionist, assumed a knowledgeable interest in the clinical details. But this must have been going on for months, Grampa; weren't you ever conscious of feeling dizzy? As if at his age a man didn't feel dizzy for all sorts of reasons. You stood up, and your head needed a second or two to get used to the change in altitude.

But Vickie and Alison had at least the virtue of being decorative. The same could not be said for Amelia Booth—a brisk, tweedy symbol of duty-bent gentility. In the old days she would have shattered sick-room calm with good intentions and calf's foot jelly. She had brought a large box of long-stemmed roses which she was arranging one at a time in the vase a nurse had produced; the eventual effect would be much the same as if she'd inserted the entire lot and let the flowers lean as they chose. "It's a great pity you won't be at Mother's party," she said. "You and Mother will get along famously. But you'll meet her at the wedding, and that's the important thing, after all, isn't it?" She stepped back to gain perspective. "There, how does that look?"

"Muchee plitty," said Mr. Ying.

In the air these days there was an unspoken suggestion, to which even Ruth seemed to subscribe, that Jacob should feel particularly grateful for having been spared to celebrate Vickie's wedding. For once he lacked the energy to disagree, though he wanted to. He was glad to be alive (though it wouldn't have been a bad way to die: without the opportunity to feel indignant or afraid), but he could think of much better reasons to be glad. If it were Morris's boy, Tommy, getting married, perhaps he'd have felt differently: *there* was a true Zimmerman. But to tell the truth, and on some subjects he told it only to Gert, he was losing interest in Vickie. She was a pretty child, not as lovely as Alison, but daintier. But marriage to this Hilliard boy would be the end of her, in a sense.

Their children would probably grow up scarcely aware that they were partly Jewish. Perhaps that was a good thing from one point of view, and undeniably it was tiresome being a Jew, particularly if you didn't have the religion to give it meaning. But tiresome or not there was a lot to be said for it. Several thousand years of urban living gave a people a sense of values, real values. Take away the Jews and in all the United States you probably couldn't staff one first-rate symphony orchestra, and even if you could the line at the box office waiting to pay admission would be pretty skimpy.

"Such a convenient thing, to have a doctor in the family," said Mrs. Booth, looking doubtfully at Mr. Ying. She was the sort of woman who would waste her money on a private room, preferring to sink into an exclusive coma rather than have a stranger nearby who could ring for the nurse.

"Oh, Uncle Morris felt simply awful that he didn't see this coming," Alison said. "He was furious with Aunt Gert for not warning him."

"Now, Alison!" Ruth said.

"Well, he thought she should have told him how much Grampa was drinking. That's the first sign with this sort of diabetes," Alison explained wisely to Mrs. Booth. "Aunt Gert is such an innocent. She said, 'But it was only *tea*, Morris. I'd have told you right away if it had been anything stronger!'"

Mrs. Booth smiled politely. "I was so relieved to know it really couldn't be serious, when my brother said he saw your Aunt Gert at the Bridge Club last night."

And where should Gert be except at the Bridge Club? The surprising part of that story was that Mrs. Booth's brother had been there. Go into the club any evening of the week and three-quarters of the players there would be Jewish. Not that that meant they were necessarily good—if Gert was to be believed, most of them were pretty dreadful—but the point was that they were there. Or at the theatre or the chess clubs or the opera or at some friend's apartment scraping out a string quartet or quietly at home reading a book. But *doing* something. A Jew would put in a good day's work and still have mental energy to spend on his pleasures. Not like most Gentiles who needed four cocktails before they could face dinner and by nine in the evening weren't capable of anything but talking nonsense or chasing after other men's wives. There wasn't any real harm in the Gentiles, by and large, except that most of them, of whatever class, were no more than four or five generations from the farm. A few hours of mental activity and they were spent, completely exhausted. To such a point that they weren't even ashamed of it. It was funny how often you heard them say, as if it proved what ferocious workers they were, Oh, I'm too tired in the evenings for this or that. All I'm good for is to stretch out with a detective story.

From what Jacob heard, Mrs. Booth's brother went to the Bridge Club to get away from a wife who drank too much.

"It's a shame Roger can't be here for your mother's party," Vickie said.

"No, not really," Mrs. Booth said drily. "He'd be wanting your attention when the whole idea is to spread you around among the old fogies. It will be all older people, I'm afraid, and I find that girls are better at that sort of thing than boys are."

"I'd rather be where I am," Jacob said. "I don't like old fogies either."

"You don't know when you're well off, Mrs. Booth," Alison said. "Grampa would be capable of turning the party into a Socialist rally."

"Well, something always happens at Mother's parties. There was the time when that Fairchild woman went around urging us all to have our faces lifted. She insisted that it had made an entirely new woman of her, which is the foolish sort of remark that begs for comment. Her husband, who is old-fashioned without being farsighted, finally threw a glass of brandy in Freddie Ames's face, so of course Freddie dined out for the next month on the story of what he'd really said, and never repeated himself once. But I can't promise you anything as entertaining as that. You'll probably find it quite dull."

"Oh, I'm sure not," Vickie said. "Everybody's been telling me what a remarkable person Mrs. Langstaff is."

"I daresay they have," said Mrs. Booth. "But did you ask any of them what they meant by it?"

So for the sake of a smart-aleck question you exposed your family to outsiders! It was for small reasons like this that Jacob felt that Vickie was moving backwards on the evolutionary scale. As yet the Gentiles had only a hazy understanding of what civilization was: they put their emphasis on automobiles and air conditioners and actually had the innocence to call this a standard of living. The true standard was what use you made of the years of living, knowing what was important. You built a family. And if people were to be secure, that family was a unity to the world whatever might go on when the blinds were down. The attitude might be old-fashioned, but the fact remained that more Jews were psychoanalysts than went to them. If you had any sense you worked eight or ten hours a day at a job you could take some pleasure in, whether or not you got rich at it (by and large it was only the Jews who were underprivileged in talent who bothered to get very rich, for lack of anything better to do with themselves). And above all, to the extent of your own capacities, you made the most of the culture around you. *This* was civilization, and even the most barbarous Jews (the majority) had a curious instinct for it. When they got their chance they might make fools of themselves, as the newly prosperous always did, but also they took out season tickets to Carnegie Hall, set their daughters to studying the fiddle, sent their sons to the most exacting schools—and not merely for snobbish reasons but because all tradition insisted that a richer life was to be found somewhere in these directions. They might not comprehend it themselves, but they knew it would be true for their children.

Whereas his great-grandchildren who were Hilliards would never really be much at home in this world: working at jobs they didn't particularly like in order to support families they didn't know how to enjoy, always guiltily at a loss for what to do with their leisure. Helpless with puritanism, alcohol and Philistinism in a world full of music and art and literature and a thousand different ways to stretch the brains they'd been born with. Well, perhaps he wasn't being fair. Roger's father was a writer and Vickie's grandfather was a Zimmerman, so perhaps there was more hope for their children than for most. But it would be a bitter day when the thought of playing patriarch at such a wedding was the best reason he could find for being glad to be alive.

"When will they be letting you out of here?" Mrs. Booth asked.

"I expect Uncle Morris wants to be sure the insulin balance is just right," Alison explained importantly.

"They're giving me practice sticking needles in myself," Jacob said. "My own son laughs at me every time I wince."

"You'll get used to it," Ruth said.

"Why should I get used to it?" he inquired. "A man was never intended to be a pin cushion."

"Well, I'll run along now and leave you to your family," Mrs. Booth said, and let the other women make a fuss over her nobility in having come uptown. She wrapped herself up, gathered together the packages which showed that the expedition had not been one of altruism alone, paused in the doorway to reprimand Jacob archly for having given them all such a scare.

"Velly plitty flowahs," Mr. Ying assured her, a kindly man atoning for his roommate's lack of cordiality. "Come again soon, chop-chop."

3

Just after the Second World War, when such properties could still be acquired cheaply, and before Mrs. Langstaff had discovered her mania for keeping constantly on the move, she had bought a charming villa in Cap d'Antibes with the intention of settling there. Although nowadays she was rarely in residence for more than a month or two in the spring and perhaps another month or six weeks in the autumn, the villa yet remained her most permanent address and had proved, in several ways, a most profitable investment. Attractively furnished and efficiently staffed, it rented during the summer months for a price which more than covered the annual upkeep and the servants' wages. For the remainder of the year, whether or not Mrs. Langstaff was there, the villa was at the disposal of her many peripatetic friends, with a certain priority going to friends who kept commodious apartments in Rome, Paris, London or New York, country houses here or there, or yachts. Mrs. Langstaff had an ingrained dislike of stopping in hotels, and a limited income, but by judicious deployment of her hospitality she contrived to spin about the globe in good style at little more expense than the cost of her passage.

For this visit to New York she had the use of the apartment of the Wendell Knipes, who obligingly had extended their stay on the Riviera through the month of May. The Knipes' apartment was perhaps not the most ideal setting for Mrs. Langstaff's uncompromising femininity, for the scheme of decoration derived from Wendell's acquisitive habits during his various postings as Ambassador—the walls glittered with a virile collection of scimitars, yataghans and machetes, stilettoes and krises—but it had the advantage of a perfectly enormous living room overlooking Central Park, a room designed for extravagant cocktail parties. The first twenty guests had huddled in one corner for companionship; it was only with the arrival of forty more that the party spread out to occupy the room. Today, at least, Mrs. Langstaff's choice seemed a sensible one, but Stephen Booth blinked at the picture of his small and stately mother-in-law alone at night in this vastness festooned with exotic cutlery.

The party buzzed and shrilled and clattered as all such parties seemed to do regardless of the age level involved, which in this case was rather high. Raising the average was a perennial sprinkling of Hilary Langstaff's old friends, thinning year by year, sere and apt to be a bit doddery. (A few of them had never established Stephen in their minds; when reminded that he was Amelia's husband they would take it for granted he was 'that writer fellow,' and be proud of their knowledge that he was writing plays these days. They would be doubly bewildered this year since Owen Hilliard had been invited: a stand-in for his absent son: a consolidation of the clans.) Most of the guests were the gleanings of Mrs. Langstaff's near-quarter-century of widowhood, the greater part of them New Yorkers or part-time New Yorkers though they might originally have been acquired at the casino in Cannes or during a cruise in the Aegean. Collectively they had a shiny, well-bred, ageless elegance, and you thought of them as maturely youthful, like yourself—the proper age to be—until Vickie Fortescue came dancing by, and then suddenly you realized that everybody else in this room was on the wrong side of the slope, slipping irretrievably downhill, and you were slipping with them.

An observation the human spirit denied to the last: it was with no sense of decline that these people fell upon old acquaintances, set about gaining new ones, or insinuated themselves into the clusters about the celebrities Mrs. Langstaff had produced as seasoning for her party. As an experienced hostess she knew that the more useless people were themselves, the more pleased they were to claim familiarity with the accomplished and had provided two actresses, a diplomat from the United Nations, a superannuated poet (the only sort her guests were likely to have heard of), a prima donna, Owen Hilliard, and a bishop notable for his Christianity.

Thus most of the guests, as well as meeting Vickie and her parents, were under notice that Mrs. Langstaff expected to be feted entertainingly in the weeks to come. If she followed her usual custom, she would give, the evening before her departure, a very small dinner party for those friends who had best lived up to their responsibility. But a few people were there to satisfy more devious purposes of their hostess. She had somehow captured in mid-flight a pair of transatlantic friends, Lord and Lady Arnstein: charming, highly cultured, gracious, and doubtless somewhat bewildered by it all, never suspecting that they were Mrs. Langstaff's first line of defense against unthinking anti-Semitism, she being of the belief that snobbery was a more powerful force than prejudice.

As a rule Stephen was content to find his own pseudoanthropological amusement in cocktail parties, but here he could never escape the knowledge that he was under Mrs. Langstaff's all-seeing vigilance. He was not intimidated by his mother-in-law (as was Joan Langstaff, for example); he had learned that he could divert her with jocular, pedantic teasing as long as he behaved himself at her parties. In her, her daughter's weakness for social manipulation had been developed to a high art. Mrs. Langstaff always appeared to be enjoying herself heedlessly, but she was in constant catalytic circulation, encouraging the withdrawn, damping the argumentative, blending the unlikely, never missing a thing. He might maneuver to keep at the opposite end of a crowded room, screened by taller men, and the instant the guests were gone she would be onto him: "Stephen, I do think you might have been a little more courteous to Miss Frothingham. I know she's lost what few wits she once possessed, but she *is* Amelia's godmother, she detests her only nephew, and I've never seen the value of flying in the teeth of Providence."

Even the most rational of men might permit himself one superstition, and Stephen's was that his mother-in-law could see around corners. Accordingly he endeavored to appease her by playing what he believed to be the true socialite: paying irrational compliments, talking nonsense, listening admiringly to gossip, misinformation and opinions that would have embarrassed even his more backward students. And all the while, today, he was wondering which of these people might be able to lead him to his half brother, Eliot Clay. For this world was merely the conservative, respectable quarter of Eliot's world; the two overlapped; there were likely to be half a dozen people here who knew Eliot and one or two who knew him quite well. The difficulty was, which ones?

In the week since the need for him had arisen, Eliot had neither phoned in nor made an appearance. Although exasperating, this was not surprising. In the grip of a new enthusiasm, such as the notion of developing a vocalist of his own, Eliot was inclined to stay away until he could report success or until he could feel that his initial promises of glory had decently receded and he could return unconcernedly, explaining that he'd decided the idea wasn't really worthy of him.

Normally, except for one occasion when there had been some legal papers for Eliot to sign, this hadn't mattered in the slightest. But for the past week Stephen had found himself growing daily more apprehensive, uneasy, distrustful of his original bland assumption that Eliot could remove his dilemma with a wave of the hand.

If Joyce had only nagged at him, thrown a few fits of hysteria as he would have expected her to do, that might have led him into righteous indignation and taken the edge off the sense of pressure that he felt. What she was doing was infinitely worse. With an air of submissive gratitude she had surrendered her misery into his keeping. Each day she arrived early and drudged late, so the Bushmen would not suffer from the days she would eventually lose. And since in her own mind the problem no longer existed, she was beginning to permit herself the luxury of second thoughts. Twice in the past several days, towards five o'clock he would hear her industry slow and stop and find her looking dreamily out of the window. When he asked if something was wrong, he got a flood of daydreams: suppose she went ahead and had the baby after all. A little boy all her own, to bring up, to love and cuddle and cherish. . . .

A less responsible person would have seized the excuse to wash his hands of the matter then and there; Stephen wanted to and hadn't the courage. He knew that Joyce was indulging in the merest fantasies, that it would be a cruelty both to her and to the unborn child to take her seriously. Joyce might relish the picture of herself dandling an animated doll at her knee, but she simply wasn't a girl to thumb her nose at her prudish little segment of society; all her neuroses would be exacerbated beyond measure by the upbraidings, reproaches and sniggers she had brought on herself, and the bastard child would inevitably be the victim. On the other hand, to let her go ahead and have the baby with the purpose of giving it up, she who could not afford to drop discreetly out of sight for five or six months, would be to expose her to all the torments without a hope of recompense —just the way to unbalance her completely.

These arguments were so clear-cut that they could have been gainsaid only by the unthinking or bigoted religious. But they weren't the arguments he could use with Joyce. He could scarcely *tell* her that she would inevitably cripple any child she had under these circumstances, and, besides, she was just the sort to persuade herself that motherhood would be a sort of therapeutic shock treatment. So, taking a leaf from her own book, he reminded her that a disclosure of her condition would no doubt be the death of her mother. She agreed earnestly, assured him of her steadfastness, and yet—perhaps because, at least subconsciously, such a fatal consequence didn't really seem such a bad idea—she went right on daydreaming.

Stephen was terrified that if he didn't locate Eliot soon, get the arrangements for an abortion firmly pinned down, Joyce might change her mind, or simply procrastinate until it was too late. He was terrified, not only out of humanitarian concern for Joyce and the child, but also for purely selfish reasons. His imagination had been at work. He could see Joyce stubbornly refusing to name the father of her unborn child—which would lead Mrs. Neilson straight to the conviction that *he* must be the guilty party. Since Mrs. Neilson's only friends, left over from the days of her good health, were wives and widows of other faculty members, this would be fully as catastrophic as if he'd asked around among his colleagues for the address of a good abortionist. Another man *might* believe in his innocence, but there was no charity for a male in the trade union of aging matrons.

Eliot would have to be found, and quickly. Without him, Stephen felt appallingly helpless. In desperation he had thrown out a couple of feelers of his own, raising the question most academically around some of his younger colleagues, not particular intimates of his, with a vague idea that somebody might be tricked into showing off his sophistication. It had been a foolish plan, for he never would have dared entrust Joyce to a practitioner discovered so haphazardly, and for his pains he had earned only a few glances of deep suspicion and the information that these things were more difficult than they used to be: the police had been cracking down recently. None of this had contributed to his peace of mind and had made him all the more frantic to locate his half brother.

Rooting through old address books, deciphering names and telephone numbers which had been crossed out, he compiled a list of some dozen friends' apartments where Eliot had perched for a time. Over the course of a couple of evenings he kept calling these numbers methodically until he got an answer. Twice he had to apologize to people who had come by their telephone numbers recently and had never heard of Eliot. The others, who knew of Eliot, sometimes explained briskly that they had no recent knowledge of his whereabouts or made fruitless suggestions, but quite as often led Stephen into the most grotesque conversations.

"Oh, come now, my lad," said a mellifluous baritone, "if Eliot has forgotten to get in touch with you that's a pity, but you really mustn't go chasing after him. It gives quite the wrong impression, you know, makes you seem overanxious. A show of indifference is much more effective, I assure you."

"You don't understand," Stephen had said, so shaken at being addressed as 'my lad' that he hadn't paid much attention to the rest.

"What a very pleasant voice you have!" said the baritone. "Would you like to come over for a drink while I call a few people who might know where Eliot is?"

Thereafter Stephen had begun by explaining he was Eliot's *brother*, without even mentioning the semidetached nature of the relationship. Even this did not necessarily save him from embarrassment.

"I'm afraid I simply don't believe it," said the amused contralto belonging to somebody down on Stephen's list as Miriam Warren. "Eliot wouldn't have kept a brother concealed from me. What did you say your name was?"

"Booth. Stephen Booth. Professor Stephen Booth," he added, trying to introduce a note of dignity.

"Oh, no! That's too delicious. Do you mean Eliot's name is really Eliot Booth?"

"We are half brothers, actually, Mrs. Warren—"

"Call me Miriam," she suggested. "Everybody does."

"I don't want to trouble you more than is strictly necessary—"

"But it's calling me Mrs. Warren that makes it all seem so unlikely. Eliot would never have spoken of me as Mrs. Warren, not with a straight face he wouldn't. If you're really a professor, I expect you've read Bernard Shaw."

"I'm sorry, I couldn't make out whether it was Mrs. or Miss," Stephen said. "I located your name and phone number in an old address book; Eliot borrowed your apartment some time ago, didn't he?"

"That was the winter I spent in Palm Beach," Miss Warren said reflectively. "For all the good it did me I might just as well have stayed home. Even the amateurs down there have a professional outlook, and the competition's too rough for a small-town girl. I'm from Oklahoma, originally. But I'll say that Eliot kept the place in lovely shape. Can you imagine?—he even repainted the kitchenette himself!"

Some time later, for Miss Warren was disposed to be talkative, it transpired that she had last seen Eliot one evening at the Blue Angel a month or two ago; just after Christmas, come to think of it, because she'd been wearing her new bracelet and shown it off to him. But she promised faithfully that if she ran into him in the next week or so, she'd tell him to get in touch with his brother, the professor. ("If you really *are* a professor; that's the part that still doesn't seem convincing.") Stephen had collected a number of such promises, but with each passing day he had less faith in them. For one thing, the impression he'd gained of these people was that they would never remember such an undertaking unless it was quite fresh in their minds. In the second place it was now apparent that Eliot had dropped from sight for the time being. "Yes, I noticed he wasn't at Sascha's party the other evening and wondered what had become of him," somebody had remarked. It was these incommunicado stretches of hard work which permitted Eliot to keep pace with his well-to-do playmates; all very laudable, Eliot-fashion, but how did you catch up with somebody who was designedly hiding from his friends?

"And just suppose," Joyce Neilson had said, with the fatuous expression of one who believed that Nature's secret purpose was the reproduction of neurotic spinsters, "just suppose it was a dear little girl. . . ."

A week of this was enough to drive a man to his wit's end. So now, miserably, Stephen prowled through his mother-in-law's cocktail party trying at the same time to remain in that lady's good graces and to match up her guests' names against those which had figured in Eliot's scandalous anecdotes often enough to stick in his mind. Here, for example, in the group of which Stephen was temporarily a part, was a rubicund, grey-haired gentleman named Kerrigan, bland, cheery, unctuous. If the woman chattering away at him was to be trusted, his given name was Brian. But he had, this gentleman, a nervous habit of twitching his upper lip as he spoke, a nibbling motion, distinctly rabbitlike. Wasn't it plausible, even likely, that in other circles he answered to the nickname of Bunny? There was a whimsical, party-giving Bunny Kerrigan who had cropped up frequently in Eliot's chronicles. Admittedly it was difficult to picture this sober-suited Kerrigan deploring some friend's unsavory divorce as the same fellow whose method of raising money for the Red Cross was to dress himself in a Roman toga and auction off seminaked call girls to his guests—but this difficulty Stephen could dismiss as an impediment in his imagination. Much more troublesome was the question of how to invite this gentleman to acknowledge the identity. Some such off-hand inquiry as 'Are you Bunny Kerrigan, by any chance?' might be egregiously offensive if in reality Bunny was some distant scape-grace cousin held in contempt by all right-thinking Kerrigans.

He had just laboriously arrived at the conclusion that the tactful inquiry was 'Are you *related* to Bunny Kerrigan?' when one of the vagrant eddies in the room swept Kerrigan away to another quarter, and, simultaneously, Stephen was forced to notice that he was being summoned by his mother-in-law. She neither beckoned nor inclined her head, but her resting gaze, one eyebrow slightly elevated, some-how held all the imperative demand of a policeman's whistle.

Mrs. Langstaff was a small and slender woman but very erect, with pale, shrewd blue eyes and a high-bridged, beaky nose. In these days of blueish tinting her hair was startlingly white, almost paper white, carefully shaped into soft scalloped curls that lay caplike on her finely boned head. She never appeared in public without a black velvet ribbon at her throat, and she affected an ivory-handled ebony cane, memento of a long-ago automobile accident but no longer necessary, a symbol merely, the emblem of her fragile-dowager imperiousness.

"Yours is a tiresome sex, Stephen," she greeted him. Her voice had harshened with age, but her speech was clipped and meticulous; she drove Amelia to distraction by pretending ignorance of the commonest slang. "The Fortescue woman may have no background at all yet she's perfectly sure of herself and everyone finds her delightful. She has the alien charm of a homebody. But look at Charles, will you."

Obediently Stephen looked at Charles. Backed against a wall just beneath some oriental broadsword which hung with its glittering point downwards, Fortescue was a natty, contemporary Damocles—resigned to the situation but not relaxed. He stood with a cocktail in one hand and a canapé in the other, looking as if he didn't know quite what to do with either one, and listened in baffled courtesy to the prattling of one of Mrs. Langstaff's oldest friends.

"He's all right at the moment," said Mrs. Langstaff, who regarded ennui as contagious and one unoccupied guest as the first symptom of a party's disintegration, "but there's a limit even to Meg Wyatt's good nature. When he's left alone, he just stands there. He doesn't make any effort. You would never believe his mother was a Haynes and his father was from the Tuxedo Park branch. Forty years of business destroys a man's social fibre. I'm afraid you will have to take him in hand, Stephen."

This was the sort of demand that made Stephen quail. It was one thing to find himself standing beside somebody, strike up a conversation on impulse, perhaps stumble on topics of mutual interest—but quite another to bear down upon a fellow guest under explicit instructions to be sociable. Then he could never think of anything to say; even when he knew the other person reasonably well his mind became an arid desert. The Fortescues would have heard the latest news from Roger at college, and except for the approaching marriage what did he and Charles have in common? He could imagine the two of them standing there, exchanging desultory observations on the animated throng about them, each contributing to the other's depression. Suddenly, as a mercy, he remembered that hour in the bar on Sixth Avenue with Mr. Rivkin from the Chess Club, while Mr. Rivkin told some story of the swindles of one of Charles's employees. What was the fellow's name? Something alliterative. But it didn't matter: he was the man Roger would be working under, and Fortescue would know whom he meant. The details of the story were still sufficiently clear in Stephen's mind; he had thought about it from time to time, wondering what he would do with it, but this was the first opportunity to do anything. The last few times Stephen had stopped by the Club Mr. Rivkin had not been there to hear of Stephen's growing reluctance to meddle in matters which he didn't really understand. Now the reluctance was abandoned in the relief of having a handy conversational gambit.

"All right," Stephen said graciously, but as soon as he had committed himself he began to fear for lost opportunities. "In a few minutes," he added. "There's someone I have to talk to first."

"Who?" asked Mrs. Langstaff with the forthright rudeness of the very old. She was not curious, merely alert to hamstring any effort to escape.

He had no one specific in mind and looked for inspiration among the latest arrivals. People came and went. On a Friday afternoon there would be several such parties, and the frenetically social would plan to look in on each one of them. Cries of adoration to the hostess, then a butterfly circuit of the room, hovering, flitting, affirming their popularity by the speed with which they must whisk it away. And then off again before Stephen could catch up with them: Has anybody here seen Eliot? "Freddie Ames," he said. "By the time I get free of Charles he'll be two parties further on."

"I had not realized that Freddie was a favorite of yours," Mrs. Langstaff said drily. "Well, don't be long. And don't fear that I'll leave you with Charles indefinitely. If you can't arouse him to a little more conviviality, I'll send Douglas to your rescue." For the duration of a party her son and son-in-law were aides-de-camp.

There was humiliation in an appeal to Freddie Ames, whom Stephen had never liked—liked still less for Freddie's ability to make him laugh. Freddie's purring epicene malice could be clever; that was the affront: he dazzled you with word trickery till you felt you were conniving at the cruelty. Physically he repelled: something was unnatural when pudginess was combined with fluid grace: Freddie had the coarsened felinity of an altered tom. But of all the people there he was the likeliest to provide a lead to Eliot. Freddie knew everybody; it was his only acknowledged occupation, though there were rumors that he received flamboyant Christmas presents from the more eminent gossip columnists.

"Freddie!" Stephen said defensively, catching him on the wing.

"Stephen, dear boy; no doubt you're quite at home among this shiny display of primitive phallic symbolism," Freddie said. "I warned Wendell that the sight of so many naked blades would make anybody suspect there must be a cuirass on the premises, but of course he missed the point." He made as if to move along, never imagining that he was in demand in this corner.

"You know Eliot, don't you?" Stephen said. "Eliot Clay, my half brother."

"But did I know of the relationship?" Freddie wondered, cocking his head, looking at Stephen with lively curiosity. "I suppose I must have. I've admired him for his uphill struggle from respectability. Heart-warming evidence that a man can lift himself by his own jockstrap."

Stephen had long recognized that Freddie went out of his way to be vulgar to the people he suspected of disliking him. "Have you seen him recently?" he asked patiently.

"As a general rule it would call for considerable ingenuity to avoid seeing Eliot," Freddie said. "But now that you raise the question—no, I haven't. Quite unnerving, when I stop to think of it. In New York we are so careless with our public fixtures. Have there been any unidentified bodies?"

"When he gets to working he sometimes drops out of sight for a time; I expect that's what's happened," Stephen said. "The difficulty is that I'm very anxious to get in touch with him." He fought down the impulse to sarcasm; that would be a losing battle. He humbled himself. "I was hoping you might have a constructive suggestion."

"It's quite possible I'll be seeing him the beginning of the week. At all events, some people who are bound to know where he's gone to cover. I could pass the word along."

"I'd be extremely grateful," Stephen said. But it was hateful to think that his peace of mind, the future stability of Joyce Neilson's life, might depend on the reliability of this flibbertigibbet. "It's really terribly important," he stressed.

"Don't jostle me with your urgency, dear boy," Freddie said. "The weightier the message, the likelier I am to mislay it. I'm already under enough of a handicap in the race against Father Time, and responsibilities are so aging."

4

Past a certain stage of adolescence when the herd instinct is still in force, most people, individually, will deny that they enjoy parties of more than eight or ten people. When a general conversation is no longer possible, they aver earnestly; a party is a dead bore: you never really get a chance to *talk* to anybody, the standing about is uncomfortable, the din gives you a headache. Having thus affirmed their status as discriminating, born conversationalists, these same people, masochists to a man, add another half dozen cocktail parties to their engagement calendar and plan themselves to give the largest party of the lot to pay off all their obligations.

So it has to be seen as admirable the way, as at Mrs. Langstaff's, a whole roomful of people who detest cocktail parties will grit their teeth and put on a good show of enjoying themselves. There are bound to be exceptions, of course. The odd misanthropist who declines to play the game. The coarser souls who are not disheartened by crowds. Ruth Fortescue fell into the latter category: she was, quite unashamedly, having a delightful time. Never would she have permitted herself the disloyal thought that Charles cramped her style socially, but she did like *people* a great deal more than he did, and that was the truth of it. Not intimately, necessarily: Ruth was chary of friendship. Just meeting them, chatting with them, getting a taste of new personalities. That was the joy of parties, especially other people's parties when she had none of the worrying to do. And a party like this, where all the people were extremely well-bred even by her rather exacting standards (some of Charles's associates, especially on the scientific side, tended to be boorish), and when everybody was busily complimenting her on her Vickie: a party like this was absolute heaven.

Yet this description of Ruth's pleasure, though perfectly accurate, makes her sound more ingenuous than in fact she was. In one corner of her mind she was very well aware, if she stopped to think of it, that probably a third of the people in the room were of a sort to resign from a club if a Jew were admitted. But why, for goodness' sake, should she stop to think of such a thing? She was enjoying herself; she had never been a person to go searching for indignations. To her, anti-Semitism was simply one of the incomprehensibilities of life, like electricity but less useful. Until an affront forced itself upon her notice (whereat she quietly retreated, unlike Gert who could be as prickly as their father), she preferred to deny its conceivability, and to disregard what might be being said out of earshot. And an affront this afternoon was unthinkable. These people were too polite, and their anti-Semitism was part of a private mythology, undismayed by a lifetime of never meeting a Jew who matched up to the caricature, sustained by legend, anecdote and the unshakable conviction that

that vulgar woman who always pushes past you to hail the only taxi on a rainy afternoon is almost certainly Jewish.

And superficially, at least, Ruth was right to think of these people as kindly and well-bred. To meet briefly, fleetingly, each of them was attractive in his or her own style: suave, pontifical or cheery; charming, brittle or sardonic. If there was vice in them, it wasn't a sort to appear on such short acquaintance; if there was malice in what they said, it was so smoothly spoken that most of it went right past Ruth's head.

"I don't see Joan Langstaff here this afternoon," said Mrs. Partridge. "She's not sick, is she?"

Ruth (whose mind naturally flew to her father who was still grumbling in the hospital but due to return home on Monday) took this for kindly solicitousness and hastened to reassure Mrs. Partridge, thereby dashing that lady's hope for the gossipy news that Joan was shut up again, in for another cure. Herself so gentle, Ruth was perhaps the one person in the room who would go away with the impression that she had spent the cocktail hour among gentlefolk.

At the far end of the room—beyond the shingle of balding heads, a world of temper away—Charles Fortescue had fallen into the depression that was giving concern to his hostess. Yet he was not one of the frustrated conversationalists nor, as a rule, was he misanthropic. Charles, as a matter of fact, was suffering from a curious sensation of *déjà vu*.

He had not come to this party disposed to be unsociable; to be strictly accurate he had come mechanically, without giving the matter a thought, as was rather common for him. The Charleses of this world surrender the greater part of their social life into the hands of their wives: they are firmly told that Wednesday evening is to be preserved against the calls of business, and as a rule promptly forget the reason; when Wednesday comes they are told which suit and necktie to put on, and it may not be until they are in the taxicab that it becomes clear to them whether this is the evening they are to have a quick bite at Sardi's and then see that play about incest, or is the evening for dining with the Harry Browns. As long as the wife plays fair, doesn't crowd in too many visits to her more detestable relatives or friends left over from school, such an arrangement saves wear and tear on a man's already overextended memory. Since Charles knew himself to be pampered (he was even obliged to be temperate in his dislikes, for a momentary spasm of indignation in the cab coming home one night could result in his wondering, some months later, why they no longer saw anything of the Harry Browns), he was content to let Ruth make plans for both of them and took it for granted that he would enjoy himself wherever she led.

Today she and Vickie had picked him up at the office, so they might all arrive together. On the way uptown Vickie had chattered in semipretended fear of meeting Mrs. Langstaff: Roger had evidently described his grandmother as a holy terror. Charles had been amused by this, had expected to like old Mrs. Langstaff (as, indeed, he instantly did), and had thought of the party ahead as the usual initial tedium followed by a few amusing encounters.

He had been betrayed by habit: a habit acquired in the quasi-social atmosphere of business conferences and conventions where one met so many new people with a minimum of opportunity to learn whether they were worth knowing. His first impulse was to find out what a man *did*. This was a defense mechanism. He had learned that men in the 'human' side of a business—personnel, public relations, advertising—were apt to be pretty poor value, whereas among the business and scientific executives he would generally turn up a few who were stimulating company. But in any case a man's work was the most interesting thing about him, so Charles had allowed this custom to extend into his personal life, and it had never let him down until today.

Perhaps it was unfair to generalize from the first handful of people he had spoken to, but it appeared that most of the men in this room didn't *do* anything at all, or, if they did, it scarcely seemed worth mentioning. ("I collect books," one young man said sweetly, unashamed.) Although Charles had not found himself in such a setting in years and years, it was not really so very surprising when you stopped to think of the people that Mrs. Langstaff was likely to know. What had shaken him was the sudden realization, just as he was beginning to enjoy the oddity of it, that this was the world he had grown up in.

To all intents this was the same sort of party he had ambled through, proud and sure-footed, when he was Vickie's age. This was the world he had been bred to, had doubtless expected to take his place in—until that day in his last year at college when his father's death sent the imposing-seeming but flimsy financial house of cards atumbling. For years his father had been drinking the capital; faced by the spectre of Prohibition he had plunged wildly into debt to stock his cellar against the most optimistic view of his liver's life expectancy. Charles had been left with almost no assets except the one on which it was illegal to raise money; the collateral family pulled the strings to get him a promising job and washed their hands of him.

In retrospect, Charles recognized that the timing had been fortunate. A few years later the shock would have been that much greater: he might easily have wasted his life resenting his 'bad luck.' But a boy at school in those less pragmatic times had been so immersed in school life that 'afterwards' was an unreality, and one form of afterwards little more disconcerting than another. He had made the transition without a struggle, fortunate again in that he had found his work absorbing from the very first.

He had made a good executive. Not a brilliant one, perhaps, but he was in a field where brilliance was less important than a commanding grasp of detail. It took no genius to recognize when the world market for copper was rising, that the time had come to open the new mine at Torracho. But a new camp, apart from all the technical planning involved, meant a whole sweep of sudden promotions, the reshuffling of men in six other camps without disruption of the work. Something of an artist in management was needed to see to it that everyone who could reasonably expect a promotion ended up satisfied, while the plodders were kept to jobs that ran themselves and the enterprising and resourceful men got all the more ticklish assignments.

An engrossing business, and though at times Charles complained fervently, he knew that he had been more or less happily engrossed in it for the better part of forty years. Not much given to introspection, this was the first time, confronted by an apparition of the life he might have led, that he wondered what the devil he would have done with himself for all those years without a job to keep him busy. What did these men do with their time? No doubt it was a foolish question. With an unaccustomed burst of imagination Charles supposed that they saw him as a slave to his office, a pathetic toiler deprived of their splendid freedom. But trying to stretch his imagination a bit further, to conceive of that expanse of time with the affairs of Andean C & Z magically subtracted—with all those hours to be filled somehow with parties, time-killing games, gossip, pointless journeying, frittering hobbies—this was more than he could manage. A lifetime later he was stunned by the narrowness of his escape.

It was a dying world, of course; in another generation or so society wouldn't have room for people who didn't pull their weight. And just as well, too, in his opinion, though that opinion was based neither on morality nor economic principles: just that the pleasures of idleness seemed outweighed by the perils of boredom. He had no evidence for this; as already suggested, the people around him, far from betraying the canker of ennui which should be corroding their souls, gave every sign of being delighted with life. Secretly convinced that he knew better, that the party was a hollow sham, Charles stood aloof, pitying, chatting politely with the people Mrs. Langstaff passed on to him from time to time evidently under the curious impression that they would particularly interest him.

But rescue was on the way, and without any further machinations on the part of his hostess. Passing nearby, in company with a large-framed, dark-haired young woman, Owen Hilliard caught sight of him and held on high an amber-lit highball glass, calling, "Just as I promised you: ginger ale!" With a vague mutter of apology to Mrs. Wyatt, Charles elbowed aside a couple of wastrels and pounced. For today he was willing to take Owen at his own evaluation as a conscientious drudge.

5

In his coming Charles gave the impression of an oppressed, dignified tourist in some backward land breaking free of a host of importunate natives to fall on the neck of a fellow countryman. He came so precipitately that he was upon them before he noticed that he was awkwardly encumbered for acknowledging an introduction. There was no convenient surface for his cocktail glass. He glared at the fragment of pastry-encrusted sausage in his other hand, started to raise it to his lips, thought better of this, made a half-hearted effort to accommodate cocktail and sausage in the same hand—but all with unflustered equanimity. As a last resort he sketched a bow at Carol.

"How do you do?" he said.

"Carol is the witness to my virtue," Owen said, sipping ginger ale.

"Is that why you brought me?" she asked.

"Mainly to protect me from the debutantes, but there aren't any. It's a long time since I was at one of these parties. The dialogue hasn't changed, but the cast has aged."

"Without maturing," Charles said.

"Yes, you looked as if you'd had a surfeit of small talk," Owen said.

"I don't mind small talk if it's *about* something," Charles said.

"What do you say to a woman who's given her life to breeding Afghans?"

"I'd have fled, just as you did," Carol assured him.

"You have to be in practice," Owen said. "Like everything else today, frivolity's become a full-time occupation."

"I'm used to people who do things I can understand," Charles agreed. He looked at Carol. "Are you in the theatre, too?" he asked hopefully.

"Good heavens, no!" she said, much amused. "Does Owen usually show up with an actress in tow?"

"It seemed like a very plausible guess," Charles said with heavy gallantry. But he had been disappointed. He had so obviously wanted Carol to be an actress from that wicked, bohemian world he liked to believe in. And his disappointment stirred Owen to mischief.

"No, Carol is just an old, old friend," he said.

"The cast has aged," she murmured.

"As a matter of fact," Owen finished casually, "we were married for a while." He got the effect he was trying for: he had shaken Charles to the depths of his conventional soul. During one of their lunches together Charles had admitted that he found it astonishing that Owen and Amelia had remained on such easy terms. Commendable and convenient, but astonishing. To his way of thinking, evidently, a divorce was the worst sort of emotional upheaval, bitterly fought out and leaving a lasting vindictiveness in its wake. There was no telling whether Charles had had bad luck with his divorced friends or had been conditioned by childhood memories; one might suspect that Charles's father had been the sort of man who would have raised his son on spiteful stories of what an unspeakable bitch his mother had been. But whatever the cause, there it was: by rights Owen should have borne a grudge towards Roger's mother, so his fondness for her was one more symptom of the exotic slovenliness of the life he led. From this point of view, it was somewhat venturesome for Owen to come at all to a party given by his former mother-in-law. For him to come with still *another* ex-wife on his arm was more than Charles could take in his stride.

"You were . . . ?" said Charles, with the uncertain smile of one who may be missing the point of a joke. His self-assurance was much too well fixed to leave him floundering for long; he recovered almost at once. "Oh, then you must know Roger!" he said to Carol, heartily. But in that instant his glance had skidded sideways as if he half expected to see Amelia bearing down on them, coming to denounce this outrage to her mother's hospitality. The reality would have been quite beyond Charles's imagining. Amelia had looked at Owen in mild surprise but had greeted Carol warmly, saying how sorry she had been to hear of Carol's husband. "I thought of sending a note, but I was afraid it might seem rather. . . ." And Amelia had ended on a vague gesture that indicated the complete breakdown of etiquette in these situations. At one time, resolving the problems of Roger's vacations, Amelia and Carol had inevitably seen a good deal of one another. But did a woman write a note of condolence to her ex-husband's second wife on the occasion of a subsequent husband's death? *That* was the sort of dilemma modern society threw up; not the melodramatic tensions conceived by Charles's conventionality.

To Owen, Charles's conventionality had become fair sport, to be shocked on principle—and this was the unexpected but direct result of Melmoth's visit. Being made privy to a man's hidden past apparently gave one a curious sense of familiarity with him, a covert kinship. Overnight Charles had ceased to be a stranger whose stuffiness ought to be treated respectfully. The stuffiness itself had stood revealed as something very different from the usual calcification of conservative attitudes. Charles, after all, had once been a violent rebel. He had tried to escape, and when this hadn't worked he had tried to pull the prison down on his own head. He had failed again, even more miserably, leaving someone else to pay the price of his rebellion. So he had surrendered; he had crept home and made a fresh start. And he had blocked away the memory of his failure behind methodical bricks of orthodoxy. A model marriage, a model family. The dignity of achievement, the solidity of success. The chameleon safety of conformity, layer upon layer. He was like a lapsed Communist, striking exaggerated postures of sanctimony to deny the past.

But Owen could not take the façade seriously, although by this time it was doubtless quite real, far more real than the long-lost rebellious adolescent. This didn't matter to Owen. The rebellious adolescent was part of his awareness now; he had become the family friend whose recollections of juvenile misbehavior prevent him from honoring the actual adult. He had become, more precisely, the disreputable, knowledgeable half brother in the play he was writing— pushed into this position by Charles's very insistence on thinking of writers as a race apart, amoral and unconstrained. If someone treated you as irresponsible, you tended to respond irresponsibly. So, like the fictional half brother, Owen pricked at the pomposity that condescended to him.

"Yes, Roger is my favorite ex-stepson," Carol said. "I was hoping he might be here today, though Owen said there wasn't a chance."

"He's too busy even for love letters," Charles said. "But not too busy to answer the telephone, apparently. Vickie must be running up quite a bill on the line to Princeton."

"It's a long time since I've seen him," Carol said. "I still can't picture him as all grown up, about to get married, start work. . . ." She turned to Owen. "Come to think of it, I still don't know what sort of job he's getting."

"Actually, he's coming to us at Andean," said Charles, to whom it would never occur that the greater part of New York wouldn't have the least idea what Andean might be. Owen winced, sensing trouble ahead.

"Oh?" said Carol. "Mining? Has he taken an engineering turn?"

"The advertising end," said Charles. "We have a small department, and there happened to be an opening."

"I see," Carol said. Briefly she glanced Owen's way: an expressionless glance which nevertheless accused him of having suppressed this information deliberately. And this was probably true. Carol shared the Village prejudice which considered advertising as the natural refuge of the incompetent, and he hadn't been in a mood for arguments. "Or, rather, I don't see," Carol corrected herself. "I wouldn't have thought a company like yours would do much advertising."

"We all do it," Charles said. "We're public relations minded, as long as it's paid for with money the government would tax away in any case. Why, at the last Board meeting somebody wondered whether we shouldn't have a television show. No one could think of a single reason why we should, but that didn't prevent us from discussing it for half an hour. Have you ever done any work for television, Owen?"

"Once," said Owen. "Just once. Never again."

"I would think it paid pretty well."

"Not well enough to cover the wear and tear," said Owen. "First you write something, then you strike out every line that might offend anybody. That leaves a lot of holes."

"It's your public relations in action," Carol explained. "If Andean were paying for the show, you wouldn't want any viewer's sensibilities to get hurt."

But Charles didn't care about the ins and outs of television; he pounced on what he took to be a fresh clue to Carol's place in the scheme of things. "Are you a writer, then?" he asked with hope renewed.

"According to Owen, I'm not even a good critic," she said, smiling. "I work in an antique shop."

If this was a second disappointment to Charles, at least it offered him meat for conversation. He assumed without hesitation that if Carol sold antiques she must be interested in the subject, probably an authority on it. He, too, had some acquaintance with antiques: his wife collected the damn things. As treasurer to this collection he had picked up some of the terminology and formed a few opinions. Every time he and Ruth came back from Europe, they brought with them some cabinet or panetière guaranteed to be several centuries old. He privately suspected that these were whittled out of orange crates during the long winter months, in preparation for the tourist season. He didn't want to be didactic about this; he was open to correction by anyone who knew better, but he doubted if as much furniture had been made during the time of Louis XIII as was imported every summer. . . .

Because Carol was Carol, or perhaps simply because she was a woman, she humored Charles in this vein. If the man wanted to talk about antiques, then she would oblige. Owen soon became bored and restless. This was the first time, he realized, that he had seen Charles out in the open, among strangers, away from any of the sources of his security; Charles's fundamental lack of ease had never been so visible. He had enormous poise and self-assurance, of course, but these were solitary strengths; he had no ease with people. His treatment of Owen as a symbol of bohemia was not the peculiarity it seemed, but part of a characteristic pattern; he was treating Carol in just the same way. There was much that was interesting about Carol, but none of it had to do with antiques. She had a cultivated taste but no special training; she might as well have worked in a bookstore or an art gallery (as at different times she had), and she would have been precisely the same woman. Either this eluded Charles, or he shied away from it. He addressed himself to the Antique Dealer, as with Owen he spoke to the Writer. He kept people at the distance of their vocations, presumably because he found them safer and more comprehensible that way; he had said as much himself, 'I'm used to people who do things I can understand.' Work enforced a measure of conformity; professional emotions were as straightforward as ambition or envy. It was only after hours that a person relapsed into eccentricity, became a private person with all a private person's irrational impulses and devious motivations. Having once been betrayed by his own individuality, perhaps it was logical that Charles should never be able to trust anybody else's.

That Carol had been thinking along somewhat the same lines became apparent a few moments later when a random eddy in the party providentially swept Charles away from them, deposited him in the keeping of Stephen Booth. Carol gazed after him reflectively before she turned to Owen. "It isn't shyness, exactly, is it?" she said. "But I can see why you're intrigued by him."

"Have I said I was intrigued by him?" Owen asked.

"Well, you keep speaking of him, as if you were trying to puzzle him out," she said. "And he *is* unexpected for what he is. As if he'd rented a double portion of confidence and fallen behind on the payments."

"You're being intuitive," he protested.

"I have to be, if nobody ever tells me anything," she replied. "Couldn't Roger have found himself an honest job?"

"There aren't many honest jobs for a boy who's done his thesis on the poetry of Andrew Marvell," Owen said irritably. "He could teach, I suppose, but he hasn't the dedication for starving. Hell, he might have gone to work for one of the news magazines. There are dirtier fates than advertising."

6

Outside, the evening was raw and drizzly, yet as the air in the room grew blue with cigarette smoke someone was sooner or later bound to open one of the windows. These were designed to look like French windows and ought to have led somewhere, to a balcony at least—but there was no balcony, no room for a balcony: only four absurd inches before the stone balustrade, a space useless except for collecting dirt and flying leaves from the park in autumn, some idiot architect's way of adding ornament to his façade.

The smoke thinned out. A few women in the vicinity of the open window began to fumble for stoles that weren't there. Amelia Booth caught a glance from her mother and went to start the room on a new cycle of stuffiness. But before she closed the window, she stood there for just an instant, looking at the scene below.

Darkness had fallen but it wasn't a true darkness. This was one of the evenings when low-lying clouds caught all the light of the city and sent it back, diffused and ghostly. Central Park lay before her: the glistening, crouching bulks of trees, the pin points of light, singly and in streamers where ran the transverse roads. A precise oblong of countryside penned in by looming, grey, window-lit buildings topped here and there by flashing signs. More directly beneath her the avenue was cut off by the balustrade, but she could see the sidewalk opposite, where umbrella tops hurried to and fro or gathered in clusters to wait for the next bus.

It was one of the many aspects of the metropolitan scene so familiar to Amelia that she could scarcely be said to have *seen* it at all. She had grown up in this city, lived here all her years; what she saw was not so much a place as a lifetime. She did not orient herself in space: there, on her left, were the towers of Central Park South; in front of her, beyond that building-block skyline, was the river where the great ships lay in harbor; on her right, northwards, if you continued far enough you came to Harlem, a region as unknown to her, except in glimpses from trains emerging aboveground to pause at 125th Street Station, as the shores of Tierra del Fuego. But Amelia located herself by periods of her life. Somewhere straight ahead of her, on the other (or wrong) side of the park, was where she and little Roger had lived for a couple of years, victims of the wartime housing shortage. On her right, up towards the museum, was where she had gone to school. On the left, where the sky was brightest, the playground of her adult life: the region of the great shops and the fine restaurants, Broadway and the opera and the offices of the different causes she had served—and beyond, the Village where she truly lived.

But this area where she stood now was her girlhood, forever her girlhood. Behind her, halfway to Madison Avenue and a few blocks down, was where she had first lived, in a town house which had ceased to exist even before the Second War. These sidewalks below had sparked to her roller skates; Central Park had then been *her* park, romance, enchantment, adventure. She had a fitful memory of a rustic open-air pavilion which served some unknown grown-up function in the summers and in the winter had been the scene of shrieking games of Prisoners' Base. She had no idea whether it still existed in this city where yesterday's landmarks were so lightheartedly obliterated, where it was never possible to revisit a memory and find it unchanged. The speed of change was dismaying; also, if she let herself be morbid about it, was the thought that tomorrow morning other little Amelias would be playing the same games down there, and she was a middle-aged woman.

The Depression had come, her father had had reverses, and the town house was sold. But they took an apartment on the Avenue only a block or so away, and the park was still hers, though now for less childish purposes: riding lessons and skating parties in the winter. At what point had the park ceased to belong, become an expanse of uninteresting greenery to be sped through, unseeing, the quickest route to a visit in the Eighties? She had strolled there with Owen in the first days of that long-ago overwhelming love. At night they had sat on the benches outside, perhaps the very ones she saw below her now (if anything in this city was so enduring), holding hands, talking, stealing kisses when the avenue was deserted for an instant, postponing the moment when he would deliver her to her front door. Remarkably adolescent, when you recalled that neither of them had been exactly a child; remarkably sweet.

She could remember (and was it this random recollection which had provoked a twitch of nostalgia?) a fragment of one such late-night, park-bench conversation.

"Tell me," Owen had demanded out of nowhere, "don't you feel at all sorry for Guy Abercrombie?"

Already she had learned to treat his question thoughtfully. He distrusted impulsive answers, so she gave the same answer a few seconds delayed—taking credit for ratiocination while she wondered what he wanted to be told. "I suppose I am in a way, intellectually," she had said. "It was never a formal engagement, but I know Guy took it for granted. And he's somebody who'll always be shaken by the loss of anything he takes for granted." This last, with its ring of a profound insight, had pleased her at the time.

"But he's such an awful fool!" Owen had cried out in the crisp night air. "Not to make sure of you when he had the chance!"

"There's a policeman down the block keeping a doubtful eye on you," she had said, understanding now that Owen was imagining what *he* would feel if he were in Guy's shoes, which was quite silly really because the two men were utterly unalike, and it was difficult to remember that only a few weeks ago she had thought herself in love with another man. The past had shattered; Guy was scarcely recognizable among the fragments. She would feel sorry for him if Owen insisted, but it seemed an irrelevant emotion. "Perhaps he'd have made sure of me if I'd encouraged him to," she had said. "I expect I knew if I waited, you'd show up." Owen had hooted with laughter, but she had defended her logic: there must be some good reason why a girl procrastinated until something clicked in her heart and she knew that her future was settled for ever and ever. . . .

Amelia sighed for a time when life had seemed so clear-cut, closed the window on the early evening and her girlhood, and turned back to a room where Owen flirted with one of his various ex-wives and Guy Abercrombie, grown bald and paunched in a pointless fidelity, stood with her mother mourning (for lack of another victim) the demise of good breeding. "In Europe," Mrs. Langstaff was saying, "it would be quite unthinkable of people to wait till their hostess's back was turned and then slip off without saying good-bye. Yet unless there is a singularly large assemblage in the bathroom, fully a dozen have done precisely that."

The room had emptied out considerably. The party hoppers had long since departed; the suburbanites trickled away to catch their trains; the remaining guests would hang on till the seven-thirty rush for dinner engagements elsewhere. It was hoped that no unperceptive bore would hang on much past that hour, since Mrs. Langstaff had reserved a table at l'Aiglon for eight o'clock. A table for six— Owen's temporary reinstatement in the family did not extend to dinner.

"It's been a less eventful party than usual," Amelia said, to prevent herself from embarking on the old argument that the world was no worse off for the loss of the punctilio her mother was so fond of.

"You and Guy have been so absorbed in one another that you missed the excitement," Mrs. Langstaff said. "Audrey Fischer made one of her more expansive gestures and sliced away the end of a finger on one of Wendell's swords. She was talking to Dr. Hewitt at the time, but he simply dithered; apparently away from the operating table the sight of blood makes him squeamish. Stephen was standing right there and instantly fell into a dispute with General Ordway about whether the sword was a falchion or a scimitar, if those are the right words. All three of them seemed satisfied to let Audrey bleed to death on Wendell's carpet; it was one of the caterer's people who finally led her off to the bathroom. Her opinions of modern chivalry are quite unrepeatable."

7

For years Madge had been his defense against office problems; now the office problems had become his defense against Madge—a barricade against any more talk of the wedding reception. Coming up in the elevator a few evenings after Mrs. Langstaff's party, Charles had prepared the most provocative point of departure he could think of: with any luck this new dilemma of his might last them through a peaceful evening.

"Has it ever occurred to you," he called after her as she went to fetch the cocktails, "how often a person is better off for *not* knowing something or other?"

"Are you discovering that ignorance is bliss?" she asked from the kitchenette.

"I suppose I am, in a way," he conceded. "It's a cliché I've never thought made much sense."

"It's part of every woman's basic equipment," Madge said. "We learn early that we'd prefer not to know what you're up to behind our backs."

"Oh, *that*," Charles said, with an irrational twinge of guilt. "I wasn't thinking of anything of that sort."

"I didn't suppose you were, but it's why a cliché to you is profound philosophy to us." Madge returned with the pitcher of cocktails and a plate of tempting canapés. She was wearing a robe of luxuriant red; a sign that either she was in a good mood this evening or that she sensed a need to boost her spirits. "What have you found out that you wish you hadn't?"

"That Bruce Bigelow has been taking kickbacks. I still don't know on how large a scale."

Madge thought about this for a moment. "You've told me less of him than most of the others," she said, "but from what you've said it doesn't seem entirely in character."

"It isn't, and then again it is—that's part of the problem," Charles said heavily. "He's a decent man, fundamentally, and I'm fairly sure that's why he's been stealing. Am I a worse executive for understanding that there can be greater loyalties than to Andean C & Z?"

She smiled at him, but didn't bother to reply.

"He isn't a Jew, of course," Charles went on, "but he has that same sort of passionate paternalism I seem to associate with Jewish men.

Perhaps I'm wrong. I have the impression that most men are fond of their children but only up to a point, it never becomes obsessive. If they lose their children by divorce or something of the sort; it's no *great* tragedy. But never mind that. Bigelow is one of the exceptions. He has three boys, and they're the center of his whole life. And how he came to have custody of them is tied up with his coming to work for Andean."

The character of Bigelow's wife was outside the scope of Charles's knowledge; what was certain was that the marriage had been an unfortunate one which eventually became intolerable, and the couple split up. However, knowing that a divorce would mean that his wife would gain custody of the boys and that would pretty much be that, Bigelow had insisted on a separation and refused to be budged. He had no desire to remarry and was fairly sure that sooner or later his wife would get tired of a decorous celibacy.

At this time he had been working in one of the big advertising firms—Young & Rubicam, J. Walter Thompson: Charles couldn't remember which—but not in such an exalted capacity that would let him support himself, his wife and children separately, *and* pay for full-time private detectives. Apparently Bigelow bought what assistance he could and spent his nights skulking around his wife's apartment, bribing elevator men, bribing servants, hovering just out of sight. It took most of a year but eventually his wife blundered, blundered with a foolishness that seemed almost wilful: running off for a fortnight in Albany with her latest boyfriend, leaving the children in the care of a none-too-bright sixteen-year-old Negro girl. Here was information really worth paying for, and a few days later Bigelow knew for sure that the couple was registered in a hotel as man and wife. Exercising his right to see the children, he questioned the eldest boy tactfully and was able to establish that the newly acquired 'Uncle Harold' had several times stayed the night, even breakfasting with the boys. Now Bigelow had more evidence than he needed. When his wife returned, he was waiting with an ultimatum. Either she would agree to an Alabama divorce on his terms, conceding him full custody of the boys, or he would drag her through the New York courts on a clear-cut adultery charge and prove that she was an unfit mother.

"I'm sorry, but that all sounds like a pretty filthy trick to me," Madge said.

"You're taking the woman's side of it?" Charles inquired.

"I'm bound to."

"Without any more idea of what she was like?"

"That doesn't seem so terribly important to me," Madge said. "She was a victim of the rotten masculine legal quibble that because a woman gets tired of sleeping alone, she can't be a proper mother to her own children."

"As far as you've gone I suppose I'd agree with you," said Charles, "but I think there's a great deal more to it than that. We can only guess at Mrs. Bigelow's character, true. But unless she was a very stupid woman, she must have known how much the boys meant to her husband, that he'd go to any lengths to get them back. Unless she was a very obtuse woman, she must have had some idea she was being spied on; I can't believe that Bigelow was that subtle in his amateur investigations. So unless the children meant shockingly little to her, her behavior was certainly remarkably irresponsible, to say the least. And surely it's another rotten legal quibble that permits any woman, however stupid, obtuse or irresponsible, to bring up her own children *unless* she indulges in sexual peccadilloes. Why should that be the only test of her suitability as a parent?"

"So you think what Bigelow did was perfectly upright and admirable?" Madge asked.

"I haven't said anything of the kind," Charles replied. "Give me some credit. But I'm sure he was convinced that the boys would be better off with him than with their mother, and the events *seem* to bear him out: he was the anxious one and she the irresponsible. And there's one other bit of evidence that she didn't think much of the kids except as a weapon to use against their father. When she was caught out, she didn't even try to put up a fight except for a minimum of alimony. She gave up, went off and got the divorce on Bigelow's terms."

By then Bigelow was beginning to discover that he had bit off more than he could comfortably chew. He had plunged heavily into debt; he had let his job slide. In any case his salary was not sufficient for the new responsibilities he had undertaken, since, among other things, he would have to hire a full-time housekeeper to look after the boys while he was off at work. He was a sound advertising man, both imaginative and painstaking, but without the flair that would take him up quickly through the ranks of a large organization. He had to strike out on his own, and his best chance was with some company that had its own advertising department, or, better yet, was about to start one. This was where Andean C & Z had come into the picture. Old Clarence Barbour had just then advanced his scheme for bombarding the stockholders with uplifting propaganda, and Andean was seriously considering the notion that this, together with such institutional advertising as they did, might most effectively be handled from within the company. Bigelow was one of the first men interviewed. A brash and energetic young man, he had been perfectly outspoken about his situation: peddling both his capabilities and his expectation of a substantial salary.

"We offered him a good deal more than he was making," Charles said. "He thought it over for a few days, probably looking around to see if he got any better offers, then snapped at it. At the time I felt we were doing pretty well by him. Looking back, I doubt if he would have agreed. Perhaps the truth is that he simply isn't worth the kind of salary he needs."

Because he still had to contribute a certain amount to the support of his ex-wife. He had to provide an apartment large enough for himself, three rambunctious boys and a housekeeper. He had to pay the wages of the housekeeper. And on top of everything was the matter of schooling for the boys, an ever thornier problem for New Yorkers. Since the public schools are of no conceivable interest to the politicians except as a source of graft, they have been allowed to deteriorate to the point where there is only one elementary school in all Manhattan considered at all possible by anxious parents—so of course family-sized apartments in this neighborhood are always at a premium. For Bigelow, determined to give his children the best, this inevitably meant three sets of private-school fees. . . .

"I'm guessing at some of this, of course," Charles said, "but I'm pretty sure I'm right. There's no suggestion he blows the money on chorus girls or gambling, and everybody in the office agrees that he's the worst bore on earth when he gets on the subject of those three boys."

"So he came into Andean figuring the company could foot the bill for his expenses?" Madge said.

"Possibly, but I doubt if it was that cold blooded. In most respects he's conscientious to a fault. Who knows how these things get started? When the debts mount up past a certain point, no matter how you diddle your budget there are going to be still more debts next month. I don't know."

"You still haven't spoken to him, then?" she asked.

"How can I speak to him when I haven't any notion what I'm going to say?" Charles demanded irritably.

"You can't let him go on getting away with this."

"All right, I can't. But that doesn't solve anything. It's a mess. For years the department has consisted of just Bigelow and a couple of girls, but now there's going to be more work. There's to be a company paper for one thing, and we have a new refining technique that can stand some advertising in the right places. So Bigelow gets an assistant, and no one could raise an eyebrow if I brought young Roger Hilliard in for the job. However, now if I call Bigelow privately to my office, tell him what I know and ask him to resign without a fuss, everyone will believe that I'm slating the department for my son-in-law. Whoever is brought in to replace Bigelow will be regarded as a stop-gap appointment, and that's hell for morale. I *know* it's silly; the kid is still wet behind the ears, but that's how people think. On the other hand, if I make it public why Bigelow is being dismissed, the poor son of a bitch will never get a decent job again. It may not be so important what you do these days, but nobody has any use for a man who gets caught doing it."

Suddenly, irrelevantly, Madge burst out laughing. Charles gaped at her in astonishment, but half a moment went by before she could explain: "And you've invited *him* to the wedding reception!"

"Oh, come now," he said, disgruntled. "That's not very helpful."

"I know it isn't," she admitted, sobering gradually. "I'm afraid I'm not going to be much help on this, Charles. I simply cannot feel the sympathy you obviously feel for this man. You don't *want* him fired."

"He's done a good job and he's fitted in well," Charles said, now a trifle defensively. "Some of these advertising characters get to believe they're the most important part of any company, but he's made himself into a real member of the team."

"Then you'll figure out some way to get around it," Madge said. "If his department's to be expanded, then I expect he's due for a good raise. You'll have him in quietly and point out that you expect that raise to be offset by a sudden drop in some of the costs. You won't like it. The puritan streak in you will keep insisting that he ought to be punished, and your imagination will keep stumbling over those three little boys. It's what you'll do in the end."

"I'm not so sure," Charles said. "That isn't really very satisfactory from any point of view. From then on every expensive idea of his would be complicated by his knowledge that I'll probably be wondering if there's something in it for him. No, it seems to me that at very least I'll have to suggest that he look around for another job. A man who's still in a good position can generally find another if he wants to."

"But what if he can't?" Madge asked. "You've said he's probably not worth the salary he needs; the reason he's done so well at Andean is that he's fitted in *there*. Suppose he can't do as well anyplace else. Are you going to give a man a nice raise on the understanding that if he doesn't quit in six months he'll be fired?"

"That's exactly why it's such a mess," Charles said aggrievedly. "*Now* do you see why I wish I'd never heard of those kickbacks?"

"How did you hear of them?"

"For God's sake, because Roger Hilliard's stepfather spends his spare time playing chess! It's precisely the sort of bloodless thing he would do. Can you imagine anything so stupid? If Stephen Booth weren't too much of an intellectual snob to stay home watching television, I might have some peace of mind for a change." He told her the story of Mr. Rivkin as he had heard it at Mrs. Langstaff's party, but Madge wasn't interested in the details, saying merely: "Well, I suppose Professor Booth felt obliged to pass it along to you."

"There's no telling what that one feels," Charles said darkly. "He didn't just tell me the story; he used it to illustrate a batch of half-baked theories about what he called 'contemporary ethics in the business community.' I didn't understand half of what he was saying because somehow or other a lot of American Indians kept creeping into the conversation. But he knows as much about the 'business community' as I do about the moon."

"You don't like him much, do you?" Madge said.

"I certainly don't *dis*like him; it's just that he seems to live in a great grey fog of abstractions. A sandwich isn't something to eat; it's a striking symbol of dietary something or other. But he's a nice little man. More than anything, I feel sorry for him, married to that wife of his."

"Is she really so bad?"

"She's a pestilence," Charles said. "You've no idea what Ruth's been going through. Mrs. Booth is quite prepared to take charge of Vickie and Roger's life down to the last detail."

"You know, I expect that's partly because of her headaches," Madge said. "I can see that it would make a person terribly impatient with practical matters, always knowing that five minutes later she might be flat on her back for hours, not able to cope with anything."

"That's no excuse. When kids get married, the sooner they learn to fend for themselves the better. And what it must be like for Stephen Booth to live with that sort of behavior day in and day out—no wonder he hides among his theories. A man has a right to a certain. . . ." His voice trailed away and he looked at her in bewilderment. "What headaches?" he asked. "I couldn't have told you about any headaches because I'd not heard of them myself till just this moment."

Madge hastily reached for a cigarette, avoiding his eyes. "I assumed they were common knowledge," she murmured.

"*What's going on here?*"

"Nothing's going on. You said yourself I should get out more, find some new interests."

"And?"

"So I've gotten interested in the League for International Disarmament."

"Oh, no you haven't!" he said flatly. "Not you, Madge, never. You aren't fooling either one of us. People in difficulty, yes. Hospital patients and crippled children, yes. But a lot of utopian windbags, no. It's so far out of character that it's silly. I know perfectly well what you're up to, and it won't work."

"It's short notice," Madge conceded, "but you cannot imagine how pleased she is to have such a willing worker. We're getting intimate very rapidly—witness my knowing of her headaches. In another week it won't be at all surprising if she thinks to invite me to the reception, even without any prompting on my part."

"Then you'll just have to refuse," Charles said wearily, the contentment gone from his evening.

"Charles, this isn't fair! It was you who gave me the idea."

"Oh, my God."

"You did. You said the trouble was that I could only be there by your connivance. That's precisely what you said. But that won't be so if I've been invited by the bridegroom's mother."

Her yet-lovely eyes were hollow with pleading; for once there was a flush of color in her gaunt cheeks. It was obvious how important this was to her, and he was going to feel a beast for refusing a request she had taken such pains to make appear reasonable. "Look, my dear," he began quietly. "How many times have you yourself told me that it isn't the truth that matters in this life, it's what other people believe to be true?"

It was a wretched business. Over the years he had seen Madge elated and Madge depressed, but it was remarkably seldom, come to think of it, that he had seen her weep.

8

Some time later that same evening Freddie Ames slipped away from a not very entertaining dinner party and took a taxicab downtown. As always on one of his rare visits to Sean Ghio's, he had the taxi leave him at the corner of Fifth Avenue and Twentieth Street, and although he detested walking, went the rest of the way on foot. It was the expected precaution. Cab drivers have a way of noticing if periodically they arrive in herds at some out-of-the-way address, and whatever cab drivers notice comes sooner or later to the attention of the police.

Several dim and silent blocks away Freddie turned up the steps of an undistinguished brownstone. Most of the building served as small and inscrutable offices, and at this late hour appeared quite deserted, but he pressed confidently at the button beside the discreet plaque which read 'S. Ghio: Dance Studio' and a moment later the glass-paneled door buzzed his admittance.

For a number of years Sean Ghio had been the chorus boy most sought after by the choreographers of Broadway musicals. Not only was he a superb dancer technically, but also he possessed that gift of personality—at once cheerful and energetic, amusing and disciplined —which could captain a mixed bag of temperamental boys and girls into a unified and hard-working team. At the peak of this career he had 'retired' to become equally successful as a coach. Five, six and even seven days a week his vast studio echoed with the exertions of his students, but each Monday evening the studio was transformed into the home of New York's least publicized and (in its own way) most exclusive club.

There was no assurance that Eliot Clay would be here this particular evening, but the possibility that he would be, the greater likelihood of finding someone who knew where he was hiding out, was what had brought Freddie. He was virtually incapable of refusing to do a favor, even for someone who disliked him. His life was a complicated ledger of indebtedness; living in the smallest of apartments on the slenderest of incomes, he could never repay directly the constant hospitality which was, both literally and figuratively, meat and drink to him. He paid in small services. He was jester, go-between, extra man, messenger, anything useful, anything but baby sitter. Conveying this urgent message would leave both Stephen Booth and Eliot Clay in his debt; Freddie had no immediate use for their gratitude, but no doubt that the day would come. New York was like that: sooner or later every asset was negotiable.

This was an old building, thick-walled, and utterly silent as Freddie mounted the smoothly scuffed stairs. Not until he pushed open the heavy door at the top of the last landing did the sounds of the party finally leap out at him: the brisk clattering of voices and in the background a rhythmic thumping from the record player. Sean himself was not in sight, nor was this unusual: whenever a show full of students was about to open, he would most likely be found hovering maternally at the final rehearsals. The club had taken on the impetus of an institution and functioned just as smoothly in his absence, its character fixed by a common determination to keep this retreat unspoiled.

At one period Freddie had come here regularly, but with the passage of time he had found the atmosphere less congenial. He had been obliged to recognize that a place like Sean's was properly a meeting ground for younger people; the competition between older members tended to become bitter and acidulous, and a visit without a specific rendezvous in view was to risk running a gantlet of the singularly unattractive epithets that attached to the aging queen. This evening he had no intention of staying for very long and was greatly relieved that he spotted Eliot Clay immediately, sitting at a small table in the far corner of the room in earnest colloquy with Bob McEvoy, who ran The Cellar d'Or. Freddie stared at this unlikely twosome for a moment, and turned back to the bar, exchanging felinities with his acquaintances without giving much exertion to his wit. He turned in one of his tokens for a highball in a plastic glass (drinks at Sean's were strictly rationed, to avoid the late-night hair-pulling brawls on the doorstep which could attract attention from a passing prowl car) and then crossed the tiny dance floor to Eliot's table and pulled up a chair. "As I very much doubt if this is the love match of the century," he remarked, "I'm bound to remind you of the club rule against talking business."

"Blessings, Freddie; that's just what I've been telling him," Bob McEvoy said, producing a fresh cigar, lighting it. He was stocky, bullet-headed, crew cut and cultivated a butch act which might, just barely, impose on a matron from White Plains. "Possibly you can persuade the creature to be reasonable."

"I'm giving him the chance of a lifetime," said Eliot, so absorbed that he had scarcely troubled to nod at Freddie.

"Somebody offers me the chance of a lifetime on the average of twice a day," McEvoy said, and no doubt was speaking the truth. The Cellar d'Or, his creation, was a mid-town supper club noted for its discovery of fresh talent, rivalling The Blue Angel in popularity. Since a newcomer who made a success at either place had vaulted right to the top in a single go, there was no lack of aspirants; the difficulty was culling them out. "Look, Eliot, I'm already giving you more than you can decently ask. I've said I liked your girl, and I'm taking it on trust that you can lick away the rough spots in another few weeks."

"You needn't have any fears on that score."

"All right, fine," said McEvoy. "I'm giving her the spot, and you can spread the word as much as you like, even if it means a flood of tatty columnists all expecting their drinks on the cuff. But if Dorian holds over for a fourth week, and he probably will, I simply cannot headline anybody else. That's final. Dorian has a very uncertain temper, and I'm morally positive that he carries a switch blade."

Eliot thought this over for a moment. "Suppose Dorian fell sick that first evening," he said.

"Then I'd send your song bird on stage to perform a strip tease," McEvoy replied pleasantly. "I know Dorian is an old flame of yours, but if you played a trick like that on me, I'd call up the Vice Squad and tell them you'd been soliciting my customers in the gent's lavatory."

"I do relish these little glimpses of the seamy side of the entertainment world," Freddie said.

"Freddie, keep out of this," Eliot said.

"But I'm confused," Freddie complained. Eliot's intensity fascinated him; it was a novelty to come across someone displaying such naked sincerity. "Do I gather you've descended to the ranks of what I believe are known as flesh peddlers?"

"I'm tired of hearing my songs given that little something extra by people who haven't anything extra to give."

"Then why not sing them yourself?" Freddie asked.

"I've offered him the top spot for that any time he wants it," McEvoy said.

"And I cannot and will not perform for a straight audience," Eliot said. "The idea revolts me. We all know I'm no vocalist, but I can camp my way through a song and that's all good fun among friends. But to go on stage to camp for the sniggering of the great unwashed is the most degrading way of earning money I can imagine."

"Gently, gently," said Freddie. "No one is twisting your arm. Here comes the Equity crowd."

It was a few minutes before midnight, three-quarters of an hour after the last curtain call on Broadway, just time to wipe away the grease paint, change into street clothes and taxi downtown. The room was filling up quickly now with the after-theatre crowd from both sides of the curtain; for a while the activity at the tiny bar became frantic. There was mild amusement to be had from the arrival of half a dozen extremely pretty chorus girls, who had no doubt passed the evening inspiring misplaced lubricity in masculine hearts. Sean Ghio came sweeping in, scattering greetings like largesse, and after a hasty inspection of the room made his way to their corner. He was in his late forties now, and close at hand he looked it, but his body was still as lithe and graceful as his youngest pupil's.

"Good evening, my dears," he said, plucking a nearby chair and coiling himself around it, disdaining so plebeian a gesture as sitting down. "I hope none of you bought tickets for Gary's new show. I told him he was quite mad to think of a May opening. He insisted that novelty was everything, and he hoped to catch the critics by surprise. I think now he hoped to catch them on vacation."

"Hopeless?" McEvoy asked.

"Well, Alec has a dance routine that would normally bring down the house, but it's in the second act so I don't suppose anybody will ever know. Thank God for television; it does take up some of the slack between flops. But that's not the point at the moment. This looks well on its way to being one of those prim and starchy evenings. I don't want to impose too far on your good nature, Eliot, but I've not noticed that you *mind* being the center of attention, and a couple of songs should loosen things up a bit."

"It's very sad," Eliot said. "My throat is dry and dusty from arguing with Mother McEvoy, and I've already drunk up my quota."

"I'll have someone bring you a nice glass of Coca-Cola, on the house," Sean said. "If you're very lucky some rum will get splashed in it by mistake." He uncurled himself and went off to spread the word that Eliot would be singing: it was contrary to the spirit of the club to cry out master-of-ceremonies announcements.

"Favoritism disgusts me," McEvoy said.

"What really disgusts you," Eliot retorted, "is the thought of liquor being splashed about instead of measured out by an eye dropper at so much the drop."

"Eliot," Freddie put in quickly, before the opportunity escaped him, "did I know that Stephen Booth is your brother?"

"It's not a scandalous relationship," Eliot said, "so it might have escaped you. Why?"

"Apparently you've been neglecting the poor fellow. At a party the other day he clung to my lapels and whined when I said I might know where to find you."

"Is something the matter?" Eliot asked.

"He didn't entrust me with the details," Freddie said. "We were having cocktails in a medieval armory on Fifth Avenue, and when he actually started to reach for a cutlass, I said I'd pass the word on."

"I'm never so popular as when I've no time to see anybody," Eliot grumbled.

"I promised you'd give him a ring," Freddie said. "If you let me down, I'll come and catcall at your protegée's debut."

"My new career is opening up new vistas of blackmail," Eliot said. "Very well; thank you, Freddie. I'll uphold what passes for your honor."

There was an abrupt drop in the noise of the room as one of Sean's lads switched off the phonograph. At this signal the unoccupied tables were quickly taken, and when Eliot started for the battered upright, the little dance floor was soon covered by the younger men in a variety of decorative sprawls. Several called out for their favorites among Eliot's repertoire. The Auntie's Lament, Eliot. No, The Bachelor Queen of England. As soon as Eliot had his back turned at the piano, Freddie slipped discreetly from the room, collected his coat from the vestibule and started down the stairs. He had never been able to understand how people could welcome with such enthusiasm the fiftieth reappearance of the same stale witticism merely because it was set to music.

PART SIX

1

Playwriting, Owen Hilliard had once remarked to somebody, was a form of applied schizophrenia.

He had been speaking of the actual process of writing, which was all that seemed to interest most people. It never occurred to them, or they were uninterested in the fact, that a devil of a lot of plotting and scheming had to be got through before the writing could properly begin. In a hundred ways you had to anticipate a play's rigorous limitation: that everything to be conveyed must be carried through dialogue. The actors would take credit for bringing the play to life, but the relatively straightforward emotions they could project across the footlights were of surprisingly little help to the dramatist, who had all the problems of making their behavior intelligible. The actress whips herself into a splendid rage, the actor registers ineffectual resignation—but for the scene to have any meaning the reasons behind her fury, his weakness, must already have been established. Every scene rested on the scenes that went before, so the first scene of all carried the weight of everything that followed. The contriving had to be meticulous.

But Owen was already past that stage and into the first act, working slowly and carefully, trying to make every line tell. This first act would have to be strong enough to break through the skepticism he was bound to encounter. On Broadway a man was quickly pigeonholed. Owen's reputation as a playsmith was high, none higher for the moment. The news that he had found a novel he wanted to adapt would have prompted several producers to reach for their checkbooks. The news that he was working on an original of his own would merely stir up memories of his past failures. Nevertheless, his standing as a craftsman was such that a really powerful first act, plus a synopsis of the rest (and this was all he would have time for) ought to lure a couple of thousand in option money out of one of the producers who had battened on him in the past.

So Owen was at his typewriter applying his schizophrenia to the problem that no two people say the same thing in quite the same way, and what was worse, any given person might contradict himself a hundred times between breakfast and bedtime—in short, he was writing dialogue. For example, a character was shown arriving home from the office to discover that his unloved half brother had unexpectedly reappeared after a long absence. The man's response to this unwelcome visitor would be reserved; so much was determined by his nature. But would his first words of greeting be offhand or sarcastic or faintly defensive? Would he say 'I'd have thought by now you'd be tired of that silly beard,' or 'I don't know whether there's time to thaw out a fatted calf,' or 'If it's money you need, you've picked a rotten time to turn up,'—and even if one of these was approximately right, was he likely to express himself in just those words?

The simplest way out of this dilemma was to put yourself into the man's mind and play around with the various possibilities until one came to seem natural; then you withdrew and changed over to the identity of the half brother to find the appropriate response. Once the characters had been clearly conceived, this was no great problem for a disciplined schizophrenic. Owen simply pressed the proper mental button and for the time being he *was* somebody else, somebody with that background living this sort of life and caught up in these desires and anxieties. When he was working well, the illusion could momentarily become very convincing, so that when the telephone in the next room began to ring he expected it to be answered by the quaintly accented German housekeeper who would presently appear at the door with a comically garbled message.

He was perfectly sane. When the phone went on ringing one second longer than necessary, he did not pause to be annoyed at the housekeeper. He simply got up from the desk in his small, book-lined study (which sometimes served as Roger's bedroom), walked through to his bedroom next door and picked up the receiver, once again Owen Hilliard who had never employed a German housekeeper in his life.

"Hello," he said grumpily.

"I hope I haven't disturbed your work." It was Amelia.

"You have, but it doesn't matter," he lied, spending no great effort to make the lie convincing.

"Well, if I call in the morning you complain I've waked you up, and any other time of day you may be working. What's a person to do?"

"You could write me letters," Owen said. "Our autocratic telephone company won't give me a phone that switches off unless there's another in the apartment that can't be switched off; they offer us a fine democratic choice between too much service and none at all." He stretched out on the bed and lit a cigarette, no more than half listening to the small voice that chattered tinnily in his ear. He was still caught up in the scene he had been working at; his created characters were more vital and alive to him than this importunate female he had been married to a generation ago. Only when it filtered through to him that she was being more urgently demanding than usual did he force himself to the surface of untidy reality.

"Nowadays," he said intelligently, "there's a splendid arrangement whereby you fly someplace in June and pay for it the following November."

"Not for honeymoons, there isn't," Amelia said. "It's an offensive idea, even if they'd let you get away with it, which I doubt. And the woman down on the Islands wants a deposit. And I'm going to be able to save you quite a bit of money furnishing their apartment, but it will take cash. I've let you put me off as long as possible, Owen."

"But you haven't let me work," he said. "If you'll just let me get some work done, in another few weeks I ought to be solvent again. There's a very promising iron in the fire."

"I'm not talking about a few weeks from now. It's this evening you have to sit down at your checkbook. Tomorrow morning at the latest."

"Oh, I'll write you all the checks you like, if you don't mind their going bounce, bounce, bounce."

"Now look here!" she said impatiently. "You've allowed me to go ahead—"

"I haven't allowed you to go ahead with anything," he interrupted her. "You've simply gone ahead, the way you always do. I've warned you time and again I couldn't see where the money was to come from, but it didn't suit your plans to pay any attention."

"You've always been one to exaggerate how poor you are," she said. "It's left over from your childhood; a lot of people who were young during the Depression are like that."

"None of that, now!"

"Well, it's true. You think by crying poor you can keep down the overhead. But this is your only child, Owen, and we have to assume it's the only time he'll be getting married."

"You're welcome to inspect my checkbook yourself," Owen said wearily. "Like most people in analysis you've reached a point where you can no longer distinguish between a fact and a neurosis. To keep myself out of jail I just paid the first slice of this year's income tax as well as the due hunk of back taxes. The first of the month brought a mountain of Roger's bills at Princeton. And by one of those unlovely coincidences, the quarterly installment of Barbara-the-Bitch's alimony is due on the fifteenth."

"Let her be the one to wait for a few weeks."

"Have you ever tried to work with process servers banging at the door?"

"Then borrow," Amelia said unsympathetically. "I'm sorry to nag, Owen, but this is really too ridiculous. In another few months Roger will be off our hands for good, earning his own living. If he gets into trouble then, you can be just as hardhearted as you please, and I shan't say a word. He has to learn to manage. But his wedding comes first, and I'm not going to let him suffer just because you can't seem to get by on an income that most people would consider affluence."

"There wouldn't have been any suffering if you hadn't led him to expect a rich boy's send-off!"

"Yes, I know, a weekend at Atlantic City would have served nicely. It isn't until the third honeymoon that one goes to Venice and then wonders why there isn't a cent left over for one's son. . . ." Amelia's voice surged on, ruthless, logical, irresistible. Though the facts had not altered, Owen knew that at any moment he was going to give in, simply because he could not support any more of the argument; knew, too, that Amelia had undoubtedly been relying on this from the very first. Women were wonderfully accurate at assessing a man's weaknesses: Amelia would never have dared take this attitude if he had been defending a principle, but she knew that in practical matters he hadn't the conscience for a sustained struggle. Hazily he guessed at how long Barbara-the-Bitch would wait before calling her lawyer and tried to match this guess against his estimate of how long he would need to finish the first act, but this was mere procrastination.

"All right, all right," he said. "We both know I'm marked down for the slaughter; let's not take a high moral tone about it. How much do you need right away?" With unladylike efficiency she rattled off the figures, and he jotted them down on the back of an envelope, wincing. For the sake of his own self-esteem he made a stand on one item: "There's no need to get that *now*, for God's sake; they won't be getting back to town till mid-July. All right, I'll send you a check to cover the rest in the morning."

At this submission her manner altered abruptly: the implacable tone disappeared from her voice; she became cheerful and soothing, asking after his work and remarking on how lovely Carol had looked the other day at Mrs. Langstaff's party, all in the manner of a kindly mother mollifying a child with candy after a much-needed scolding. As Amelia got older it became more apparent that her emotions had no real validity except as a means of achieving her own way. When her chummy-chummy mood went on longer than was strictly necessary, Owen suspected there was something else on her mind, and, sure enough, eventually it appeared.

"Owen, you seem to have been getting quite cosy with Charles recently."

"He amuses me."

"Somehow I can't quite believe that, but it's no concern of mine," she said. "Look, we need somebody like him—the good solid Republican businessman type—up on the platform at the L.I.D. convention. Several somebodies, in fact, but he'd be ideal. Do you think there's any chance of getting him interested?"

"I very much doubt it," Owen said vindictively.

"Why?"

"Oh, just a hunch," Owen said. He had no idea what Charles's opinions on disarmament might be, but it seemed probable that someone with the story of Sophie Melmoth in his past, just waiting to be dredged up by an inquisitive reporter, would shun the limelight of controversial platforms. "I may perfectly well be wrong."

"What would be the best time to approach him, do you think?"

"Oh, after the wedding, I'd say. Isn't a man traditionally supposed to go through a psychological upheaval when he gives a daughter away? You just might catch him with all his defenses down."

Dazzled these days by anything that harked to the subconscious, she was properly impressed by the profundity of this advice, which Owen had thrown out with offhand malice. After a few more well-bred protestations of sorrow at having had to badger him, she rang off. Owen lit a cigarette and continued to lie on the bed, brooding. He had no need to look at his bank balance: even before this latest demand it had been touch and go whether he could cover the next installment to Barbara-the-Bitch. So she would have to wait, and there was no hoping that she would wait graciously. With luck she might be out of town—she was often jaunting off for a week or two here or there—and that might give him a little leeway. But not much, probably, and not to be counted on. If he couldn't see another hunk of cash coming in within the next fortnight, he would have to borrow again. The thought depressed him terribly. Only recently he had worked his way out from the position of paying interest on money he had borrowed to pay interest on money he had borrowed.

One of the many reasons for his financial predicament was the heavy load of life insurance which he carried, and now that Roger was virtually finished school, about to strike out on his own, it seemed that Owen might cash in, recover what he could of the investment. But he knew he would never bring himself to do it. He was not yet an old man; one of these days he might well find himself with a new set of responsibilities. And this was the only sort of estate he would be able to leave. A man who owned a grocery store or a piece of land which accidentally sat on top of gold or oil or coal could leave his property to his great-grandchildren. The creative person could not. A composer, an inventor, a writer, could within his own lifetime see his creation become public property. In principle Owen thoroughly approved of this act of socialism; what made it sheer brigandage was that the government made not the slightest allowance for this eventual sequestration, taxing the socialized creator at the same rate as the capitalist entrepreneur. What was almost worse, the writer could struggle along on a shoestring for twenty years and then make a killing the twenty-first. Presumably this success was the outcome of his long, grim apprenticeship, but did the tax authorities take that into account? Not at all. He was punished to the hilt for the pleasure he had given and had to settle for the satisfaction of knowing that if his work became an enduring classic his grown children would not see a penny of the profits. Since Owen had first been earning money at all, he had carried as much life insurance as he could afford, and a bit more. It was part of the bourgeois streak in him that, in the old days, Carol had deplored.

He glanced at his watch. Seven twenty, and for the time being his mood was shattered; it would be useless to go back to the typewriter just yet. There were limits to self-discipline: in a few hours his mind would erect some sort of blockade against the anxiety of money, money, money, and he would be able to work again, but he had to give himself time. He went to the kitchen for ice and fixed himself a drink, studied the contents of the refrigerator, especially the freezing compartment, to decide what he would throw together for his dinner.

Drink in hand, he wandered into the living room. This wasn't one of the days when his cleaning woman came in, so the room reeked of unemptied ashtrays, and everything lay just as he had left it hours before when he retreated to the study to work. The remains of a make-shift brunch still sat on the coffee table amid a litter of the morning mail, over towards the wastebasket the floor was strewn with little balls of envelopes and ads, crumpled and hurled. Somehow the newspapers had unleafed themselves and scattered themselves over several armchairs. Opened books and magazines lay about, and the glass from this morning's nightcap stood on the edge of a book-case shelf and would no doubt prove to have left a ring on the wood. A soiled shirt dangled from the Chinese wall screen near the hall door: the collar button needed reinforcing, and he had left the shirt there to be sure to remember to call it to Mrs. Brigg's attention, but at the moment it contributed the finishing touch to the room's atmosphere. Admittedly, when he was working he tended to let tidiness slide, but even so it was remarkable that since Mrs. Brigg's departure yesterday evening one man could all unconsciously have reduced a room to a state of such depressing squalor.

Impulsively he turned on his heel, went back to the bedroom, and dialed Carol's number, feeling guilty as soon as he heard the rhythmic buzzing of his distant summons. "Is this a bad time to be calling?" he demanded.

"Why should it be?" she asked.

"I still don't know the hours you keep when I'm not there. You could be feeding Lois or expecting guests."

"Lois went to bed half an hour ago, and I'm not expecting a soul. Is anything wrong?"

"No. . . ."

"Isn't your work going well?"

"It was going beautifully till half an hour ago when Amelia called up screaming for vast sums of money for Roger's honeymoon and all. Now I badly need to be cheered up."

"Then hold on just a second," she said. "There's something on the stove I'd better turn down to a slow simmer."

He stretched out again on the semimade bed (his own handiwork), bunching the pillows under his head, already relaxing in this long-distance evocation of domesticity. Carol's offhand mention of a pot simmering on the stove was symbolic of the new Carol. In the old days she had been impatient of the niceties of cookery as something unworthy of her time; she had preferred to eat out when possible, at home contenting herself with chops, roasts, hamburgers, salads, whatever could be put together with the least fuss. In the interim years she had learned to take pride in her cooking. This could not have come from the need to fix simple meals for Lois, so it must have been the doing of the shadowy Andrew—a thought which Owen declined to pursue. It was odd the way the mind shied away from the particulars of a love's other relationships. He could not resent Andrew, and the civilized man in him was pleased by the idea that the marriage had been a happy one, yet details which his imagination could take hold of were an assault that offended the uncivilized part of him.

"It might be a bit skimpy but I think dinner would stretch to two," Carol said. "Would you like to come down?"

"What a foolish question! Of course I'd like to come down. But I mustn't and I shan't."

"*Just* for dinner?"

"But it wouldn't be just for dinner," he said. "Oh, I don't mean that I wouldn't be able to withstand other temptations if I struggled very hard, but I'd spend the rest of the evening thinking happily about you, and that's no way to get any work done. This way I keep you firmly in your place as a disembodied voice."

"Should I ask questions about Amelia's badgering?"

"No, I think not: that would just get me depressed all over again. Your function is to soothe my fevered brow by telephone."

"Bright and lively chatter on command at all hours? Except that my mind is a perfect blank."

"Don't be negative," he urged her. "Tell me of Lois's latest head-on collision with the English language. Tell me something hilarious that happened at the store today. I'm easily amused. I suppose what I really want is just to hear your voice for a while. After a day spent listening to the babble inside my own head, I begin to feel like a radio playing on and on in an empty room. Do you have a drink?"

"I have a drink," she said. "I'm comfortably curled up on the sofa in the living room. When you called I was just beginning Chapter Seven of *The Huddling Place*."

"Good Lord!" he said, pleased and touched. "How is it?"

"Have you never reread it?" she asked.

"I've never reread any of them. By the time you've written a book, revised and rewritten it a few times, and finally done all the proofreading, you've had quite enough for one lifetime. One of the hells of playwriting is that you have to do all that and then sit through rehearsals till every line comes to sound detestable. But I thought *The Huddling Place* was one you liked least."

"I felt that way at the time," she said. "Now I'm beginning to think I was mistaken. Without question it's the least *effective* of your novels, but I can see now this is mainly because it was also the most ambitious. You tackled more than you knew how to handle—and yet you didn't really miss by so very much. I'm not saying you could come back and turn this into a great book; you'd probably have to reshape it from the very first page. But I keep getting the feeling that your next novel would have been something truly impressive. Haven't you ever been tempted to write another book?"

"Not really," he said. "Oh, I've played with the idea from time to time, naturally, but my mind has lost the habit of thinking in those directions. When I was writing novels, ideas came to me novel-shaped—I don't know any other way to express it. It's why short-story writers always fumble their first attempt at something longer: you can sense the short story at the center, and the rest is just elaboration. For the past eight years or so I've been thinking from a playwright's point of view. I react to things in terms of dialogue and action, and I suppose my mind simply glides over anything that can't be handled in those terms."

"It seems a pity," she said.

"Nothing of the kind," he said cheerfully. "Let's face it, darling, I have a rather small talent that needs to be husbanded. Better that I do one thing capably than that I splash around trying to prove that I can do everything at once—and nothing very well."

"You're capable of so much more than doing 'one thing capably,'" she retorted sharply, "but it's no way to cheer you up, quarreling with your lack of confidence. Honestly, Amelia ought to be strangled for depressing you just when your work was going along so smoothly."

273

"Well, she complained that there didn't seem to be *any* safe time to call, and I have to admit there's some justice to that."

"I hope you realize that's the only reason I never call you," Carol said. "There are stretches when the shop is empty and I get to thinking about you and it's all I can do to keep my hands off the telephone."

"I'm a selfish lout, aren't I? Calling to be cheered up and never available to return the compliment."

"Oh, I don't need cheering up. If I called it would be a lot more selfish than that. It's just that at times I haven't enough to keep me busy and I get to thinking of something you said the other evening when I hadn't the energy to argue. Or something funny's happened in the shop and I know if I don't tell you about it right away I'll forget—as I have. Or just that it occurs to me that I shan't be seeing you till Thursday evening and it seems a long way off."

Owen wriggled into a still more comfortable position. Carol's voice was soft and caressing in his ear; with very little effort he could conjure up the image of her wide-browed beauty. There were so few anxieties to being in love with Carol: he felt enfolded by a commonsense affection which partook of her maternalism yet was utterly distinct, leaving their adult dignities unmarred. "It's the thought of Thursday that keeps me virtuous this evening," he said.

"I was afraid you might feel that you ought to call it off, to keep working."

"No, I know how to deal with my conscience," he told her. "I warn myself that the motor is in grave danger of overheating—that I simply must take time off to have the sparkplugs cleaned, the oil changed, the carburetor adjusted—"

"What a romantic way of putting it!" she said admiringly. "There isn't a woman living who wouldn't be proud to be compared to a service station."

"I have to use that sort of argument with my conscience," he explained. "If I try anything more romantic, it sniggers unpleasantly and asks whether I'm not getting a little old for that kind of nonsense."

"It seems to me you have a very unfriendly sort of conscience," Carol said. "Mine never argues with me except when I go past a candy store."

With Barbara-the-Bitch, as he all too vividly remembered, though she had been younger and still unscathed by life, any sort of teasing had been out of the question: she hadn't understood it, had felt

274

there must be malice in it, and adopted postures of defense. This had quickly made any sort of personal conversation almost impossible, for Owen believed that constant flattery was encouragement for children and condescending to a love degraded it. Teasing was the relaxation of his love. He needed to feel that affection created an enclosure where people might shed their daily weight of armor, where reticences and weapons were left outside, since within were only peace and frolic and the paper arrows of coquetry. With Carol he felt that way. She had a self-assurance which could scarcely be bruised; Owen had never known her to be hurt by anything less than the rare calculated insult—and this was all the more remarkable since her background could have given her no cause for feeling unassailable. Yet with her he could talk foolishness without feeling foolish; he could outrage all the decencies and be sure that only his love was heard.

2

"Well, let's get it over with!" Alison said.

"Get what over with?" Morris Zimmerman asked.

"The scolding. Everyone else in the family has had a go at me. Now it's your turn."

Morris smiled at his niece, the acknowledged beauty of the family, sitting so erectly, bristling with defiance. He had a certain sympathy with her position and very little liking for this assignment. They had hounded him into it. They had a superstitious belief that a doctor's words carried special weight—but why, except when he was doctoring? "Have you made it so clear to the others that you still think of yourself as a child?" he asked.

"But I don't!"

He shook his head. "I would argue with somebody or discuss something with him. If I was feeling particularly stuffy, I might read him a lecture. But scolding is for children."

"Well, then when do you all stop treating me like a child?" she demanded. "No, don't answer that, Uncle Morris. You'll just say, when you start acting like a grown-up. But since you're all convinced in advance that if I'm fed up with Ben and want a divorce I must be acting like a child. I can't win."

"Yes, well, let's forget the other scoldings, shall we?" he suggested. "When people are upset they tend to say a lot of foolish things—

well-meant, no doubt, but foolish." It occurred to him that perhaps this was his most helpful function: to try to clear the atmosphere of too much kindly, officious interference. Older women had a way of bustling about, impatiently spring cleaning their way through a mess of bruised young sensibilities, making things worse as often as not. If there was some manner in which Alison and Ben could get together again, they would probably find it themselves, given half a chance—and if not, there was little any outsider could do. "I haven't the slightest intention of scolding you," he promised her. "I'd just like a clearer understanding of what has gone so drastically wrong."

"That's what every single one of you says," Alison retorted sullenly.

"I expect so," he agreed, and waited, relying on the history of their closeness since Phil's death to have its effect. He was sure that he had always treated her straightforwardly; he had been her refuge from the overmothering that a motherless child attracts. It would be surprising if she could retain her defensiveness for very long, without encouragement.

"Well, it's true," she said, and then, as if conceding that at least she would stay for a while, she kicked off her spiky shoes and tucked her stockinged feet beneath her—still frowning, still not relaxed, but perceptibly less hostile. "You all say that you just want to understand. And God knows I've tried to explain. I'm not clever with words. For that you have to go to Ben: he can take anything I say and twist it around till he's proven I've as good as confessed I'm a spoiled and selfish little bitch even if all I've done is ask whether he wants another cup of coffee. And *that's* one of the troubles, if you want to know. Ben is a genius at that game and I'm not. But all the same I've done my best to explain. I've explained till I'm blue in the face. And they don't really listen at all. Once they've made sure that Ben doesn't come home drunk every night and knock me about, they know I'm in the wrong and they don't try to understand what I'm saying. They simply store up little nuggets of my words to use as ammunition against me—to show that I must be exaggerating or that I have the wrong attitude towards marriage generally."

"Um, yes," Morris said. "I can believe there's been a good deal of that."

"You ought to hear me when I'm with Aunt Ruth," Alison said with a harsh little laugh. "It's really very funny. I know she wants to be sympathetic, and it hurts her to feel I must be in the wrong. So I tie myself into knots trying to say exactly what I mean and some of it is pretty complicated but that doesn't matter: in the end what Aunt Ruth has heard is always a cliché. There's nothing I can do. Sometimes I think it would be kinder in the long run if I told her something she could understand—that I'm in love with another man, just for example. She'd be disgusted, maybe, but she wouldn't be so bewildered."

"Would there be any truth in it?"

"No."

"Quite sure?"

"You've heard about Paul, obviously, and that means you've been listening to dear Ben," Alison said contemptuously. "I had a feeling he'd try to spread that story around. It's typical of Ben. He's not capable of believing that his wife could become fed up with him in her own right. Oh, no. That would mean admitting he was somehow at fault. It's much more comforting to believe that somebody else has corrupted my feeble little mind."

"Still, I gather that Paul exists."

"Oh, of course he exists. I'd imagine that whenever a reasonably attractive girl gets tired of her husband a Paul will turn up to hold her hand, if he has to crawl out of the woodwork. But I haven't gone to bed with him, if that's what you mean."

"Why not?" Morris inquired curiously.

"Believe it or not, because he's married himself with a couple of kids. He makes it pretty obvious that his wife is a cold fish. If that's a line, it's a silly one. I may be flattering myself, but I have a strong hunch that if he found things so much more satisfactory with me he'd follow me out to Reno no matter what I might say, and that's more of a responsibility than I want right at the moment."

"Meaning that you still haven't decided whether you're in love with him or not?"

"Meaning approximately that, I suppose," Alison admitted. "In any case it had nothing to do with my wanting a divorce. It's just something I'll have to think about when I become sure of myself again—and that seems a long long way off."

"Sure of yourself?" Morris repeated doubtfully.

"Oh, for Heaven's sake, Uncle Morris! Do you think I'm a hard-boiled little halfwit the way all the others do? I'm sick and tired of everybody assuming I'm the sort to throw over a marriage out of simple petulance. I'm going to love it, kicking my heels in Reno for six weeks and then building a new life from scratch, nobody to hold onto and my own family lined up in righteous disapproval. Ooooh, I'm looking forward to it all!"

"Now don't *you* go scolding *me*," he said.

"Well, it's so unfair! Just because I had to be born into a family where too many people have been too damn lucky with their marriages."

Yet as Alison carried on about the lack of appreciation she had met with in life, Morris found that despite his good intentions he was no better than the others. He listened, but he couldn't seem to hear the originality she found in her complaints: they sounded shallow and captious in comparison with the real anxieties which he lived with day in and day out. On the one hand, Alison's resentment of criticism; on the other, the knowledge that old Jacob's life must now be reckoned at a year or so at the outside, and the problem of what would become of Gert when he died. It was out of such realities, not the vagaries of romance, that a middle-aged life was constructed. His son's inability to settle on a profession: that was a worrisome reality. The fact that up in Boston his daughter was not picking up after her delivery nearly as quickly as he would have expected—that might be a reality, too, although probably it wasn't. Susan was a healthy girl, she was in the best of hands, there was nothing he could do for her that wouldn't have been thought of already. Ever conscious of his own inadequacies, he fought against the tendency to think of all other doctors as semicompetent; by an effort of will he had kept himself from fussing. But until he saw Susan with his own eyes next week, when she and the baby came down for their promised visit, the apprehension would drag at him.

And apart from these purely private concerns, just outside a man's front door waited a whole world of tragedy. The tragedies of patients, the tragedies of friends. The daily horrors that leapt at him from the newspapers, evidence of the insane world his grandchildren would have to grow up in. . . .

Against a background of these preoccupations, the question of whether two spoiled young people could resolve their differences seemed ludicrously trivial, and it took an exertion of tolerance to remember that for Alison and Ben everything else would remain trivial until this dilemma of their immaturity was decided one way or another.

"If you've really been so unhappy all along," he said, "why didn't you get out years ago?"

"There's pride," Alison said. "You hate to admit that you've made such a fool of yourself. And then everyone sits on the sidelines telling you that these little adjustments are inevitable; we've all been through them, dear, a little give and take and everything will straighten out."

"We weren't just being glib," he protested.

"I suppose not, but just look at you!" Alison replied. "Aunt Ruth has the easiest nature of anybody alive; she'd have been just as happy with any husband who wasn't an absolute monster and who gave her a couple of children to keep her occupied. And she thinks everybody else must be the same. She looks back and remembers that twenty-five years ago Uncle Charles spoke to her crossly one evening so she's come through all the vicissitudes of marriage and why can't I?"

"Well, perhaps Ruth isn't the most imaginative of women," Morris said. "But I think you'll grant that I've tried to be understanding."

"Oh, you've *tried*, Uncle Morris," Alison agreed with a touch of condescension. "You've been more help than anybody, but just the same you've never understood, except academically. How could you? After being married to Reba all those years? I don't think anyone whose marriage has been truly happy can imagine what happens when everything turns sour."

And what was a man to say to a remark like that? Within any family there were certain legends that carried more weight than any appeal to the truth, and Morris's marriage was such a legend. Beyond question, Reba had been a saint. More questionable but never questioned were the corollaries that Morris must have been wonderfully happy married to such a woman, and that his resistance to any idea of taking a second wife was a tribute to Reba's memory. It was too late now to begin arguing with these propositions, but in another sense it had always been too late. Reba had captured all hearts as easily as she had captured his; her goodness was such a palpable quality that a man forfeited all sympathy if he ventured to struggle against it. After some initial restlessness (quickly forgiven him for Reba's sake) he had learned to accept gracefully the martyrdom of his happiness.

For there were certain drawbacks to living with a saint, and especially if the saintliness was based on that impregnable innocence which is less charitably known as stupidity. Reba had had the disposition of an angel—which included the angelic prerogative of knowing right from wrong and the angelic instinct for always being in the right. Knowledge, experience, intelligence could make no headway against angelic intuition; it was pointless cruelty to quarrel with the loving devastation of someone whose intentions were bonded for purity. When she had died—swiftly, tragically, nobly—Morris had been smothered under the heartbroken commiseration of those who hadn't had to live with her.

Then, if at any time, would have been the moment to puncture the myth—perhaps. He had kept silent deliberately, telling himself that no purpose would be served by a belated disloyalty: there was some value in the example of an ideal marriage, but none in the revelation of one more marriage held together by the usual mixture of inertia, desire for peace, and concern for the children. He told himself this and knew that he lied. Within the family Reba's canonization had been completed by her fortitude in the face of a ravaging cancer. Her sublimity was fixed and out of reach: he would have succeeded only in proving that he had been unworthy of her.

So now he was forever trapped within the confines of that legend: a man of such riches that he could never conceive of the afflictions of poverty. "Still, it's worth while trying to help me understand," he told Alison. "I might be able to stop the others from badgering you."

"What do you want from me?" she asked fretfully. "The whole long saga of our differences all over again? None of them is very impressive by itself. It's the atmosphere they've left behind. The scar tissue. Why shouldn't it be enough that we're two people designed to make each other miserable?"

"Ben doesn't seem so convinced of that."

"Don't you believe it!" Alison said. "His ego is just shaken up because *I* was the one to call it quits. That should have been his privilege—at a more convenient moment when he had a nice submissive substitute ready to step into my shoes."

"Well, then, what exactly made you decide to call it quits when you did?" Morris inquired.

"Realizing that I didn't have any hope left that things were ever going to get better. Realizing that I could still get out with no great harm done to anybody, which would stop being true the day I discovered I was pregnant."

"That's not exactly what I meant," Morris said. "Those realizations didn't come to you in the middle of a peaceful Sunday afternoon, did they, suddenly, out of nowhere?"

"There was a quarrel," she admitted. "Does it matter? There's nothing special about the straw that breaks the camel's back. As a matter of fact, it began as an argument about Roger and Vickie."

"Oh?" Morris said encouragingly.

"Ben was in one of his starchy moods, insisting they were both much too young to be getting married. Especially Roger—just out of college and taking up his first job while still in the middle of his honeymoon. According to Ben it will be months before he's the slightest use to the company. He'll get by only because he's Uncle Charles's son-in-law."

"I imagine there's some truth in that."

"Oh, that isn't the point," Alison said, impatiently lighting a fresh cigarette from the butt of the last. "Ben is very proud of his job; he's proud that he worked his way through college and got where he is without help from anybody. All very admirable, of course. But it kills him with jealousy when anyone has things the least bit easier."

"I see," said Morris. "Did you point all this out to him?"

"You're just as bad as all the others," Alison complained. "No, I *didn't!* At least not until he went on to say that Vickie was too ignorant and too selfish to be any help to Roger: she'd only make it five times as hard for him to do a decent job. And that was directed straight at *me.*"

"Yes," said Morris, sighing, imagining the rest.

"I know it *sounds* childish; that's why it's so hard to explain. It's never the quarrels themselves; it's the thing in the air after years and years of them. Whatever we started out with has all been used up; there's no joy left in it anywhere. We sort of wander around in an irritation looking for excuses to scratch at one another."

"I'm not arguing," Morris said. "I'll even try to stop the others from bothering you. Go on out to Reno—you might just as well. What troubles me is where you'll go after that."

"You're a lamb, Uncle Morris," Alison said, brightening. "Don't worry about me. I can look after myself."

"A little too effectively, I suspect," he said, but she was too relieved at escaping a scolding to notice.

3

Eliot Clay's latest hideaway proved to be far east on 56th Street, only a few blocks from the Fortescues': a new building looking as if it had been patched together out of plate glass and prefabricated terraces. The lobby boasted of luxury within, with patterned marble flooring and flamboyant modern lamps. Stephen Booth went up in the self-service elevator, once again escaping the fate of being trapped helplessly between floors, which he knew would some day overtake him. He traced the sequence of numbers down richly carpeted hallways until he found the door he was looking for. Here the meanness beneath the ostentation revealed itself: inside a piano was playing, a girl was singing, and Stephen could hear them both almost as clearly as if the door stood ajar.

The girl's voice was a light yet throaty contralto that carried the simple melody without effort and gave a curious sense of wistfulness to the words:

> In a pinch I'd be keen
> With 'Begin the Beguine'
> Or any old ditty
> That wasn't obscene:
> I'm tired of being risqué. . . .

The music stopped; there was a less audible murmur of talking, and Stephen thought this was the moment to press the bell. Apparently he was wrong. The piano gave forth an aggrieved discord as if a hand had slapped down on most of an octave. An instant later Eliot opened the door. "Hi, I didn't expect you so early," he said, but making a visible effort to be cordial.

"It's my free morning," Stephen apologized.

"No matter," said Eliot. "Just give me five minutes more and I'll be free for as long as you like." He turned back, leaving Stephen to close the door and follow him.

The living room was conceived in the same spirit as the lobby downstairs and seemed scarcely more personal: whoever lived here must have thought it in poor taste to possess anything older than last year. The furniture, of shapely woods, sculptured foam rubber and curiously textured fabrics, all spoke with a Scandinavian accent. The small upright piano was painted powder blue, presumably to match the skin tones of the nude hanging on the opposite wall.

Beside the piano stood a slip of a girl, no more than nineteen or twenty at first glance, though an easy self-assurance suggested that she must be rather older. Her white blouse, grey skirt and loafers contributed to the school-girl effect. Her hair was jet black; she had a mane of it falling straight back below her shoulders, and her skin was swarthy; she had enormous dark eyes, a snubbed nose, a wide slash of a mouth, and the general appearance of an intelligent monkey. She gave Stephen a glance of speculative indifference, obviously taking it for granted that he was one of Eliot's confreres.

"Pay no attention to this gentleman," Eliot instructed her as he returned to the piano bench. "He's merely a talent scout from Hollywood. If he takes a fancy to you, he'll offer you millions and millions of dollars. Just forget that he's there."

The girl threw Stephen a quick grin to show she wasn't taken in by this nonsense, but he obeyed the cue to make himself inconspicuous and subsided into an armchair.

"All right," said Eliot briskly. "We'll run through the last chorus. Get it right, and you're off to your fitting. The thing here is the vocal switch. You start off in your most lyrical, little-girl voice. Halfway through you start getting brassier and brassier. By the time you get to the last line you should really be hitting into it, and that should cover the laughter—assuming you get a laugh. Then pull back hard for the repeat. Okay?"

"I think so," said the girl.

Eliot began to play. His melodies were usually very simple, mere vehicles for the lyrics, but he prided himself on his accompaniments, as elaborate or delicate as the song required, and often with dazzling little musical interludes to separate the stanzas. Now he played a brisk elaboration of the tune Stephen had already heard, which slowed and started to double back on itself. Eliot gave a tiny nod, and the girl began.

> I'd much rather sing
> Some three-quarter thing
> Concerning a romance
> That blossoms in spring
> From a Rodgers and Hammerstein play—

"Bear down," said Eliot.

> I'm sick of the smirks
> On the faces of jerks
> Who find double meanings
> Where no meaning lurks,
> I'm tired of being risqué!
> Hey, hey—
> I'm tired . . . of being . . . risqué.

She had sung to the whole room—her gaze wandering across Stephen's face as if it were one among many—and standing easily, without gesticulation, till at the very end her arms rose spontaneously to accept a great bundle of applause. Now she let them fall and turned anxiously back to Eliot, who was frowning over the keyboard as if still listening to the echoes of her performance. "Much better," he said finally. "That 'Hey, hey' should be more of a sigh instead of an imperative summons for horse fodder, but other than that it was fine —vocally. I don't know why you were waving your hands about unless it was to impress my brother, but we'll work on that later—in front of a mirror, duckie, so you can see just how out of place that gesture looks. Now run along to your fitting, and try to get back here by two thirty. And make damn sure they've fixed the neckline of that red dress: you're supposed to look like a pro, all right, but not *that* sort of pro. I've rewritten some of the words of the blues number; you can memorize them on the bus going over. . . ." Still rattling off instructions at high speed, he bundled the girl into her gay spring coat and out of the apartment.

Then he spun back into the living room and grinned his enthusiasm down at Stephen. "She's really going to be first-rate, that kid," he said. "Could you sense it?"

"I thought she was excellent," Stephen said. "I couldn't even see anything wrong with that gesture you were so sarcastic about."

"Not for that song," Eliot said flatly. For an instant he posed motionless at the center of the room, a lithe graceful figure in tight black slacks and yellow pullover, with the sort of lean chiseled good looks any man would be grateful for. Then he lifted one hand slightly, palm upwards, sketching a vague gesture of appeal. "Something on that line, I'd think," he said, "but she'll have to find it for herself. That arms-high gesture should be saved for songs that end on a full sustained note—it lifts the ribs and makes breathing easier, and God knows these kids don't have the vocal training that gives them any breath to spare. There may be a beer in the refrigerator; I know you won't settle for some of my tea."

This meant iced tea, which Eliot drank incessantly while he was working, regardless of the season. "Nothing for me, thanks," Stephen said.

"She has the intelligence and the humor, and she's actually eager to learn!" Eliot said. "You can't imagine how eager. For most of a month now I've been working that kid like a slave, and she keeps coming back for more—which is the way it ought to be, but Lord what a rarity!" He had prowled the room till he found a tall glass half filled with melting ice; now he bore this off through a door at the far end of the room. "Mostly it's been a matter of clearing away a lot of bad habits she's got into. They're so desperate to be noticed, those poor kids. . . ." His voice faded as he went on to a further room. Break their silly necks for something. Mumble managers and double-mumble agents. Copy all the worst mannerisms of. (Slam of a refrigerator door.) Waste is heartbreaking. "People are so pathetically *eager* to be entertained," Eliot said, re-emerging with a fresh glass of tea, "but not one in a thousand has the least idea why one performer leaves them cold and the next sends them into raptures. Talent, they say glibly. You point out that the first performer had a far better singing voice, or whatever, than the second had—and they take refuge in something equally incoherent about 'personality.' Twaddle, of course. When you know these people you know that off stage most of them have no personality to speak of, and what there is, is likely to be detestable. So what's the answer? A modicum of talent, a lot of showmanship, a modicum of luck, a huge helping of genuine self-confidence—not the put-on sort. And there's one of the catches: you need self-confidence to be a success and success to be self-confident. Of course some of them start out with an invincible self-confidence built in, which means they're uncommonly gifted or uncommonly stupid or occasionally both. But it doesn't have to work that way. Am I boring you?"

"Not at all," Stephen said politely, reminded of his impatience.

"I've been cooped up with that girl for a month, and I suppose I've been dying for an opportunity to boast to someone about what I've been doing. Teaching has been the least of it, though she's had to relearn practically everything. How to hold herself, what to do with her hands, how not to flirt with the audience. Above all, to rehearse a song till she could sing it in her sleep—yet still make it sound as if she loved every word of it. Well, that's all basic. But I've also made myself into her self-confidence—all she needs for the time being, and I couldn't have done that if she weren't smart. She'd have gone home in tears after the first lesson. I've been an absolute brute, Steve. I've been sarcastic, I've been bitchy, I've staged scenes, I've developed nuances of disgust that nobody ever thought of before. But she understood from the beginning that I'd be infinitely tougher on her than any audience she'd ever face, and it worked. She turned herself inside out to win that first grudging word of praise —but, my God, when it came! Now when I'm satisfied, she's convinced that she's really good. And when I finally allow myself a little modified enthusiasm the day or so before her debut she's going to walk out on that stage *knowing* she's bound to knock them dead. That's the theory, anyway, and it's going to be an awful shock if I turn out to be wrong. I've been on the sidelines of this racket for a long time now and I think I know all the tricks, but this is the first time I've taken a chance on failure. Before, if a song didn't go over, I could always blame the singer. Not this time. It's the test of whether I'm just another dilettante. I swear I've lost ten pounds in the last three weeks."

Despite himself, Stephen was touched. Albeit affectionately, he had always regarded Eliot as a dilettante in every sense of the word: someone who played on the shores of life and never got his feet wet, avoiding even the responsibility of a fixed address. There was something pathetic and impressive in finding that Eliot still wanted to take himself seriously, even if in such a trivial matter. Stephen searched for something constructive to say, to prove that he had not merely been waiting to interrupt with his own anxieties. "That song she was singing," he said. "Isn't it a little, well, blasé for a girl as young as that?"

Eliot hugged his knees with laughter. "You've lost your eye for the girls, Steve. How old do you think she is?"

"Twenty?"

"She's closer to thirty and twice divorced. No, when she's made up and dolled out, Jo doesn't look like any dewy-eyed innocent—that's no problem. Well, to hell with it, but keep your fingers crossed for me. And tell me why you had me tracked down to Sean Ghio's."

"Where?"

"The hangout where Freddie Ames finally caught up with me. And since I called you the other day two other people have passed along your message. You must have had search parties out all over town."

"There's this, for one thing." Stephen reached in his pocket and threw over the wedding invitation which had been sitting on the hall table for several weeks.

Eliot gave him a bewildered glance, puzzled over the ivory envelope for a moment before he opened it. When he saw the contents he snorted. "Oh, come *on*, Steve! For God's sake!"

"I expect you'd forgot all about it."

"My demi-step-nephew's marriage!"

"That's one way of looking at it," Stephen said mildly. "But there are times when you have to be reminded that you belong to the human race, and this is one of them. The invitation must be answered; there's not much time. And you ought to think about a wedding present, though I suppose you could wait till after they're settled down and produce something more practical than the seventeenth silver table lighter."

"That part's all right; I'll have Sandy dig up something original," Eliot said. "But do I have to *go?*"

"You do," Stephen said with a flat voice of an older brother, never quite sure whether his authority still prevailed.

"I can't abide these baroque rituals, you know that."

"No one will notice whether you're at the church. The reception is what I care about. It's just another party, Eliot; I expect there'll be dancing, and you're fond of that. But even if you were going to be quite wretched, I'd want you there."

"You have a morbid sense of family feeling," Eliot said, and Stephen accepted this since his true reasons were in such a muddle. Because Amelia had wished that Eliot might be excluded and would feel vindicated if he failed to appear, that was a small part of it. Uppermost in Stephen's mind, probably, was a long-held feeling that Eliot for his own sake should never be allowed to escape too far from a sense of normal family solidarity. There had to be some haven from the gathering loneliness of the homosexual life, somewhere he was accepted for no cleverer reason than that he belonged. Finally, Stephen had his own yearning for companionship, anticipating that at the wedding reception he was going to feel like a redundancy. With the bridegroom's father very much in evidence, what *raison d'être* was there for a mere stepfather? By himself Stephen would be almost a gate crasher; with Eliot there, a clansman at his side, his presence would acquire a certain tribal dignity.

Grumbling, perhaps animated less by pure fraternal loyalty than by a sense of indebtedness, Eliot finally gave in. "When *is* the bloody thing?" he muttered, scowling at the fine engraving. "Well, it could be a lot worse. All right, I'll uphold your quaint notions of family honor, Steve." He glanced about; then propped the cards against a driftwood table lamp, where presumably they would not be overlooked. "But don't ask me to believe *that's* why you had half New York on my trail."

"No," Stephen said, wondering if unconsciously he had arranged that little show of ascendancy before having to appeal for a younger brother's help. "I'm in something of a jam."

"And you've come running to me? There's a switch," Eliot said happily, yet without malice. "Which of my many talents are you in need of?"

"I think it's called the willing suspension of disbelief," Stephen said. "I need help in finding a reliable abortionist, and I'd like the help from someone who will believe that I'm not responsible for the necessity."

Eliot's face was wholly without expression. He sipped at his iced tea; he lit a cigarette. "Who's the girl?" he asked.

"Is that what will determine whether or not you believe me?"

"Oh, no, I believe you already. With me, if you'd knocked up a girl you wouldn't lie about it; I'm sure of that. You'd be far likelier to boast."

"Scarcely," said Stephen. "It speaks of a lack of elementary prudence I shouldn't be proud of. Is there any good reason why you should know who the girl is? No, I expect that's stuffy; if I couldn't trust your discretion, I shouldn't be here at all. It's Joyce Neilson."

One of Eliot's eyebrows arched exquisitely, and his mouth twitched. "Your secret is safe with me, Steve," he said earnestly.

"It's not my secret, damn it."

"Oh, you *are* turning into a pompous old creature," Eliot said, now laughing openly. "You may not be the most virile man on two feet, but if you wanted a holiday from Amelia I don't think you'd go hunting in the attic. To tell the truth, if it had been one of your students I'm not sure I'd really have believed you all the way, though I was ready to pretend. I could see why you might feel obliged to lie, even to me. But I give you credit for better taste than . . . Joyce. Do you know who the bankrupt seducer actually was?"

"I wish to God I didn't," Stephen said bitterly. "Have you met Arthur Vaughan? He's the wretched little man involved with Amelia in this newest crusade. In and out of the house all the time. And since Joyce threatens to have a nervous breakdown if he's told of her condition, I have to go on being polite to him." This was a real grievance to Stephen, all the more exasperating because it seemed insoluble. He had begun by liking Vaughan. The man seemed something of a prig, but he had a clear-headed fervency that was not unimpressive: Stephen had pitied him contending with Amelia and treated him cordially. Now his liking was altered to loathing. This was not entirely a logical reaction. On the surface Vaughan was guilty of little more than a certain sexual irresponsibility; he might be accused of hypocrisy; yet the sensible view was that a man need be no less high-minded for an occasional veniality. But Joyce's still-unexplained abomination of her lover was no less contagious for being neurotic; the violence of her feeling simply underlined her defenselessness. She was patently not the sort of girl with whom any sane man ventured on casual carnality—and far beyond that Stephen took it on faith that in some fashion Vaughan had behaved despicably towards her, or she believed he had. It made little difference which; it was still on the order of brutality to a child, and Stephen's sense of decency was outraged. Yet for him suddenly to reverse his behavior towards Vaughan, to reveal any part of the contempt he felt, would have demanded an explanation, and he was expressly forbidden the explanation. "I have a physical longing to kick the little beast out of my house," he complained. "It's very frustrating."

"If he's to be kept out of the secret," Eliot said, "who's going to pay for all this? Do I have three guesses?"

"Joyce has some money saved up."

"How much?"

"I don't know, exactly," Stephen said. "If it's not enough, I suppose I'll have to make up the difference with an advance against her salary."

"Of course you'll *have* to! You've spent the last few years complaining about the girl, what an incompetent pain in the neck she is, and now you're making sure she'll be with you for life."

"What would you expect me to do? Seize the excuse to get rid of her?"

"Oh, no," said Eliot. "I'd expect you to do just what you're doing. The truth is, you prefer it this way. You're in love with responsibilities."

"Not this one!"

"All of them," Eliot insisted. "The messier the better. They give you the illusion of being a pillar of strength. I grapple your loyalty with hoops of steel by borrowing money periodically. If I ever paid it back, you'd feel cheated."

"Try," Stephen suggested.

"No, you'd just take it for the good of my character and then we'd both be the poorer. But this notion of paying for Joyce's abortion. . . ."

"I'm not paying for anything. It's only a loan. I'll stop it out of her salary."

"Except you won't," Eliot said, shaking his head. "Within a month you'll be feeling guilty about how little money she's taking home, and you'll invent some excuse to raise her pay. Not that you have the money for that sort of game. It's a nervous affirmation of your manhood. . . ."

And here, Stephen suspected, was the key to his relationship with Eliot. As brothers they were bound to quarrel, but so dissimilar were their natures that their separate reproaches roared harmlessly by like two trains passing on parallel tracks. It was an exercise in futility to accuse a man of fecklessness if he had persuaded himself that a sense of responsibility was an aberration, something to be ashamed of. So their squabbles could never be heated, and in fact were little more than displays of fraternal affection. "At least you might put me out of my anxiety first," Stephen protested. "Are you going to be able to help me?"

"Oh, *that*," Eliot said with a dismissing wave of the hand. "Nothing easier."

"Are you really so sure? I've gained the impression that things have become more difficult recently: the police have been tightening down."

"That happens regularly," Eliot said. "They take time off from shaking down shopkeepers and restaurateurs and rush off to jail with some broken-down old doctor who's developed the shakes. It gets a maximum of fanfare so we'll think we're guarded with unsleeping vigilance. But it never has the slightest effect on a noble profession."

"That's a weight off my mind," Stephen said. "I've been particularly anxious that Joyce gets to somebody who is reasonably respectable. . . . Well, you know what I mean."

"Don't think of this as a hole-and-corner business," Eliot said. "It isn't at all, necessarily, depending on what you can afford. That's why I asked who was paying. Hell, a few of the fashionable private hospitals work wonders in the name of curettage."

"I'd not even thought of a hospital," Stephen said. For the moment he was happy: instead of a troublesome urgency, abortion had become a sociological abstraction.

"Don't be naive," Eliot said. "If money is no consideration at all, you can send a girl into a perfectly good hospital here in the city—almost any hospital at all, except possibly the Catholic ones—and the operation will be performed by a qualified surgeon."

"There are limits to what I'll believe."

"It's perfectly true," Eliot replied. "I've known of it two or three times myself, and I'll tell you how it's done. The most recent case was also a girl named Joyce, as it happens, but she doesn't bear any resemblance to that female hobbledehoy you keep upstairs. This Joyce's family have money leaking out of all the crevices, but that didn't stop Joyce from getting herself pregnant by somebody already well married. Mildly annoyed, she trotted around to the family doctor with her dilemma. He hadn't got where he was by treating his wealthier patients to righteous lectures: he talked with Joyce for a while and told her she seemed seriously disturbed by what had happened. This was a slight exaggeration, since nothing much could disturb Joyce except the prospect of missing a good party, but she was just smart enough to agree that, yes, indeed, she was terribly upset. Forthwith, her doctor called in the services of a psychiatrist or a psychoanalyst—I never remember which is which—perhaps not one of the finest in the city but certainly one of the more successful. He's a fast man at diagnosis, and it took him no time to decide that Joyce was *very* seriously disturbed. Psychoanalysis was indicated—he would accept Joyce as a patient—and in the meantime he would recommend a therapeutic abortion for the sake of her mental health. So into the hospital Joyce went, ostensibly to have a cyst removed; in due course the cyst was attended to by a first-rate surgeon, and everybody was happy. As I recall, Joyce even put in a couple of sessions on the analyst's couch, strictly for laughs, before she got bored."

"You surprise me," Stephen admitted. "I don't see why he'd take a chance like that."

"He hadn't taken a chance at all," Eliot said. "Joyce is down on his books as a regular patient, and he's entirely entitled to recommend an abortion for a disturbed patient. If, afterwards, she decides to abandon analysis, that certainly isn't *his* fault—he can't compel anybody to keep coming. As long as he doesn't have too many such capricious patients in a year, and I imagine he rations himself discreetly, nobody is permitted to raise an eyebrow."

"But I'm taking it for granted he was paid off on the sly."

"Both doctors were. There was a handsome 'consulting fee,' delicately requested in cash. I assume it was divided according to the strictest medical ethics."

"To men of that standing the money can't be that important."

"To men of that *tax* standing it can," Eliot corrected. "The government makes criminals of us all. A thousand dollars that finds its way straight into your pocket has no legal existence: it's worth more than five thousand that comes across the books in the ordinary way —and even the very big boys put in a lot of hard work for five thousand dollars. A few such favors to your more valuable patients and you can buy a diamond bracelet for that blonde without even a ripple in the family exchequer. Catch on?"

"To the point where you're beginning to unnerve me again," Stephen said. "I'm in no position to help with the purchase of diamond bracelets."

"I didn't suppose you were—I was just showing off my knowledge." Eliot laughed. "Actually it's rather quaint: your appealing to *me* on a matter like this."

"You've described your friends. I hope they're not all in such an exalted financial bracket. And that means getting back to the hole-and-corner aspect of the business, doesn't it?"

"In a way, yes. But that doesn't mean disreputable."

"I've been curious about this," Stephen said. "It's something you don't think about until you have to cope with the problem. But you take it for granted. In spite of all the laws, it's an accepted part of urban living, New York living, almost as normal as the speakeasy used to be. Well, that's an exaggeration, but you know what I mean. It's something one knows about, happening all the time. This is a mildly promiscuous era: girls get into trouble every day. On some levels the girl has the baby and gives it for adoption; above a certain level the baby simply never materializes. Somebody always knows somebody, which seems remarkable when you stop to think of it. A lot of doctors will agree that the present laws are criminal, but that's a far cry from taking a chance on wrecking your career and serving a jail sentence besides. So one tends to picture a bleary, shaky-handed old lush who's been struck off the register for incompetence. Not very reassuring. And not very accurate, either, I'd gather from your attitude."

Eliot stretched out flat on the sofa and blew smoke at the ceiling. "Joyce will spend a night or two at some pleasant establishment on Long Island or over in Jersey, known locally as a respectable nursing home or boarding house—something of the sort that accounts for occasional such comings and goings. Her problem will be disposed of by a highly qualified doctor who may have some anxieties about the police but none at all about being struck off the register, for the simple reason that he—or more probably she—has never been on it. Not in this country. Refugees, Steve: they were still trickling in right till the end of the war, and a lot of them were first-rate doctors. Unless they had influence in the right places, they found they couldn't practice here unless they were prepared to go back to school for a year or more, which many of them couldn't afford to do. For the most part they gave up and found other jobs. But I suppose the thought of all that training and experience going to waste would be particularly offensive to a woman's practicality—at least the best ones mostly seem to be women. Perhaps a female revenge against a society that doesn't take women doctors very seriously anyway. I don't know. But from all reports it's hygienic, painless and safe. You haven't anything to worry about."

"How much will all this cost?"

"Four or five hundred," Eliot said. "That's quite standard, I believe. But I'll ask around." Nonetheless he lay there peacefully, making no move towards the telephone, oblivious to Stephen's hope of returning home with an appointment made, a date fixed. "There are drawbacks to the life I lead," he added reflectively, "but at least I miss some of the anxieties. At times it must be a nuisance to be normal."

"For a woman, perhaps," Stephen said. "Men suffer very little."

"Well, either there's the worry that the girl might get pregnant," Eliot argued, "or else somebody has to rush around taking precautions, and that's bound to have a blighting effect on the mood, it seems to me."

This was the one way that Eliot could be annoying, and from time to time he appeared to do it quite deliberately. Clearly it was better that inverts be reconciled to their position, follow their bent openly rather than furtively, but they became tiresome when they began to suggest that their lives were richer, freer, finer than those of ordinary men—and they all came to it sooner or later. "I'd like to get this organized as soon as possible," Stephen said with some asperity. "Coping with Joyce is more of a problem every day."

Eliot gave him a glance of tender mockery, perfectly aware of his brother's reactions. "You'll probably have to cope for another week or ten days," he warned. "These things have to be arranged well in advance. The good ones want to give a girl a check-up first, to make sure there won't be complications."

"All the more reason for getting started right away, I should think."

"After lunch," Eliot said. "Not before. The people I know aren't worth talking to till the day's second Bloody Mary is behind them."

4

Gretchen darling—
   This is going to be a difficult letter to write. . . .

Except that they were all difficult and always had been. Some
women wrote effortlessly, words streaming across page after page.
Madge envied them. Letters had always been drudgery to her, perhaps because she had never for very long had someone at a distance
with whom correspondence could be a joy. She still remembered
from her schooldays in England the letters from her father—rambling,
wise and funny—but she had generally replied with hasty schoolgirl
scrawls to say that everything was fine except that she had broken a
finger playing lacrosse. After her marriage, when her father went
back to Chile, the correspondence began again and for a little while,
scarcely more than a year, she had poured onto paper all the excite-
ments and exasperations of her life with Virgil. Then her father had
died, and that was that.

Since then, letters were only the routine obligations of her life.
Seventeen years of letters to Mother and Father Blair, for example.
Virgil hated writing letters, yet his parents were the sort who fretted
unless they heard from him periodically; he had pushed the task onto
her. So once a week for all those years she had settled down dutifully
to create a letter to the couple in Urbana, Illinois, whom she had
met precisely once: on the honeymoon trip she and Virgil had taken
two years after their wedding, when she was far gone in pregnancy.
Gretchen had been born in Urbana, Virgil wanting to preserve for
his son the possibility of becoming President.

Father Blair, lean and shy, taught algebra in a local high school
and coached the basketball team; there was another child, a married
daughter living in Ohio. Mother Blair tended her emptied home,
subscribed to the Book of the Month Club, and played mah-jongg
with a circle of friends who disapproved of card games. Scarcely an
eventful life, yet each week she filled both sides of three sheets of
airmail stationery, with afterthoughts and inquiries written length-
wise in the margins. The last batch of peach preserve was a decided
success, and Terry Bliss (an old friend of Virgil's, and I think you
met him, Madge dear) is finally getting married, and William's team
is such a disappointment this year, and the sweater for Gretchen is
going more slowly than I expected. . . .

For seventeen years, replying had been the bugbear of Madge's life, because she was expected to come up to Mother Blair's epistolary standards. A hurried note would never do: back would come the plaintive observation that surely, living such an unusual, exciting, exotic life, Madge could never be at a loss for things to tell them—they were interested in *everything*.

And, although Mother Blair had tried earnestly to make their relationship a close one ("With no mother of your own, dear, and Virgil has always been a harum-scarum boy—there'll be times when you'll need a shoulder to cry on"), Madge had never felt free to speak her mind, to tell the truth. What would be the point of it? Suppose one time she had written: 'I'm alone this evening, as I have been these past half-dozen Saturdays. In the mistaken conviction that he is a shrewd poker player, Virgil is off with the bachelors playing for higher stakes than we can afford. Before leaving he seemed annoyed that he wasn't still a bachelor himself, so he could lose his own money as he liked without being made to feel guilty. . . .' There was a small splinter of reality, yet except for the relief she might have given her exasperation, what good would have come of writing it? The Blairs would have been duly upset, but there wasn't a thing they could do. And if in their well-meaning innocence they had tried to do something, had written a reproving letter to their son, the situation would simply have been made several shades more unmanageable.

Life in a mining camp high in the Andes was no exotic adventure. Especially for a woman it tended to be a lonely routine with few pleasures and many discomforts. Obliged to compose gay weekly chronicles of this existence, inhibited from mentioning her inner cares and annoyances, Madge had found herself forced to creations of demure hypocrisy. 'We drove up from Lima this morning,' she would write, she who had made such trips a thousand times but now looking for an oddity that might strike an outsider. 'As he always does, when we were well up in the mountains, Virgil stopped the car every so many miles to let a little air out of each tire. He's explained this to me again and again, but I'm always afraid that before we reach camp the tires will be absolutely *flat*.'

This gushing idiocy was no part of her real nature: it was a character that settled upon her each time she sat down to her weekly chore. So many pages had to be filled, the illusion of communication maintained, and by this coy elaboration of trivialities the job got done. Yet it was the worst possible practice in correspondence, and perhaps was one reason why her closeness to her own daughter had eroded so rapidly as soon as Gretchen went off to school, when for nine months of the year their only contact had been by mail. She had never never known how to express herself warmly and naturally on paper. She didn't now.

. . . These last years, unhappily, we have drifted further apart than can be blamed on the overnight journey between us. To a great extent I am sure that has been my fault. . . .

But was she really sure of anything of the sort, or was that just one of the verbal bribes you paid for sympathy? I'll accuse myself a little, first, so that you'll be less defensive. Where was truth to be found in the words of people who had once lived on terms of innocence and omniscience?

Madge sighed and looked up. Over the desk was a solid bank of photographs of the earlier Gretchen, all shapes and sizes, each in its separate frame—Charles had spent one evening arranging and rearranging them, fitting them together till not an inch of wall was visible —it was funny to think of the mysterious pattern of nails that would remain when the pictures were taken down.

There was Gretchen in her play pen, Gretchen on her tricycle— though God knows there hadn't been much space to ride it. Gretchen wide-eyed in communion with a baby llama; Gretchen comical in overalls and a miner's helmet far too large on the afternoon when Virgil took her down into the mine; Gretchen solemn with the responsibility of a .22 rifle. All the phases of Gretchen until she was thirteen. Elsewhere about the apartment were later pictures —the wedding portrait, Gretchen and Bob with their children—but here over the desk was Madge's daughter. An enchanting child, earnest, outgoing, affectionate. She had given Virgil a sense of worship: the emulative tomboy. And she had given Madge a sense of adoration and rapport, for beneath the boylike mannerisms (really the only sensible response to that rough countryside, where a prissy girlishness would have been sadly out of place) the emergent female had always been clearly defined. Gretchen had been a little *girl*, a darling girl, a friendly girl, perhaps the least complicated satisfaction in her parents' lives.

This had all changed by the time Gretchen came home for her first summer vacation—changed so radically that they were forced to wonder whether Gretchen had all along sensed the tensions and antagonisms they had tried so hard to keep concealed from her. Now her attitude was one of 'A plague on both your houses.' Her father was to be scorned for just those qualities she had formerly worshipped. And her mother, by some bizarre twist of logic, was to blame for their living where they did. In retrospect Gretchen's childhood had suddenly become dreary, miserable; the world was a lush and civilized place, and why should *she* have been condemned to grow up in this bleak outpost?

They had taken this as a phase of adolescence which would quickly be outgrown; there was no other way to take it, though in time they found they were wrong. The frenzied bitterness of that first summer month (mid-winter in Peru, to add to Gretchen's grievances) was never repeated, true, but neither did she return to anything like her former trusting adoration. A part of the normal pattern of growing up, one might say, but Gretchen seemed to work at exaggerating the pattern. She cultivated reserves of stubborn selfishness, she withdrew into herself, she treated her parents (at best) with an impatient affection which declared them such failures at the gracious art of living that their opinions were not to be taken seriously. And incessantly she dreamt of her release, her eventual escape into the elegance and abundance that was her birthright. Against this dream, compounded from vacations spent with classmates, Gretchen measured her parents' life and found it wanting in every respect. Even Madge's cooking—a proud legacy from her Danish mother which had triumphed even over water's bland refusal to boil an egg at an altitude of fourteen thousand feet—was sniffed at for the lack of the fresh vegetables and fruits, the packaged, frozen, cellophaned variety of a handy supermarket.

It should have been possible to joke and jostle the child out of such nonsense, but Madge and Virgil had been hamstrung by a sense of guilt, a feeling that they *had* shortchanged their daughter, though not in the fashion she imagined. If only Gretchen had had the security of a completely happy home, surely this revulsion would never have been so extreme. Now they were being punished for all the ragged edges of resentment that had come to Gretchen's notice, and they lacked the conscience to respond naturally. They had cajoled and wheedled for a return of their only child's respect. And it seemed to Madge that sixteen years later she was still wheedling: 'To a great extent I am sure that has been my fault—'

. . . though these last few years it has been ill health, mainly, that has kept me from getting out there as often as I would like. You, on your part, have never shown the least understanding or sympathy for my relationship with Charles. . . .

And that was putting it mildly.

Where in her upbringing had Gretchen come by her rampant prudery? Not at home, certainly. Madge and Virgil had quarrelled about many things but not about sexual morality. It wasn't a question of what a person did but who got hurt by it: this was the attitude Gretchen had grown up with. Everyone knew that Dick Mayo was having a torrid affair with a young English divorcée down in Lima who would forfeit her alimony if she remarried. Dick was a bachelor, so who suffered? Almost everyone knew that Lisa Hardy was sleeping with the camp's Peruvian doctor, but a tacit conspiracy kept the news from her husband; it wasn't till the couple abruptly eloped, leaving two small children to Ted Hardy's alcoholic mercies, that their conduct became reprehensible.

Yet within this climate of live-and-let-live Gretchen had somehow all unknown manufactured a private puritanism which had erupted in full force at the discovery that her mother had become, in effect, the mistress of a married man. Evidently the very idea was disgusting, shaming, humiliating. In her first outrage, quivering with nineteen-year-old fury, Gretchen had even threatened personally to confront Ruth Fortescue with the facts—a suggestion so barbarous that for the moment Madge had literally been struck dumb. Yet this was the same girl who on another occasion, some years later, had admitted with contemptuous indulgence that when her husband was off on business trips, he doubtless played around. "I can always tell when there's been a chippie," she had said (and wasn't the expression twenty years out of date?), "because otherwise when he gets back he's a frightful nuisance the first few days." The gulf between mother and daughter had become unspannable.

In time Gretchen had learned to accept Charles's existence, though always with a stiff-necked disapproval, and when shortly after her marriage she began her campaign to get her mother to live in Chicago, it was clearly with the intention of ending this degrading relationship. The motives behind her attitude had never been very intelligible. Disrespectful of her father's memory and all too aware that that marriage had been less than ideal, she could scarcely have expected her mother to keep her widowhood a holy trust for the next life. Neither was Gretchen naive enough to believe that a woman's life ended at some birthday. Her reaction was more intensely personal than that, and what aroused her deepest impatience was any suggestion that Madge had quite simply fallen in love with Charles and therefore had very little control over the consequences.

To Gretchen, evidently, love was something which led comfortably to the good things of life—or else was a contemptible indulgence.

Which implied not merely that she had never been in love but that the very idea frightened her. And on this score Madge looked back guiltily on her marriage and wondered how it might have appeared to a certain type of strong-willed little girl trapped in the middle.

For there was no questioning the love in that marriage: it was the one constant, irrational grace in a stormy mismating. From any objective point of view they should never have married at all, Madge and Virgil. Their characters were utterly dissimilar; their ideal of happiness met at no common point. He was that supreme egoist of virility: a man's man, always wanting to be off killing something or other, risking his neck in boyish wagers, chafing at domesticity. So that she, by nature more a lover than either nest builder or mother, had been driven into the false position of nagging at him for some sense of responsibility. Their life together had been one long succession of turbulent battles and equally turbulent reconciliations. Yet throughout, scarcely affected by time, continued the illogical, compelling tie of their love—making all the rest worth while. Or so it had seemed to them. Perhaps a child, with a child's pragmatical selfishness, would have drawn the lesson that love was a treacherous and inconvenient compass.

After Virgil's death, which had come as both a tragedy and a release, Madge would have laughed at the idea of embarking on another love affair. It was shocking, a sad brutality, the relief she had felt in finding that her heart was her own again: she was her own mistress, free to make her own plans, decisions. Briefly she had exulted in this illusory freedom. Illusory, because a heart with the habit of loving had no self-sufficiency; without knowing it, she was running water suddenly dammed up, but a dam could never be high enough—somewhere there had to be an outlet. If not Charles, someone else. It had happened to be Charles.

Were the Gretchens more happy with their docile, circumspect emotions? You couldn't imagine Gretchen satisfied with one small furtive fraction of a man's life, but while Madge would never have chosen the same position for herself she could not entirely disclaim the choice. Perhaps she could not control the impulse of her heart, but at least she had some say in the opportunities she permitted it. Whatever reasons Charles had given himself twelve years ago for believing that the best way to tell her of Andean's settlement would be over an intimate dinner at Gaston's, there must have been some answering hypocrisy in herself. She was a grown woman; she could perfectly well have preferred to see him at his office and that would have been the end of the matter. So there it was. Possibly she had thought of herself as immune, but a person always had to take responsibility for self-ignorance.

She had fallen in love—the usual, feminine, unanswerable reason for complicating life. Worse, she had fallen in love with Charles for a quality which he would instantly, indignantly, have disclaimed. He appealed to the maternal in her as Virgil had never done, and this was the more ironic because she knew, though he had never said so openly, that Charles was inclined to scorn Virgil as an overgrown adolescent, unworthy of her. That estimate had a superficial plausibility, missing the fact that within his own limitations Virgil had been a complete person, joyfully, masterfully at home in his own world. Charles had twice the intelligence and twenty times the maturity—and was at home nowhere, except within his own mind. Poor dear, he could never be entirely at ease with other people: there was a core of shyness which he had never overcome. In an odd way this had probably been the making of him as an executive, for he had grown skilled at compensating for his lack. He stored up information about people as a substitute for understanding them; he manipulated them with infinite consideration as an apology for not liking them. But, personally, there was a lonely and frightened little boy hiding somewhere within the grand and dignified edifice.

Of course this was only one aspect of Charles, the most immediately endearing, perhaps, but scarcely the most important. Glorious had been the relaxing into the keeping of someone with a compulsive sense of responsibility; gone were the days when all the niggling obligations preyed upon her mind if they were to be taken care of at all. Charles resolved the mysteries of her income tax, reinvested her modest inheritance, periodically straightened out her checkbook —all as automatically as he changed a fuse. Trivialities to him, but the sense of dependence was a luxury she had not known since her girlhood. He was endlessly thoughtful (oh, the bliss of it!), wise and amusing and gentle and generous. And she had loved him for the past twelve years or more, living almost contentedly for the evenings they could spend together, the stolen weekends. An unsatisfactory relationship, which at least had kept staleness at bay. There was little point in assaying a love, yet possibly, just possibly, there might be more worth in a little bit of Charles than exclusive right to many another man. But this was one of the many understandings that could never be expected of Gretchen.

. . . but this is not meant as a reproof. I know that you have thought it selfish of me to insist on living my own life in my own fashion. . . .

Madge stared in dismay at the embossed sheet of pale blue stationery. She knew if she tore it up she would lack the courage to start again, but the awkward empty sentences mocked at communication. All the things she so desperately wanted to say were getting lost in her efforts to win a sympathy which was probably not there to be won. Apologizing for Charles, apologizing for wanting to live her own life! And to what end? A maudlin hope that Gretchen would discover empathy, or be seized by a sudden sense of the narrowness of her own life and conceive some better dream for *her* children. They would find their own dreams. This letter was a mistaken necessity: it would have to get written somehow or other, but it would serve no earthly purpose; there was nobody to receive the message. The Gretchen to whom she might have spoken her heart had never come to maturity, the Gretchen for whom she had once held such high hopes. . . .

You brought forth a child knowing that one day it might trample underfoot everything you believed most important; that was part of the bargain you made with life. You hadn't the right to hope, but you tried to cheat on that part of the bargain, just a little, pitching your ambitions deliberately low—you didn't ask for talent or genius, fame or fortune—only, perhaps, that your child would have the courage to live its life to the full, unashamed and unafraid. So, of course, all wittingly, Gretchen had curled herself into the dreariest oblivion of middleclass security, where the emotions all were cautious and the opinions conventional, things of the spirit neglected and vegetables overcooked.

And so one generation twisted to the next. Probably one or another of Madge's grandchildren would turn his back on that converted swampland of comfortable mediocrity—and break his mother's heart in the process. It was a curious law of nature. These last few days she had frequently found herself thinking of Bruce Bigelow and the three sons for whom he had sacrificed so much: peace of mind, integrity, even his sense of decency. For the moment he had possession of what he had paid for: the physical presence of three young boys, no doubt adorable and admiring. But they would grow up and grow away, indifferent to all the investments he had made in them. In fabricating their own characters, they would expose one by one all the inadequacies of their father's; they would grow critical surely, condescending perhaps, contemptuous possibly, but independent certainly. This was the reward he could look forward to: three young strangers who bore with him in varying attitudes of tolerance and affection, forever a little impatient with the man who held all the keys to the days of their predignity.

How would he look back on the decisions he had taken to reach this end—the conniving, the ruthlessness, the swindling? Probably without too much self-pity, for that was the nature of the animal: the memory of your own betrayals warned you not to expect any better. Still, it was the ultimate tragedy that an intimacy which had once promised to give so much meaning to life should seep away entirely, leaving only the habit of loving and a sense of loss, of bewilderment, of noncommunication.

Such was the ill success of a lifetime of living that when she wanted to reach out to all that would endure of her, all that had given her a knowledge of permanence, she could only write with sad self-conscious flippancy:

. . . but perhaps you were lucky not to have me as a millstone around your neck. I'm not the grandmotherly type, Gretchen, I'm really not. This afternoon I saw Dr. Donoval again. . . .

5

Conscientiously, once every month or six weeks when some errand brought him to mid-town on a matinée afternoon, Owen looked in at the theatre to make sure the cast was behaving itself. By rights this was the director's task, but Bruno was a very busy and very popular young man and tended to get all wrapped up in each new project. Nonetheless, you couldn't let these things slide. The theatrical business would be simplified if actors could be relied on to go on giving the performance they had been rehearsed in, but they could not. Privately they were all convinced that the author had no ear for dialogue and the director was a fraud, and that they, with their natural genius, could greatly improve the original design. Left to their own devices for a while, they would improve a play until the audience wondered audibly what the critics had been so enthusiastic about.

So at a little after four o'clock this Wednesday afternoon, on the way to an appointment with his agent, Owen stopped off at the theatre, waved to old Eddie on lonely duty at the ticket window, slid quietly through one of the doors and took up his place at the rear of the orchestra and off to one side, looking across the heads of the audience to the lighted stage beyond.

This was familiar routine by now, yet it never failed to give him an exhilaration, seeing hundreds of people rapt, laughing as one man, caught up in a world of his devising. He envied them their whole-hearted absorption. These days, much as he loved the theatre, he could seldom escape from a professional detachment which was constantly being caught by technical details. He couldn't help noticing a clever piece of 'business' or a false note in the dialogue: he was intensely aware (as so few reviewers seemed to be) when fine direction or brilliant performances obscured the essential shoddiness of a play. All this was educational, no doubt, but it spoiled the fun and made him pathetically grateful for the rare show which for a few hours could revive his old innocence.

His own plays, of course, held not the slightest charm for him at this point. Through endless weeks of rehearsals and try-outs he had revised and rewritten, scrapping passages that 'didn't play,' inventing fresh dialogue for scenes that needed to be built up, till even his brightest lines came to seem stale and hackneyed and he wondered that anybody could ever respond to them. But a good director, and Bruno was very good, had the same vision as the writer's but translated into terms of pace and movement, and eventually the play had come to life. No longer just the idea which had once excited Owen's imagination, however; it was the production as a whole which came to matter and how the audience reacted. Now Owen scarcely heard the words he had labored over: the movement of the players about the stage told him exactly what was going on, and they might have been speaking Chinese for all he cared. He was conscious only of the *effect* of what was happening. Here the audience should be gripped, there moved, there waiting for the release of laughter—and any alteration of this pattern could damage the whole.

He had timed his arrival to Denise Durrell's big scene in the second act, suspecting that she might be the weakest link in the cast, and he saw immediately that his suspicions had been well grounded. Too much publicity had not agreed with her. She thought of herself now as the star of the play, and like many an actress before her had decided that this made *her* the most interesting thing on exhibit. She had added a host of little gestures and grimaces ('growing into the part,' as she would probably defend herself), she was pausing in her lines to give them more effect, and she was upstaging the other actors abominably, forcing them to play to her. Denise Durrell was on cunning display, and *The Cascade* suffered. This was an anxious moment in the play, the laughs were carefully spaced to heighten the mood; now by her own exertions Denise was evoking more laughter and the tension had virtually disappeared.

Yet listening to her in private you would have believed Denise the most dedicated of actresses, eager to subordinate herself to the needs of a role, always thinking of the good of the play. Or perhaps this was just the pose she adopted with a playwright. He had never made much sense of Denise as a person. She was constantly appearing in new guises—one time a hoyden, the next a languishing Lilith—as if trying out different personalities for the role of mistress. And this was true of the species as a whole: actors rarely seemed as sure of themselves as when somebody else had written the dialogue. It had been an exhausting love affair, trying to keep pace with the permutations of her character; he was getting too old for that sort of game. A little peace was what he wanted, and with Carol there might be peace.

Anyway, Denise was Bruno's problem now, and he must be sent over here as soon as possible to appreciate what havoc was being made of his meticulous design. Also, the new lad who had replaced Gordon in the hoodlum's part still seemed wooden, although this too might simply be a consequence of Denise's cavortings. A few fresh rehearsals were badly needed, and however busy he might be Bruno would have to fit them in.

Leaving an audience happily unaware of its betrayal, Owen went out to the dazzling afternoon. It was a lovely spring day; Polly's office was only a few blocks eastward, between Fifth and Madison, and he decided to walk. A rarity for him, but then he was rarely so aware of the attraction of fine weather. It was dreadful how in the city seasons wheeled about, noticed mainly for the inconvenience they brought. First it was too cold without steam heating (which played hell with one's sinuses), and then it was too hot without air conditioning (which encouraged head colds), and in between were the intervals when you never knew what to wear and could be confident only that whatever you decided on would prove wrong. No doubt spring and autumn duly brought their days of glory, usually to pass unheeded because of prior, enclosed commitments. Such days were reserved for children, for the old men on public benches hun-

gry for the feel of sun, for lovers with their senses all alerted. . . .
Well, there was his excuse for this afternoon. But periodically Owen
sensed the aridity of a life so cut off from the grand cycle of nature,
and for a time he would dream of one day having a house upcountry
somewhere in the mountains; a house enclosed in trees which would
yearly die and be reborn, and with a garden which he would tend
himself, learning the mysteries of a compost pit, forking and weed-
ing and watering and keeping himself wonderfully fit, and providing
an occasional fresh vegetable for the pot. A part of him was convinced that he would be a richer man for this contact with fundamental realities, but it was an intellectual conviction only—on a
plane with the belief that some time he *must* settle down and read
Finnegan's Wake through to the end—and he knew that nothing
would ever come of either dream. He had long ago sold his soul to
this city; the bustle and stimulation had entered into his blood; he
was tuned now to a quicker rhythm than the slow march of the seasons and he had no real desire to change.

The street through which he was walking was the center of the
jewelry trade (for New York was unexpectedly medieval in that certain guilds had captured certain districts of the town: the great gar-
ment trade within twenty square blocks, the toy makers down near
Twenty-third Street, the out-of-print book shops along lower Fourth
Avenue). Here, nearly every store at street level dealt in jewelry of
one sort or another—the window displays competed in promises of
bargains within—and the windows of the floors above spoke of precious and semiprecious stones, the importing of clocks and watches,
and the tiny manufacturies whence came the public's gewgaws. It
was easy to forget to what an extent New York reached out into the
country: in half a dozen offices along this street Mr. Louis Melmoth
of Actonsville, Connecticut, would be known as a valued customer
who each year bought so many engagement and wedding rings, so
many bracelet charms and strings of cultured pearls. Doubtless it
was from this block that he had come uptown that afternoon to pay
his call on Owen. . . .

The thought was mildly disconcerting. Melmoth was not the out-
lander he had seemed; business would bring him to the city from
time to time; he found it worth while to take a city newspaper. Inevitably he would hear of Owen Hilliard's newest play, most probably he would read a review of it. He would know at once where the
story had come from. The next time he came to town he would be

drawn irresistibly to the theatre, to see what had been erected on his sister's death.

And what would he make of it, that strange, grey little man? Owen had altered the superficial details, but it would mean nothing to Melmoth that the preparatory school had been removed to New Hampshire and the girl's father become a tailor instead of a jeweler. The essential story stayed the same, had to stay the same—the misfit schoolboy and the dreamy, unsuitable town girl; the autocratic father who precipitated the catastrophe, the influential school which shielded the boy from any consequences. It was Melmoth's old tragedy; it hung like a pall over the entire first act (almost completed now), and its revelation would be the first act climax. From then onward every situation, almost every line, would hark back to the long-ago death of the 'tailor's' daughter. For two and a half hours Melmoth would be caught up in the history which was already an obsession with him. Would he leave the theatre purged, feeling that at long last his sister had been avenged? There was a glib and unlikely outcome for you! He was far likelier to write a letter to Charles Fortescue claiming to have been the inspiration of the play. . . .

But on this bright and hopeful May afternoon Owen was able to put aside these speculations about what would happen so far in the future and so very problematically. Adolescent suicide pacts were in the public domain, after all, cropping up in the tabloids all the time. If need be, he would deny all knowledge of Melmoth and take refuge in a claim of coincidence. Charles would believe him; Charles must think of Melmoth as more than a little mad and therefore as nobody whose word he would accept in preference to that of a friend, the father of his son-in-law. The devil with it. What mattered now was that the play was coming along superbly. If necessary, he could feel guilty much, much later on.

Between Fifth and Madison in the Forties there still remain, among the towering new monstrosities, a number of older six and eight story office buildings; on the fifth floor of one of these were the offices of Marx and Spurgeon, one of the best of the small private literary agencies. The waiting room, where drudged two old-faithful secretaries, so much a part of the establishment that they greeted Owen by his first name, was furnished in standard blond office modern, but Polly Spurgeon's office, where he was waved a moment later, was a contrived period piece, though of no clearly ascertainable period. Her desk was a delicate antique with all modern impedimenta— push buttons, intercom, telephone—either disguised or hidden away.

The carpet was modestly threadbare but told of Persia; the wall was hung with Fragonard cartoons; on the mahogany bookcase was a cupid-supported enameled clock which tinkled the quarter hours. The armchairs were comfortable, but cleverly designed to lay claim to an antiquity they did not possess. It was a lady's office. Polly would die defending her position as a gentlewoman who had somehow strayed into the hurly-burly of business.

"Owen, dear, you're just on time!" she greeted him in her croaking voice. "I've finished my chores for the day. Just give me a chance to powder my nose and we'll slip around the corner for a comfortable drink, out of reach of this beastly telephone. All right?"

Polly Spurgeon was a tall, thin, highly strung, birdlike woman in her middle fifties, grey-haired, with protuberant eyes, a receding chin, and a sharp little bill of a nose, yet the lively, nervous intelligence of her face made her attractive. Though warmly affectionate with the clients she was fond of, she was known in the trade as something of a dragon, for her invincible gentility covered a sharp impatience with stupidity and a steely determination. The force of her character was evidenced by the fact that in a world where everybody called everybody 'Darling' on first meeting and switched to first names a moment later, she was called Polly only by her chosen intimates and Miss Spurgeon by the rest. In private life she was Mrs. Felix Weaver, but who Felix Weaver might be, whether he still existed or in fact had ever existed at all, was a mystery unsolved even by her closest friends. Any effort to inquire into this side of Polly's past met with a blunt, ladylike hint that some misfortunes were too private to bear discussion. Nevertheless the rumor persisted that Felix Weaver was a fiction born of Polly's known dislike of unlisted telephone numbers, which she was forever mislaying: in this fashion she had her home telephone in the directory, but listed where only personal friends could find it.

When Polly had cleared away the day's grime, they went 'around the corner' to her usual after-office hideaway: the gloomy, semideserted cocktail lounge of an Edwardian hotel, where a knowledgeable waiter hurried over with a full bowl of salted peanuts and inquired only what the gentleman would have to drink, taking it for granted that Miss Spurgeon would have 'the usual.'

"You are a trial, my pet," Polly announced, settling back and fixing a cigarette into a holder which was supposed to filter away the harmful qualities of tobacco. "I've had the Coast on the telephone twice this week already; they're really anxious to have you do the adaptation on *Cascade*. And well as I know your feelings, I haven't the heart to give them an unqualified No. You're going to give in one of these days, you know."

"Not this time," Owen said amiably.

"These high and mighty principles of yours are a lot of rubbish," she declared, and proceeded, not for the first time, to prove her point. Owen allowed her to scold him without demurring. The relationship between an author and his agent was a curiously delicate one—essentially businesslike, yet if it were to be successful it must be so much more than businesslike. Owen had been with Polly for almost twenty years now, and as was the rule rather than the exception there had never been a contract between them: in any moment of petulance he had been free to go elsewhere. She negotiated his contracts, protected him from producers and publishers, looked after his foreign rights, acted as a buffer against a thousand different nuisances and interruptions. If anybody had to be discourteous or disobliging to the outside world, it was Polly who did the dirty work. She served him as critic and editor, troubleshooter, business manager; in short, looked after him generally. For all this she took ten percent of what he earned, so their interests were intertwined. Her desire to see him make as much money as possible was a natural part of 'looking after him'; that her own income would go up in the process was doubtless a part of Polly's consideration, but not the venal part that Carol imagined. After all, if he took this assignment in Hollywood, nine-tenths of the profits would be his; by Polly's standards it would be a dereliction of her duty not to urge him to jump at the chance. Suppose she didn't. Suppose, for example, that his present streak of success ran out, that he lost his touch, that five years from now he turned on Polly and snarled "For God's sake, why didn't you *make* me go out to the Coast when I had the opportunity?" By the tacit nature of their relationship he would be in the right. He was the independent one, following his wayward star; it was her part to keep his feet as firmly on the ground as possible. He was free to make all the mistakes he liked, but she had earned the responsibility of pointing out the error of his ways.

So he accepted her scolding in good part, waiting until she arrived at her usual peroration: Where did he suppose Shakespeare would be working if Shakespeare were alive today?

"Writing speeches for one of the wealthier politicians," Owen said. "All right, Polly, I don't doubt there's wisdom in every word you say. But it's not what I want to talk about."

"Nothing sensible ever is. I expect you've been working on that new play and can already smell the Drama Critics' Award."

"It's coming on beautifully."

Polly inspected a peanut before popping it into her mouth; since the arrival of her 'usual' (sweet Vermouth over ice), she had been making ladylike but unremitting inroads on the bowl. "Well, it would be nice if you had a play all of your own," she conceded dubiously. "I'm tired of seeing half the loot go off to somebody else."

"The first act should be done by the beginning of next week," he said. "Another day or two to do a quick synopsis of the rest. And then I want you to see what sort of option money you can get me. I'd like to be quite sure I'm not wasting my time. Not that I have any doubts, but you know how it is. And, frankly, I need the cash."

She looked at him quizzically.

"Roger's wedding," he explained. "I'd always thought it was the bride's father who suffered, but it turns out to be not as one-sided as I'd believed."

"Oh, of course. I'd not really forgotten," Polly said. "It's down on my calendar, and barring calamities I'll be on hand. Just yesterday I stopped in at Steuben and sent them a crystal vase—and then went back to the office and wrote it off as a business expense."

"Clients are cheaper than other sorts of friendship," Owen said.

"I don't admit to any other sort," Polly retorted grimly. "All right, so you want an option. If your enthusiasm isn't just the usual form of writer's puerperal fever, that shouldn't be too difficult. Though it's not the best time of year: people are still nursing their bruises from last season. Let me think. Eli is scouting about over in England; Buzz is in the hospital and the word is that he'll have to keep away from excitement when he comes out, *if* he comes out. There's Mark, of course, and they say that he's sitting on a bundle of fresh Texas money."

"Mark sits on everything till the last possible moment," Owen said. "He hasn't any taste of his own; he never jumps at anything till his spies tell him one of the other boys is about to take the plunge. I can't afford to wait, Polly. I need a fast reaction."

"The only fast reactions in this town are negative," she said automatically, still running down her mental list of available producers. "The Blatt woman's a possibility, so is Dave. Fletch is on the lookout, but since he dropped so much of her money in that musical, his wife is taking a personal interest in his hobbyhorse. . . . Well, anyway.

If I'm going to scout the path for you, you'd better give me a clear idea of what the play's all about."

She was the only person to whom Owen talked freely of a work in progress. He would give various reasons for this inhibition, but the true one was that he had a childish dislike of anticipating a climax: he wanted a work of his to unfold naturally on the audience (even when that audience was a solitary reader) with all its twists, tensions and surprises still unexpected. He had long ago learned that this attitude was wasted on Polly. She was more truly the professional than he, in one sense; able to clear her mind of any previous impressions, able to bring to a seventh version exactly the same objectivity she had brought to the first, though all novelty had long since disappeared.

So quite unselfconsciously he began telling her the story of the play, giving the situation as it existed when the curtain went up, sketching out the main characters and their interrelationships, mentioning the minor characters primarily in terms of function. "There's a dialect part German housekeeper. I started out thinking of her strictly in terms of comedy relief, which is needed, but she's turned out to be a lot more than that. She's the spirit of common sense. When emotions are rawest she brings in a plate of sandwiches; when melodrama arrives she wants the day off to visit her sister in Hoboken. She's the reminder that life goes on." He dwelt at some length on the atmosphere of the first act leading up to the as yet unwritten revelations at the end. . . . And as he talked he found himself forming new ideas of how best to deal with that critical scene between the two half brothers. Then, more briskly, he went on to outline the action of the two succeeding acts, finally admitting that he was still of two minds about how to handle the denouement, but had no doubt that that problem would solve itself when the time came.

Polly listened impassively, conveying peanuts to her mouth in rhythmic succession. When he had finished she turned and beckoned to the waiter for another brace of drinks. "Well, you may have something there," she said noncommittally. "As you tell it, it sounds a bit contrived and mechanical, but that's no criticism. So do most melodramas when you strip them down to the plot line."

"I don't think of this as a melodrama," Owen said, mildly shaken. "This time I'm serious, Polly."

"Well, it all depends on how you treat it," she replied. "If you haven't learned your trade by now, you never will."

"Wait till you see the first act," Owen said confidently.

"I'll tell you one thing, though," Polly said. "That central character

—I think his name is Amory, though a couple of times you slipped and called him Charles—"

"Amory," Owen said.

"Yes, well he's going to be hell to cast, I warn you. He's the main figure; he *behaves* unsympathetically throughout—towards his son, towards his half brother, towards the Puerto Rican girl—yet he has to hang on to a fair share of the audience's sympathy just the same. It takes a first-rate actor to bring that off, a real star. But it's just the sort of part that any star in his right mind will refuse."

"I don't see why."

"Oh, don't you?" Polly croaked cynically. "Because the play's going to be stolen right from under his feet by that disreputable, wisecracking younger half brother. Your hero's a stuffed shirt, so the real interest is going to center on the scapegrace who helps the young lovers along. I'll bet he has most of the good lines, too."

"Most of the funny ones," Owen admitted.

"Splendid," Polly congratulated him. "So we'll need a star who is eager to play second fiddle to one of the lesser characters. Easy. While I'm attending to that, perhaps you'll find me a shy politician."

It was a technical problem which Owen was chagrined to realize he had lost sight of in his enthusiasm. The star system had to be catered to. Occasionally, in a limited revival of Chekhov or Sheridan, a well-known actor or actress might take a juicy but subordinate role, anticipating unlimited kudos for such dedicated self-sacrifice, but as a rule they were frantically jealous of their standing. They counted and compared the number of their 'sides'; before a play could be produced there was endless wrangling about whose name would appear above whose in the billing and in what size type. An actor hired for a secondary part might never reach Broadway if in the out-of-town tryouts he attracted too much notice for the liking of the acknowledged star. Polly was absolutely right: they would need someone first rate for the part of Amory, someone whose personality would dominate the stage, who could play the bastard yet keep you aware of the crippled, lonely soul within. . . . Yet most actors capable of such a performance would be frightened off by the flashy appeal of the younger brother's part.

They discussed how best to remedy this. Even on the basis of such a brief synopsis Polly was ready, as always, with constructive suggestions, ways to make the part of Amory more attractive from an actor's point of view, ways to deglamorize the half brother. She even suggested that in a pinch Owen might cut out the half brother's better lines for the time being, planning to replace them gradually later on, during rehearsals, as belated inspirations to strengthen the play. Once an actor's ego had expanded into a large, complex role he could watch such alterations almost indulgently, confident of his ability to hold the stage; it was only beforehand that he was insecure.

In time the peanut bowl was empty. They had talked through the worst of the rush hour and now taxis were available again; Owen put Polly into one, promising her the first act by next Wednesday at the latest, then hailed another cab for himself. Slowly, in jerky spurts, he was carried uptown, his mind seething with fresh ideas towards the new day's work which was finally about to begin. He made no particular effort to straighten them out, knowing from experience that that job would be done for him half unconsciously at the back of his mind; he let his thoughts wander, looked at the people out strolling along the Park in the long bright evening, courtesy of daylight saving.

As he climbed the stairs of his apartment house, he was vaguely aware of a telephone ringing steadily somewhere in the building; when he reached his front door he realized the phone was his own. Alarm immediately swept over him: in the city if a phone wasn't answered within half a dozen rings, one normally gave up, called again later; this senseless determination could only mean trouble.

He fumbled clumsily with his keys, cataloguing calamities. Roger or Carol—they vied for precedence in his anxiety. Roger down at college: a sudden, drastic illness. Carol in hysterics: Lois had been rushed to the hospital. Carol or Roger, Roger or Carol. . . .

Finally he got the key to work. He hurried through the cheerless, darkening living room. The bell still shrilled from the bedroom beyond, and his imagination now was in full morbid stride. Roger with a broken back. Carol struck down by a crosstown bus. Lois vanished between school and home in the ghastly way that only little girls could vanish. Further down on his scale of fears: Barbara-the-Bitch was punctually on the warpath. Amelia was calling to say that Vickie had died, eloped, proved to be with child. . . .

He ran the last few steps, snatched up the receiver.

It was no one he had thought of.

"Thank God I've got hold of you," said Charles Fortescue, but in a voice so thick with panic that it was a moment before Owen realized who was speaking.

PART SEVEN

1

Charles sat motionless in the armchair. He badly wanted a smoke but his mouth was dry and gummy and the energy to go and fetch a glass of water was beyond him; he simply sat. His left arm lay in his lap, the sleeve pushed back, his wristwatch visible. Merely by dropping his eyes he could see how much time had elapsed since he had spoken to Owen, but he tried to keep himself from looking. The minute hand was frozen. If he could prevent himself from looking a little longer, just a little longer, forcing his mind on through the bleak maze of misery, then a couple of minutes would surely have gone by. . . .

He was in something very much like a state of shock—perhaps a state of shatteredness would be more like it. He was no longer the Charles Fortescue he had come to recognize.

People who are chronically more or less at the mercy of their environment, forever on the edge of calamity, find means of compensation. They acquire fatalism or they shelter behind a father figure or they merge themselves in some dream or religion that gives promise to their insignificance. In the last resort they can always take refuge in hysteria, which for all its appearance of futility is actually a survival characteristic: when reason cannot find a solution there is always the possibility that unreason may. But it was a very long time since anything had occurred to remind Charles of man's essential helplessness.

He was not an arrogant person, yet he had insensibly come to believe that he was in command of his life: this was a consequence of the ordered urban existence he knew. At home, at the office, he was surrounded by people who made it their business to smooth his path. If Charles decided on a trip, Andean's travel manager booked passage and made reservations, Ruth did all the packing—and Charles went. If the rain fell from heaven, it fell not upon Charles Fortescue but on the doorman who hailed the taxi and then held forth the protective umbrella. Since his wishes were never immoderate, there had come to seem a lulling inevitability about their fulfillment: by and large his world went as he wished it to, and had done so for many, many years. Charles was not an arrogant man, was notably a kindly and considerate one, but too many years of satisfied expectations had given him the assurance of arrogance without the concomitant strength. Catastrophe found him undefended. He had neither philosophy nor faith to sustain him; he was alone in his self-sufficiency. Yet he was too restrained, too inhibited, to indulge in a fit of hysteria.

He sat benumbed by self-pity. All those comfortable years now seemed an elaborate snare leading him to this moment of disgrace. A part of him already accepted that disgrace, tormenting him with pictures of Ruth's bewilderment, Vickie's disgust, Peter's contempt. . . . But that was only a part of him, the whimpering child. There was also a desperation which scuttled through the anguish insisting that there must be a way of escape somewhere, had to be, *had* to be.

He permitted himself to look. Seventeen minutes, almost eighteen. And then he hadn't thought to check his watch until some time after he had hung up the receiver. Say twenty-one minutes. How long did it take a taxi to cross the Park?

Originally, his appeal to Owen had been the result of a frantic process of elimination. He needed help, but where to turn for it? His conventional business friends were struck out in a body. Morris Zimmerman was unthinkable. Never had Charles felt so lonely. He had thought of a host of unlikely acquaintances and rejected them before he thought of Owen, who then instantly appeared his only hope. The friendship was still green, but they were bound together by the forthcoming marriage. Owen was a bohemian, a man of the world. Without thinking any further, Charles had called—and had known his worst moments when, for what seemed like a long, long time, there had been no answer.

Now it was gradually coming to him that his choice had been a cunning one. Owen was no part of Charles's real life, yet he had more claim on Owen's loyalty, for the next few weeks at any rate, than he could have made in mere friendship's name. Owen was three times divorced with no family of his own; Owen was an artist living on the outskirts of propriety. He should have no scruples about helping, if Charles's addled wits could just think of the best way to make use of him. . . .

The doorbell rang.

Charles heaved himself up, lunged across the room cursing himself for his lethargy: he ought to have been waiting right by the front door. He swung open the door, seized Owen by one arm and drew him inside; then eased the door shut again. "Did anybody see you in the hall?" he demanded with soft ferocity.

"I don't think so," said Owen.

Relieved, Charles stepped back, belatedly embarrassed by his behavior. He hated to be handled by other men. "I'm sorry," he apologized. "I'm not myself."

"I'd gathered that." Owen's concerned expectation was a demand.

"How much did I explain over the phone?"

"Not a blessed thing."

Charles turned back into the living room. The burden of explanations suddenly unnerved him. He had always despised people who blathered on about themselves. The prospect of baring his private soul to another person, and particularly to a man, was a humiliation. He would as soon have stripped naked in public. Yet now there seemed very little choice, and he wondered if he would come out of this encounter with any shreds of self-respect left about him, able to look Owen in the eye. The last didn't matter so much: Owen's friendship was expendable.

"I don't even know where I am," Owen remarked. He was standing in the archway, still holding his hat, looking about him with heavy-lidded curiosity.

"This is the apartment of an old friend of mine, Mrs. Blair," Charles said in a rush, and then stopped.

"Yes?" Owen said, waiting for more. Finally he put his hat on the hall table and took a few prowling steps into the room. "Mrs. Blair is out?"

"She's in the bedroom," Charles said dully, gesturing at the door. He had returned to his armchair, his accustomed shelter. "She's dead."

In the echoing silence the refrigerator out in the kitchenette gave its preliminary shudder and hummed into life. Owen blinked and looked about him. Instinctively he reached for a cigarette, but thought better of the impulse. When he turned back to Charles, his expression (to Charles's imagination) had become hard and mask-like. "How?" he inquired.

"Nembutal, I expect," Charles said. "At least there's an empty bottle on the floor beside the bed."

"You have to call a doctor," Owen said harshly. "You can't be sure."

"Suppose it turns out to have been a heart attack? That won't make any difference."

"I mean you can't be sure she's dead, you fool! Sleeping pills are tricky; everybody knows that. You aren't a doctor."

"Good God, what imaginations you people have!" Charles said, angry in his turn. "Do you think I'd just be sitting here? She's been dead for hours; she must have done it late last night or early this morning. Rigor mortis has set in." That phrase, the legacy of a lifetime of reading detective novels, slipped out with an ugly glibness yet didn't appear to satisfy the other man. Owen still glared down at him coldly, without the slightest sympathy, with an incomprehensible look of indignation. Why should Owen be indignant?

"There's no doubt she's dead, and not much doubt it was the sleeping pills," Charles repeated. "You can see for yourself, if you insist."

As soon as the last words were spoken, he regretted them, was seized by a dread that Owen would take the offer literally. The thought of Owen (who presumably found his mistresses among pretty young things Vickie's age) looking down at Madge's haggard features, seeing as an outsider with no memory of how lovely she had been, seeing only a gaunt old woman, shamed him dreadfully. Yet to identify that reaction was to despise it, despise himself. He realized now that since the initial moment of horror he had been thinking entirely of himself, of how her suicide could bring his comfortable world crashing down about his ears. Scarcely more thought for Madge than if she had gone off inconveniently for a weekend. This was how he repaid the person who had loved him more deeply than any other. Ruth loved him, of course, but in part she loved the husband who sheltered her and fathered her children: it was a pampered love which cost her very little. Madge's love had cost her everything. She had still been in the prime of life, a handsome woman before her illness. She should have remarried; undoubtedly she would have remarried. If it had not been for him, she would have had a full, normal life. Instead, for his sake, she had settled for all the disadvantages of clandestine living. There had been so many places they could never go together, so many things they could not do. (He would buy her tickets for the plays he had enjoyed, and she would go with one of her lame-dog friends; afterwards they would talk of the play for hours, reminding one another of the best moments, creating shared memories of what they could not share.) She had even been limited in her choice of friends, not really but effectively, because she lost patience with the people she had to keep isolated from the important side of her life. She had spent so much of twelve years merely filling the hours between their stolen, hurried meetings. And because she was Madge, and loved him, she had accepted all this almost without demur.

Except that she had wanted to go to the wedding reception, to get a glimpse of Vickie and Peter. This was the one thing she had ever asked of him. And he had refused, impatiently, implacably.

"I think you'd better explain why you called me," Owen said. "You'll have to ring for a doctor anyway, and he'll attend to the formalities."

"I can't," Charles groaned. "Oh, dear Christ, what a mess it all is! And it's my fault." His guilt was crushing him; he wanted to punish himself. Madge had taken the leap that terrified him, Madge had ceased to exist, there was nothing left of her but that stiff and empty body in the other room—and all he had thought of was what a scrawny old woman she would look to somebody else. "All my fault," he repeated, twisting the knife in his self-contempt. "She kept begging me and begging me and I wouldn't let her go."

"Where?" said Owen.

"To that idiotic wedding reception!"

"What the devil. . . ."

"Well, I couldn't!" Charles complained. "It wouldn't have been fair to Ruth. In all that time she must have had her suspicions. And if somebody there had recognized Madge. . . ." He knew he wasn't being coherent, but he took it for granted that Owen was following him. "You know the sort of coincidences that happen in this bloody town," he said pleadingly. "There will be all sorts of people there, perhaps somebody who'd seen us together. I couldn't let her go."

"You aren't making sense," Owen said disappointingly.

"In twelve years it was the only thing she ever asked of me. . . ."

"*How long?*"

"Twelve years." The number seemed to startle Owen. "That's why it meant so desperately much to her," Charles went on, explaining. "Hearing about Vickie and Peter all that time, never being able to meet them. My children—it was natural. And she thought it was the one chance she would have."

"You still aren't making sense," Owen said flatly. "People just don't kill themselves for reasons like that."

"You don't understand, it was the *only* thing she'd ever asked me for," Charles said, finding comfort now in the abasement of confession. "I've just been realizing that now. I gave her things, of course, but she never asked, never even hinted. Probably she felt that she hadn't the right. She had some money of her own, so it wasn't terribly important. But I had to notice for myself when she needed something. That television set there: it was only by luck that I found out she was thinking of getting one of those cheap, portable models. She wouldn't have told me. She loved to get presents as long as they were surprises; if I came when she wasn't expecting me, that counted as a present; she knew that I loved her and gave her as much of myself as I could. If she'd asked for things maybe she'd have felt kept. And when finally she did ask for something, something she wanted dreadfully, I refused her."

"None of that matters," Owen said impatiently. "Dammit, Charles! don't you have the least idea of how people work?"

"What do you mean?"

"I've never heard such rubbish. No grown-up woman kills herself because she can't go to a wedding reception. There has to be a real reason, too. Didn't she leave a . . . Oh-oh, I think I'm finally beginning to catch on." Owen had been pacing the carpet; now, after a hard stare at Charles, he turned with brusque resolution and went straight to the bedroom door, and opened it. He fumbled for a moment, and then the light within flashed on, the harsh overhead light which Madge never permitted.

Charles sat where he was, trying to fight off the numbness, trying to order his thoughts, but mentally following Owen into the bedroom, reliving his own moments there. He himself was conditioned against using the overhead light, but when he arrived there had still been enough daylight filtering through the heavy blue drapes for him to fumble his familiar way to the bedside lamp. He had known immediately that she was dead; the discovery of her stiffness had come later, only as the result of an impulsive effort to take her hand. And he wished once more that he had not given Owen permission to look on Madge in her final defeat, but there was no shame left in this feeling: only a tender, defensive pity. It was a betrayal, exposing her to a stranger who would see only impersonal facts, the haggard, implausibly blondined head lying on the frivolous pink pillow—and not the infinite pathos of those still-lovely eyes staring blindly at the wall opposite. (Charles had wanted to close her eyes, but he had already been caught between his desire to flee and the knowledge that he could not; feeling that anything he did might prove the wrong thing to do, he had done nothing.) At least she was fully made-up. It was noticing this that had given Charles the clue to appreciate the meaning of the empty tumbler on the bedside table, and to look for, and find, the bottle which had held sleeping pills. In the ordinary way she would never have gone to bed with her make-up on; she had oiled and creamed her face religiously every night. Now there was a smudge of lipstick on the pillowcase, and her mascara had run a little, as if she had cried for a while before falling asleep for the last time. . . .

Owen reappeared in the doorway, snapping off the light, pulling the door quietly shut behind him. "That was a sick woman, Charles," he said gently.

"Not recently," Charles said. "Several years ago she had a severe illness, and she never really got her strength back. It changed her. She was such a lovely woman before, you've no idea."

"Do you know what was wrong?"

"She hated talking about it; she hated the very idea of illness. Something to do with her insides, but it wasn't . . . you know, it wasn't serious."

"All the same, that's where the answer is," Owen said positively. "They may have told her at the time that it wasn't serious, or she may have lied to you. You'll find that she'd just learned it was getting worse; there wasn't any hope left. Pain to look forward to. It must have been that, something of the kind. Not the nonsense about your forbidding her the reception. You've no need to feel guilty."

Charles shrugged. He couldn't understand why Owen seemed to consider this so important; he couldn't see that what Owen said made any real difference. If Madge had had the reception to look forward to, she would have waited. It was only a couple of weeks away, now. A few more weeks of being, with something to hold on to. Instead, she had died in the bitterness of her last request having been refused. She had been alone, denied, desolate. "She didn't leave a note for me," he said. "Not a word. I've looked everywhere."

"That seems strange," Owen admitted, frowning.

"To hell with how it seems!" Charles burst out. "Do you realize what it will mean? There will be an autopsy now, and an inquest. I'll be dragged in. And the newspapers will get hold of it; they always do."

"Yes, I see."

"You don't see," Charles contradicted him. "You don't see the half of it. They go grubbing around in the old files. And for someone like me, even that isn't necessary. They always have our obituaries ready, just in case. Tom Bingham over at F & F dropped from a heart attack last month, and only a few hours later the morning papers were out with five tidy paragraphs, all the shifts in that shifty career, everything, even that he had been a track star back in high school. Somebody had already done the grubbing. They have the information stashed away against the time we make news by dying or absconding to Caracas with the petty cash. And there's a story here, just the sort the tabloids gloat over. It was a long time ago, I was only a kid; you'd think it would be forgotten. But it's there, waiting to be dug up again."

Owen nodded. "I know of that other matter," he said shortly.

"You do? Then you ought to realize what I have to expect," Charles said. For the moment he was only briefly surprised to learn that Owen had come upon the story of Sophie Melmoth. It seemed inevitable somehow; he accepted it. Perhaps there was a certain logic to his acceptance: he himself, when the possibility of Vickie's engagement first arose, had made some inquiries about this Owen Hilliard. Financial inquiries, essentially, and damned uninformative the replies had been, but it was the natural thing for a father to do (even knowing what little control he had over his daughter's decisions), and he took it for granted that Owen would have made similar inquiries about himself. Except that Owen, being an artist, would have peculiar friends, would have fewer contacts in the business community but would know people like newspapermen and gossip columnists who might not have access to Charles Fortescue's credit rating but could hunt for his name through the archives of tragedy that passed as 'news.'

If he reasoned at all, it was some such train of reasoning that lay behind Charles's unstartled acceptance that his secret was no secret, but the truth was that he had never had any great faith in the completeness of his escape. His dignity had always been the dignity of a refugee waiting to be tapped on the shoulder. A man dragged his past behind him; an unsteady structure always ready to topple and engulf him. "It's a fine splashy story," he said bitterly. "They don't care how many lives they ruin, just so that for a few days they can sell a few extra papers—all in the name of keeping the public informed. God! The Fatal Loves of Charles Fortescue, or Why Don't They Ever Leave Suicide Notes?"

Owen mumbled something, but Charles wasn't listening.

"It's not this that's so terrible," he said, gesturing at the bedroom door. "Not by itself. I can't be ashamed of Madge. It will be a nasty shock for Ruth, but I expect she's had her suspicions—and, anyway, she'd not be the first wife to learn that her husband's been unfaithful. It's only the publicity that will be so hard on her; she'll forgive me the fact more easily than she'll face up to her friends and family knowing about it, pitying her. But dragging this other story out of the past, dancing up and down on it. . . ."

"Doesn't your wife know about that?"

"Why the hell should she?" Charles demanded. "Why should anybody? Oh, I suppose I'm sorry now that I never told her. It will seem as if I was hiding something, and that's considered a bad sign these days. I've never understood why. We all have things we'd rather keep hidden from ourselves, and why give other people the right to remind us?"

"I suppose they *are* bound to turn up the story?" Owen said doubtfully. He was looking blindly at the bank of photographs of Gretchen, over the desk.

"Of course they're bound to," Charles snapped. "If they don't think of it for themselves, there's a madman up in Actonsville who'll be delighted to remind them. And it's precisely the kind of thing they revel in. It wasn't much of a story at the time. I was only a youngster, a stupid, miserable youngster."

"And there was a war on."

"That's right. But now? There's nothing they like better than a solid, moderately prominent businessman. Have you noticed? There's no juice left in it when a film star gets caught in the wrong bedroom. Everybody expects that. But an executive from some company that doesn't do too much advertising—there's the ideal target. Put him in the pillory, bring up the dead past as witness against him, peel away the respectability. It's all good clean fun, what they call a public service. And every fresh bit of muck they can throw at him is a boost to their own shoddy, drunken, prying egos. It'll be lovely for Vickie, coming just a couple of weeks before her wedding. And there's no limit to how nasty they can make it sound. Even back

321

when it happened there were some people to say I'd killed Sophie."

Owen had lowered himself into the straight desk chair and lit the cigarette he had denied himself earlier. "Well, and did you?" he asked, watching with cold, hooded eyes. Charles could no longer remember why he'd been so sure that Owen would be understanding and sympathetic.

"I don't know," he said resentfully.

"What?"

"It's the honest answer!" Charles flung at the other's incredulity. "If you mean, did I literally, physically pull the trigger, I don't know. I suppose there must have been a time when I knew, but I'm not even sure of that any more. Did you never get into a mess when you were a kid and have the whole adult world come crashing in on you?" Suddenly, for the first time in many, many years, he could see that starkly antiseptic little room where he had wept away his childhood. "They gave me some sort of dope at the hospital; I guess I must have been hysterical. When I woke up there were a couple of men in the room—lawyers. They'd already learned a lot and they didn't ask me what had happened; they told me. Bit by bit. Some of it right, some wrong. At first I'd argue with them, and maybe they'd accept a part of what I said but then they'd pull me up short; no, it couldn't have been like that, it must have been like this. They were positive. They were grown men. One of them had a square, black beard, I remember. Their intelligence cracked like whips. They would start the story for me all over again, putting in some of the bits I'd given them so there was a little less for me to argue with; it sounded more correct. Then I'd sleep some more or cry some more. This didn't happen all at once, you understand; it went on for a couple of days. While they kept notes and could always prove to me when I was getting confused: I'd said something quite different a session or two before—or so they would claim, anyway. My God, Owen, for the next few years I thought about it all the time. I dreamt about it. I relived it. But I relived it a dozen different ways, and I never knew which one was real. I know we met that afternoon in a crazy determination. I remember that Sophie was frightened of the thought of the pistol; she didn't want to see it, she wanted me to do it when she wasn't looking, and I hadn't the courage for that—and what happened afterwards is lost. Whatever the truth was got lost in that hospital room forty-five years ago; you'd have to look for it there. Two generations ago, Owen. Two generations!"

"A terrible thing to live with," Owen muttered. "It might almost have been better if they'd left you with some memory of the truth."

"But you don't *live* with something like that," Charles said querulously.

"To some extent you'd be bound to."

"It's something that happened, it's part of the past, you know it's there. But when you stop understanding it, you stop thinking about it." He resented Owen's expression of knowing better. "Do you lie awake brooding about your adolescent humiliations?"

"I didn't have anything quite so—"

"Don't be superior; it's exactly the same thing," Charles struck in. "You change and you go on changing till you can't recognize the youngster you used to be. There was a boy named Charles Fortescue and the records insist that we're the same person. But I've no contact with him, no sympathy. I can't even make sense of him. Why did he stalk around wrapped up in self-pity; why did he work so hard to make himself loathed by the other boys? Don't ask me! It's all very easy to say that he wasn't too happy at home, but that's all the more reason to look for happiness somewhere else. I can understand his falling in love; I could understand it if he'd chucked school, run away with Sophie, found a job someplace. . . ."

"You're talking from a different world," Owen said impatiently.

"Of course I am, that's just the point," Charles said with equal impatience. "You said I'd be bound to live with the memory. Well, I can't go burrowing back into the mind of that tortured adolescent. I couldn't even if I wanted to. He's grown alien and contemptible. Because he couldn't have what he thought he wanted, he decided he was better off dead and persuaded somebody else to go with him. Christ! Compared with that, the fact that he chickened out at the last moment almost seems healthy. There's nothing bewildering about cowardice. But it's all the behavior of a total stranger, and you can't go on flinching for that indefinitely. The boy who could feel those feelings is as dead and distant as Sophie."

"Not quite," said Owen.

"He can be disinterred," Charles said bitterly. "That's what it will really amount to. Those damned ghouls." The unfairness of it sickened him. He had suffered and suffered terribly at the time and for long afterwards. That suffering might now seem as remote and incomprehensible as all the rest, but it was undeniably a fact: he had paid heavily. And now a wholly different Charles was to pay all over again, and a new set of innocent victims as well. . . .

"Knowing all that," Owen said, "I'm surprised you didn't turn on your heel and clear out. Let somebody else make the discovery. When a woman kills herself, they don't make much of it; there would have been a fair chance that your name would never have come in at all."

"I couldn't do it," Charles said, sincerely uncertain now whether he would have had the heart to walk away, if that had been possible, leaving Madge lying there in the dark. "In any case, it would only have made matters worse. I was seen letting myself in."

"Oh, Lord," Owen breathed.

"She wasn't expecting me this evening," Charles explained, tormenting himself with the irony: he had thought to please Madge with a surprise. "Ruth called up in mid-afternoon. Morris's daughter is in town; there's the new baby to be fussed and cooed over. I'm not much for that, and Ruth always gives me the chance to beg off. So I came here, figuring I'd take Madge out for dinner. I always ring the doorbell, and it took me a moment to realize she wasn't going to answer. Madge is never out for very long, and I decided to come in and wait. But I was slow remembering which key it was, and it all added up to enough time for that snoop down the hall to find an excuse for a quick trip to the incinerator. I had the door open by then. So they'd know that somebody had been here and left without taking any action. That's not just a crime, it looks suspicious. There would be the devil of a hue and cry."

Owen was snapping his fingers impatiently. "But *that's* why there wasn't any note!" he exclaimed.

"What?" Charles said blankly, feeling stupid.

"She wasn't expecting you!"

"Not till Friday evening, and there wasn't too much chance of that."

"Then she was counting on being found by somebody else. Is there a cleaning woman?"

"Mondays and Thursdays."

"Tomorrow morning, then," Owen said triumphantly. "And of course she couldn't leave a note for you here: that would have dragged you right into the middle of it. Don't you see? She wouldn't do that; her instinct would be to protect you. I expect you'll get a letter at your office in the morning's mail."

"Probably you're right," Charles said, unable to share Owen's enthusiasm for this deduction. Actually, the prospect filled him with dismay, seemed almost to add to the burden of his anxieties. He would have to alert Mrs. Peabody's curiosity by warning her that he was expecting an important personal letter: in the ordinary way he received no private correspondence at the office. She was accustomed to opening everything that came and would not be put off by copperplate handwriting and the word *Personal* in the lower left corner since nowadays charity appeals often came in just this guileful fashion.

And then—call it callous of him—he could not foresee anything but anguish in the letter itself. If it had arrived as intended, as a farewell and warning and explanation for a shock, that would have been different: he would have sat alone in his office shaken and unhappy (and a tiny bit relieved), mooning sentimentally over the past, rediscovering what a fine woman Madge had been, adjusting himself to his loss. Now the warning would come too late; the shock had already been met in its most brutal form, the explanation become virtually irrelevant. The letter would come into a life that was crumbling apart, bringing discomfort and guilt because he wouldn't have the emotion to spare for Madge's last good-bye.

And finally, he couldn't see that Owen's deduction bettered the situation in the slightest, so why the triumph? "Yes, I suppose you're right," he repeated heavily. "Does it make much difference?"

"It explains why there's no note."

"What good does that do now? If I'd got her letter today! But no, not in this town. It takes them thirty-six hours to carry an envelope a dozen blocks."

"Could you have stood the waiting?" Owen asked curiously. "A suicide note doesn't have to mean that the attempt succeeded."

"You have the damnedest mind," Charles protested. "Is this how you help a friend? I could have. . . . Oh, I don't know. If I'd had any notion of what to expect, I'd have come with key in my hand and that bitch down the hall wouldn't have had the chance. . . . Owen?"

"Mmm?"

"Look, she didn't see *me* letting myself in."

"You said she did."

"A man. A man's back."

"She must know you by sight."

"She only moved in a couple of months ago; that's one reason she's so curious. And I've never ridden up in the elevator with her or anything like that."

"Is this why you called me?" Owen demanded.

"I only thought of it just now."

"Well, stop right there!"

"Now, wait. . . ."

"Charles!" Owen began warningly, and then paused, seeming to reconsider. For a moment he played with his cigarette lighter, flipping it over and over; his eyes, watching the movement, were hidden. Finally he said: "Let's hear what you have on your mind."

"It's quite simple, really," Charles said, and it seemed to him that he was asking very little, the sort of favor that cost a man nothing and therefore wasn't even cause for gratitude. He had arranged a job for Owen's son; it hadn't cost him anything to do so and it might even prove a benefit to Andean, but still it was a kind of favor though he had not expected any thanks for it. "All that matters now is that there be *a man* to phone for a doctor, explain things to the police. Don't you see? Any man but me. Without me it goes back to being an ordinary run-of-the-mill case of suicide. There's no story in it, no scandal."

"I'd not even met the lady," Owen pointed out.

"Who's to know that?" Charles asked. "She hadn't any friends to speak of, especially these last few years. There'll be no one to argue about how well you knew her. Anyway, why should anybody bother? You'd have a key, and that's all that would count."

"And then, as you say, the newspapers have a way of getting hold of these things," Owen said reflectively. He was regarding Charles with a steady, inquiring gaze; there was no way of judging what he was thinking. "It's nothing I'm proud of," he added, "but I'm in the papers rather more than you are, as it is."

"There'd be no story."

"Whenever somebody's involved who can be passed off as a celebrity, there's a story."

"But you haven't anything to *lose*," Charles said cajolingly, for this was the real point. It was the film star in the wrong bedroom again: nobody paid any attention to what scrapes a writer got into. They were artists, they lived in a different world. A writer could be a flagrant homosexual or boast of having taken dope, and no one thought any the less of him. "You haven't even a family to think of."

"Don't be too sure of that," Owen said.

"Roger knows the facts of life, I'm sure."

"I wasn't thinking of Roger. There's a chance that I'll be getting remarried."

"I'm delighted to hear it," Charles said automatically, "but that can't make any difference. You've been divorced for years, account-

326

able to nobody. And Madge could simply have been an old friend of yours. I'm sure you can think of all sorts of perfectly innocent reasons why she should have given you a key . . . you're a writer."

"It's not so easy to maintain a familiarity that never existed." Owen gestured at the photographs over Madge's writing desk. "There will be relatives turning up, I imagine, expecting explanations."

"A daughter out in Chicago—and she's a cold-hearted bitch if ever there was one. She won't even come East to the funeral, most likely."

"You're going too fast, Charles."

"I know the girl, I tell you."

"Then she knows you, and what the hell was *I* doing in her mother's life? It may not be difficult to think of innocent explanations, but who believes them?"

"Does it matter what anybody believes as long as nobody gets hurt?"

"Perhaps not," Owen said, "but you're not thinking one step further than getting yourself out that door. If you can just get away, leaving me holding the baby, you figure I'll have to go through with this scheme of yours whether I like it or not. Which I don't. For one thing, I'd have no confidence in bringing it off. I'm not an actor, Charles. I'm not even a very good liar."

But for the first time Charles was scenting escape. His difficulties had seemed impassable; now there was a path. Owen's objections were merely so many obstacles in the way, which would have to be brushed aside, trampled down if necessary. With the knowledge that there *was* a way, Charles's mood had turned from despair to confidence. He had spent the better part of his life dealing with other men's objections and getting his own way in the end. "Nobody is going to cross-examine you, Owen," he said reasonably. "This is a tragic thing, the sooner forgotten the better. All Gretchen will care about is avoiding any scandal. She won't stir up any fuss, I promise you."

"Your promises won't do me any good if it turns out you're mistaken."

"I just don't see what's frightening you so."

"You don't see that it's a damned awkward position you'd be putting me into?"

"Not really," Charles said sincerely. "You aren't answerable to anybody for your past actions. And however peculiar things may appear, people will believe you. That's your advantage. You're an *artist*.

You'll get the benefit of every doubt, which nobody gives to an ordinary businessman."

"Now we're getting somewhere," Owen said with an edge to his voice.

"Oh, come now, that's meant as a compliment," Charles said persuasively. "You don't seem to appreciate how lucky you are. I'm not suggesting that you may not be every bit as moral or high-principled as the next man—possibly more so. But you're in a different category; you're like a millionaire who can dress just as shabbily as he pleases, and people charge it off to eccentricity and respect him none the less. He hasn't a position to keep up, and neither do you. You know that's true, Owen. There can't be anything peculiar about *whatever* you may do because you aren't expected to conform in the first place. An artist could have a pocketful of keys to women friends' apartments and it wouldn't necessarily mean a thing: he could still be perfectly faithful to his wife or sleeping with the boy next door. Isn't that so?"

"I had a feeling it was coming to this—that I don't have a reputation to lose," Owen said. "Perhaps that's true. But why should you be so sure that I haven't any self-respect either?"

"What the devil has this to do with your self-respect?" Charles asked, astonished.

"I don't even know that I can explain," Owen said distastefully. "It's not that I have any particular respect for the dead or that I mind telling fibs to the cops. But all the same, doesn't it strike you as rather a degrading masquerade, what you're asking of me? Posing as something I've never been. Telling a string of lies where I could be caught out at any moment. Leaving a daughter—and I don't care how much of bitch she may be—with an odd memory of her mother. Exposing myself to contempt and ridicule. All in order to shuffle a poor woman underground with a minimum of inconvenience to you."

"*Inconvenience!*" snarled Charles, narrowly averting a full-voiced bellow. "If I'm pulled into this and they dig up that old story, they'll crucify me!" It disgusted him that a man couldn't follow elementary logic. "How much do you think would be left of me? Companies don't like it when an executive makes front-page stories for the tabloids. I'd find myself retiring several years sooner than I expected and with no chair on the board to keep me occupied. Have I done anything to deserve that? What will be left of my marriage; what will happen to Peter and Vickie? Don't think you aren't concerned in this too—you are! Vickie's not one of your tough little bachelor girls —she's still practically a child—she adores me. Can you imagine what it will do to her, seeing her father dragged through a mess of this sort, all that horror of forty-five years ago mucked up for people to gloat over? That's the girl your son is supposed to be marrying in a couple of weeks. Do you think she'd be able to go through with it? Do you think Roger would thank you for your qualms of self-respect? God damn it, Owen, you aren't a priggish, small-town deacon. This wouldn't cost you anything that *matters*."

He stopped short, feeling that he could go no further short of getting down on the floor and grovelling to the son of a bitch. In the sudden hush they heard the slam of a door in the hall, and then a clatter of young voices that surged and faded down the corridor, reminding them of where they were, the world outside, the passage of time. He glanced at his watch, was incredulous to find that less than half an hour had elapsed since Owen's arrival.

"This has already cost me more than you'll ever know," Owen said.

There was no sense to the words, but the tone was that of a man who has been forced to swallow reason.

"It's just luck that you haven't done still more damage in the world," Owen went on reflectively, "and then gone your way leaving other people to pick up the pieces. That's what other people are meant for—they taught you that lesson early on, didn't they? But there has to be a limit to what's done in the name of propping Charles Fortescue back up on his pedestal." Abruptly Owen stood up, looking around him.

Charles had paid no attention at first. When you've pushed a man further and faster than he wants to go, you have to let him sputter a bit to reassert his own ego; any good executive knew that. But Owen's sudden look of determination was all wrong, and in an instant Charles reverted from confidence to desperation. "Now wait a moment!" he barked.

"Where's the telephone?" Owen demanded. "I hope to Christ it isn't in the bedroom."

"What do you think you're doing?"

"Getting you out of this mess if I can—but without playing cat's paw. Or scapegoat. As the case may be."

"But who do you want to call?" Charles asked anxiously. "You can't be highhanded about this."

"Highhanded, am I? That's a laugh. I happen to know somebody who can probably keep this out of the papers if anybody can do it, that's all. Oh, there it is—" Owen had sighted the telephone, but Charles, heaving himself out of the armchair, got there first; protected the telephone with his bulk. He had no confidence in any hare-brained, impulsive scheme of Owen's. The man was a dreamer, a romancer, with no real understanding of practicalities.

"We can't rush at it like this," he insisted. "Who *is* this person?"

"His name is Elmendorf. Tony Elmendorf. He's with the District Attorney's office."

"Then he's out of the question," Charles said. "Anyone connected with the City government would be fatal, don't you see? I'm a Republican."

"Well, this fellow is an Existentialist," Owen replied sardonically. "That makes you brothers of a sort."

It was added evidence of Owen's irresponsibility that he could try to be funny at such a moment. "I assume he's a good friend of yours," Charles said. "All right. Why can't you arrange things between the two of you, then? Leave me out of it altogether? That would be much safer. Otherwise you're putting me at the mercy of a perfect stranger."

"It's the people who know us that have no mercy," Owen said. He stood a pace away, controlled in his patience, but looking perfectly capable of hurling Charles aside. "You have a legitimate claim for sympathy," he said levelly. "I expect you'll get it. Particularly since I've never begged a favor from Tony before. But only if it's very clear that everything is open and aboveboard. Running away is precisely how to make sure of a mess. Now let me at that telephone, Charles. This is the help you wanted, whether you can recognize it or not."

Still Charles hesitated, utterly unconvinced, feeling that everything was out of hand and disaster only a matter of time. But it was evident that he had lost all control over the situation; the plan so captiously rejected had exhausted him; he had nothing else constructive to offer. What Owen was doing was probably all wrong, but at least he was doing *something* and doing it with a resolution which Charles suddenly realized he was powerless to resist. He was empty, drained of will; his gesture of barricading the telephone was a sham, the petulance of impotence. If Owen pushed at him, he felt as if he would topple stiffly, like a wooden soldier. So finally he turned away, turning his back on his fate. He started towards the shelter of his armchair and then veered, making for the kitchenette and the liquor cabinet. Behind him he heard Owen's quick, incisive dialing, and then a waiting silence.

There was Irish there, of course, several bottles—Madge had catered faithfully to his tastes—but Owen probably wouldn't like Irish and Charles both lacked the moral courage to drink alone and felt some blind instinct either to placate the other man or to involve him more deeply as an accomplice; he scarcely knew which. He took a bottle of Scotch and two glasses and returned to the other room.

"Damn!" Owen said, replacing the receiver. "This is going to take some time. Where's the telephone book?"

"Bottom shelf to your left—no, further over." He half filled one of the old-fashioned glasses with whisky. "There's still time for you to see that it's safer my way," he said, without hope. "Here."

Owen accepted the drink, glanced distrustfully at Charles's grasp on the bottle. "I told you that running away wouldn't help."

"What an incredible prig you are! I'm having *one* drink—I need it." He poured himself more than he had intended and went back to his chair; watched sullenly while Owen flipped through the pages of the directory, found the number he was looking for, dialed again.

"Hello, Harry?" Owen said. "Has Mr. Elmendorf been there?—this is Mr. Hilliard. . . . How long ago? . . . That's fine, did you get any idea where he might be heading? . . . Right, thanks a lot." He hung up, glanced at his watch. "We should have him by eight, if not sooner. I'm pretty sure where he's having dinner."

"Will we have to tell him about Sophie and all that?" Charles asked.

Owen found a new number, marked it with his finger before he looked up from the telephone book. "I don't think so," he said. "Not in detail, anyway. Just that there's an old story the papers could dig up and throw at you."

"That's something," Charles said.

"Do you care so much?"

"Perhaps you've told him already."

"I haven't, no." Owen shook his head slowly. "I don't gossip. But I'm curious. According to you, those emotions were burnt out forty years ago. You haven't even thought of Sophie in years and years."

"I don't suppose I'd recognize the girl if I bumped into her in Heaven," Charles snapped, feeling obscurely tormented. "What do you want me to say? It's nothing I'm proud of, even if I can't spend a lifetime feeling guilty. As you seem to expect I should. You're the one who doesn't understand how people work!"

"You may be right at that," Owen said. He sipped at his drink. After a moment he began to dial again.

2

All the standard methods of cheering somebody depended, in the last analysis, on an appeal to the future. Tomorrow would be a better day, every cloud had a silver lining, God was in His Heaven and all was for the best. But take away these consolations of optimism and there was little left to offer a person but stale crumbs of philosophy. So it was with Joyce Neilson. Stephen could feel sorry for her, was tired of feeling sorry for her, but he wasn't much good at comforting her. Joyce was crying again in the attic study overlooking Jefferson Mews: not sobbing, not weeping, for this was a minor affliction among all the rest, but snuffling away from time to time, adding to the gloom and dampness of the drizzly day outside. And what was there of cheer to say to her? Before very long she would be rid of an embarrassment, but her life would not be any the better for the anguish she had experienced, if anything rather the worse. There was no silver lining to be pointed to. If God were in His Heaven, He (like everyone else) had long since lost any interest in Joyce.

"It was such rotten luck, that that was the soonest they could take me," she had said, and this was the cause of the snuffling. "I'd been so looking forward to the wedding."

Since Joyce would now be attending neither wedding nor reception it was foolish to go on resenting Amelia's conventional inflexibility: as a colleague and 'friend' (however much disliked) Arthur Vaughan was included in the reception, too, whereas as a family employee Joyce had been invited to the wedding alone. In all fairness, this arrangement had not seemed to dissatisfy Joyce. Perhaps she sensed she would be a lost soul at a party. The wedding was what appealed to her. The exultant music that set the scene, the breathtaking arrival of the bride, the sonorous language, the symbolic gavotte of giving and taking in marriage, the throat-choking, eye-misting moment when the new couple came down the aisle—an orgy of vicarious emotions for Joyce, picturing herself in each phase of the ritual she would never take part in. The secondhand happiness of the damned.

For damned she most certainly was: damned by a weak and unendearing personality. Homelier girls and stupider girls were getting married every day; girls who would quickly disclose facets of ruthlessness or bitchery that Joyce was quite incapable of. Colder girls found happy love affairs; girls less well educated or less conscientious found interesting careers for themselves; more fractious and spiteful girls could have hosts of friends. Joyce sidled awkwardly through life, loved only by the mother who had somehow taught her to distrust her femininity, her very self. In a crowded, competitive world where personalities jostled for the room to breathe, where strength of character was the only accepted excuse for a lack of charm, Joyce either had never learned the necessity to 'sell herself' or she had never been convinced that there was anything to sell, and this was the one sin for which there could be no mercy. Nobody had the time or patience, or perhaps the self-assurance, to prospect for spirit among the shy and shrinking; the adolescent's temporary permit to be gauche was soon withdrawn—and thereafter was only popularity or its converse, failure. A contemptible failure: excuse could be found these days for the alcoholic and the juvenile delinquent, the dope addict, the pervert and even the habitual criminal, but who had sympathy to waste on the incorrigibly unlovable?

Somewhere in the past Joyce had doubtless reached out a clumsy, imploring hand to life . . . but no, that would never do, we can't have any begging; it offends our vision of the national character. We prefer above all the easygoing charm that can pass for sincerity while leaving all our prejudices unruffled, we can admire cleverness as long as it is at someone else's expense, we have a certain respect for hardness, egoism and guile, we are secretly a little envious of arrogance—but begging we cannot tolerate. It makes us uncomfortable: we look the other way and talk a little faster, ashamed that a fellow citizen should be so lacking in self-respect. Thus rejected, Joyce had learned to live in anticipation of the next rebuff; all the contortions of her personality were only evidence that she could not even learn to cringe gracefully.

And what lay ahead for her, this nonstarter in the race for admiration? Joyce's latest misadventure would surely have extinguished the last of her faith in her womanhood: to give herself was to invite betrayal and anguish; this was the only lesson she had gained. Her emotions would have to be watched suspiciously for their treacherous inclination to give her over to the enemy. She would retire still further into herself, erect still more barricades of awkwardness against the pain outside.

333

Cheery words of comfort to such a person would be false to the point of cruelty. Instead, Stephen thought to distract her. As a small child could be diverted from mischief by calling its attention to some neglected toy, so he hoped to make Joyce forget this newest misfortune by talking of one which time perhaps had meliorated. He left his desk and went to sit in the armchair which normally stood near the great trapezoidal window for his hours of reading, but which for the past few weeks had been moved near to Joyce's desk so that at least Stephen could be comfortable in his discomfort. "You know I don't begrudge the money," he said half truthfully, "but you've never given me a single reason why Arthur Vaughan should be allowed to get off scot free."

For a few seconds it appeared as if he had made a mistake: Joyce stared at him in dismay and her face started to crumple. Then her lips tightened, her head tossed, she found strength in a gust of resentment. "I don't see why I should have to talk about something when I don't want to," she said.

Stephen's curiosity assured him that his course was therapeutic. "It might help to get things off your chest," he said.

"And you'd like a nice tidy case history, with no loose ends," she retorted accusingly.

This was so close to the truth that Stephen might have been embarrassed if he had not devoted a professional lifetime to the proposition that a professor was *never* disconcerted, not even when caught out in a failure of memory. "You've made me connive at a policy I find illogical," he said. "That entitles me to an explanation."

"Logic hasn't anything to do with it. I just couldn't bear to ask him for anything."

"Pride can be misplaced," Stephen said sagely.

"I don't know about pride," Joyce said. "There are lots of things I don't know about. Pride. Shame. I wouldn't even give him the satisfaction of knowing he was that much of a man." For a moment she was silent, her lips tightening spasmodically; then she began to speak again, slowly at first, then a whole spate of words came pouring forth, and for a while Stephen could scarcely make head or tail of what she was saying. She was not hysterical; apart from a slight working of her mouth she appeared calm, but the ideas came tumbling out all in a jumble. "A few mannerisms don't make a neurotic," she said, and much later on Stephen worked out to his own satisfaction a train of associations which could have led to her next remark: "I might have been better off if Daddy had been a plumber." She was not talking to him, she was not talking to herself; this was an out-pouring of old grievances, efforts to rationalize her unhappiness, all mixed up—though in a fashion that was doubtless emotionally co-herent within her own mind—with the miserable story of her love affair. To interrupt her would have silenced her with selfconscious-ness; Stephen kept silent and tried to swim with the verbal tide.

From the frequency of its appearance the phrase 'piling Pelion on Ossa' had evidently some bitter symbolic significance, and eventu-ally Stephen realized what it was. An only child, her father's darling while he lived, Joyce had grown up in the world of intellectual jar-gon and academic catch phrases. To Bob Neilson that old-fashioned classicist, 'Pelion on Ossa' would have been a handy and graceful short cut; to his daughter it would have been part of everyday con-versation, and the ideas flying about the dinner table the common-places of life. Yet Joyce would never have had the intelligence to run with the very brightest children, where such eccentricities might have passed unremarked, and among her peers her modes of speech, the familiar opinions she defended, would have seemed the most detest-able of affectations. Pelion on Ossa, indeed!

She was like a rich child whose parents have fallen upon hard times: unable to afford the best, unable to appreciate the second best. At least this (by implication) was how Joyce accounted to her-self for her loneliness. She was an intellectual snob without an in-tellect to suit; it wasn't her fault if she felt ill at ease and superior with people who were ignorant of the patter that was second na-ture to her. She had sensed an answering loneliness in Arthur Vaughan. Loneliness was a bond between people, and surely there had never been such a city as New York for breeding loneliness. She was tired of her friends; she knew that within a mile there must be thousands of people she could like better, but how did one go about *meeting* them? Arthur had seemed sensitive and understanding, and above all they spoke the same language. And she had felt sorry for him.

"You aren't on guard against someone you feel sorry for," she said. "He never lets you forget that crippled foot; he makes jokes about it, really clever jokes, so that you laugh with him and think it's wonder-ful that he hasn't any bitterness. He makes fun of himself and he's interested in you. Somehow there's the idea that it's the tall and handsome men who are so clever with their flattery. Ugliness is like a kind of sincerity, and after a time you forget you had ever thought he was ugly. Mother was having a good period just then: she was all right in the evenings as long as the television set didn't break down and I didn't get back too late." Vaughan had encouraged her in the small disloyalty of complaining of her mother's demands, encouraged her to believe that he had recognized a complex and fascinating personality still waiting to be awakened. "It's irresistible, you know, suddenly discovering that you're interesting; I suppose now I'd have made a fool of myself for any man who made me believe in that. But he was so sympathetic and intelligent and . . . wistful. I wanted to make up to him for all the years. It didn't seem as if I was thinking of myself at all. I wanted him to love me, of course, but that was because I felt sure I could make him happy. I'd always been frightened before, but now being frightened was selfish, and I told myself I had as much right as any other girl. You find the first excuses, and after that everything is out of control."

She made a gesture of ineffectuality and then looked down at her hands. "It would be stupid to say I didn't know what I was doing, yet I did and I didn't. I'm not stupid, and these days you can be only just so innocent. But it was all new, and what you've heard and read and what you feel takes you just so far. All I cared about was pleasing him; that was all I had to go on. If it pleased him it was all right. But then all of a sudden it wasn't all right. Nothing had changed except that overnight, very subtly, he began to shrink away. He didn't say anything, not then, but he made it appear as if, well, he'd been putting up with these things for my sake. He made me feel beastly and unnatural. I don't think it was true, and even at the time a part of me sensed that it probably wasn't true: that he'd had what he wanted and was trying to put me off this way. But I couldn't accept it. I wanted to believe that it was all my fault in some fashion that I couldn't understand, that I could make it go right again if I tried hard enough. And the harder I tried the more openly he shrank away. At the end he was terribly apologetic about it, but he couldn't help himself, he said. He was perfectly willing to take most of the blame; no doubt he was more inhibited than most men."

"What an absolute son of a bitch," Stephen said, all scientific detachment gone.

"I told you he was a monster," Joyce said in sullen vindication.

"It's as good a word as any. But I hope this hasn't set you thinking that other men are all like that."

"Arthur wasn't like that, either, when he wanted something."

Stephen felt rebuked—and helpless. Joyce was quite intelligent enough to realize that the sly cruelty with which Arthur had discarded her had only been a personal quirk. The fact remained that she had confided herself to someone whose only intention had been to discard her. The moral to be drawn was not that men were sadistic but that any man spending his flattery on Joyce would probably have only one end in view and eventually would drop her, more gently than Arthur, perhaps, but just as firmly. A paranoid moral, but in Joyce's case probably justified. In her relationship with Arthur she had doubtless made every mistake in the book, yet none stupidly or ignorantly; stupidity and ignorance alone had never stopped a woman from walking sure-footed through a love affair. The trouble was that Joyce had been brought up to regard herself as a thinking person; she had a modest faith in her intelligence, and her intelligence was just sufficient to muddle all her instincts. In any emotional dealings, even with herself, she would be sure to make the worst of both worlds.

Yet over the past weeks, in the course of seeing her through her troubles, Stephen had acquired a grudging sympathy for Joyce. He liked her no better: she was invincibly unlikeable. He pitied her if anything rather less, for pity was a contemptuous feeling and out of keeping with his new, exasperated respect. He would go on being just as annoyed by her instability and her grotesqueries. But he had come to accept the responsibility she represented, and no longer chafed under it. A bond of dependency once acknowledged could be stronger than a bond of affection: he felt closer to Joyce than he had ever felt to Roger, for example, who was easy-natured and well-mannered, whom he was fond of, but who had always held to the independence of being Owen's son. Joyce had become a sort of emotional pensioner, someone he would worry about gratuitously until the day he died. Eliot was slightly mistaken: he did not *welcome* responsibilities, but once they were there he could take a masochistic comfort in them. They were his defense against the dehumanizing egoism that was the sickness of the city.

"Well, there's no good in brooding about it," Stephen said briskly, putting aside the thought that if there were any brooding going on he was the cause of it, flattering himself that at least he had put a stop to the snuffling. "Right now the important thing is to keep yourself as busy as possible, believe me." In one breath he had discharged two sets of obligations: occupational therapy was just what Joyce needed, and the revisions of the last chapter still waited to be typed up. "I promise I'll save you a piece of the wedding cake."

But he found that this generous afterthought undid all his good work, and he was obliged to start again from scratch.

3

They met by arrangement in a cocktail bar a few blocks from Charles's office; two men each with a burden of resentment that the other would never understand. The place was empty except for a few local all-day drinkers; it was the dead hour before people start dropping in for a quick one on the way home from work. Owen arrived first. He picked one of the little three-sided cubicles, put the suitcase on the rear seat and piled his coat and hat on top of it, ordered an extra-dry martini without lemon peel from the apathetic waiter, and sat down where he could keep an eye on the door. He had nowhere to go, nothing to do with his time, but he was in a mood to get furious if Charles kept him waiting. His sense of charity was overspent; he was feeling imposed upon. The very least the other man could do was be on time.

Several minutes before the hour, Charles came. Stolidly, not hurrying, but to give the man some credit he was grey, as if the past two days had been long and anxious. The anxiety would have been all for his own skin, but that was the way of the world. The dead were dead and safely out of it; the survivors suffered first and mourned later, if they mourned at all. As he marched the length of the room, Charles's gaze traveled ahead, trying to extract intelligence from Owen's features. From his post at the bar the waiter sidled the short leg of the triangle, arriving at the same moment, exposing the extent of Charles's disquietude. For a moment Charles stared at him helplessly. The waiter could not be willed to disappear, an order was necessary to get rid of him. Doubtless Charles wanted a drink, but it took an effort to bring his mind to choose among the possibilities. "Irish on the rocks," he said eventually, and dismissed the waiter from his mind.

"Well?" he said to Owen. It was a sharp and impatient word, fit for an underling who was tardy with some report.

"You're here, so you got my message."

"That didn't tell me anything."

"It's all right," Owen said reluctantly. Charles's attitude was the last straw: he didn't deserve to get off so easily. He should have been kept in suspense for a while, toyed with, cat-and-mouse fashion.

Owen hadn't the heart to do it. But he might have known that another man's opinion of what was all right—an artist's opinion!—would not carry much weight with Charles.

"What happened, exactly?" he demanded. He put his coat and hat on a nearby chair, slid into his seat across the table: a capable executive ready to make a businesslike assessment of the pertinent information.

"Just what Tony said would happen, I suppose," Owen said. "I don't know how these things work. The medical examiner's report came through as expected. The cops are happy with the contribution to the Widows' and Orphans' Fund. It's just another routine suicide—there were four all told in the city that same night. No story, no publicity."

"There's still nothing to keep that Lieutenant from talking."

"Charles, you think this is unique because it happened to you. It's a big town. Hardly a night goes by without somebody dropping dead in the wrong bedroom. If it isn't a crime, if he isn't a crook or a movie star, if somebody has just the least bit of pull, even the widow never finds out. They're used to hushing things up when it doesn't matter. So Tony says, anyway."

"Umm," said Charles, still not satisfied. His drink arrived; he sipped at it absently. "Did Gretchen come?"

"No."

"There. I told you she wouldn't." But Charles was startled by his accuracy as a prophet.

"She just happens to be sick in bed with the mumps," Owen said drily. The irony pleased him: Charles's bogey kept offstage by a belated attack of a childhood disease. Who had ever heard of Nemesis down with the mumps? "Her husband flew in yesterday evening."

"I've never met him." The unknown was a new threat.

"He's very cooperative, Tony says. All in favor of the quiet life. He wouldn't have cared if his mother-in-law had a dozen boy friends as long as he could get things tidied up without any fuss."

"Madge always said he was an unfeeling bastard."

"I should think you'd be grateful that he is."

"'As warm and progressive as a glacier.' Those were her very words."

"He's being reasonable, that's what counts," Owen said. "He's having the body sent out to Chicago. And he spent the morning going through the apartment. There were a number of things of yours."

"I don't care about that."

"Whether you care or not, there they are." Owen gestured with his head.

"What?"

"In the suitcase."

All Charles's conviction that something was bound to go wrong focused on this offending object. "But I don't *want* it," he said plaintively. "Any of it."

"He couldn't be expected to know that," Owen said. "You might have sued, for all he could tell. I have a receipt for you to sign, beginning 'One pair of ruby cuff links. . . .'"

"Madge gave them to me years ago. I can't suddenly start wearing cuff links that Ruth has never seen before."

"And he couldn't just turn them over to the Salvation Army. You might be reasonable, too."

Charles still stared at the suitcase in horrified fascination. "Oh, this is terrible!"

"You had worse worries the other evening. There's the receipt."

"The receipt doesn't matter."

"It matters to *me*," Owen said angrily. He was accustomed to such egoism in other artists, but in a businessman it struck him as outrageous. "I promised I'd have it back this evening. You're supposed to check over the contents before you sign, but you can suit yourself about that."

"But what the devil am I going to *do* with that thing?" Charles moaned, making no motion towards the receipt. "Can you imagine me sauntering into the apartment with an unexplainable suitcase in one hand?"

"Isn't there someplace in the basement you can leave it?"

"With Vickie going off and Peter due back from college?" asked Charles, intolerant of anyone who lacked his masterful grasp of details. "Ruth is in and out of there twice a day."

"Well, your office, then."

Charles reached out a forefinger and tested one of the brass catches. It flew open. "Not even locked," he said glumly.

"Do I have to think of everything?" Owen snapped. "Check it at one of the railroad stations."

"And what then? It would just have to be reclaimed. After a few weeks they open things up, and God knows what's in there to identify me. Letters, maybe."

"Don't you understand, Charles?" Owen asked. "I don't really care *what* you do with the suitcase. That's your problem. Mine is the receipt. Once you've signed that, for all I care you can throw the damn thing away!"

"How?" Charles asked simply.

Both men looked at the suitcase. Large, off-white, unscratched, valuable looking.

"It's a nice new suitcase," Charles observed. "If it were precious to me, it might very well get stolen. But if I *tried* to walk away from it? A dozen busybodies would rush to protect me from myself."

"There must be ways. . . ."

"Could you dump it in a litter basket and walk away casually?"

"Maybe not," Owen conceded. "In some respects this is an inconvenient town." With Tony Elmendorf's macabre anecdotes fresh in mind he nearly added that it made you feel sorry for a murderer with a corpse to dispose of. He stopped himself in time.

"I'm extremely sorry to impose on you any further. . . ." Charles said.

"Hey, wait! I've already lugged the thing over here."

"I know, but it's the only sensible solution."

"Why *my* place?"

"It's safe. I can go through the bag at leisure. Tear up letters, throw things away where they won't have any connection with me."

"Look, I'm supposed to have the receipt at the Plaza at seven," Owen said aggrievedly. "It'll look damn queer if I show up clutching the suitcase after you've signed for it. That means a trip all the way uptown and back. Don't you have any other friends?"

"Fewer than you might expect, and they're mostly Ruth's too," Charles said. "But that's not really the point. Wouldn't it be the height of stupidity to drag still another person into this, at this point? Still another set of explanations?"

"Oh, hell!" Owen said.

After waiting to make sure there was nothing more to come, Charles took this as surrender. "I really am most apologetic," he said with a proper show of contrition. Then, to celebrate having got his own way once again, he finished off his whisky and summoned the waiter. "Another Irish," he ordered. "Make it John Jameson, this time. And . . . what was that, Owen? A martini?"

"Extra dry, without lemon peel," Owen said sullenly.

"An extra-dry martini without lemon peel," Charles repeated in the tone of one announcing his intention of picking up the check. "No ginger ale today, Owen? You're not working?"

"No."

"That's something else I have to apologize for, I'm afraid."

Owen said nothing; Charles could apologize as often as he liked, and it made no difference. That he wasn't working was certainly Charles's fault in a way—if not the way Charles thought—yet the small voice of justice kept insisting that Charles wasn't to blame. If a man flung upon a window, blowing over a beautiful house of cards he hadn't known was there, he wasn't to *blame*, was he? Even though you might hate him for it for the rest of his life. That was more or less how Owen felt, and an unsatisfactory way it was to feel. He wanted to resent what Charles had done to him, but whenever he paused to ask himself just what it was that Charles had done, the answer was . . . precisely nothing.

All through that grotesque scene at Charles's mistress's apartment, with the woman lying dead in the other room, one part of Owen's mind had been concerned with the question of how well his play would survive this interview. A petty concern, but the presence of tragedy didn't alter the man you were. Even as he had tried to grapple with the situation as it was, he had known that he was being forced deeper and deeper into an undesired intimacy with his central character: never again could he stand back from Charles and tease. Henceforward they were bound together; Charles would be looking over his shoulder as he tried to write. This was what Owen had worried about. The reality had proved far worse than his fears. Much later that same night—after Tony Elmendorf had come and picked up the pieces, had gone along to Owen's apartment for a nightcap, had eventually exhausted his stock of cynicisms and departed for home—despite his weariness Owen had forced himself back to his play, to reread what was already written and think of the scenes he had planned, hoping to recapture some of the enthusiasm that had gripped him earlier in the day. It wasn't to be done.

Nor was the difficulty simply the old obsession which had kept him from ever writing about Tony. If that had been the case he could have cursed his bad luck, cursed Charles (however unfairly), and put the project aside for some later date. But it wasn't that at all: it was far more deadly. Somehow, in the course of that evening, he himself had changed, his outlook had changed. The scenes which yesterday had seemed vital and exciting and psychologically sound, now stood revealed as merely glib. They were slickly written, yes, but they were shallow and artificial. The very idea of the play was artificial.

Whereas another man might have found something powerful to do with the aftermath of an incompleted suicide pact, he had scamped the issue. He had contributed nothing but the mechanical trickery of having the situation double back on itself twenty-five years later. Polly had put her finger on the trouble with the word 'contrived.' She had said everything would depend on how well he brought it off, and in a commercial sense this was true. Probably (without the thought of Charles looking over his shoulder) he could still have given the story sufficient plausibility to carry it through an evening. With the help of good performances on the stage he might have tricked an audience—as audiences were growing accustomed to being tricked—into believing that they were watching a real play. It happened often enough. People went to a show, thought it was excellent, and a month later were mildly surprised to find that they couldn't remember anything about it, except that So-and-so had been excellent as the alcoholic father.

Well, that wasn't at all the sort of play he had dreamt of writing. Yet as he looked over these scenes he had written so confidently, seeing now at the same time how very effectively they would 'play' and how little they said and how false they were—only the facile theatricality of a man who has learned all the tricks of the trade—he was forced to wonder just how often he *had* written this sort of play, and whether he was really capable of anything much better. Not only had this one play come tumbling down about his ears, but his very belief in himself as an artist was called in question. . . .

Yet how could Charles be blamed for this? Charles was simply Charles, blundering his blind, self-protective way through the world. He meant no harm. In his blundering he might push open a window on reality; if somebody else's dreams got caught in the draft, that was an unfortunate accident. Charles meant no harm, he merely occasioned it; he was as innocent as a force of nature. When he looked back and noticed the wreckage in his path, he would apologize, if he saw the need for apology at all, for quite the wrong reasons.

"I know this has been a bothersome interruption to your work," Charles said, reinforced by the second whisky. "I'm sure I don't have to tell you how grateful I am for all you've done."

In no mood for graciousness, Owen simply shrugged.

"If I haven't seemed properly grateful," Charles explained, "it's only because I've been so upset."

"That's all right," Owen said. "Let's not forget the receipt."

Charles obediently unfolded the paper and took out his pen. But he didn't just scrawl his signature. The actual sight of the list

343

brought on second thoughts. "It would be a pity to chuck some of these away," he muttered. "That's the only practical traveling kit I've ever found. And the cuff links. . . . Those cuff links, Owen. There's no reason why you couldn't get some use out of them. I'd be glad if you kept them."

All the bile in Owen promptly overflowed. "I don't need to be *paid* for my services," he said disagreeably.

"It wasn't meant that way," Charles said in astonishment.

"It was a damned offensive suggestion!"

"It certainly wasn't meant to be," Charles said. His expression was a curious mixture of antagonism and distress. "Perhaps I'm not accustomed to feeling grateful. But those cuff links mean something to me, you know. I don't like to think of them in the pawn shops. If I can't have them, it would please me to know they were being worn by someone who . . . who was. . . ." His voice faded away. There was no end to that sentence. 'Who was my friend,' he had probably intended to say, or something like it, and had lost courage. The offer had been a token of friendship, inept and ill-timed as might have been predicted. Charles would assume that somebody who had seen him through a scrape had proved his friendship and was entitled to friendship in return. Even though he had no clear idea of what was expected of him, Charles would do his best.

"I'm upset too, I expect," Owen said wearily. "We can leave the cuff links till you come for the suitcase, can't we?"

4

Trains do not stop at Princeton but several miles away, at Princeton Junction, and the trip is completed in one of the rattly coaches of a small spur-line shuttle known to generations of undergraduates as the P.J. & B.—standing for Princeton Junction and Back. People who have made this trip a few times quickly learn where it is best to get on the train in Pennsylvania Station to avoid too much walking at the other end. Thus it came about that without any particular pre-arrangement the Booths and the Fortescues found themselves in the same car, and then, inevitably, by force of courtesy, sitting across the aisle from each other.

"But where is Vickie?" Amelia asked.

"Oh, she went down yesterday," Ruth said. "There was a party at Roger's club."

The car filled up rapidly, and the unusually high proportion of middle-aged couples, often with adolescent children in tow, suggested that there were quite a few others here bound on the same errand, to attend their sons' graduation ceremonies. The children were in festival mood, excitable and talkative; their parents had a look at once smug and bemused, as if suddenly wondering where all the years had gone that they should have sons fully come to manhood.

From the window seat Ruth leaned across her husband. "Isn't Owen coming down?" she inquired.

"I have no idea," Amelia said. "He's been working hard recently, and when he's in a fit of working nothing less than an explosion can move him."

"I shouldn't think he could bear to miss it."

"Owen hasn't much use for ceremonies. He'd probably say that if Roger *hadn't* graduated there would be some reason in his coming down."

"We do things not to disappoint a child," Ruth said, "and nine times out of ten it turns out they don't care one way or the other. But if we fail to do something, that always turns out to be the one time they care dreadfully."

With common impulse the two husbands got tired of being talked across and stood up. Ruth was sent to sit by Amelia, and then the men sat down together to read in peace, Charles with his copy of *Time* and Stephen with a pocket edition of Prescott's *Conquest of Peru*. Next on the list of his labors was *Our Brothers, the Incas*.

The arrangement was not one that Amelia would have chosen, but she determined to make the most of it. For the past month she and Ruth had been constantly at loggerheads; Ruth was clearly of the opinion that she was not losing a daughter but acquiring a son and was prepared to mother the young couple until such time as they distracted her with grandchildren. This war was by no means over, the worst battles lay in the future, in due course Roger would have to be warned what to expect and how best to deal with it. But for the time being a truce was in order. No differences of opinion must arise to mar the wedding; the two mothers must present a common front of harmonious indulgence. Such a reversal of attitude was no strain on Amelia, but she recognized that Ruth, as a simpler person, might need to be cajoled into understanding that hostilities had been suspended. To this extent, although the prospect bored her, Amelia welcomed the opportunity to be charming.

"You must be a wreck," she said sympathetically. "The bride's mother has all the worst of it, I know."

"Who was it that had to run so fast just to stay in the same place?" Ruth asked, sighing. "That's what I feel like. I go to bed exhausted, and yet I can't feel I've accomplished anything: I'm always a bit further behind than I was the day before."

"I can imagine," Amelia said warmly, untruthfully.

With the slightest of jolts the train started, pulled away from the lighted platform.

"When all this is over," Ruth said, "I keep promising myself that I'll just go to bed and stay there for a few days. But I know I'll never be able to do it."

"I've made myself the same promise," Amelia agreed. "After half an hour I always get restless."

"It wouldn't be restlessness with me," Ruth said. "All Peter's things still have to be attended to. He's spending the summer up in Vermont, you know." For this graduation did not mark the end of Peter Fortescue's schooling. Some six months before he had faced up to the realization that life was not an endless succession of classes, football games and houseparties and had perceived within himself a yearning to become an architect. So far as Amelia knew there was not the least reason to believe that Peter was in any way fitted to become an architect; the ambition could be as ill-conceived as that of someone tone deaf determining to be a composer; but Peter's pronouncement was accepted by the Fortescues as proof of both talent and calling, and the boy would commence his new studies in the autumn.

"He's lucky to have a few more summer vacations to look forward to," Amelia said.

"This isn't a vacation, exactly," Ruth replied, a shade defensively. "The father of the friend he's visiting is a building contractor. Peter will spend the summer working for his keep as a sort of general helper —getting a firsthand knowledge of how houses are built from the foundations on up. He had the idea himself, made all the arrangements. I must say he's shown more enterprise than I would have expected."

Amelia's impulse was to wonder whether a pianist would benefit by a few years in a piano factory, but she knew this for simple querulousness: architecture was probably different, and Peter certainly would be no worse off for knowing how concrete was poured and bricks laid. The truth was that she resented the very possibility that

346

Peter might be discovering a genuine vocation while Roger was vanishing into the underbrush of industry. "Peter's a very sensible boy," she said. "I know Roger's going to miss him."

"Well, Roger will be busy making new friends," Ruth said.

"It's hard to think of Roger grown up and married, with a place of his own," Amelia said. It wasn't hard at all, but this seemed the sort of maternal rubbish that Ruth would find engaging.

"With girls you see it coming further ahead," Ruth said. "I've always known Vickie would be off and married before she was twenty."

"She's remarkably mature for her age," said Amelia.

"I'm not so sure about that," Ruth said, struggling with the temptations of the compliment.

"Oh, she *is*," Amelia insisted. "Very levelheaded, down to earth. Roger's a lucky boy."

"They pick up all the mannerisms for public display," Ruth said drily. "All I've seen of Roger so far is an earnest, amiable, beautifully mannered young man. I expect you could add a few details to that picture if you had a mind to."

"I don't suppose we're ever really fair to our own children," Amelia said. "We can't help remembering every folly, all the anxieties. . . ."

"Is that it?" Ruth wondered. "When I look at Vickie I don't think of the girl who read somewhere about sucking eggs and thought she'd use the vacuum cleaner for the messy part, as she called it."

"Well, you know what I mean," Amelia said after a courteous laugh. "We may not think of those incidents, exactly, but we don't forget them either. They're right there making it difficult to realize that yesterday's child has finally grown up."

The train had emerged into the unlovely Jersey morning and was now slowing down for Newark station.

"Oh, *grown up*," said Ruth. "Well, grown up is exactly what Roger and Vickie are not, and except when they're around I really don't see the point of pretending otherwise."

"If you feel that way, I'm surprised you approve of the marriage."

"How else do people finish their growing up?" Ruth asked simply. "But it's not something that happens overnight. Heavens, they've never really been off on their own before, either one of them! And that's why, I must admit, I'm not as happy as I might be with this wedding trip you and Owen have planned for them."

"Don't tell Owen that," Amelia said. "He'd be very hurt."

"Oh, it's very handsome of you," Ruth said hurriedly. "Extremely generous. They should have a wonderful time. But just the same, and I don't mind how silly you think I am, I know I'm going to worry."

"I can't imagine why. They'll be well looked after."

"It seems like such a long time. I know it's good for them to have a chance to get used to one another, but still, it's a whole month. All sorts of things can happen. And so far away."

"That's part of the idea, I would have thought."

"I was looking at the atlas the other evening," Ruth said. "I've never had any sense of geography. If somebody had asked me where Jamaica was, I'd have put it somewhere around Bermuda."

"No, much farther south."

"It's on the other side of Cuba," Ruth said darkly.

"Oh, for God's sake, Ruth!" Amelia snapped. The train was bustling through the Jersey countryside; the day ahead seemed long, and she decided that the trip home would be time enough to concentrate on being charming. "They aren't going to *walk* there, you know."

5

Before ten o'clock in the evening The Cellar d'Or simply did not exist for people in the fashionable world. At that hour, guided by the migratory instinct that governed their lives, they would begin to come swarming by the taxi load from all corners of the city, to clatter down the seven gilded steps, to be greeted by Bob McEvoy if they were habitués, to be taken in hand by a headwaiter who would shoehorn them into place around one of the countless little tables that crowded the floor, each the size of a modest pizza pie. Their orders for drinks would be attended to with miraculous dispatch, considering the sidling, twisting and stretching required of the waiters. After a time the lights would dim and on the stage would come the first of McEvoy's hand-picked entertainers, to sing to them, to make them laugh, or possibly, by way of variety, to perform magic tricks to a sophisticated patter. Between performers the lights would come up for twenty minutes or so, giving waiters a chance to work, allowing early patrons to pay their checks and leave, instantly to be replaced by newcomers stopping in after the theatre. This pattern would repeat itself until two in the morning. Under the dominion of the efficient waiters, who had a way of whisking away any glass that was less than half full, enormous quantities of liquor were consumed, and very little food. Occasionally someone who had hurried ill-fed to a theatre would order a sandwich, and be astonished to find that it was really quite edible.

Although the chairs were wretchedly uncomfortable, and the tables so small and crowded together that in the course of an evening you were sure to get a neighbor's drink in your lap, this was so much a part of supper-club custom that the habitués had probably never noticed that along two walls at the Cellar d'Or there was a series of quite comfortable little banquettes, each fronted by a table almost adequate for two. Early in the evening, long before the fashionable hours, these were almost the only tables in the room. They were properly damasked then, and dinner could be ordered from a small but dependable menu. The stage was occupied by a relaxed trio of musicians—piano, bass and muted sax—who wandered good naturedly through old show tunes. Since the front half of the floor was cleared of its tables, there was ample space for dancing.

Thus the rare couples who were content to spend the evening in one place could dine well, could talk without having to compete with a blaring band, could dance, if by this they meant gliding sociably about the floor in each other's arms instead of cavorting exhibitionistically, and late in the evening, just when conversation might be flagging a bit, they would be served up the best of entertainment. This arrangement, a relatively recent innovation of McEvoy's, had not yet been discovered by out-of-towners and was far too sensible, too old-fashioned, to be popular with true New Yorkers. So dinner hour at the Cellar d'Or still had the added advantage of rarely being crowded. It afforded, in fact, the nearest thing to a romantic atmosphere to be found in any public spot in town, and since Owen wanted all the elements on his side this evening he had phoned ahead in mid-afternoon for a reservation.

They had the quietest of corner tables, he and Carol. They had dined well on filet mignon, garlic bread and salad, while the trio (primed with a five-dollar bill to the pianist) played tunes from *Kiss Me Kate* and other shows they had seen together, and while Owen, in a ferociously expansive mood, talked of everything under the sun except the things he meant to talk of when he sensed that the right moment had arrived. They had danced quietly and contentedly for a while until the trio, no doubt corrupted by one of the other diners, switched to something with a more Latin rhythm; whereupon they grinned at one another, in acknowledgement of Owen's limitations as a dancer, and went back to their table where coffee kept hot over a candle flame and two bubbles of brandy waited.

"My! I can't remember when I danced last," Carol said.

"Nor can I," lied Owen, who had had to affirm his youthfulness in just this fashion all too often with Denise Durrell. "Just the same, you're still the only person who's ever made me enjoy it."

"I've never understood that," she said. "You're quite good, really. You have a perfect sense of rhythm."

"So they tell me," he agreed. "So they've been telling me all my life, but it doesn't seem to register. The trouble is that I don't *feel* like a good dancer. Except with you. I'm always working at it; I can't just relax and go with the music." He was not listening to what he was saying; he was admiring Carol: slightly flushed from the food and the warmth and the exercise, looking particularly lovely—and also particularly touching. He had noticed that she was wearing the same dress she had worn the last time they went out together. Tricked out differently: another belt, another pin—but surely no woman would have two black dresses so much alike. The thought that at her age she should have to practice such economies outraged him; he longed to fill up her lap with money, command her to set forth the next morning and turn the shops inside out until she had a whole wardrobe of pretty new things. Instead, taking advantage of the surge of impulse, he blurted: "There's something I want to ask you, Carol."

"I *thought* the air seemed just a bit electric," she replied happily, refilling both their demitasse cups.

"Perhaps I ought to lead up to this gradually," he raved, "but there doesn't seem much point to that. It would still come to a surprise at the end, and a lot of explaining to do." Now that he was fairly started and there was no drawing back, he felt frightened. At his age a man was supposed to know what he was doing, but too many times before he had thought he knew, he had been just as positive as he was now, and he had been mistaken. You pushed your way through life doing your best to make your decisions appear sensible ones, thoughtfully considered, maturely resolved, yet always you were at the mercy of so many moods, urges, emotions which never even reached the surface. How did a man persuade himself that one particular woman out of all the thousands held the keys to his contentment? Was there anything of rationality in this process, or was it simply that, as someone had once said, you fell in love, no matter with whom, when you reached the need for being in love? Certainly a man gave clearer thought to the least of his workaday problems than to this moment which could so easily mean the destruction of all peace of mind for years and years to come. He didn't think at all, perhaps, but depended upon instincts which he might once have possessed but which he had long ago exchanged for the tidier machinery of logic. He blundered ahead, hoping in the teeth of all the evidence about him that he would prove to be one of the rare lucky ones. And he had to blunder ahead, for to let himself be frightened by all the uncertainties was to anticipate death. "What it comes down to," he said, "is what would you think of a honeymoon out on the Coast?"

"What?" she said in bewilderment.

"I said you'd be surprised," he reminded her. "But the timing is quite ideal. School is over. Lois can stay with your father. Or she could come with us, if you'd prefer it that way? Why not? I'm not sure how long it will be for; not more than a few months, I should think. We'll find a place near the water, and Lois can learn to swim. It's high time she learned to swim. You'd both get brown and healthy. And when my work out there is finished we'll pick up some sort of car—I expect we'll have needed one anyway—and drive back slowly across the country and look at the Grand Canyon and all the places we've never seen. What do you say?"

"Now, wait a minute. . . ."

"No, don't wait! Be impulsive. Say you think it's a tremendous idea."

"But I've never been so confused in my life," she said, laughing uncertainly. "Owen, be serious."

"I'm deadly serious."

"But what's become of your play?"

"There's a woman for you! She gets a proposal of marriage, and she asks, What's become of your play?!" Owen spoke teasingly, but he was unreasonably disappointed. He had known there would have to be explanations, elaborate explanations, but he had hoped that they might be left till later. He had teased himself with the thought that Carol would accept his proposal unquestioningly, sensing his own uncertainties and his need for her enthusiasm. It had been too much to ask for, he knew that. He couldn't blame Carol. But it seemed to him that when a man made his gallant, defenseless plunge into the future he should be reassured promptly, and he was obliged to hide his disappointment. "The play? Oh, the bubble burst, that's all."

"But it was going along so beautifully!"

"It seemed to be," he agreed. "I'm afraid it was only a pipe dream, and the person from Porlock walked in."

"Who?"

"You've forgotten the story," he told her, forcing himself to calm down, gesturing to the waiter for more cognac, accepting that this would have to be done the long way around. "Coleridge one evening drank his glass of laudanum or smoked his opium, I don't recall which, and dreamed a golden dream of Kubla Khan. Remember? When he awoke, the poem was all there waiting in his mind. He was writing it out, when somebody from the nearby village of Porlock rapped at his front door—and by the time Coleridge got back to his study the rest of the poem had vanished from his head. Something of the kind happened to me."

"That's ridiculous!" she said. "You don't work that way. You plan ahead, you always know exactly where you're going."

"And there are times when I can't get there, just the same," he said. "I had a jolt the other evening, and maybe it opened my eyes. When I got back to my study I could see very clearly that this wasn't any *Kubla Khan* I was writing."

"Honestly, Owen!" she exclaimed, her face clearing. "This *always* happens!"

"It's different this time."

"It's always different and always the same." For the moment she was the brisk housewife, happy to be dealing with a routine problem. "You get stuck, you have a bad day, and you decide the whole thing's a great mistake and you should have stuck to your father's hardware store. I've never known it to fail."

"By now I ought to be aware of my little tricks," he said. "This isn't a case when I need to have my hand held and be told how terrific I am."

"You're sure?" she asked, studying him. "You're really sure? You've fooled yourself before."

"I'm sure."

"It wasn't any good at all?"

"Worse than that: it was quite good. Very, very slick. Superbly hollow."

"All right, then, you got off on the wrong foot," she said decisively. "That can happen to anybody. And I suppose dear Polly caught you when your defenses were down."

"You're always seeing Polly in the shadows." He found it was one thing to reach a decision, be proud of having reached it, and quite another to explain that decision to someone who at the outset was bound to think of it as contemptible.

"Then it's the nonsensical business of Roger's honeymoon," she said. "But that doesn't make sense. You could borrow the money if you really wanted to, couldn't you?"

"I suppose I could. And I could thumb my nose at Polly. But what I can't do is go on kidding myself any longer."

"Poor love. You *are* in a bad way." Carol was tender with misunderstanding.

"It's not discouragement, if that's what you mean," he said steadily. "My feelings are still a bit mixed up, but on the whole I'm smug."

"Smug?" she asked, and Owen took a deep breath.

"Because I've finally stepped off the merry-go-round, which is something that people like me don't often do. We spin around thinking we're going somewhere, and it's only the years flashing by."

"If that isn't discouragement—!"

"How do you discourage an artist?" Owen inquired sardonically. "It's a nice question. The mediocre tailor soon learns how bad he is, but how does the mediocre artist learn? You can sneer at him, neglect him, starve him to death, and none of it matters. Posterity can always reverse your verdict. Didn't the same things happen to Melville and Moussorgsky and Modigliani? The list goes on and on."

"I wouldn't say you'd exactly been starved or neglected."

"It might have been better for me if I had been, but I doubt it," he replied. "I'd just have been stubborner, most likely. There's a scrubby gallantry about failure. You march nobly off into the sunset convinced that one day the entire Twentieth Century will be held in ridicule for having failed to appreciate the genius of Owen Hilliard. Phooey! That mirage is the consolation prize of every second-rater in the business."

Carol was finally beginning to realize that this was more than just another passing fit of depression and was becoming indignant. "But you can't just suddenly decide you're a second-rater," she protested. "You can't!"

"What difference does the word make?" he asked. "What I've decided is that it's time to give up the idea that one morning I'll wake up to find that I've written a masterpiece. Because I never will, unfortunately. A sad admission, but there it is."

"At your age!" she jeered.

"Oh, I know the whole rigmarole of self-deception," he said. "I know it better than anybody, Carol. I've lived with it all my life."

Illusions were waiting ready-made for every age. You started out knowing you would set the world on fire before you were out of your twenties, but in time you learned to despise that ambition. Early talents had a way of burning out equally early, so you told yourself. Maturity was the thing; a reputation that gathered slowly lasted longest. Next year, or the year after, would come the rewards of discipline. And imperceptibly your heroes changed from the youthful prodigies to those whose talents flowered later in life. You talked less of Shelley and more of Marcel Proust or Bernard Shaw—how much of Shaw would be remembered if he had died at fifty? It was a comforting question, but the comfort was usually a fraud. . . .

"The merry-go-round never stops," he said. "There's always the hope that next time around you'll grab the brass ring. And getting off means leaving behind a large investment of dreams; thirty years' worth in my case. That's why it's so tough. Maybe my failing is that after all this time there's still a streak of New England sanity in me. And it says that thirty years is long enough."

"So you're giving up."

"Nothing of the sort! I'm accepting my limitations."

"It comes to the same thing," she said flatly.

"Be gentle with me, Carol," he said. "I still feel raw in places." His glass was empty and the cognac had only made him thirstier; he caught their waiter's eye and ordered a long scotch for himself; Carol was still nursing her brandy. "Undeceiving oneself is a remarkably uncomfortable process," he added, appealing to her sympathies. "I've had a rough couple of days. Growing pains, I suppose."

Her right hand was available and he took it gently, held it, trying to help her over the hurdle of her old prejudices. But it was still too soon. She smiled faintly, affectionate yet impatient. Her hand was unresponsive, and a moment later she needed it for a cigarette. "I might understand better . . ." she began, and then shook her head. "What started you thinking this way?" she asked.

"Oh, I expect it's been creeping up on me for some time. Working with other men's ideas, telling myself that I was building myself a reputation that would pay off when I got back to my own work. It made sense of a sort. And then I had my fling at writing an original —and got my nose rubbed in the fact that there's something missing in me."

"Confidence, mostly. I've always said so."

"No shortage of confidence," he said. "Technically I'm a damn good writer, and I know it. I'm a far better craftsman than most of the writers whose stories I tinker around with. But they all of them have something I don't have. A quality of temperament? Of sympathy? Of vitality? I don't know, but I can feel it's there. And I'm not a kid any more. Perhaps the old dog can learn new tricks but he can't change his nature. All right. I'm a craftsman, period. Either I face up to that or I go back to pretending that I'm one more unappreciated genius."

"So the only answer is to go running out to *Hollywood!*"

"That's not quite the same as selling my soul to the devil."

"The way you've always felt, it's just as bad," she insisted fiercely. "You'll be miserable."

"Owen suffering among the swimming pools?" he asked, hoping to arouse her sense of the absurd. "Darling, darling, you can't make a tragedy of this, however hard you try."

"Just after you've finished saying it's too late to change your nature," she retorted. "Do you think you're going to be so comfortable getting along without your integrity?"

"That's still in place," he said, mildly nettled. "But from now on it's the integrity of any other hired hand. Neither more nor less. My part is just to do a good honest job of work."

"And then sit back and watch them turn it into one more marshmallow."

"Perhaps my being there will make a difference, perhaps not. Either way they'll pay me handsomely, and I'll pocket the money without a lot of adolescent soul searching. I've come of age, Carol! That's cause for celebration, surely."

She shook her head. "I can't see celebrating because somebody quits taking himself seriously."

"I'm sick and tired of these snobberies," he said harshly. "Haven't I modestly declared myself one of the best craftsmen in the country? But work isn't to be taken seriously any more."

"I'm not a snob."

"Of course you are," he said. "It's not your fault; it's become the national disease." He gestured at their waiter, just departing. "We even have to bring in Europeans to staff our restaurants because we've decided it's demeaning to wait on table. Our ambition is to trifle at white-collar anti-jobs because anything that smacks of an honest day's work is contemptible. And the same state of mind has crept into the art world. Every man has to be a genius or he won't play. And since there isn't enough genius to go around, we take refuge in anti-art, where we may or may not be appreciated but at least we can never be found out. All right, that's the fashion, and if I were a real artist that's probably where I'd be: writing anti-plays about anti-characters who speak a sort of anti-dialogue."

"Now you're just sneering," Carol said.

"The revenge of the impotent? Well, perhaps. Yes, you're right. I've given up my membership, I'm an outsider now, I don't have any right to make fun of my betters."

"I didn't mean it that way," she said contritely.

"No, but you're absolutely right, just the same," Owen replied, following up his advantage. "It takes some getting used to, my new condition. I've spent a long time in my caterpillar dreams, expecting to wake up a butterfly, and there are still moments when it's hard to remember that the wings aren't there."

"You can make me cry for you, if that's what you want," she said in a small voice, and he was startled to see that she meant it. Her eyes were liquid with tears.

"But that's the last thing I want!" he cried, forgetting for the moment that they were in a public place. He dropped his voice again. "You're acting as if some calamity had overtaken me, as if I'd altered, and I haven't. That's what you must understand. I'm the same guy I was yesterday, just a few dreams lighter."

"But. . . ."

"No, wait!" he insisted. "Or it'll get all out of perspective. I wouldn't *stay* out in Hollywood even if anybody wanted me to—you needn't worry about that. I'm coming right back. A play is meant to be played to an audience: not tricked onto celluloid and shut up in a can, a finished thing, forever unaffected by the people who see it. Neil was on the phone this afternoon talking about a novel that sounds promising—he's sending it around in the morning. If I like the feel of it, I'll fool with the idea over the summer, and get down to it in the autumn. If not that one, there'll be something else. And if there's a film to be made of it later on, I'll angle for that job too, and why not? There are new techniques to be learned, lots of nice green money to play with, crazy people to meet. . . . It should all be fun, as long as you don't take the swimming pools seriously. Twenty times as much fun if you're along; we laugh at the same nonsense. Dammit, Carol, it could be a ball! So why don't you stop looking so solemn, say yes, and we can make this a *real* celebration!"

An unexpected voice above them said: "But how utterly delightful to see the two of you together again!" They looked up, dazed at being jerked so abruptly from their private world. It was Eliot Clay, sleekly elegant, beaming down at them.

"The years whisk by, Carol, and you don't look a day older. That's a secret you should share with the rest of us."

Owen was casting about for some way to sweep aside this gadfly, but he was too slow.

"Look, my poppets," Eliot prattled, "is this a private celebration? That's the one word I overheard, I swear. But would you mind dreadfully if I joined you? Be frank, as long as the answer is that you'd love to have me. Otherwise I'll spend the evening off in a corner by myself, gnawing on my fingernails—terribly disfiguring and leads to blood all over the keyboard. You couldn't do that to me, could you? No, I thought not."

He waved over their waiter at the same time as he appropriated a chair from one of the other tables, set it into place. "Bring these nice people another round of whatever they're drinking, and I'll have a gin and tonic. Back in a minute," he added, and went off through the door that led backstage, to the dressing rooms.

"Damn!" said Owen, inwardly cursing the interruption in much stronger terms, for he was sure that Carol had been on the point of weakening. "Have you no sales resistance at all?"

"But I like Eliot."

"I like Eliot, too. There are times when anyone is a redundancy."

"Perhaps," she said. "I thought we might be glad to have him around, to keep us from glooming at one another."

Owen's heart lurched, but he refused to panic. "If you think you can turn me down that easily, you're mistaken."

"It's too much for me to take in all at once," she replied, evading the finality.

"Nonsense, my sweet. You aren't a schoolgirl fumbling her first proposal. This has been in the air for some time. Until this evening you'd have been all in favor."

"What confidence you have is in the wrong places."

"It's the idea of Hollywood that's making trouble," he declared. "My God, Carol, you can't let that spoil everything for us."

"It isn't Hollywood," she said. "Not in the sense you mean."

Her face was closed; Owen looked at her in loving exasperation. Although he had argued with Tony he had privately agreed with his friend's conviction that Carol would jump at a proposal. Not for the cynical reasons, but because he had sensed that she felt as he did: that they belonged together now that each was a little older and

357

wiser than when they had broken up. Nor had he changed his mind. "Perhaps you're right," he said. "It's my fault. I shouldn't have thrown all this at you so suddenly. I should have come to you sooner."

"Can you think I'd have helped you get to where you've gone? I'd have fought you every inch of the way!"

"That's just it." In distress, his instinct was for solitude: he withdrew into his troubles. Carol saw only the end result of his brooding; she could not imagine what he'd been through these past few days, as he read over all his work of the past ten years, looking for some evidence that he was wrong. But now it seemed obvious that if she'd shared in that torment of self-seeking she would share, too, in the inevitability of his recognition, and the triumph. "Do you suppose I didn't fight?"

"I'm not supposing anything," Carol said unhappily, "except that perhaps it's a mistake ever to try to start these things up again, once they've gone wrong. There are too many old memories getting in the way. I can't forget that last time I drove you crazy propping up your faith in yourself. Now you're telling me it was all a waste of time."

"One way and another, we've both lost a lot of time," he answered. "I'm trying to get us off on a fresh footing."

"But not this way, Owen, I need something to believe in. Having a ball just isn't enough. There has to be more to living than growing up and then helping your own children grow up and then dying. I need something to believe in."

"Can't you believe in art without having a pet artist in the house to inspire?"

"You're missing the point," Carol said. "I wish Eliot would come back. You're offended and I can't blame you, and I'm feeling defensive, and in a few more minutes we'll start hurting one another."

"Should we sit here politely while you mess us up with notions left over from your girlhood?" Owen asked. "If I can grow up, so can you. There comes a time for a good hard look at reality. It may have seemed like a romantic idea once, playing inspiration, but when I said there wasn't enough genius to go around that also applied to girls like you."

"I've never wanted to play inspiration to anybody," Carol said. "That's the way you insist on seeing me."

"Put it any way you like," he replied. "You have this thing about artists, and you're upset because I won't keep up the pose. But you're a big girl now, you have a life to live, you have a kid to look after. I'm offering you a life which should be the maximum of fun, the minimum of worries, and all the chances for Lois."

"Aren't you being a bit Victorian?"

"At least I don't have to promise that love will come later. Come on, Carol! I have a right to appeal to your realism. Aren't women supposed to be the realists of this world?"

"Probably we are," Carol said. "But we have our own ideas of realism."

"Then what's yours, for God's sake?" Owen asked, exasperated. "Going on forever playing a Greenwich Village girl in a Greenwich Village that hasn't been there for decades?"

"That's what I meant about hurting," Carol said. "Are you trying to goad me into defending myself? For a woman, believing in something usually means believing in her man, and that holds true a long way from Greenwich Village. It's not always easy. But it gets pretty impossible when the man quits believing in himself."

"Then you approve of the man who's deluding himself—just as long as he doesn't stop!"

"You can put a good face on it, Owen. For anything you did you'd have reasons that sounded fine and noble. I've never known a man who couldn't convince himself that expediency was a crusade."

"Who the hell is being noble?" he demanded. "I've told you I've been through the worst few days of my life—"

"And what's new about that?" she broke in. "Every man who turns commercial has his sob story. How often have I had to listen to it? At every Village party there's the slummer in his hand-tailored suit, three sheets to the wind with nostalgia and eager to tell you how it damn near killed him to sell out."

"Just for once can't we get along without that sanctimonious jargon about selling out?"

"It was like cutting out his heart, to hear him tell it, but it was the right thing to do. A man has to face up to his responsibilities sometime. And the critics are all corrupt anyway. And if Michelangelo were alive he'd be in advertising. And the city is no place to bring up children."

"Do you honestly think I'm anything like that?" Owen asked.

"You'll give a more eloquent twist to it, but it's where you're going."

"That's to say I've changed completely, and I haven't."

"You're changing, Owen. I'd noticed it already, but I didn't want to believe it. And I didn't want to say any of this, either," she added, her voice quickening and softening so abruptly that he took it for a change of mood rather than her unflagging social sense. "I wouldn't have said it if you hadn't goaded me. And here—thank goodness!—is Eliot back again." She was able to look up at Eliot with that smile of instant, easy delight which women keep ready for emergencies.

"Come and have a spin before the floor disappears," Eliot said to Carol, and off they went, just like that. They were the only couple dancing now, which would have discomfited Owen, whereas Eliot showed an almost-professional pleasure in having the floor to himself except in that he kept chattering incessantly, proving how little attention he needed to give to the intricate behavior of his feet. In his arms, though nearly as large as he, Carol seemed light and graceful.

Nobody seeing her laughing, responding so animatedly to whatever Eliot was saying, would have guessed that she was only seconds away from a critical moment of her life, assisting (if she was to be taken literally) at the obsequies of a love. Women had a resiliency amounting to ruthlessness—at times. When they were hurt they could become the most miserable, dependent of creatures, but when they did the hurting they could walk away from their brutality with an aplomb few men could equal.

But despite the show of heart-free callousness Carol was giving, Owen still couldn't take it as anything more than a show. He had known that she would be deeply upset at first. He had known this so well that at one point he had even considered giving some other explanation for taking the Hollywood offer. Put all the blame on Roger and Vickie. Whisk Carol out there for a second honeymoon, and let her get accustomed gradually to his new estimate of his capabilities. It was what a woman, in a similar situation, would have done: sure that the end justified the means. But he had found that he lacked the courage or the cowardice, whichever was called for. With a cross-grained masculine quixotry he had demanded that Carol share the fruits of his self-discovery.

So now he had to cope with the preposterous accusation that he himself had changed. She *would* say that, of course; it went against nature to discard a love on ideological grounds. It had to be the person, the man, who had changed. And he hadn't. He was the same Owen Hilliard, obsessed by his work, loving it. Heaven alone knew what impelled a man towards being a writer; the first steps were lost in boyhood. A feel for language, a certain way of looking at people and situations, a mixture of other unguessable yearnings, promptings and possibly even complexes. Somebody encouraged at just the right moment, somebody else *dis*couraged at just the right moment, and the ambition hardened a bit more. You had your fling, and from then on everything depended on talent, perseverance and luck. But apart from all this, somewhere along the way, writing became a temperamental addiction: this was how you wanted to *live*. Work was a justification, the solitary disciplines a necessity, the evocation of scenes on paper a drug.

If a man could make a living out of this compulsion he was blessed, and however talented an artist he might be was almost beside the point. No longer hagridden by an irrelevant dream of glory, Owen knew he would love his work all the more. He would be just as conscientious but more relaxed about it, probably a lot easier to live with. It was a good life he was offering Carol, a vital and productive life that any woman could take pride in. . . .

But then Carol and Eliot came back to the table, and Carol was bubbling with delight. "This is so exciting!" she exclaimed. "Darling, just listen! Eliot has discovered this new singer. He's been coaching her himself these past six weeks and written new songs just for her."

"No, only one of the songs was written especially for Jo," Eliot said. "They're all new, though. I'd been hoarding my best things for most of a year, waiting for the right girl to come along."

"And this evening's her debut, Owen," Carol said. "You can imagine why Eliot didn't want to sit off in a corner by himself."

"I get vicarious stagefright," Eliot said.

They were united in the gaiety of anticipation.

"Well, well, so there's something to celebrate after all," Owen said ironically, but he had felt sick at the tone of Carol's voice. There were fatalities in knowing somebody too well. With another woman he would have noticed only that her manner had altered and drawn no conclusions; with Carol he could not have the consolation of such innocence. For all that she had called him 'Darling' this was her bright and social voice, a barricade of politeness. It was a voice that disclaimed intimacy, denied that intimacy had ever existed, and for the first time he felt really frightened, faced the thought of defeat. She was fast at work healing up the breaches in her self-sufficiency; she was shutting herself off from the man who had changed. He could almost hear the little doors going slam, slam, slam as she fired off questions to keep Eliot talking. But how did you find the girl, Eliot? Had she ever sung before? How did you set about training her? Eliot, the unsuspecting buffer, was happy to oblige; he and

Carol provided a model of decorous gaiety as the waiters drifted past replacing chairs and tables with well-rehearsed efficiency, readying the room for the supper-club trade.

Owen asked, "Are you going to accompany her yourself?" thinking that at least this would fix a limit to the intrusion.

"I'm not that professional, really," Eliot said. "Val, he's the pianist up there, is one of the best in the business. If she goes wrong he'll be able to cover up for her, while I'd fall to pieces on the spot."

"I think you're wise," Carol said. "Tell me—" and Owen called for another round of drinks, a double for himself. He wanted fortification against the frustration of the hours ahead, desperately needing to talk to Carol, and inhibited by the presence of an outsider. There was no way to tell a man he wasn't wanted when he so obviously *was* wanted. One of Carol's Village chums could have done it, doubtless: flinging out the rudeness in blind indifference to anything but his own wishes. But Owen couldn't, and Carol knew that he couldn't and was taking full advantage of the fact. The more Owen thought about this, the angrier he became. It wasn't fair to him, it wasn't fair to herself. She wanted to be left in peace to make a mess of her life in her own way—and her daughter's too, most likely. Camp followers of that phoney world where failure was a proof of superiority. Where artists postured for the admiration of other artists and the discomfort or humiliation of the layman, where public approval was the mark of the beast, where they talked so righteously of people who 'turned commercial' or 'sold out.' Well, it would be shameful to let her get away with it, shameful to let her retreat out of reach behind this barrage of chit-chat. . . .

"It's the pointless gestures that are so hard to get rid of," Eliot said. "You can't imagine. They *will* keep waving their hands about."

"But how do you stop someone from that sort of thing?" Carol asked.

"You don't," Owen said. "You encourage him in his folly. Strike a silly attitude and hold it till the ship goes down."

Carol gave him a sharp look before she led Eliot back to a discourse on his tutorial methods, but that was the start of an undercover battle. Eliot's presence might prevent them from quarreling openly, but this seemingly innocuous conversation, the training of a singer, proved to offer unlimited opportunities for pointed little sarcasms which could pass as general observations. Carol might lament—oh so objectively!—the money madness that spoiled many young talents, and a moment later Owen would seize upon some detail of Eliot's teaching to comment upon artists who never troubled to learn the fundamentals of their art.

For a while they were reasonably subtle about this, not that it mattered, probably: Eliot was far too sensitive to remain long unaware that he was being used as a sort of no-man's land over which the shells were flying. But, if he noticed, Eliot accepted his role unperturbed, as one familiar to him; watching them both with feline indifference, breaking in smoothly whenever the innuendoes threatened to become too flagrant. Gradually, nevertheless, the story of his protegée took second place to the cold war.

"Jo is such a delight to work with that I've grown quite terrified of losing her," Eliot said.

"But you must have a contract," Carol said.

"Of a sort," Eliot agreed. "I'm not an agent. She's mine until she pays back the price of the songs I've given her, and I've fixed that as high as I dared. My idea is that if I keep writing new numbers for her, I can keep her in peonage indefinitely, but of course if she makes enough of a hit that won't work. At any moment Hollywood could drop a bundle of money into my lap and whisk her away."

"They tell me it's a fascinating life if you don't take the swimming pools too seriously," Carol said. "Owen's going out in a few weeks."

"Oh, wonderful!" said Eliot. "Doing a film, I suppose."

"The adaptation of *Cascade*," Owen said.

"But what marvellous news!" Eliot said with warm good nature. "It's always so heartening when an old friend finally lands in clover."

"They'd invited him before," Carol said. "This was the time he . . . capitulated."

"Did you ever see what they did to that other play?" Owen asked quietly. "There's some honesty to *Cascade*. Not a great deal, perhaps, but some. This way I'll be able to fight for it."

"You won't win, of course," Carol said.

"At least they'll know they've been in a fight," Owen said. "Surely that's better than giving up in advance."

"Don't you expect they've known for years how to deal with writers who go out there with that attitude?" Carol said scornfully. "You'll be the new boy trying to tell the old hands how to run their business."

"So what? I don't have anything to lose."

"There's always something to lose," Carol said. "This time, as you said, you'll be learning a new technique. Why throw away that knowledge when another time, when you wouldn't be so green, you could fight for a play you felt more strongly about?"

"I've never lived that way," Owen protested.

"You've begun," said Carol.

Tired of playing tennis spectator to this exchange, Eliot broke in pacifically: "But nobody nowadays sees movies till they turn up years later on television," he said, "and by the time the Late Show comes on everyone is too tiddly to know what's going on." He beamed at this disposal of another dreary little heterosexual squabble. "Something has occurred to me," he said to Owen. "Will anybody be using your apartment while you're away?"

Caught off guard, Owen shook his head.

"That's a great mistake," Eliot said. "It just isn't safe to leave a place standing empty for months and months." He was volubly persuasive about this, no doubt glad to have got onto a subject without loopholes for controversy. Although Owen could see drawbacks to the arrangement, he was too depressed to put up much resistance, and a little later they drank to Eliot's acting as summer caretaker for the cost of telephone and electricity.

At last the long room was filling up rapidly. The waiters, who for hours past had been extraordinarily solicitous out of simple boredom, were now darting about at top speed, filling the orders of customers who would do their best to get full alcoholic value for the Cellar d'Or's exorbitant minimum charge. From moment to moment the din increased, as friends discovered each other across the room and bayed or shrieked their greetings, since moving about, once you had been seated, was virtually impossible in mid-room. And as the hour approached for his protegée's debut, cracks began to appear in Eliot's pose of nonchalance. He didn't fidget or squirm, but his manner became distrait and for once his facile patter showed signs of drying up. Eventually he pushed his chair back, muttering something about having a last word with somebody.

"Now don't go upsetting the poor girl," Carol said, clearly not wanting to lose him.

"Wouldn't dream of it," said Eliot. "I thought I'd go and calm down McEvoy's newest boy friend. The job of M.C. here is kept as a sinecure for the reigning incumbent, and this one is rather more scatterbrained than most." He stood up, tried to reassert his unconcern by saying casually to Owen: "I don't suppose your place has a piano."

"I'm afraid not," Owen said.

"Oh, well," said Eliot. "That way I get out and about more." He grinned at them, perhaps hoping that his absence would help to clear the air, and sidestepped neatly away between the flying waiters.

At his going Carol stiffened slightly, bracing herself against the expected onslaught, and Owen snorted mirthlessly. "You *are* defensive," he remarked.

"Who wouldn't be?" she asked. "You're just waiting to tell me what a bloody fool I am for not leaping at the chance to hook you."

"Am I?" he said, looking at her lovely profile, remote and cool. It was true that at one time there had seemed such a lot to be said, but his fervor had dissipated with the waiting, blurred by the scotches, following after the brandy, the wine, the cocktails before dinner. He was left with an overwhelming burden of pity—for Carol, for himself, or all the people in the world who went out of their way to spoil whatever happiness they found.

"There are more valid reasons for turning a man down," he said. "For a richer life, sure. That leaves a man with some self-respect. But for the glory of playing mother hen to cheap little genius fakers?"

"Now you stop that!" she said.

"What do you call them, then? The painters who dribble paint on a model and roll her across a canvas. The poets who scribble phrases on file cards, shuffle three times, and call it 'action verse.'"

"It's so easy to sneer."

"To hell with them," he said. "I'm thinking of you. You and all the other women who kiss their bruises and keep their egos patched together until a new inspiration comes along and you just remind them of a phase outgrown, you aren't worthy any longer, they tip their hats and away they go. We've seen it so many times. There's always another genius faker waiting in the wings, fortunately. But he's always the same age—have you noticed that, Carol?—while every year you're a little older."

"It's a sad picture," she said. "You can think of it sometimes, beside the swimming pool. It might take your mind off your income tax for a little while."

"So *that's* the great change you pretend to see in me!"

"It's part of the pattern, yes."

"Pattern, hell!"

"There was a time when you wouldn't have given a damn."

"There was a time when I hadn't anything to give a damn about."

"When you would have been disgusted at spending a small fortune on your son's honeymoon. When it would have bothered you to see him turning into one more huckster."

"That last crack was pretty low."

"It's the way you used to feel."

"Then I'm right to call it growing up."

"You're right to call it whatever is most comfortable," Carol said. "You're the one who has to live with yourself."

"That's no great hardship, surprisingly. It just gets a bit lonely at times!"

"I'm sorry about that, Owen." But the momentum of anger didn't permit her to sound sorry; she was far beyond that impulse to cry for him: the regret was formal and perfunctory. She had herself quite in hand again. "I'm sure you'll find someone to believe in the new Owen," she added politely. "I never could, you must see that. I just haven't the cynicism."

"Is that what it takes?" he asked, but Carol simply shrugged, and it was in that moment of spent silence that Eliot returned and slid into place, febrile with excitement. "Well, here we go, children," he said. "Hold your thumbs!" Carol looked brightly expectant, and Owen sat there all alone, studying his desolation.

It seemed to him that somebody or something must be horribly to blame for what had happened, but he couldn't decide who or what. Was he wrong, or was Carol? Was there some justice in her accusations, some new illusion in his disillusionment? Or were both of them partly right and partly wrong, both of them bound to be lost in a world where all the values had been twisted or misplaced?

The room lights had dimmed; the saxophonist and the bass player had gone, leaving the pianist to arrange a stack of accordion-pleated staff paper on his rack. Now a crew-cut young man, manlier than manly, wearing a pale blue dinner jacket, came bounding up onto the little stage to fondle the microphone and wait for a token hush. "The Cellar d'Or takes pleasure . . . one of the most exciting debuts . . . a hand for Miss Jo Desmond!"

"Jo Borsarelli, actually," Eliot murmured. "A rough translation."

Bosomy slenderness in demure white, a shy smile on the monkey face. Bowing composedly to the polite applause, turning for a last word with her accompanist.

It was his tragedy and nobody else's that he had spent the better part of his life chasing a will-o'-the-wisp. And not much of a tragedy, really; he'd had a better time of it than most, and he hadn't suffered except in his own anticipations. Now he wanted to believe that it was his triumph that he had finally faced up to himself, acknowledged that he would never be more than he already was—a competent professional, filling a need of his time, to be forgotten the moment he was out of sight. All right. But it was a shattering thing all the same, for a man to surrender the dreams that had sustained him from adolescence onwards. All his life he had lived for the day to come; now he faced a future without a future. There was agony in that, and a sort of courage. If Carol couldn't admire the courage, at least she might have shown some sympathy for the agony. Instead—

> *Being constantly smutty*
> *Is driving me nutty,*
> *I'm tired of being risqué.*

Instead she had seen only his defeat. She had not recognized his loss but only her own. And he might have known that she would react this way. Of all the women he knew, she was the one who could not accept his new translation. Her father had seen to that. In the morality play of her intelligence there were only two attitudes for the artist, dedication and cynicism: to surrender the first was to embrace the second. She had never forgiven her father for worshipping the true while practicing the tawdry. She adored her father beyond reason, yet she had never forgiven him, and one such dichotomy in a lifetime was more than enough.

So there was no other way for her to look at what he had done: he had sold out. Just for a handful of silver he left us. . . . And on that knowledge, with none of the anguished indecision which was the earmark of a man, she had torn out the loose-leaf pages of their love. Regretfully, perhaps—but, oh, so righteously. Her own childhood had been flawed by just this disenchantment, and she would never allow Lois to grow up in another such atmosphere of spiritual decay.

The long room dinned with released applause, and as if on cue, by some arrangement of Eliot's, a waiter slipped in with another round of drinks for their table. Owen reached for the new glass and drank half of it off at a swallow, and immediately knew that this was a mistake. He wanted to go home and curl up and lick his wounds in peace and solitude.

He touched Carol on the arm. "Carol. . . ."

But he had waited too long. The girl on stage was about to sing again, and Carol scarcely glanced at him. "Oh, do be still!" she whispered impatiently.

An impersonal impatience, catlike. Claws raking soul-skin of a total stranger.

She assimilated wholly. He was going, let him go, God bless him . . . he was gone. So why was he still there, embarrassing everybody with his presence? The skeleton at every feast these days, that was he. Men never knew when to make an exit, hesitating, childlike, down each step of the inevitable staircase.

He would have liked to get up and go. He could picture himself as the artist Carol wanted him to be: surging out of there in a transport of egoism, trampling the decencies underfoot as he went. But he was only the craftsman, Owen Hilliard, trapped in his sense of bourgeois respectability. He had brought a lady to dine, and there was a bill to be paid. By these small signs you shall recognize genius: genius never sits fretting impotently to pay a bill.

And not a waiter in sight, of course.

So there was to be a use for Eliot, after all. Owen reached for his wallet.

> *When you wake up to find what a fix you are in*
> *Don't reach for a knife, don't poison his gin,*
> *Divorce is a tidier way.*

Laughter sputtered about the long, dim room, laughter suppressed so as not to obscure the next comical line, as several hundred people tried to persuade themselves that these pansy jingles were the last word in sophisticated entertainment. They were having a hell of a fine time, they were really living it up; the brightly painted girls across the table would prove to be good bed fellows, the wives back home were faithful, their children thought they were the greatest men on earth, their credit-card utopia was the acme of civilization, and in the end God would be pleased to welcome the flabby articles they called their souls. It took so many illusions to keep the average man going, and to try to get along without illusions was to be the loneliest man in any crowd. Delude yourself and cheat your wife, bluff your children, bamboozle your boss, bilk the customer, diddle the expense account, barter your principles, impose on your friends, swindle your salvation for success—and you would pass forever as successful, for this was the age of the slob. But if somewhere in this foggy fog of pettifoggery you came upon yourself and recognized yourself—the modest fulfillment of out-dated promises, the forlorn striver on a short path between oblivions—and you decided to settle for yourself and make the most of it: why then, damn and despise you for a failure.

Eliot was leaning forward, beating his palms together, conducting the applause. It took him a moment to respond to Owen's tugging at his sleeve, a still longer moment to grasp the significance of the folded bill that Owen thrust into his hand. Then he scowled at the idea of anybody walking out in the middle of his girl's performance and looked to Carol for support: it was her duty to keep her escort in order. But by then Owen had struggled to his feet—only to find that one leg had gone to sleep, robbing his exit of the last vestige of dignity. He could only stand there helplessly. While Eliot pursed his prissy lips and Carol glared up at him in opaque contempt for his ineptitude. While somebody behind him muttered protestingly about people with no consideration for others. While monkey-face, undisturbed, shaped her voice to a brassy huskiness and began again:

> There was a time when love was romantic,
> Courting was leisurely and chaste.
> Now love affairs are furious and frantic,
> Sex is committed, and repented, in haste!

"Precisely so," said Owen, turning on his heel, turning his back on Carol and so many things. From there the door seemed far away, and the path treacherously narrow.

One foot before the other. Past tables where sat blobs of faces, eyes intent on the stage behind him.

Insanely the overheated room darkened, his knees were slow to respond. A resolute step or two. . . . He stopped, leaning heavily on the back of an empty chair. Forcing himself to breathe deeply, fighting the blackness in his eyes, the numbness. They passed immediately; he was looking down at his hands clenched tightly on the chair, the skin shining with bubbles of sweat. His forehead and hands felt wet and very cold. And in his ears that horrid voice, now turned babyish and almost lisping:

> Long years ago
> With my first beau
> When I was young and so was he. . . .

Fighting nausea, he straightened up and stumbled on before he was ready. Lurching past the oblivious good-time-Charlies. Brushing aside the headwaiter's outstretched, helping hand. Fleeing down a corridor of middle-aged hell from that pansy evocation of innocence—

> We kissed a bit
> And then we quit,
> We really thought that that was it,
> When love was like it used to be.

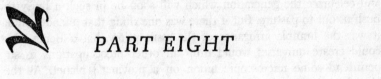

PART EIGHT

1

As the last of the guests approached the receiving line, the accordionist sent to inquire of Roger Hilliard what tune he would prefer for the opening dance. This is a crisis never anticipated even by the most foresighted of bridegrooms, and it is remarkable how the name of every melody can vanish in a trice from a well-stocked memory, apart from some wildly inappropriate exception such as "The St. James Infirmary Blues." Peter Fortescue was called into hasty conference, and while Vickie made unnecessary repairs to her make-up, the two young men decried each other's suggestions as unsuitable either to the occasion or the rheumatic joints of their seniors.

But eventually the little band burst into a few warning, syncopated bars of the *Lohengrin* march, and then—as if it were the most natural transition in the world—*segued* into "Where or When." For a moment Vickie and Roger spun in happy solemnity by themselves, oblivious to the flashing of the photographer's lamp, and then the party was properly begun with that complicated ritual of 'cutting in' which eventually calls for the first usher to cut in upon the best man who has cut in on the groom's father who has cut in on the bride's father who has by now forgotten his instructions and is dancing with the wrong bridesmaid. This arrangement might today have been still further complicated by a certain superfluity of fathers, but for the fact that only dire necessity could ever get Stephen Booth onto a dance floor.

He stood on the sidelines, as he had stood on so many sidelines in the course of his life, waiting for the initial excitement to subside and for somebody to come to talk to him. Somebody disputatious, for preference. Stephen was out of sorts and eager for argument. The church ceremonial had depressed him, as did all such barbarous survivals in a world that posed as civilized. He was willing to concede that a wedding was a good excuse for a party: let us all get drunk and celebrate the generation which will soon be in such a hurry to push us out to pasture. But if there was one thing that offended him, it was the humble arrogance of the assumption that a Being who could create universes would drop all other preoccupations to superintend some microscopic union on a provincial planet. At the church this afternoon they had been exposed to a particularly unctuous follower of this credo, who then, in relaxation from his labors, had doffed his robes to come along to the party and demonstrate that his piety was not of the dour and cloistered sort. Stephen glowered across the room at the pink innocence above the clerical collar and wondered if Amelia would get annoyed if he baited the man.

"A happy occasion," said a voice beside him, and Stephen found that the penalty for standing on sidelines was the company one met there. Excluded by his lameness from the dancing, Arthur Vaughan had come expecting companionship, grimacing an agonized delight in the frivolity just beyond his reach. "How very grown up Roger looks!"

Stephen mumbled something and considered taking to the floor.

"Would you," pursued Vaughan, "have any idea who is the girl he's dancing with?"

One of the bridesmaids: a roly-poly bespectacled girl with an unfortunate nose. Some friend or cousin of Vickie's, doubtless, with too strong a claim to be left out, yet who added nothing to the scheme of decoration. And now that his attention had been drawn to her, Stephen could see a certain spiritual resemblance to Joyce Neilson. Physically they were very different types, but they shared the overbright, overanxious homeliness which presumably gave courage to the prowling Vaughan.

In Stephen's pocket was a telegram which had been delivered just before they set off for the church. Since in this day of promiscuous long-distance telephoning telegrams generally brought word of calamity—distant deaths or the arrival of unwelcome guests—Amelia's curiosity had had to be dispelled by tedium: he had told an involved story of a mislaid thesis and a distraught colleague on vacation. The

372

telegram was from Joyce, of course, and he himself had suggested that it be delivered by hand, lest a telephoned message be accepted in his absence. 'All well,' it read. 'Back at work on Monday.'

Thus uneventfully the episode was ended, with no retributive septicemia to punish what the bloody-minded would think of as a sin. No grand tragedy, just a routine, everyday affair. Morality and Law had suffered their usual defeat, as they always would when they contradicted common sense. Well-meaning people had paid the usual price for ignoring the laws of the jungle. And the martyred saintly villain of the piece, all ignorant, all untouched, disported himself at another girl's wedding and sought introduction to his next victim.

"No, I don't know who she is," Stephen replied, and then added with refined cruelty, "I should think you could do rather better for yourself, Arthur."

"She looks the sort of girl who won't have many partners later on," Vaughan said with a tender smile that told of his solicitude for the world's underdogs. He kept a perfect dignity, wholly oblivious to any cruelty, which, in effect, had therefore never existed—a blow struck out in malice which had gone not merely wild but unregarded.

Yet the more telling phrases, trembling with indignation, which formed on Stephen's lips, would remain unspoken. He had given his word to Joyce, and that was that. From time to time it horrified him to realize that he would go to the grave still governed by the dicta of one of the most ignorant people he had ever known. His mother had had no understanding of the world and the most positive of opinions. She had been determined that her sons would be gentlemanly, and her ideal of a gentleman Stephen had become even before the age of rebellion; when that age came he had found no sensible direction in which to rebel. To be unprincipled on principle or to follow a calculated policy of boorishness would clearly have been childish at that stage. He was trapped within a code which had gone out of fashion, conditioned against accepting any other. Like any intelligent but unarmed man he had taken refuge in scholasticism. And he had gone through life giving his word charily but honoring it, always a little surprised when other people failed to honor theirs. Puzzling over rights and wrongs in a world where the distinction had been lost. Accepting responsibilities that others left lying about. Committing decencies which generally went unnoticed, and waiting for the promised answering consideration which so rarely came.

373

The perpetual victim, or so it sometimes seemed, of people who had been more rationally brought up.

2

"I wonder how many weddings I've been to," speculated Freddie Ames. "Hundreds, I should imagine. Say a dozen a year for the better part of thirty years. . . . It's a terrifying thought. The churches become as familiar as theatres, and you get so that you could handicap the performance of the star turn."

"The bride, you mean?" asked Joan Langstaff, staring resentfully at her champagne glass full of ginger ale.

"Dear me, no," said Freddie. "The bride is just an amateur, after all. The minister upstages her every time, gets her with her back to the audience, and walks off with the whole show. It's the young ministers you have to watch out for. They think they've found the ideal moment to strike a blow at the divorce problem."

"You don't hear a word they're saying," Joan said. "You just stand there in a daze, wondering whether you'll trip over the train when it comes time to turn around."

"Oh, the oratory isn't meant for the besotted couple," Freddie said. "You could mumble the Last Rites over *them*, and they wouldn't know the difference. It's for the people out in the audience who've had the time to think again and may be in need of encouragement and uplift."

"I could do with some uplift," Joan said, still looking at her glass.

"We might dance," Freddie suggested doubtfully. "I'm told that dancing with me is a very uplifting experience. Is that the right word? Edifying, ennobling? In any case, something not to be missed."

So one more couple was added to the throng. For the moment, dancing was still general. Soon the older people would begin to drop away gradually, falling into conversations, leaving the floor to Roger and Vickie and their contemporaries and a few unreconstructed souls like Tony Elmendorf and Eliot Clay. But every able-bodied man in the room knew he must have one brief spin with Vickie, and until that chore had been attended to he was available, depending on his temperament, to whoever had caught his fancy or seemed in danger of neglect.

The crowd turned and twirled and occasionally even dipped, collided and apologized. At the far end of the room Eliot Clay and

Alison, having had a chance to take each other's measure, broke into a performance of inspired jitterbugging. The couples nearby made room for them, danced in place watching, and applauded either in admiration or irony when the pair finally exhausted themselves and stopped.

"Hey, you're terrific!" Alison said, panting. "You're even better than Ben."

"I'll assume that's a compliment," Eliot said. "Who is Ben?"

"Oh, a son of a bitch," replied Alison, some of her elation vanishing. "Let's get us a drink, shall we?"

Superficially a trivial episode, yet symbolic. At any other party Alison would probably have said "Hey, you're terrific!" and stopped there; the comparison with her husband might not have sprung to mind at all, or remained unuttered if it had. But a wedding reception however large, however many outsiders there may be in the room, still has some of the quality of a great family gathering: at its center the party will be haunted by the people who are not there, who should have been there yet are not. Their absence may have become a part of the routine of living, scarcely thought of except during the reaches of a wakeful night, yet at such a party it will suddenly be vivid again. So many gaps in the tapestry.

Alison's loneliness was still a novelty. This was the first real party she had been to without Ben for years and years; it still seemed incredible that she wouldn't look up to see his hateful, familiar face disapproving of her from across the room. This was a great relief, of course. She could behave exactly as she pleased, without fear of being lectured later on about how thoughtless she had been or how selfish. Certainly she had no regrets, no faintest thought of turning back. Already she had begun her packing for a stay of several months, having decided that she might as well see something of the West Coast while she was out there. Forty-eight hours from now she would be on the train (for Alison had a natural terror of airplanes); her reservations in Reno were all arranged, and on the forty-third morning she would become a free woman again. Blessings on the whole procedure. It was just that at odd moments this afternoon she would realize that when somebody had become a habitual part of your life it seemed that you were bound to miss him, even the detestable side. Her freedom from Ben's inevitable nagging meant that there was nobody here who gave that much of a damn. . . .

Whereas it was Alison's father who haunted the afternoon of old Jacob Zimmerman sitting in state across the room—Philip, his first born. Who had grown into a great growly bearlike man, clever at business yet with a heart of mush where his only daughter was concerned. He had been the most vital of the children (as Jacob thought of them), the most physical; less clever than Morris or Gert, with none of Ruth's stubborn gentleness, yet always the dominant, the ruling, clowning eldest. And how, at a party, he had opened up, expanded until he seemed to occupy more than his share of the room! At Alison's wedding he had been in his glory. Dancing till he turned lobster red, joking, speechifying, making outlandish plans for his grandchildren; his huge shouts of laughter rising above all other noise in the room. Without him, this afternoon's party seemed almost staid: there was nobody here with the magnetism to draw this mixed bag of people into a brief unity of fellowship and celebration. Philip would have done it, but Philip was one of those scarlet smears on the countryside that mark man's effort to save a few more hours in the race with death. . . .

And though a less demonstrative Father-of-the-Bride than the missing Philip, Charles Fortescue went through the motions with the flawless assurance that comes of years of executive efficiency. He talked, he danced, he drank, he remembered names, he answered jests in kind, all with an appropriate look of grave delight. You would never have taken *him* for a haunted man, and yet, of course, he was seeing Madge behind every shoulder, looking at him in mute reproach. It was obvious now that she had been right. This was such a large, ungainly gathering that even Amelia had thrown up her hands and left it alone. Half the people in the room had no idea who the other half were and it made little difference, they were united by the spirit of the occasion; they came together, chatted, danced and separated without even exchanging names. One more person in that crowd would never have been noticed. Middle-aged women were as indistinguishable as the glasses of champagne they carried: Madge would have blended in among them, enjoyed her secret fun and slipped away—almost as immaterial in her passing as her presence here today. . . .

And Douglas Langstaff danced at his nephew's wedding and thought of his own son dead these fourteen years, dead before personality had been more than a promise, the last to carry the name in this branch of the family, the unanswerable excuse for Joan's distrust of unblurred reality. . . .

And Gert Zimmerman held communion with a young man who had not returned from war. . . .

And so it went around the room with those to whom this party was more than just one event among others on a social calendar—a milestone somehow infinitely more significant than just the union of the two youngsters at the center of it all.

There were more there that afternoon than had come through the receiving line.

3

"That very pretty child in the green dress?" Ruth said uncertainly.

There was a handful of children, preadolescents at their first grown-up party and very much on their best behavior, for the moment giving a better impersonation of maturity than Roger's college friends.

"That's Amelia's Frances," Owen said.

"I knew it must be," Ruth said. "She's changed remarkably over the past few months, hasn't she?"

"Changed? I wouldn't say so."

"Really? Somehow I had the impression she was all spots and braces."

"Braces, yes," Owen said. "You'll notice that her smiles are rather constrained. But not spots. They're very vain about that complexion."

"And such perfectly lovely hair," Ruth exclaimed, then sighed and added with apparent irrelevance, "Daughters can be very unaccountable."

"It's precisely the shade Amelia always strove for," Owen said. "The gods have a sense of irony."

Ruth gave herself a little shake, escaping from some private reflection, and beamed a bright smile at Owen—or rather (as he felt it) less at Owen personally than at her son-in-law's father. "I gather you have some congratulations coming," she said, "though I'm not entirely sure just what for. Wasn't there something about your getting remarried? I'm sorry: I've been in such a spin these past weeks, you can't imagine."

"These rumors are the plague of anyone with a past as disreputable as mine," Owen said. "All that's needed is for me to be seen with the same woman three times running."

"But Charles said. . . . Well. There's nothing to it, then? I'm sorry to hear it, but that's just the busybody in me speaking: we like

377

to think a man is so much better off for being married." Yet Owen fancied that there was just a touch of satisfaction in her manner: an only son, if he was your son-in-law, should remain safely an only son. "Don't tell me that Hollywood is just another rumor, too."

"No, I'm going. Only for a few months, of course."

"Oh, I think that should be fascinating for you," Ruth said with easy, meaningless enthusiasm. She prattled on, clearly taking it for granted that this move was a praiseworthy promotion: the nonconformist had finally achieved corporate recognition, had made it into the fold of the respectably salaried. And as quickly as possible she shifted from the abstraction of compliments to the reality of something useful and human. "Alison," she said, plucking a girl from the crowd, "Roger's father is going to be out in Hollywood this summer; there's your chance to meet some movie stars."

An unusually attractive girl. Owen remembered her from the earlier party when she had been shepherded by a surly young husband. Now it appeared that she was going out to Reno to dispose of the surly one and would then be sightseeing out West for a few months. No special plans, but she hadn't thought of getting as far down as Los Angeles. She looked up at him, merry-eyed and moist-mouthed, inviting encouragement—trying out her new freedom, less conscious of the twenty-odd years difference in their ages than Owen was. A man, after all, was a man.

Owen explained that out on the Coast, as he understood it, writers were insignificant creatures, lowlier than file clerks, and themselves met film stars only by accident. But it depressed him to recognize that he had explained all this amusingly: charm had come by conditioned reflex. He couldn't be accused of flirting back, not quite, but certainly he hadn't put the girl off. And he wasn't interested, not really. By trial and error and disappointment he had laboriously achieved the instinct which little girls were born with: he wanted a *home*. Not in the sense of a fixed place but a fixed atmosphere, an atmosphere of settled emotional ease and laughter, where he could fold and be enfolded and get on tranquilly with the years that were left. And no man in his right mind went looking for this among dissatisfied, questing girls of twenty-five or so, still whetting their personalities for the kill. No. Something a decade further along, a woman who had learned the distinction between the best possible and the possible best, who dreamt of making a good marriage instead of winning one in the great raffle. That was what he should be looking for, and he knew it. And despite himself he went right on responding to lean flanks and a firm young bosom and eyes that made promises.

So it was understood that when he had an address out there it would go from Roger to Ruth Fortescue and out to Reno. He danced with Alison, and by the time Eliot Clay cut in it was accepted that they would probably be meeting again in mid-August. Owen was left with the consolation that mid-August was two months away. By the time Alison showed up, *if* she showed up, there might be somebody sensible around to protect him. He might have been struck dead by a sports car. Anything could happen in two months.

Roger bore determinedly through the crowd, inspiring the reflection that cutaways were entirely the wrong costume for this sort of wedding. A young man who looked splendid in a dinner jacket, positively dashing in full evening dress, in a cutaway reverted to a schoolboy in masquerade, as unconvincing an imposture of maturity as Roger at fifteen wagging a white beard and creaking rheumatically in a prep-school play. Happily, Roger seemed to have no suspicion of this: he trod with the assurance of one whose manhood had been published to the community.

"Things have been happening so fast I've not had a chance to think," he told his father. "It was something Vickie just said that made me realize. You won't be here when we get back."

"By the time you notice, I'll be on the way home."

"I'm not so sure of that," Roger said. "I'm beginning to suspect I'll need some . . . male solidarity. Mother and Vickie's mother make quite a team."

"Team?" Owen asked drily, and Roger let out a bray of laughter unbefitting a cutaway.

"Well, you know," he said, gesturing. "Pulling in opposite directions, maybe. But both pulling."

"Indeed I do know," Owen said reminiscently. "My own mother was dead, but Amelia's made up for two."

"Gran?" Roger said in surprise, looking to where Mrs. Langstaff held a modest court of the nondancers. "She's a terror, of course—" proudly "—but it's all fuss and nonsense. Underneath she's a softie."

Owen held down his impatience, unsure whether this was a sign of Roger's backwardness, not wanting to be unfair. He could not remember himself at twenty-two distinctly enough. It seemed unlikely, but not impossible, that he could still have possessed this innocent attitude of 'As that person behaves to *me*, so that person is.'

"I wouldn't be much use to you even if I were here," Owen said.

"It's your own battle, and you'll just have to learn to cope. Vickie will help."

"She says it will take some of the pressure off when we have a kid."

"Possibly. Does that mean that you plan to start reproducing right away?"

"Well, I wouldn't say *right* away." Roger was given to a certain ponderous, poker-faced flippancy. "The rumor around college was that it takes nine months, sometimes longer. But there's not much point in waiting, is there?"

Every point, but it would have been a waste of time to say, Wait for a little and be sure that this marriage will last. Roger knew it would last. He knew it as every young man knows that he has the future in his hands, and he knew it more especially because he was Roger Hilliard, who had profited from his father's bad example. Roger had got on well with his stepmothers; he had made the most of having a couple of homes instead of just one, had certainly suffered as little as could any offspring of a broken marriage—and had always been politely critical of the whole arrangement. When *he* married, it would be for keeps. There was an unspoken suggestion that his father must have erred out of willful irresponsibility, lack of imagination, or a deplorably casual attitude towards marriage. However, the father had eaten sour grapes and the child's teeth were set on edge. Properly forewarned, sternly resolute, Roger could not even imagine the possibility of failure. Which would make it all the harder on him when he failed.

And why assume failure? Roger and Vickie were ordinary, decent kids; their marriage could perfectly well turn out to be an inspiring success. Perhaps. But the truth was that such marriages were rare, in this environment rarer still, and under these particular circumstances rarest of all. The most innocent samples of twenty-two and nineteen, still with so much of their growing up to do, and growing up together was one of the best ways of growing apart. Throw in the stresses of a first job for Roger and learning to keep house for Vickie. Throw in all the sudden unexpected disciplines, vexations, responsibilities and temptations that went with harnessed freedom. Add deliberately the confusion of a newborn baby underfoot even before the parents had found their own footing. Stir briskly, keep in a confined space. Oh, sure, it might all work out to perfection. But the probability was that three or four or five years from now—one or two or three kids from now—Roger would turn up some evening hollow-eyed and angry-mouthed to say that he didn't see how he could go on much longer. What would Roger's splendid determination be then but the device which had kept a marriage going till it could not possibly be dissolved? And one more household would be held together by children and financial necessity through the years of resentment and half-concealed animosity. This was the reality overlooked by Roger's bland inquiry: There's not much point in waiting, is there?

"Will you be earning enough to afford this program?" Owen inquired.

"How on earth should I know?" Roger asked calmly. "I've never supported myself before, much less a wife and all the etceteras. We'll make out somehow."

Owen groaned. "You should have got out of college in my day."

"I know all about the Depression, Dad," Roger said with an impatience suggesting that he had heard more than he wanted to hear. "It's not remotely the same. Everybody's doing this, and they manage to get by. They all agree they won't be out of hock for years. I don't even know how to get *in* hock yet, but I expect I'll learn."

"All the fundamental things are left off the curriculum," Owen agreed, the last impulse to talk seriously dying away. Instead, he marveled at the tidiness with which time disqualified a man from playing sage to his own son. Quite objectively Owen knew that he was more intelligent than Roger; he was considerably older, and therefore certainly wiser. Roger could be brought to acknowledge the intelligence, but never the wisdom; Roger would lose every argument with a graceful admission that his father used words wonderfully well, and that, after all, was his profession. Roger's collegiate opinions remained unaffected because he had access to all the flaws in his father's maturity. Owen's views came discounted in advance: his views on money colored by a distant Depression, his views on women damned by a lamentable record of divorce, his views on the world in general distorted by the odd perspective of an ivory tower. Roger's maturity was rapidly outdistancing his father's: in just a few months it would be at apogee. In a few months he would be a sage himself: a happily married man, a prospective father, a salaried citizen at the center of modern industry—and ready to explain life to anyone who would listen.

Vickie came to them through the crowd: nubility in an ivory gown. "I've been trampled by everyone but Grampa, and now I can play favorites," she announced, swaying lightly to the rhythm of the music. "Dance with me," she invited them impartially.

"Later," said Roger. "You reminded me that Dad will be away, and I want him to meet Mr. Bigelow."

"A girl shouldn't have to beg for partners on her wedding day," Vickie pouted, turning the full force of her appeal on Owen.

"I'll just make the introductions and then I'll be right back," Roger said.

"But it's really Owen that I want to dance with," said Vickie, choosing to be captious.

"Later," Roger said firmly, in the voice of one who intends to be master in his own home. Then, belatedly realizing that he wasn't in complete command of the situation, he added with less assurance, "Coming, Dad?"

And Owen hesitated for an instant, realizing that in a sense this was the last purely paternal act he would ever perform: to go along with Roger's small symbolic bid for authority or to dance away with Vickie, to remind the lad that a man has to earn respect before he can enforce it. Were these decisions ever as consequential as they seemed? This was merely the last in a long sequence of crises which had existed only within his own mind: when to chastise and when to encourage: constantly seeking a balance between the needs of discipline and the needs of a growing individuality. Always aware that whatever he decided would in some degree be wrong, because of the inherent fallacy of one person thinking for another person's welfare.

Dating back to that first time when he had looked at Roger and thought 'My God, this is *my* son!' It hadn't happened immediately. Owen's philoprogenitive instinct was not strong; he had been mildly amused but mostly bored by Roger's vegetable infancy and the slow experiments in locomotion. Not till Roger was somewhere between two and three—really talking, making sense, testing out his tiny independence—had the full terror settled on Owen. On his behavior would depend, to some extent, what sort of mess this creature grew up to be. He did not exaggerate his own importance in the scheme of things; he knew that in all likelihood the boy would grow up well enough however badly Owen bungled his fatherhood. . . . And yet that knowledge was not as consoling as it should have been. The sense of self-conscious responsibility remained. He had recalled the traumas of his own childhood, moments of betrayal or injustice which had stuck fast in his memory, yet actually incidents of such little significance that when he had reminded his father of them years later his father had found no recollection of them and denied they had ever occurred. So Owen had wondered what memories Roger would carry forward into his manhood of the times when he had been cruelly misunderstood, when he had asked for bread and been given a stone.

And this wondering had added still another level of artificiality to a relationship already artificial. Owen had dreamed of a bond of easy comradeship with his son, and when the time came there were things which seemed more important: there had been comradeship, but never entirely easy, as Owen had thought of the future and Roger had thought of today. Well, now the future had arrived, and Owen would never really know how well or poorly he had done. Their relationship had shaken into the usual deep affection tempered by deep misgivings: Roger would never be, or not for many years, his normal adult self in his father's presence; there were bound to be too many areas of reserve. Other people would get to know the true Roger and his worth; other people would hear the stories that began 'My father—' Other people would profit from whatever Owen had done that was sensible, and other people would suffer for the mistakes he had made.

So Owen grinned in apology at the girl who would suffer first of all, and went off to be introduced to Mr. Bigelow.

4

The young photographer, Bill Swan, was a man who enjoyed his work and took pride in doing it well. He had arrived at the Fortescue apartment even before Vickie had changed into her gown, and from then till the moment when the bridal couple finally drove off in the hired limousine he would have a complete record of the day. He did not mind wasting film. He knew that of the several hundred pictures he took only a few dozen would be chosen for the album, but never let it be said that a disappointed bride would later wail "Oh, why didn't he get a shot of Uncle Morris dancing with little Frances?" Bill had got it. And if one of the ushers got fried and pitched forward on his face, as often happened, Bill would get a picture of that, too. Some customers liked a touch of humor in the album.

After the first rush of dancing had subsided and before the wedding cake was due to appear, Bill set about taking the formal portraits in the smaller reception room across the hall. First Vickie alone, then Roger and Vickie together, then the couple with their respective parents, and finally a wide-angle line-up of all the members of the families. It was while taking this last shot that Bill realized that the two grandparents—Mrs. Langstaff and Jacob Zimmerman—were both unusually photogenic people and knew that his vision of this album would not be satisfied unless he had a shot of the two of them chatting together. Immediately he spoke of this to Mrs. Booth.

"Oh, dear God!" moaned Amelia, with a look of horror, but she could not deny the aptness of the suggestion, and on this day of days the bride's wishes (as divined by Bill Swan) had the force of law.

So it came about that when the others drifted back across the hall to rejoin the main party, Mrs. Langstaff and Jacob Zimmerman were left sitting side by side on a small settee, wearing expressions of stony resignation more appropriate to a wake. Bill Swan took one look at them and promptly discovered a defect in his equipment. He hurried off apologizing profusely, promising to be right back, praying that in his absence they would fall into conversation and give him some chance at an informal snapshot.

Mrs. Langstaff felt obliged to make an effort. "Vickie is *such* a lovely young bride," she offered, feeling safe from controversy on this point.

"They get younger every year," said Jacob gloomily.

"Nineteen isn't so very young."

"I can remember when nineteen meant knowing how to cook and keep house," Jacob said. "What does Vickie know?"

"She'll learn quickly enough."

"A man could starve to death while these girls are learning."

"You aren't being fair," Mrs. Langstaff said, refusing to give in. "I think the young people are to be admired for how well they *do* manage, without any servants."

"Servants?" Jacob asked incredulously.

"But then, it's quite miraculous the way all these labor-saving devices have come along just in the nick of time."

"A little honest work around the house is something to be ashamed of?" Jacob asked with such deep suspicion that the conversation died instantly. Nor was it out of any sense of social obligation that he revived it a moment later. His mind had worked on quietly underground till he arrived at another thought; there was somebody present to serve as whipping boy, so he spoke aloud. "What makes anybody suppose that young man can support a wife?" he demanded.

"Why, he has a very good job for a boy just out of college," said Mrs. Langstaff.

"He's been given a job, he can lose a job," said Jacob. "What then? What does he have to offer?"

"Roger has a great deal of character," Mrs. Langstaff declared.

"Can you buy groceries with character?" Jacob asked. "I don't trust these job-jobs. When a man is a dentist or a lawyer, you know where you are. If a man is a teacher, he may starve but at least his children will get a good education."

"Roger may not have been at the top of his class, but he's certainly not a stupid boy," said Mrs. Langstaff.

"If a man can play the oboe better than the next man, who cares how stupid he is?" asked Jacob. "If he can restore pictures or make eye glasses, who asks? Some of the stupidest men I've known were opticians, and when bad times come they go right on getting richer. People need glasses to fill out the relief forms. But what does Roger have to offer that every other healthy young man doesn't have?"

"Roger has *breeding*," Mrs. Langstaff replied firmly, and again the conversation expired, this time from shock.

And once again Jacob's restless mind brought it back to life a moment later. "I don't like these parties," he announced abruptly. "I don't think I'll go to any more of them."

"Not see your own grandchildren get married?" said Mrs. Langstaff, startled.

"It makes me feel old."

"But surely the shock comes when one's *children* get married. After that it scarcely seems to matter."

"Then you've missed the secret," Jacob said with infinite scorn. "The whole purpose of living is to be a grandfather—or a grandmother, if you like."

"I can't say I've looked at it that way," Mrs. Langstaff conceded.

"Isn't it obvious?" Jacob asked. "There are too many worries to being a parent. If one of them isn't sick another one is, if one of them doesn't need braces another has to go to summer camp and where is the extra money to come from? And, anyway, you're much too close to it all. With grandchildren it's different. You sit back and you watch. Somebody else does the worrying. Maybe you give some advice, maybe you meddle a little. Mostly you just watch. You see yourself grow up again, and this time around it's more understandable. This is when you see something of where you came from and sense something of where you are going. You see the pattern and you're still a part of it. And then suddenly they are grown up, getting married, and you feel yourself being pushed off the edge of the board."

"There will be great-grandchildren," Mrs. Langstaff said.

"I already have one—you won't find them very interesting," Jacob told her. "By then it's a repetition. And you know you won't be around to see them grow up very far, so you're more detached."

"Perhaps I'm already detached," said Mrs. Langstaff. "There are so many other things in my life: I've never taken my responsibilities as a grandparent as seriously as you do."

"No sense of family," Jacob grunted. "That's what's wrong with you people."

"Too much sense of family," Mrs. Langstaff retorted, accepting battle, "that's what's wrong with *you* people."

Jacob looked at her curiously for an instant. "So maybe Vickie and Roger will find a happy medium," he said. "Is that the answer?" And he grinned at her, a grin of such sly, elfin irony that despite herself Mrs. Langstaff threw back her head and laughed.

And at that moment Bill Swan took the picture that was to be the most beguiling in Vickie's album.

5

About his daughter, Charles Fortescue had no uncertainties. Vickie would sail through her wedding day as though she had been rehearsing for the occasion for years—as, in a sense, she had been. Girls hired out as bridesmaids in anticipation of the day when they would hold the center of the stage, and in any case they had an inborn flair for social matters which boys simply did not have. It was Peter, in his capacity as best man, that his father had worried about. Peter had reached the stage of being very proud of a poise which was not much more than skin deep; he strove for a nonchalance of comportment which, misfiring, could plunge him into grotesque humiliations. It would have been typical of Peter at the altar to hand over the wedding ring with a world-weary gesture which sent the thing flying back among the pews—and then stand there white with anguish while half the church humped and groveled to search the floor.

Later on, when the wedding cake appeared and the moment approached for Peter to propose his toast, Charles's anxiety returned. He scarcely noticed as Vickie and Roger, assisted by much hilarious coaching from the crowd, cut the cake; he was watching his son for symptoms of stage fright. The evening before he had volunteered to hear the boy in whatever he was proposing to say, but the offer had been brusquely declined, an affront to Peter's dignity. Thereafter Charles had expected the worst: Peter aiming at a witty sophistication and stammering into some unintentional obscenity, suddenly recognizing the enormity of what he had said and gasping like a stricken fish, quite unable to go on.

It was terrible, the unnecessary apprehensions your children put you through. Glass in hand, Peter spoke some half dozen sentences that *were* passably witty, and if his delivery did not quite measure up to his dream of urbanity he showed no more awkwardness than was appealing in a boy his age.

With Peter's toast safely by, Charles lost interest. He himself had been urged to say a few words, and for a while he had been tempted. He had had what seemed like an amusing idea. Never one to let the grass grow under his feet, he had already made arrangements for a man to come in the day after tomorrow to measure Vickie's ex-bedroom for built-in bookcases. A good, big desk and desk chair were on order. Filled with these long-postponed plans for his comfort, Charles had thought of stepping forth today to say that if he was losing a daughter at least he was gaining a study. He had imagined a great wave of laughter—and then common sense reminded him that most people there wouldn't have the faintest idea what he was talking about. It would have to be led up to gradually. So he had written out a few lines of introduction, revised them and expanded them, then tried speaking them aloud—and realized that he just didn't have the necessary light touch. Another man would have made it all sound funny, but he, he knew, would end up sounding as if he'd been waiting impatiently for his daughter to clear out of the house.

And there was just enough truth in this to make Charles uneasy. He was very fond of his daughter, but equally bewildered by her. These last few years she had been displaying such an exaggerated femininity (at least he supposed that was what it was) that there was no telling what to make of her. One day a hoyden, the next a bluestocking, the next a coquette. . . . She tried on personalities in the same spirit that Ruth tried on hats: looking for one that would suit her. She borrowed her opinions from whatever young man was uppermost in her mind. Since for quite a while there she had shifted young men almost as rapidly as she shifted personalities, there was no knowing what her newest enthusiasm might be. And the trouble was that Vickie could never keep an enthusiasm to herself. She shared, generously. Coming home from an exasperating day at the office, Charles would find that he was scheduled for conversion to general semantics or progressive jazz or the poetry of Gerard Manley Hopkins. Evidently a sufficiency of beaux was the true finishing school.

After a few years of this Charles had begun to long for the day when Vickie would be married and settled down, content with whichever personality she had finally adopted, and with opinions that remained fixed long enough to reveal which ones were truly hers. On this basis he was quite looking forward to meeting his grown-up daughter at long last—say in six months or a year from now. But when he thought it over, it seemed all too likely that this attitude would emerge from any speech he made, so he had declared that quite enough toasts would be proposed without his adding to the list.

Now he was glad he had kept to this decision. Stephen Booth had been prevailed on to make a toast, through some womanly conspiracy to make him feel a part of things; he produced a rambling harangue spotted with obscure jests which convulsed the collegiate group, presumably accustomed to this form of humor. For no particular reason except that he had to be the center of attention Owen made a speech, and *he* had the light touch that Charles envied, making everybody laugh with his feigned dismay at becoming a premature grandfather. Roger replied with a few well-rehearsed sentences; at least Charles assumed they were well-rehearsed, doubting that Roger was the bridegroom to extemporize such a neatly turned compliment to his mother-in-law.

And for a horrid moment it seemed that Bruce Bigelow was getting so caught up in the spirit of the occasion that he might push himself forward, glass held high, to announce how much they were looking forward to having Roger at Andean C & Z. Such a gesture would have been entirely in character for this man who had recently become Charles's *bête noire*—bluff, earnest, opportunistic, with a cultivated sincerity as unnaturally natural as a field of growing corn. Only a few minutes ago he had come bustling self-importantly over to Charles to profess that he detected great possibilities in Roger. "I've been having a heart-to-heart with the boy," Bigelow had said. "I'll confess I had my doubts; this isn't a job for just any kid fresh out of college. But Rog has stuff, he's on the ball. We'll make him into a real addition to the team." Apart from a certain eager charm,

Roger's assets were not such as to leap out at one; Charles took this pronouncement as politic on Bigelow's part. But politic merely, not cringing. Bigelow had no idea that he should have been cringing.

He had appeared in Charles's office the morning after the discovery of Madge's suicide—an unwanted apparition produced by the backstage office efficiency. Charles had merely said to Mrs. Peabody, "I'd like to see Bigelow whenever it's convenient after this shipping muddle's been cleared up." And Mrs. Peabody had determined conveniences with Bigelow's secretary and made this appointment and no doubt entered it on Charles's calendar, which he hadn't thought to look at, not after the misery of finding Madge's farewell note among the morning's mail. So there was Bigelow, bluff and hearty, unaware that he was due to be eased out of the company.

For such had been Charles's decision. Give Bigelow the chance to resign with a few weeks' notice—for ill health or whatever other reason appealed to him—on the understanding that he'd be given a clean recommendation. This wasn't the nicest of ethics, but it was done all the time: let the next company that hired a man look out for itself. Then get Bigelow's replacement in as fast as possible, to be briefed by Bigelow and firmly entrenched in the job before Roger returned from his honeymoon. That way there would be the absolute minimum of fuss: Charles's criterion for most executive decisions.

But it still needed to be done, and even at his most autocratic Charles hated these scenes: he had known men to lose all sense of dignity and weep. A rigorous firmness was called for, underlying the sympathy you were bound to feel for the other man's position; a kindly ruthlessness. This morning he felt composed of sawdust. He had looked blankly at Bigelow, wondering how to begin.

Immediately it developed that Bigelow had his own ideas about why he had been summoned. "Well, I gather you've already heard the news," he said, with the egoist's easy assumption that his own concerns were of equal interest to everybody else. "You say something in strict confidence to a few people and by the next day it's all over the office. Well, I know exactly what you're worrying about, and I promise you it won't make the slightest difference." Charles kept his head and soon realized that Bigelow had come under the impression that he was to be congratulated and cautioned on his forthcoming remarriage—he was intent on protesting that no caution was necessary. This was no giddy young girl but a sensible widow his own age, fully alive to his responsibilities. Andean's new program would not suffer. They were postponing the honeymoon till his scheduled vacation in August. "And I'll work all the better for knowing the boys are in such capable hands," he offered as the clinching argument. The congratulations, on the other hand, were thoroughly in order. This was a wonderful woman. He had known her for years. She was a compound of all the virtues. "The boys," he said at least three times, "are absolutely crazy about her." It was evident that this wedding had been waiting only on a raise in Bigelow's salary.

As a general rule this would merely have made Charles's task that much more unpleasant. Bigelow was no less of a thief because he was planning to get married.

But on that particular morning Charles had found the requisite moral indignation hard to come by. While Bigelow talked on, gracefully acknowledging Charles's unspoken congratulations, Charles had sat there reminding himself that the man had stolen, stolen from *Andean*—and the fact had seemed of very little consequence. Nobody had suffered. Pitching Bigelow's depredations at the highest they might have been, after corporate taxes and all the rest, the average shareholder's quarterly dividend check wouldn't have been affected by more than a fraction of a penny. Of course if one followed that reasoning to its logical conclusion, one could bankrupt a company in no time. But taken as a human incident, an exception, Bigelow's wrong had caused no suffering, whereas to penalize that wrong would inflict suffering in the most direct and immediate fashion.

This was no way for the executive vice-president of a company to be thinking, and Charles had been perfectly aware of that. But he had also been aware of many other things that day: all the suffering he himself had heedlessly inflicted in the course of his life. He was haunted by Melmoths. He was haunted more especially by Madge; a Madge reproachful as she had never been in actuality, telling him now, too late, how selfishly he had treated her love, taking everything and giving so very little in return. He felt now how circumscribed and lonely her last years had been and knew that there was much that he might have done, should have done, and had failed to do.

And if for a moment he was haunted neither by Madge nor Melmoths, he felt guilt for the suffering he had *almost* brought down upon Ruth and Vickie and Peter—suffering which had been averted by no virtue of his own.

He could not think of himself as a villain; he was an ordinary, well-intentioned man, perhaps more conscientious than most; yet he would have hated to add together all the suffering he had caused in his day. And feeling that way he found it quite impossible to sit in righteous judgment on another man, punish him for a venial sin of dollars and cents, very possibly dash away his chance of happiness. Madge's pathetic letter, lying on the desk, was both a demand and an excuse for amnesty.

In the end Charles had acquiesced in the congratulations expected of him and just mentioned as if in passing that there was another matter he had wanted to discuss. It had come to his attention—one of the accountants had been checking over figures—that some of the expenses in Bigelow's department were higher than they might be.

Bigelow had snapped his fingers. "Now isn't that just my luck!" he had cried with innocent grievance. "Oh, it's all my fault. A man can know a devil of a lot about advertising and still be a dope where *costs* are concerned, and some of those characters took advantage. There's a son of a bitch named Rivkin who does our printing. . . . Well, I only caught on to him a few weeks ago, and I'd hoped to get us fixed up with an honest outfit before anybody noticed how I'd been taken. I'm sorry about it, Chief, but when I first came in there was so much to catch on to all at once, and no trained staff to help, and I'm afraid I made a few boo-boos. But I'm squared away now, and with an assistant to take over some of the legwork I can promise you we'll get full value for every nickel." And he had gone off jauntily, leaving Charles with the reflection that he had merely removed the suffering beyond his own cognizance: the victim now would be the innocent unknown, Mr. Rivkin.

If he had thought to gain some sense of magnanimity from this gesture, some lessening of his guilt, time had quickly proved him mistaken. Ever since that day Charles had regretted his momentary weakness. He had come to loathe the very sight of Bigelow. Bigelow had taken on the character of an irrelevant survivor: the smug stranger who emerges unscathed from the crash where a love was killed. Except that Bigelow was no stranger to be forgotten, but right there underfoot: bustling about in his new importance, finding excuses to drop in upon Charles to discuss schemes for Roger's apprenticeship. This was Bigelow's opportunity to show his painstaking loyalty, and he made the most of it.

And every time the man appeared, he brought Madge with him: the sacrifice who had made his detestable presence possible. The even tenor of Charles's working days was doubly shattered: he not only had to bear with this persecution, but there was nobody to whom he could complain of it later on. Nobody to fix him a drink and hold his hand and set him talking about some of the really serious problems the company faced and lovingly remind him that he was too important a person to be so upset by these petty exasperations. He was alone again, and Bigelow pursued him as a symbol of that knowledge.

Pursued him even to his daughter's wedding day where he should have been most secure: in the midst of his family and his closest friends, with everybody there assembled who might be presumed to love Charles Fortescue.

6

Briefly, that afternoon, Amelia felt a surge of her old affection for her husband. Stephen was selfish, he shared in the common masculine delusion that women had been invented for man's comfort and pleasure, but he did have his own sort of consideration and gallantry. At times these irritated her. Gallantry implied that women were inferior creatures, in need of cosseting; just the sort of thing to put her back up. Consideration was different, and perhaps she had come to take Stephen's too much for granted. Certainly when someone showed a heedless indifference to her feelings it came as a shock. She was acutely aware that Stephen would never have treated any woman, on her son's wedding day, as Guy Abercrombie had treated her.

Guy had come bumbling over to her with his facile flow of courtesies: what a manly lad Roger had turned out to be, and what a charming bride he had captured. In her innocence Amelia had beamed up at him, thinking to herself that every woman should retain at least one rejected lover in her life; this was the only fidelity which made no tiresome demands. But then it developed that Guy had more to bring her than compliments; he had news as well. "I don't suppose you saw this morning's papers," he said.

"I had a nervous bridegroom on my hands," she replied. "Roger showed more imagination than I would have expected, thinking of all the catastrophes that might occur."

"Yes," he said, pursing his lips and teetering on his feet, a sudden study in portentous humbug. "It's very sad. Late yesterday afternoon Rodney died."

"I'm sorry to hear it," Amelia said automatically. As a response to the news this statement was not strictly accurate. She was conscious of no new sorrow for Rodney; that morning on the way to meet her mother at the ship she had assimilated the inevitability, and now she found that the distant memory of a strong young man who had held her in his arms was quite unaffected by the death of a flabby, middle-aged stranger. Nevertheless she was sorry to hear of his death, sorry to the point of outrage that the information should have been thrust upon her this afternoon. The maladroitness of his errand would never occur to Guy, sobered yet elated by the complacent shock of having outlived another old friend; he was merely bent on spreading the word. Stephen would not have done such a thing. Whether out of innate gentleness or that odd, womanish sensitivity of his, he would have saved the news for another time. He was even capable of understanding the basic maternal knowledge: that in giving life one gave a death as well, so that word of any man's passing came as reminder of her own child's brief and uncertain grasp upon existence. To bring this reminder to a wedding party was a cruelty no less cruel for being unintentional, and Amelia was furious.

So she disengaged herself from Guy, cutting off his description of how he had rushed around and spent the evening comforting poor Sheila (poor Sheila, indeed!) and made off across the room. Her intention was to go to Stephen, bringing him her renewed appreciation of his gentleness in exchange for some sympathy, but with each step this seemed less and less like a smart idea. To Stephen, this acknowledgment would be the same as an admission of all the past times when she had failed to give him due credit; a week from now, in the midst of one of their arguments, he would turn her words against her. For the time being their private cold war had reached an uneasy equilibrium, and it was probably better to leave things as they were, not give in to an impulsive sentimentality. There was the temptation to hope that a gesture like this, coming at just the right moment, could shift a relationship to a profounder and friendlier level, but it always worked out that she had merely given new edge to the enemy's weapons.

But while Amelia hesitated, half decided now to leave Stephen to his conversation with Vickie, Vickie darted off to spend her raptures elsewhere, and Stephen scanned the crowd until he found Amelia and then started towards her. And as he came Amelia found herself weakening, reconsidering the idea of appealing to his sympathy.

"That's a formidable little creature," he said before she could speak.

"Vickie?"

"I wonder if Roger has any idea what he's let himself in for," Stephen said, wide-eyed. "She has their life all mapped out. How many children, and in what order they're due to arrive. Presumably she's been on to God about that. Anyway, she has the names all picked out. And five years from now she expects to have a house in the suburbs; the commuting may be a bore for Roger but it will be *so* much better for the children!"

"Girls are always like that," Amelia said, smiling. "When the time comes Roger will have his own opinions."

"Opinions aren't much use in dealing with a steam roller."

"Roger has his own brand of stubbornness," Amelia said. "Stephen, can you imagine what Guy. . . ."

"You think of him as stubborn," Stephen interrupted, "because whenever he found you difficult to deal with, he simply moved over to Owen's place for a few days. That's a technique that doesn't work so well when a man has a home of his own."

"I'm not the least bit concerned about Roger's ability to look after himself," Amelia declared.

"No, you go on the assumption that man is naturally the domineering brute," Stephen replied. "Heaven knows why. In practice you generally get your own way, because when you *don't* get your own way someone is trampling feminine equality underfoot. I've never minded especially; at home I tend to believe in peace at any price. But it's not a policy that appeals to all temperaments, and I rather doubt it will appeal to Roger's."

"What are you getting at?" Amelia asked, now thoroughly glad that she'd not been given the opportunity to disarm. "That Roger would be better prepared for marriage if he'd seen you knocking me around periodically?"

"Not exactly," said Stephen. "I'm just realizing too late that I neglected my responsibilities as a stepfather. I never took them very seriously; Owen was always so much in evidence that I left things to him. But it occurs to me now that the one example of a domesticated male Roger can draw on is myself."

"Why do you suppose everyone has settled on Roger's wedding day to jump up and down on my feelings?" Amelia asked.

"I was talking of my own shortcomings," Stephen protested mildly.

"No, you weren't," said Amelia. "In your usual roundabout way you were suggesting that I've emasculated Roger to such an extent that he won't know how to deal with a wife."

"Well, you *have* brought him up as a gentleman," Stephen said, as if conceding a point.

"That's only disastrous if one hasn't the background for it," Amelia snapped, and walked away from the argument before it could bring on one of her headaches. She felt sorely put upon. She alone in this festive crowd was not to be allowed to enjoy herself, but was tormented by mutterings of death and reproached for the way she had brought up her son. This last she knew in her heart to be quite unfair. Roger was none of your sensitive neurotics but the sturdiest, stolidest of young men, with no need of object lessons in knowing his own mind. If you wanted to waste your sympathy, the one who probably needed it was Vickie, since her romantic visions of the future would soon be foundering on the shoals of masculine complacency. But Amelia couldn't see there was any occasion for sympathy. They were a well matched couple. She wasn't one of these mothers who thought no girl good enough for her son; she felt that Roger would have done very well for himself if Vickie turned out to be just half as nice as she seemed. Amelia had actually wept a little as the minister was pronouncing the binding words, quite surprising herself, for there wasn't any reason for tears. The solemn, darling child had long since disappeared; she had grown impatient with the boyishness of Roger's prolonged adolescence and was looking forward to his metamorphosis as a married man—yet she had wept as for a loss. What loss? Her own youth, perhaps. One more bewilderment in a day that was not living up to expectations.

She had come upon Charles Fortescue, that great length of conservative, unsurprising male, who beamed down at her—father-proud and filled with champagne—and asked why she was so downcast.

"Charles, I have a favor to ask of you," she said impulsively, not pausing to wonder whether this was the ideal moment, thinking only to salvage some satisfaction from a disappointing afternoon.

"Anything within reason," he said agreeably.

Against this occasion Amelia had prepared a host of compelling arguments why Charles should leap at the chance to be a speaker at the L.I.D. convention. Given half a chance, she had felt confident of being able to prove to him where his patriotic duty lay, but he didn't give her even half a chance. From the first word, almost, he was shaking his head.

"You're wasting your breath, Amelia," he said, kindly but firmly.

"Don't you see? You should go after someone in the business of making bathing suits or bedroom suites."

"But don't you believe in disarmament?" she demanded incredulously.

"Oh, I suppose we all believe in disarmament, especially if the Russians begin it," Charles said. "But until that day comes along you'll not get me up in public denouncing the policies of my best customer."

"Oh, hell," said Amelia, who had been on the point of assuring him that he was eager to show the world that American businessmen put principles ahead of profits. She wandered away, more disconsolate than ever. For the first time in years she would have welcomed the possibility of getting a little drunk, but too much alcohol was one of the things that brought on a headache.

7

There are parties and parties and in time they blend together, so that five years later one often cannot untangle what incident took place on what occasion. Freddie Ames, for instance, will not long remember at just which reception it was that the maid of honor took a drink too many, tripped and went headfirst down a flight of stairs. (Bill Swan got the photograph.) Roger and Vickie, on the other hand, will never forget—nor will they allow the unfortunate girl to forget, for the story will be one of the highlights of a unique memory. For them, today's smallest episodes will be memorable, to be cherished, exaggerated, and in time to grow fabulous. Thus, when Vickie was cornered by a tipsily maudlin ex-beau and assured that he alone appreciated her and that Roger would make her miserable, she cherished the memory of a declaration of undying adoration, and was quite put out when less than a year later the young man got engaged.

This was Roger and Vickie's wedding, of course; what happened to them was all-important, and the other people there were just a backdrop to their happiness. Parents and relatives looked on in benevolent admiration, envious enjoyment—or that was how it seemed from the center of things. In their preoccupation with one another it never occurred to them that this day was a landmark in a number of other lives as well, or that this party could and would be remembered for a host of reasons which had nothing whatsoever to do with them. It was only an illusion that life stopped short for celebrations. "Roger and Vickie's reception. . . . Oh, Lord! Do you remember? That was the party where. . . ."

It was the party where Joan Langstaff astonished everybody by not getting drunk. This was the one eventuality which had not been foreseen. That the temptations of the party would prove too much for her had been resignedly taken for granted: sooner or later she would abandon all her promises and take the fatal first drink. Thus far the prediction was accurate. Joan got herself trapped into conversation with the Reverend Dr. Kirkpatrick (who had officiated at the wedding), and after ten minutes of that worthy's unwitting demonstration of why Christianity had failed she abruptly put down her ginger ale and reached for some champagne. This vanished in a twinkling. She started on a second glass while waiting for the scotch on the rocks she had requested of a passing waitress. At this point the alert went out; it was well known that after the first drink there was no stopping Joan without a public scene, and one just had to wait for the crash. Douglas and Amelia and Stephen took turns hovering in the vicinity. From this point on all of them were too apprehensive to enjoy the party. Joan, however, had a delightful time. She achieved just the degree of tipsiness she needed to steady her nerves and maintained it with discreet sips of scotch; she was gay, talkative, flirtatious and amusing—and impeccably behaved. When the maid of honor—normally a somewhat priggish and abstemious girl, a stranger to the perils of excess—took her header down the stairs, it was Joan who took charge and led the girl away to be sick in the powder room, remarking wryly that she had more experience at this sort of thing than most. More people remembered this miracle than anything said or done by either Vickie or Roger.

It was the party where Tony Elmendorf first met a young woman who was to undermine a great deal of his cynicism—though it still remains to be seen whether her efforts to get him to the altar will prove successful.

It was the party where Morris Zimmerman was found in tears. Gert went looking for him, having noticed how long he had been missing, and being the one other person there that afternoon who knew that there wasn't a word of truth in the reasons given why Morris's daughter and son-in-law had not been able to get down for the wedding. She found him in the smaller reception room across the hall, otherwise almost empty for the moment. He was standing at one of the windows with his back to the room, staring down at nothing. His cheeks were streaked.

"You've been talking to Boston," Gert said.

"They put the call through for me downstairs."

"And?"

"I spoke to Dan," Morris said dully. "He'd just had the report from the hospital. It's . . . what I was afraid of."

"No hope?"

"A few months of knowing she won't see her baby grow up."

"But the baby's all right? I don't understand these things."

"The baby's perfectly all right." Morris wiped his face with a handkerchief, blew his nose fiercely. "Gert, I have to get up there this evening. There'd be no harm if I slipped away?"

"Not yet," she said. "Vickie would notice. She'd want to know why."

"I'm a doctor, after all. You could say there'd been an emergency."

"She knows you have somebody standing by for today. Besides, you wouldn't save any time. They'll be gone in half an hour, and then Harry can drive you straight to the airport—it's right on his way home. I'll set him to finding out what times the planes leave and getting you a reservation."

"It's not just saving time," Morris said. "It's the thought of going back in there and pretending to be happy and gay. I can't do it."

"Neither can I. And somehow we'll bring it off."

"Not if Father sees me. He'll know something's wrong. I've never been able to fool him."

"Then tell him," Gert suggested. "He's better insulated than any of us—he's had longer practice."

"It might be easier if one could only believe there was some *point* to it all."

"Of course there's a point," Gert said, deliberately misunderstanding him. "We're still paying back for all the times we were shielded from noticing what life is really like. Come along, Morris. We have to be in the background while Vickie heaves her bouquet."

And this was the party where Freddie Ames produced his best, or worst, pun of the season, depending on one's point of view. He had fallen into the clutches of a sentimental Zimmerman who was enchanted by the spectacle of Vickie and Roger posing at the balustrade as Vickie prepared to toss her bouquet to the gaggle of bridesmaids on the landing below.

"Don't they," sighed the Zimmerman to Freddie, "remind you of a couple straight out of a fairy tale?"

"Wedding parties *always* remind me of a fairy tale," Freddie replied instantly.

"Really?" beamed the Zimmerman, pleased to have found a soul mate at last.

"Of course," said Freddie. "The one that begins, Once upon a time there were four bears. . . ."

8

The roly-poly girl with the unfortunate nose was the shortest of the bridesmaids but the most determined, and she caught the bouquet. The garter was caught by a very tall young man who starred at basketball and catching garters at wedding receptions; he festooned his mirror with his trophies and was terrified of girls.

A few minutes later in a little room upstairs Ruth was helping Vickie out of her wedding gown. They were alone. Failing the assistance of the maid of honor, who was still *hors de combat*, Ruth had looked to Gert for help and got a shake of the head and a gesture which meant that Gert would explain later. This was slightly unnerving (Ruth assumed that the party had overtired Jacob), but fortunately Vickie hadn't noticed. At this stage Vickie was in no shape to notice much of anything. She was dizzy with excitement, chattering away without pause.

Had Mummy noticed the way everybody seemed to be *enjoying* themselves? Most wedding receptions were just a bore, but this one had been a real party, the most wonderful party there had ever, ever been. . . . And beginning with the drive to the church Vickie went through a recital of the afternoon's events seen from her point of view, as if trying to ensure that even the most trivial incident would be engraved on her memory forever.

Outwardly placid, Ruth went about her tasks of folding up the lace, packing away the gown. Inwardly she struggled with a sudden rush of misgivings. She recalled all the times she had remarked so smugly that she had always known Vickie would marry early, and now it seemed much too recently that . . . well, that Vickie had come tottering into the living room and fallen full length in her effort to walk in a pair of her mother's high-heeled shoes. Five she had been, or six. They had picked her up and found her mouth bloody with lipstick and her eyes bruised with mascara, reeking from the perfume she had splashed on herself. Playing at being a grown up woman. And here she was a few days later, skilled at make-up now and confident in her own high heels, but still playing at being a grown up woman, and in danger of much worse tumbles.

Ordinarily Ruth was not troubled by useless apprehensions, so it must have been the sight of Alison there that afternoon which had stirred her fears. Alison seemingly so happy and carefree while her bags were all packed for Reno, a disconcerting reminder that a wedding need not keep its promises. So it frightened Ruth to ask herself how much Vickie and Roger really had in common, only to find that she hadn't even the least idea. Nor was this because her knowledge of Roger was still limited. On examination, her knowledge of Vickie appeared to be equally limited.

She knew Vickie by her character and her nature, her emotions and her moods. . . . But what did she know of Vickie's opinions? What did she care, almost, as long as Vickie showed no signs of wanting to be a Communist? That wasn't how you looked at your children. If there was an election going on, Vickie might have decided ideas on the subject, but there were more important things to listen to than *what* she was saying. Vickie tended to be sloppy in her speech and Charles flew into a fury if somebody said 'the most unique' so there was her grammar to be corrected. Vickie tended to get excited and contradict people flatly, so there were her manners to be corrected. Vickie tended to swear too much. The ideas Vickie was expressing were the least of it, since she would very likely be saying the precise opposite six months later and be quite unembarrassed if you pointed out the inconsistency. "That," she would say airily, "was just a phase."

Children picked up their ideas here and there. For a time Vickie's had been borrowed wholesale from her adored schoolmistress, Miss Finley; later she had pilfered from her beaux. Charles, who took everything literally, would occasionally get indignant over some heresy Vickie brought home, but Ruth had never paid much attention. From her point of view it was all a lot of nonsense. But now she felt that she had been mistaken. Somewhere along the line she should have schooled herself to accept Vickie at Vickie's own evaluation of herself: as an adult whose opinions had to be taken seriously. For Vickie took her opinions seriously, unlikely as this might seem; they were the stuff which she would inflict upon Roger when the kissing slowed, and which would determine, as he found them sympathetic or perverse, how much they 'had in common.' Yet for the life of her Ruth could not imagine what Roger and Vickie would find to talk about through the long evenings, and for the first time felt a stranger to her daughter.

The difficulty was that she could not see Vickie as a woman. As a girl, yes. As a minx, a romp, a chatterbox, a brat, a tease, a flirt—oh, most especially a flirt. As all the implications of a woman, yet not a completed woman, as Vickie must see herself, as Roger must see her. And the flaw must be in Ruth's vision, for the woman was most substantially right there; now scrubbing her face and neck at the sink, dressed only in a bra and panties. Vickie would have to watch her weight carefully when she became pregnant, but for the moment she had a perfectly lovely body, as long as you weren't ashamed of the curves God meant a woman to have. But it added to Ruth's feeling of remoteness to realize that she didn't even know how experienced or inexperienced that body might be. Out of old-fashioned prejudice she preferred to think of her daughter as still a virgin, though all one read and heard of young people these days made that seem improbable—but the humiliating fact remained that she didn't know. It was another of her failures as a mother. She had always been absolutely forthright with Vickie (if you improved over your own upbringing you thought you had solved everything), vaguely assuming that frankness would beget frankness. Somehow it hadn't worked that way; Ruth had remained poised with conscientious answers to questions that were never asked. And when belatedly she had introduced the subject herself, she had met a Vickie bristling in defense of her sophistication, contemptuous of the idea that there was anything she didn't know. Thereafter Ruth had confined herself to making sure that Vickie got home at a respectable hour and to telling occasional edifying anecdotes about girls who got themselves into trouble.

As a result Ruth today had no idea whether Vickie's babbling revealed a nervous apprehension of the night ahead or heedless unconcern for a familiar experience. Either way Ruth felt at fault: if the former, she had been a neglectful mother; if the latter, a permissive one.

"Do you know what really frightens me?" Vickie said, interrupting herself so appositely that Ruth felt a surge of communion with her daughter.

"What, dear?" she asked gently, prepared to dispel a whole nightmare of lurking sexual terrors.

"It's that flight tomorrow morning. I've had a horror of planes ever since Uncle Phil was killed."

"Nonsense," Ruth said briskly. Her own fear of flying was well disciplined, since Charles's vacations usually allowed of no other form of travel. "It's nowhere near as dangerous as driving."

"Oh, I know all about statistics," Vickie said. She was dressed now, in the pretty blue silk they had found at Bonwit's, making up her face at the mirror. "I just don't want to become one."

"At least you won't be going over any mountains; that's the most worrisome part."

"These days it's whether some passenger has a homemade bomb in his luggage."

"Don't be silly," Ruth said sharply. "There's nothing to worry about. You'll have Roger's arm around you and before you know it you'll be there."

"I know, I know. It's just that if I don't have something to worry about I feel as if I'll take off, myself."

"But you won't forget to cable as soon as you get there," Ruth added.

Vickie laughed. "You're a great help! There's no need to worry and it's safer than driving and that's the eighty-seventh time you've reminded me to cable!"

Ruth smiled at her absurdity, at the general absurdity of fretting over your own children long after they had stopped being either children or your own. Perhaps she had reason to feel guilty, but she wasn't equipped temperamentally to feel guilty for very long. She had done her best. She had wanted Vickie to grow up—*all* the way up. This was all that mattered. And it meant letting go and letting go, standing back and giving the child room to be herself. . . . Until finally you stood back for the last time and watched her get married and go off with someone else to complete the process. For in Ruth's philosophy getting married was very much a part of growing up: the last stage and the most important. Learning to live in tandem, taking the responsibility for someone else. And then the joys and cares of your own children. This was all still part of growing up. The bachelors and the spinsters of this world never really ripened, to her way of thinking; they simply aged, like pickles, in the brine and spices of their solitary egoism. And the divorcées, too, like Alison: she had not even tried to go on growing up; she had thought herself a finished product and expected to bask indefinitely in Ben's delight at his good fortune.

Well, it was Vickie's turn now, and what happened over the next few years would probably be the real test of how good a mother Ruth had been. The mistakes wouldn't matter if she had succeeded in giving Vickie some sense of values for the business of living, if Vickie could learn that "we" was more important than "I," if she went on maturing, if she didn't come running for sympathy every time things got difficult. For there would be difficult patches, of course, and it remained to be seen how well Vickie had learned the lesson that even a spoiled brat could be adorable until something was demanded of it. Only time would tell—and Ruth now realized that the period ahead would not be empty, as she had thought, but filled with anxieties: watching and waiting and trying not to meddle. The last would be all the harder for knowing that Amelia would never be missing an opportunity. Ruth supposed she would have her lapses: she could not expect to be an ideal mother-in-law any more than she had been an ideal mother, but her intentions would be of the best and surely that counted for something. Her intention was to leave Vickie to fight her own battles. She would simply have to keep reminding herself that she had bred up a daughter to be proud of, who could stand on her own feet, who had all the makings of a woman.

"Are we ready?" Ruth asked, clicking the suitcase shut and then looking around the room one last time to make sure they hadn't overlooked anything.

Vickie turned away from the mirror, and Ruth saw that her eyes were swimming with tears.

"Oh, my dear . . ." she cried in sudden panic, forgetting both pride and resolutions.

"I'm not going to cry. I'm not," Vickie said calmly. "It would just be too silly to have to do my make-up all over again. I'm perfectly all right, perfectly in control of myself. Oh, damn! Oh, Mummy, it's just that I'm so *happy!*"

9

Bill Swan got his closing shot of Vickie and Roger smiling back through the rear window of the limousine; there was a burst of cheering, a final hurling of artificial rose petals, and then the car pulled away from the curb, merged with the other traffic, turned the corner and vanished.

Until this moment, captive of the afternoon's orderly progression, Owen had been gripped by a sort of ritual elation. Abruptly it was gone, leaving him let down, almost depressed. Briefly he stood on the sidewalk, wondering what to do with himself. Then he went back inside in search of Tony Elmendorf; they could have dinner together and find some way to kill the evening.

But near the head of the stairs he found his friend in such intent conversation with an unfamiliar dark haired young woman that Tony either failed or refused to meet Owen's eyes. The party was dying, but gradually. Some of Roger's and Vickie's friends were working hard to keep it alive. People stood about finishing off conversations, making plans to get together next week, waiting for wives or husbands to come back from the cloakroom. Ruth and Amelia were near the door of the main reception room to say good-bye to those who were already leaving. Owen got a drink (during the party, out of some vague sense of responsibility, he had been unusually abstemious), wandered across the hall to the smaller room and sank into one of a pair of unoccupied armchairs. The three-week interval before he was due to fly West stretched before him like a void: he had nothing to do, nobody he particularly wanted to see. The thought of Carol ached like a sore spot in the mouth that the tongue could not leave alone. Tomorrow, no doubt, he would pull himself together: have Polly get him some theatre tickets, make plans and engagements. He might even, since there was plenty of money now, fly over to London to see what they'd made of the West End production of *Cascade*. He liked London; it was so decidedly a man's city. But just at the moment even the thought of London failed to stir him. He felt ambiguous, neither working nor resting from work well done; he felt lonely and adrift.

Charles Fortescue appeared in the doorway, evidently equally at loose ends. He glanced around the room, hesitated, decided that after looking Owen squarely in the eye he could scarcely withdraw, and came over to sit in the other armchair. "Well, I'd say this went off pretty well," he said with the hearty uncertainty of a man whose checkbook has been pillaged and who wants some assurance that he has had his money's worth.

"I suppose so," Owen said. Since that meeting in the cocktail bar they had seen one another only at family gatherings, and that would probably be the pattern from here on. Owen supposed their antagonism would eventually wear itself out in semiformal familiarity.

"Haven't you been enjoying yourself?"

"Up to a point," Owen said. "But would you have any idea what we've been celebrating?"

"What's that?"

"I've been sitting here wondering what the devil we've been celebrating," Owen said, realizing that Charles was . . . not drunk, certainly; not even tight, perhaps, but sure to be one or the other by the time he finished the glass he had brought with him.

"Something to do with a wedding, I believe," Charles said cunningly.

"No, not that," Owen replied. "It doesn't make sense. A man in his right mind doesn't rush out to celebrate because he's bought a ticket on a horse race. He waits to see whether the horse wins."

While he thought about this, frowning, Charles fished in an inner breast pocket for a cigar. "You're in . . . a funny mood . . . Owen," he said between the starting puffs. "Do weddings usually have this effect on you?"

"I've never been at my son's wedding before."

"Let's hope you never are again."

"All right, let's," Owen said agreeably. "But it's a possibility and we both know it, and that's why I asked the question. I've been celebrating *something* this afternoon. It's gone now, but I could feel it at the time. There was actually a lump in my throat when the car drove away. And it's not just because Roger and Vickie got married. Nobody has the slightest idea whether that was a good thing or not. More likely not. My God, Charles, look at the people who were here today. Look at your friends. Look at us. It's funny—the first time we met I envied you for possessing just the sort of domesticity I've always wanted."

Charles glanced about and cleared his throat. "Whatever you may believe," he said gravely, "I consider myself a happily married man."

"That's nice," said Owen. "When are you coming around to clear out that suitcase?"

"It's a hell of a time to bring *that* up," Charles said, blinking. "I've been meaning to call you."

"I'll be leaving town in a few weeks. Possibly sooner."

The cigar waved deprecatingly. "I've been giving you a chance to reconsider about those cuff links."

"Perhaps I deserve them as a keepsake," Owen said. "All right, I accept. They'll remind me of what a happy marriage is really like."

"You're an offensive son of a bitch," Charles said, but without heat: if you gave yourself into another man's hands you probably had to expect a certain amount of insolence.

"But is it the sort of happy marriage you're hoping Vickie will have?" Owen pursued. "What Vickie doesn't know won't hurt her either, of course."

"I used to think writers were more sensitive than other people," Charles grumbled. "Anyway, you're all wrong. There are lots of excellent marriages, even from your point of view. There's Ruth's brother, Morris. His wife has been dead five years now, poor creature, and he's never even looked at another woman. That should give you some idea."

"I don't say there aren't exceptions," Owen said. "Occasionally the horse does win. But what the hell? Were we celebrating today because we were so frightened that there won't be anything to celebrate later on? That sounds all wrong. No, if Roger and Vickie give me the opportunity, ten years from today I swear I'll throw them the biggest, gayest, splashiest party I can afford. There's sense in that."

"I probably won't be around to enjoy it," Charles said gloomily. "There's your answer right there, I suppose. We don't know how these things will turn out so we hope for the best and celebrate while we can."

"No, there has to be more to it than that," Owen insisted. "There was something in the air. You must have sensed it, too. A rare, real gaiety. An affirmation of something or other. For a couple of hours there everybody who was capable of being happy *was* happy. I know I was. Didn't you feel it, Charles?"

"Of course I did," Charles said, "and it didn't surprise me at all. But then I don't take as cynical a view of Roger and Vickie's chances as you appear to."

"Is it cynicism? Think of all the marriages you've known. How many have broken up? How many others might just as well have broken up and are held together only because splitting up would be even more inconvenient? Those are the failures. The only marriages that matter are those where two people have built a unity that is larger than the sum of its parts. I'm not talking about romantic love or sex or even community of interest. Just unity. Harmony, if you like. You can sense it sometimes entering a strange apartment: My God, here is a place where the people still *like* one another. It comes as a shock. Where would you fix the percentage, Charles?"

"It wouldn't be very high," Charles admitted.

"Fifty percent?"

"Certainly not that. Not in New York, anyway."

"Thirty, then?" Owen asked. "Twenty? Ten, five, two? It doesn't much matter where you fix the figure; the odds will still be pretty heavily against Roger and Vickie. Just because they're our children and we like to think they're special doesn't alter the odds. All right, and *that* was part of the atmosphere this afternoon, too. Everyone is aware of it, even Roger and Vickie. They aren't stupid. No matter how confident they are, they can't help knowing that millions of people have felt precisely the same way—and ended up in the divorce courts. It's been a part of the air they've breathed since the day they were born. But if all we had to celebrate was a long-shot possibility, what *were* we so happy about?"

"Oh, I don't know," Charles said irritably. "I guess there's something symbolic about it when your kids get married. You think of grandchildren and the future. It's a sign that life moves on and a part of you is moving with it."

"I daresay that has something to do with it," Owen agreed. "Yet if that is what we were celebrating, you and I, it brings us down with a thump to a womanish view of reality. Because it's much the same as saying that nothing we've done with our lives is quite as significant as our share in producing those children who got married this afternoon."

"I never said anything of the sort!" Charles said, with such indignation that he had to brush away cigar ash.

"It's probably true, you know," Owen went on tranquilly. "We cling to a sense of our importance, but we're neither of us the stuff that leaves a mark on history. If you'd never been born somebody else would have managed your mining company, and just about as competently. As for me, though I pride myself on my imagination I cannot imagine anyone foolish enough to revive one of my plays a century from now. So there we are. You will be a name in the files, a photograph on the board-room walls, for a while. I will be a part of the annals of Broadway's most stagnant era. But through Roger and Vickie we have made a unique contribution to the future. I admit that this is a distinction we share with every other fertile man on earth, but at least it's something, and latent with unimaginable promise. We might still win a footnote in the history books, Charles —as grandfathers of the first man to set foot on Mars."

"What rubbish you do talk," said Charles.

"Oh, there's sense at the center," Owen said. "But not enough sense. I still feel there's something missing."

"Why don't you go and talk to Ruth's father," Charles suggested. "Old Jacob's been going to these parties upwards of fifty years. He should be able to tell you what they celebrate."

"The wisdom of the very old is astringent wisdom," Owen said vaguely, and fell silent, for the thought of old Jacob was the thought of death, and already that afternoon Owen had several times had to eject the subject from his mind. For this was the dark side of an off-spring's marriage: if it spoke of a specious symbolic immortality, it also whispered of corporeal mortality—and if Owen had heard those whispers, how much louder they must have sounded in Jacob's ears! There was a sentimental belief that an old man's dying moments would be comforted by the spectacle of his progeny crowding around him, but Owen doubted it. Dying was a selfish moment: if the man believed in Heaven, he was doubtless worrying about the good standing of his own soul; if he believed in extinction he was probably offended by the sight of all those uncouth strangers who would enjoy tomorrow's sunlight while he would not. Owen believed in extinction, so Roger's wedding had been a reminder that he was now at least two-thirds of the way towards that moment when the switch would be pulled and the universe would go out. He disliked such reminders; he disliked the whole idea, but there seemed no good alternative. The intelligent man was caught in the dilemma of being strongly prejudiced in favor of his own ego, yet not to the point where he could contemplate its perpetuation throughout eternity. The soul was a cruel idea conceived by someone too unperceptive to notice that the only things fixed in an individuality were the flaws: the weaknesses and shortcomings, sins and frailties. Wash these away and nothing would be left, for all else was changed. Each past self was a stranger, bound to its brother only by a dreadful similarity of inadequacies: the soul. Yesterday's virtue was a sentimentality, yesterday's idealism an embarrassment, yesterday's love a sorrow or a humiliation or a guilt. Yesterday's dream was always a paradise far, far better lost. Nothing was permanent but stupidity—and a man who could believe that he would recognize himself (or abide himself) with the stupidity lifted away was a man who believed in hell. So it really made no difference whether you thought of oblivion or of returning your soul to the godhead whence it was borrowed: extinction was still extinction. The hope of old age was the triumph of dying a bankrupt.

But when his own moment came, if he identified its coming, Owen knew that he would not be one whit gratified or consoled by the thought of progeny who would carry his seed down the generations. He himself would be quite as extinct as any celibate, and instead of murmuring patriarchal benedictions he would probably die cursing all the questions that still remained unanswered. So, feeling as he did, it was obviously not merely the prospect of grandchildren which had given him this afternoon that curious sense of vitality and elation.

A herd of Andean executives and their wives came to say good-bye, rousing Charles from his lethargy; when they had gone he turned a glazing eye on Owen and said: "Well, now that you've succeeded in depressing us both, have you decided what we were celebrating?"

"Possibly," Owen said uncertainly, groping his way through the labyrinth of words. "It hadn't anything to do with Roger and Vickie, except indirectly. It was ourselves that we were celebrating. The perpetuation of ourselves."

"That's what I said," Charles replied. "Grandchildren."

"Not in that sense, or at least that's only a part of it," Owen said, with gathering assurance. "What I'm getting at is something quite different. It's that today, at last, we stopped being onlookers and took up our places in the pageant."

"What pageant?" Charles asked suspiciously.

"The blind quest," Owen said. "The twisting, straggling march of man's creativity. Call it history, call it comedy. We create civilizations and they demoralize us. Always and forever, there is the collapse between the vision and the reality. We create gods and they abandon us. We create economies and they beggar us. We create governments and they betray us."

"That's the Democrats," said Charles. In the other room the band was signing off with "Auld Lang Syne," and one or two hardy souls were singing.

"Yet none of it matters," said Owen. "We never learn. There is always a new vision. We create new gods and new governments, convinced that one day we will create something finer than just another barrier against the brother without or the barbarian within. This is our pageant, mostly ludicrous and just a bit superb. Women are a part of it all their lives, while we bustle about importantly, shifting the scenery. But once in a while we have our own roles to play as Everyman; just for a moment we become a part of the age-old gallantry, and we are moved. That's what happened this afternoon, Charles. We were on stage, with all our fathers' fathers as audience, acting the middleman between the past and the future. Performing the ritual of handing along the torch of hope to singe the fingers of the next generation. The gods sniggered, I daresay, but I got a lump in my throat."

"You've put it into fancy words," said Charles, "but it's just what I said before: Life moves on. It strikes me as a damn dull reason for a party."